Blue Jackets
The Log of the Teaser

by

George Manville Fenn

Blue Jackets
The Log of the Teaser
by George Manville Fenn

Copyright © 2024

All Rights reserved.

ISBN: 978-93-68092-76-6

Published by

DOUBLE 9 BOOKS

2/13-B, Ansari Road
Daryaganj, New Delhi – 110002
info@double9books.com
www.double9books.com
Tel. 011-40042856

This book is under public domain

ABOUT THE AUTHOR

George Manville Fenn was a very productive author of novels, a writer, an editor, and an educator from England. He was born on January 3, 1831, in Pimlico, London. He mostly learned on his own; he taught himself Italian, French, and German. During the years 1851–1854, he went to Battersea Training College for Teachers and then became the head of a state school in Alford, Lincolnshire. In the early 1850s, Fenn started to write short stories and pieces for newspapers and magazines. The Old Forest Ranger, his first book, came out in 1856. Afterward, he wrote more than 100 books, many of them for teenagers and young adults. He was one of the most famous writers of his time, and his books were well-liked and read by many people. He also worked as a reporter and writer for Fenn. Among the newspapers and magazines, he worked for was The Boy's Own Paper, which he ran from 1866 to 1874. He worked hard to make children's books better and was a strong supporter of education and reading. The Englishman Fenn passed away on August 26, 1909, in Isleworth.

CONTENTS

Chapter One
We Jolly Sailor Boys

"Come along, boys; look sharp! Here's old Dishy coming."

"Hang old Dishipline; he's always coming when he isn't wanted. Tumble over."

We three lads, midshipmen on board HM clipper gunboat the *Teaser*, did "tumble over"—in other words, made our way down into the boat alongside—but not so quickly that the first lieutenant, Mr Reardon, who, from his slightly Hibernian pronunciation of the word discipline and constant references thereto had earned for himself among us the sobriquet of "Dishy," did catch sight of us, come to the gangway and look down just as Double B had given the order to shove off, and was settling the strap of the large telescope he carried over his shoulder. I ought to tell you our names, though, in order of seniority; and it will make matters more easy in this log if I add our second handles or nicknames, for it was a habit among us that if a fellow could by any possibility be furnished with an alias, that furnishing took place.

For instance, Bruce Barkins always went by the name of "Double B," when, in allusion to the Bark in his family name, he was not called the "Little Tanner," or "Tanner" alone; Harry Smith, being a swarthy, dark-haired fellow, was "Blacksmith;" and I, Nathaniel Herrick, was dubbed the first day "Poet"—I, who had never made a line in my life—and later on, as I was rather diminutive, the "Gnat."

One can't start fair upon any voyage without preparations, so I must put in another word or two to tell you that there were two logs kept on board the good ship *Teaser*—one by the chief officer, and in which the captain often put down his opinion. This is not that, but my own private log; and I'm afraid that if the skipper or Lieutenant Reardon had ever seen it he would have had a few words of a sort to say to me—words which I would rather not have heard.

It was a gloriously fine morning. We had been dodging about the coast on and off for a month on the look-out for piratical junks and lorchas, had found none, and were now lying at anchor in the mouth of the Nyho river, opposite the busy city of that name. Lastly, we three had leave to go ashore for the day, and were just off when the first lieutenant came and stood in the gangway, just as I have said, and the Tanner had told the coxswain to shove off.

"Stop!" cried our tyrant loudly; and the oars which were being dropped into the pea-soupy water were tossed up again and held in a row.

"Oh my!" groaned Barkins.

"Eh?" cried the first lieutenant sharply. "What say?" and he looked hard at me.

"I didn't speak, sir."

"Oh, I thought you did. Well, young gentlemen, you are going ashore for the day. Not by my wish, I can assure you."

"No, sir," said Smith, and he received a furious look.

"Was that meant for impertinence, sir?"

"I beg pardon, sir; no, sir."

"Oh, I'm very glad it was not. I was saying it was not by my wish that you are going ashore, for I think you would be all better employed in your cabin studying navigation."

"Haven't had a holiday for months, sir," said Barkins, in a tone of remonstrance.

"Well, sir, what of that? Neither have I. Do you suppose that the discipline of Her Majesty's ships is to be kept up by officers thinking of nothing else but holidays? Now, listen to me—As you are going—recollect that you are officers and gentlemen, and that it is your duty to bear yourselves so as to secure respect from the Chinese inhabitants of the town."

"Yes, sir," we said in chorus.

"You will be very careful not to get into any scrapes."

"Of course, sir."

"And you will bear in mind that you are only barbarians—"

"And foreign devils, sir."

"Thank you, Mr Smith," said the lieutenant sarcastically. "You need not take the words out of my mouth. I was going to say foreign devils—"

"I beg pardon, sir."

"—In the eyes of these self-satisfied, almond-eyed Celestials. They would only be too glad of an excuse to mob you or to declare that you had insulted them, so be careful."

"Certainly, sir."

"Perhaps you had better not visit their temples."

Smith kicked me.

"Or their public buildings."

Barkins trod on my toe.

"In short, I should be extremely guarded; and I think, on further consideration, I will go to the captain and suggest that you have half-a-dozen marines with you."

"Captain's ashore, sir."

"Thank you, Mr Herrick. You need not be so fond of correcting me."

I made a deprecatory gesture.

"I should have remembered directly that Captain Thwaites was ashore."

"Beg pardon, sir," said Barkins, touching his cap. "Well, Mr Barkins."

"I hope you will not send any marines with us."

"And pray why, sir?"

"We should have to be looking after them, sir, as much as they would be looking after us."

"Mr Barkins, allow me to assure you, sir, that the dishipline of the marines on board this ship is above reproach."

"Yes, sir. Of course, sir. I only thought that, after being on board the ship so long, sir, they might be tempted, sir."

"I hope that the men of Her Majesty's gunboat *Teaser* are above all temptations, Mr Barkins," said the lieutenant harshly. "There, upon second thoughts, I will not send a guard. You can go."

The oars dropped with a splash on either side, and away we went among the hundreds of native boats of all kinds going up and down the river, and onward toward the crowded city, with its pagodas, towers, and ornamental gateways glittering in the morning sunshine, and looking wonderfully attractive to us prisoners, out for the day.

"Don't speak aloud," I whispered to Smith, who was gathering himself up for an oration respecting the first lieutenant's tyranny.

"Why not?"

"Because the men are listening, and one of 'em may report what you say."

"He'd better," said Smith defiantly. "I'm not afraid to speak. It was all out of his niggling meddlesomeness, so as to show off before the men." But all the same he spoke in a low voice that could only be heard by our companion who held the lines.

"There, never mind all that bother," cried Barkins. "I say, how would you like to live in one of those house-boats?"

"I call it pretty good cheek of the pigtailed humbugs to set up house-boats," cried Smith. "They imitate us in everything."

"And we don't imitate them in anything, eh?" said Barkins. "Hi! look out, old Chin-chin, or we shall run you down," he shouted to a man in a sampan.

"My! what a hat!" cried Smith. "Why, it would do for an umbrella. Port, Barkins."

"All right; I won't sink him. Pull away, my lads."

"I say," I cried, as we rowed by an enormous junk, with high poop and stern painted with scarlet and gold dragons, whose eyes served for hawseholes; "think she's a pirate?"

"No," said Barkins, giving a look up at the clumsy rig, with the huge matting-sails; "it's a tea-boat."

As she glided away from us, with her crew collected astern, to climb up and watch us, grinning and making derisive gestures, Barkins suddenly swung round the telescope, slipped the strap over his head, adjusted it to the proper focus, as marked by a line scratched with the point of a penknife, and raised it to his eye, when, to my astonishment, I saw all the Chinamen drop down out of sight.

"Yes, she's a tea-boat," said Double B decisively, "and heavily laden. I wish she had pirates on board."

"Why?" cried Smith. "They'd kill all the crew."

"And then we should kill them, make a prize of the junk, and have a lot of tin to share. Bother this glass, though! I wish I hadn't brought it."

"Why?" said Smith; "we shall have some good views from up yonder, when we get to the hills at the back of the town."

"Ain't got there yet. It's so heavy and clumsy, and the sun's going to be a scorcher."

"I'll carry it, Tanner," I said.

"You shall, my boy," he cried, as he closed it up, and rapidly slipped the strap off his shoulder again. "Catch hold. Mind, if you lose it, I value it at a hundred pounds."

"Say five while you're about it, Tanner," cried Smith. "Why, it isn't worth twopence—I mean I wouldn't give you a dollar for it. But I say, my lads, look here, what are we going to do first?" continued Smith, who was in a high state of excitement, though I was as bad. "Start off at once for a walk through the city?"

"Shouldn't we be mobbed?" I said, as I slung the heavy glass over my shoulder.

"They'd better mob us!" cried Smith. "If they give me any of their nonsense, I'll take tails instead of scalps. My! what fools they do look, with their thick-soled shoes, long blue gowns, and shaven heads!"

"That fellow in the boat is grinning at us, and thinks we look fools, I said."

"Let him!" said Barkins. "We know better."

"But what are we going to do?" I said. "I hate being in a crowd."

"Oh, they won't crowd us," said Barkins contemptuously. "Here, hi! you sir; mind where you're going. There, I thought you'd do it!"

This was to a young Chinaman, in a boat something like a Venetian gondola, which he was propelling by one oar as he stood up in the bows watching us, and was rowing one moment, the next performing a somersault in the air before plunging into the water between the port oars of our boat with a tremendous splash.

I did not say anything, thinking that it was a case of running up against a man, and then crying, "Where are you shoving to?" but leaned over the side, and caught at the first thing I saw, which happened to be the long black plaited pigtail, and, hauling upon it, the yellow, frightened face appeared, two wet hands clutched my arm, and, amidst a tremendous outburst of shouting in a highly-pitched tone, boats crowded round us, and the man was restored to his sampan, which was very little damaged by the blow inflicted by our stem.

"Give way, my lads," cried Barkins, and we rowed on towards the landing-place, followed by a furious yelling; men shaking their fists, and making signs suggestive of how they would like to serve us if they had us there.

"I'm sorry you knocked him over," I said.

"Who knocked him over, stupid?" cried Barkins. "Why, he ran right across our bows. Oh, never mind him! I daresay he wanted washing. I don't care. Of course, I shouldn't have liked it if he had been drowned."

Ten minutes later we were close in to the wharf, and Smith exclaimed—

"I say, why don't we get that interpreter chap to take us all round the place?"

"Don't know where he lives," said Barkins, "or it wouldn't be a bad plan."

"I know," I cried.

"How do you know?"

"He showed me when he was on board, through the little glass he wanted to sell you."

"Why, you couldn't see through that cheap thing, could you?"

"Yes, quite plain. It's just there, close to the warehouses, with a signboard out."

"So it is," cried Smith, shading his eyes; and he read aloud from a red board with gilt letters thereon—

Ching
Englis' spoken
Interpret
Fancee shop

Just then the boat glided up against the wood piles; we sprang out on to the wharf, ordered the men back, and stood for two minutes watching them well on their return for fear of any evasions, and then found ourselves in the midst of a dense crowd of the lower-class Chinese, in their blue cotton blouses and trousers, thick white-soled shoes, and every man with his long black pigtail hanging down between his shoulders.

These men seemed to look upon us as a kind of exhibition, as they pressed upon us in a semicircle; and I was beginning to think that we should end by being thrust off into the water, when there was a burst of angry shouting, a pair of arms began to swing about, and the owner of the "fancee shop," whose acquaintance we had made on board, forced his way to our side, turned his back upon us, and uttered, a few words which had the effect of making the crowd shrink back a little.

Then turning to us, he began, in his highly-pitched inquiring tone— "You wantee Ching? You wantee eat, dlink, smoke? Ching talkee muchee Englis'. Come 'long! hip, hip, hoolay!"

Chapter Two
A Piece of China

Ching flourished his arms to right and left, forming a lane for us to pass along, and we followed him for the few dozen yards between the landing-place and his place of business; but it was like passing through so much human sand, which flowed in again behind us, and as soon as we were in the shelter of the lightly-built bamboo place, crowded round the door to stare in.

But Ching had regularly taken us under his protection, and, stepping into the doorway, he delivered himself of a furious harangue, which grew louder and louder, and ended by his banging to the door and fastening it; after which he turned to us with his little black eyes twinkling, and crying—

"Allee light. Ching light man light place."

We all laughed, of course, and the Chinaman joined in. Then, growing serious directly, he looked from one to the other.

"You likee dlink?"

"No, no, not yet," cried Barkins.

"No likee dlink?" said the Chinaman wonderingly; and then in a voice full of reproof, "Sailor boy likee dlink."

"Oh yes, by and by," cried Smith.

"Ah, you wantee buy fan, shawl, ivoly? Fancee shop."

"No, no, we don't want to buy anything now," cried Barkins. "We'll pay you—"

"Allee light," cried the man, brightening up, for he had looked disappointed, and he held out both hands for the promised pay.

"Oh, come, wait a bit," I said. "We want you to take us and show us the shops."

"No, no. Shop no good. Bess shop—fancee shop, Ching."

"Oh yes; but we want to see the others too, and the streets."

"Stleet allee full dust—allee full mud. No good."

"Never mind," said Barkins; "we want to see them, and the temples and mandarins' houses."

"Pliest shut up temple. Want muchee money. Mandalin call soldier man muchee, put all in plison. No good."

"They'd better," cried Smith; "why, the captain would blow all the place down with his big guns."

"No blow Ching fancee shop down. Englis' spoken. Good fliend."

"Look here, Ching. Shut up shop, and come and take us all round the town to see everything, and we'll each give you a dollar."

"Thlee dollar?" cried the man, holding his head on one side, and raising three fingers.

"Yes," we cried, and once more his hand went out.

"What can't you trust us?" cried Smith.

"No tlust. All pay leady money. Go 'board. Fo'get."

"Oh no, we shan't," I cried. "And look here, Ching, after we've been round the town we want to go to the theatre."

"'Top flee day to go to fleatre?" he said.

"Three days! no. We must be back on board at sundown."

"No go fleatre—no time."

"Never mind the theatre, then," cried Barkins. "Now then, off we go. And I say, boys, let's have something to eat first."

"Wantee something eatee?" cried Ching, making for a canister upon a shelf.

"No, no," cried Smith, "not that. We want a good dinner. Do you know what a restaurant is?"

"Lestaulant?"

The Chinaman shook his head.

"Wantee good din': eat muchee soup, fis', cakee?"

"Yes, that's right; come along."

The yellow-faced man went softly to the door and listened, while we glanced round at the collection of common Chinese curios, carvings, lanterns, sunshades, stuffed birds, bits of silk, and cane baskets which filled the place, till he came back to us with a cunning look, and his eyes twinkling, as Smith said, "like two currants in a penny bun."

"Too muchee men all wait," he whispered. "No talkee talkee;" and, making a gesture to us to be very silent, he led us through the back of his shop into a smaller room, closed and fastened the door, and then led us through another into a kind of yard full of boxes and old tea-chests, surrounded by a bamboo paling.

There was a gate at the end of this, and he led us through, fastened it, and, signing to us to follow, led us in and out behind houses, where we sometimes saw a woman or two, sometimes children at play, all of whom took refuge within till we had passed.

"Big clowd outside, wait long time," said Ching, with a laugh; and directly after he led us along a narrow alley and out into a busy street, which was crowded enough, but with people going to and fro, evidently on business, and though all stopped to look, and some followed, it was not a waterside crowd of loafers, but of respectable people, moved by curiosity to watch the barbarian sailors passing along their street, but paying most heed to me with the heavy glass.

I'm getting an old man now, my lads—the old boy who is writing this log; but it all comes back as clear to my mind's eye as if it were only yesterday: the narrow, busy street, with men shuffling along carrying packages, baskets of fruit and vegetables or fish, cages too containing birds, and all in the same way slung at the ends of a stout bamboo placed across the bearer's shoulder, and swinging there as if the man were carrying curious-looking pairs of scales.

The shops were as bright and gay as paint and gilding laid on their quaint carvings could make them, while on their fronts hung curious lanterns, banners, and signs covered with Chinese characters, all of which I longed to decipher, and at which I was ready to stop and stare, till Ching bade me imperatively, "Come 'long."

"Chinaman no fond love English sailor allee same Ching. Don't know better. Come 'long."

This drew my attention to the fact that among the faces full of curiosity there were plenty which greeted us with a heavy, dull scowl, and, recalling the fact that we were only "foreign devils," according to their teachings, it seemed better to obey our guide, though we were all bitten by the same desire to stop and inspect the various shops and stores we passed.

Ching led us farther and farther away from the riverside, and past enclosures at whose gates stood truculent-looking, showily-dressed men, who carried swords hung from a kind of baldrick, and scowled at us from beneath their flat, conical lacquered hats. And I noticed that our guide always hurried us past these gateways, peeps through which were wonderfully attractive, showing as they did glimpses of gardens which looked like glorified, highly-coloured representations of our old friends the willow-pattern plates.

One in particular was so open that Smith stopped short, heedless of the presence of three fierce-looking Chinamen, with showy robes and long pendent moustachios.

"Look here, boys," he cried. "What a game! Here's the old bridge over the water, and the cannon-ball tree, and the gold-fish pond, and—"

"Come 'long," whispered Ching hurriedly; and he caught our comrade by the arm, forcing him onward as the guards scowled at us fiercely.

"Here, what are you up to?" cried Smith, resenting the interference.

"Take velly much care of Englis' offlicers. Big mandalin live there. Men sword velly sharp—cut off head."

"Bosh!" said Smith shortly; "they'd better."

"Oh no, they hadn't," cried Barkins. "We don't want to take you on board without any head."

"But they daren't hurt us," cried Smith bumptiously. "We're Englishmen, and our gunboat is in the river. I'm not afraid. Why, there'd be a war if one of these men interfered with us. Our people would land and burn up the place."

"No," said Ching quietly. "Send letter to mandalin. Why you men cut off little offlicer head?"

"Here, who are you calling little officer, Pigtail?" cried Smith indignantly.

"Mean young offlicer," cried Ching hastily. "Say, Why you men cut chop young offlicer head off? Mandalin say, Velly solly. He find out who blave was who chop young offlicer head, and give him lichi."

"You mean toco?" said Barkins.

"No; lichi."

"What's lichi?" I said.

"Tie blave up along post, and man come velly sharp sword, cut him all in 'lit pieces while he live."

"And do they do that?" I asked, in horror.

"Neve' find out blave who chop off head," said Ching, with a queer twinkle of the eyes. "No find blave, no can give him lichi."

"Sounds pleasant, Poet, don't it?" said Barkins.

"Horrid!" I cried, with a shudder.

"Moral: Don't try to peep into mandarins' gateways, Blacksmith," continued Barkins.

"Bosh! it's all gammon. I should like to see one of them try to cut my head off."

"I shouldn't," I cried, laughing; "and he wouldn't."

"No," said Ching perfectly seriously. "Velly bad have head chop off. Head velly useful."

"Very," said Barkins mockingly. "Well done, Chinese Wisdom. I say, Herrick, why is a mandarin like the Grand Panjandrum?"

"Because he plays at the game of catch, catch, can and can't catch the man who cuts off the English fellow's head," said Smith.

"Wrong!" cried Barkins. "Now you, Poet."

"Because he's got a little round button on the top."

"Good boy, go up one," cried Barkins.

"Hallo! what place is this?"

"Velly good place, eatee drinkee. All velly nicee nicee."

"Here, I say, Ching," cried Smith, "gently; any one would think we were babies. Stow some of that nicee nicee."

"Yes! Stow all along inside, like ship. Allee good. Come 'long."

For we had reached a showy-looking open-sided building, standing a little way back in a well-kept garden, with rockeries and tiny fish-ponds, clipped trees and paved walks, while the large open house displayed tables and neat-looking waiters going to and fro, attending upon well-dressed Chinamen, whose occupation was so much in accordance with our desires, that we entered at once, and Ching led the way to a table; one of the waiters coming up smiling as soon as we were seated.

"Now then," cried Barkins, who was full of memories of hard biscuit and tough salt beef, "what are we going to have to eat?"

"I don't know," I said, looking round uneasily. "What have they got?"

"Here, let's make Ching order the dinner," cried Smith. "Look here, old chap. We can have a good dinner for a dollar apiece, can't we?"

"Velly good dinner, dollar piecee," he replied.

"That's right," said Barkins; "we don't have a chance every day to spend a dollar upon our dinner. Go it, Ching. Tell the waiter fellow, and order for yourself too. But I say, boys, we must have birds'-nest soup."

"Of course," we chorussed, though Smith and I agreed afterwards that we rather shrank from trying the delicacy.

Ching lost no time in giving the orders, and in a very few minutes the man bustled up with saucers and basins, and we began tasting this and tasting that as well as we could with the implements furnished to us for the purpose, to wit chopsticks, each watching the apparently wonderful skill with which Ching transferred his food from the tiny saucers placed before him, and imitating his actions with more or less success—generally less.

We had some sweet stuff, and some bits of cucumber cut up small, and some thick sticky soap-like stuff, which rather put me in mind of melted blancmange with salt and pepper instead of sugar, and when this was ended came saucers of mincemeat.

"'Tain't bad," whispered Barkins, as we ate delicately. "Peg away, lads. We're pretty safe so long as we eat what Pigtail does."

I did not feel so sure; but I was hungry, and as the food did not seem to be, as Barkins said, bad, I kept on, though I could not help wondering what we were eating.

"I say, Ching," said Smith suddenly, "when's the birds'-nest soup coming? Oughtn't we to have had that first?"

"Eat um all up lit' bit go," replied Ching.

"What, that sticky stuff?" I cried.

"Yes. No have velly bess flesh birds'-ness for dolla'; but all velly good. Nicee nicee, velly nicee."

"Don't!" cried Smith excitedly.

"Let him be, Blacksmith," said Barkins; "it's only his way. Ah, here's something else!"

I looked at the little saucers placed before us, in which, neatly divided, were little appetising-looking brown heaps, covered with rich gravy, and smelling uncommonly nice.

"What's this?" said Barkins, turning his over with the chopsticks.

"Velly good," said Ching, smiling, and making a beginning.

"Yes; don't smell bad," said Smith. "I know: it's quails. There's lots of quail in China. 'Licious!"

I had a little bit of the white meat and brown gravy, which I had separated from a tiny bone with the chopsticks, and was congratulating myself on my cleverness, when it dropped back into my saucer, for Ching, with his mouth full, said quietly—

"No, not lit' bird—lat."

"What's lat?" said Barkins suspiciously.

"No lat," said Ching smiling; "lat."

"Well, I said lat. What is lat?"

Smith put down his chopsticks. I had already laid down mine.

"What's the matter?" said Barkins, who kept on suspiciously turning over the contents of his saucer.

"He means rat," whispered Smith in an awful tone.

"What!" cried Barkins, pushing himself back with a comical look of disgust upon his face.

"Yes, lat," said Ching. "Velly good fat lat."

Our faces were a study. At least I know that my companions' were; and we were perfectly silent while our guide kept on making a sound with his mouth as he supped up the rich gravy.

"Here, hold hard a minute," said Smith. "I mean you, Ching."

"Yes?" said the Chinaman, with a pleasant smile; and he crossed his chopsticks, and looked at our brother middy inquiringly.

"What was that we were eating a little while ago?"

"Clucumber; velly good."

"No, no; before that."

"Birds'-ness soup; velly cost much. Not all birds'-ness. Some shark-fis' fin."

"I don't mean that, I tell you," cried Smith in an exasperated tone of voice. "I mean that other brown meat cut up small into the brown sauce. It was rabbit, wasn't it?"

"Oh no," said Ching decisively; "no labbit. Lit' mince-up pup-dog. Nicee nicee."

Smith turned green, and his eyes rolled so that he actually squinted; while Barkins uttered a low sound-like gasp. As for me, I felt as I remember feeling after partaking meekly of what one of my aunts used to call prune tea—a decoction made by boiling so many French plums along with half an ounce of senna leaves.

"Oh gracious!" murmured Barkins; while Smith uttered a low groan.

"You both likee more?" said Ching blandly.

"No!" they cried so unanimously that it was like one voice; and in spite of my own disgust and unpleasant sensations I felt as if I must laugh at them.

"Oh, mawkish morsels!" muttered Barkins.

"You feel you have 'nuff?" said Ching, smiling. "Oh no. Loas' suck-pig come soon. You eat velly much more."

"Not if I know it," whispered Smith to me. "I don't believe it'll be pig."

"What then?" I whispered back.

"Kid."

"Well, kid's nice."

"Get out! I meant baby."

"Ugh! Don't."

"It's too late to say don't," groaned Smith. "We've done it."

"Hold up, old chap," I whispered. "Everybody's looking at you."

"Let 'em," he groaned. "Oh, I do feel so ill!"

"Nonsense! Look at Tanner."

He turned his wild eyes upon Barkins, whose aspect was ludicrous enough to make him forget his own sensations, and he smiled a peculiarly saddened, pensive smile; for our messmate was leaning towards Ching.

"Don't eat any more of that," he said faintly.

"Eat um all up; velly good."

"Can one get a drop of brandy here?"

"Dlop blandy? No. Velly nicee 'lack."

"What's 'lack?"

"No, no 'lack! lice spilit."

"'Rack!" I said—"arrack?"

"Yes, allack," said Ching, nodding.

"Let's have some—a glass each," said Barkins; "and look sharp."

Ching summoned one of the smiling waiters, and the order was given. Then for the first time he noticed that we had not finished the contents of our little saucers.

"No eat lat?" he cried.

I shook my head.

"Velly good!"

"We're not quite well," said Smith.

"Been out in the sun too much," added Barkins.

"Ah, sun too much bad! Lit' dlop spilit make quite well. No eat lat?"

"No, no!" we cried in chorus.

"Velly good," said our guide; and in alarm lest such a delicacy should be wasted, he drew first one and then the other saucer over to his side, and finished their contents.

Long before this, though, the attendant had brought us three tiny glasses of white spirit, which we tossed off eagerly, with the result that the qualmish sensations passed away; but no recommendations on the part of our guide could induce us to touch anything that followed, saving sundry preparations of rice and fruit, which were excellent.

The dinner over, Ching took us about the garden to inspect the lilies in pots, the gold and silver fish, fat and wonderfully shaped, which glided about in the tanks and ponds, and then led us into a kind of arbour, where, beneath a kind of wooden eave, an instrument was hanging from a peg. It was not a banjo, for it was too long; and it was not a guitar, for it was too thin, and had not enough strings; but it was something of the kind, and evidently kept there for the use of musically-disposed visitors.

"You likee music?" said Ching.

"Oh yes," I replied dubiously, as I sat using the telescope, gazing right away over the lower part of the town at the winding river, with its crowds of craft.

"Why, he isn't going to play, is he?" whispered Smith. "We don't want to hear that. Let's go out in the town."

"Don't be in such a hurry," replied Barkins. "The sun's too hot. I say, our dinner wasn't such a very great success, was it?"

Smith shook his head, and just then Ching began to tune the instrument, screwing the pegs up and down, and producing the most lugubrious sounds, which somehow made me begin to think of home, and how strange it was to be sitting there in a place which seemed like part of a picture, listening to the Chinese guide.

I had forgotten the unpleasantry of the dinner in the beauty of the scene, for there were abundance of flowers, the sky was of a vivid blue, and the sun shone down brilliantly, and made the distant water of the river sparkle.

Close by there were the Chinese people coming and going in their strange costume; a busy hum came through the open windows; and I believe that in a few minutes I should have been asleep, if Ching had not awakened me by his vigorous onslaught upon the instrument, one of whose pegs refused to stay in exactly the right place as he kept on tuning.

Peng—feng—peng—pang—pacing—pang—peng—ping—pang—peng— paang.

Then a little more screwing up.

Peng, peng, pang—pong.

Ching stopped, nursed the instrument upon his knee as if it were a baby, pulled out the offending peg as if it were a tooth, moistened the hole, replaced the peg, and began again—screw, screw, screw.

Peng—peng—ping—pang—pong—pung—pungh—pungh—poonh— poingh—pank—peng—peng, peng, pang—pang—pang,—peng.

Just a quarter of a tone out still, and he tried again diligently, while my eyes half closed, and the Tanner and Blacksmith both nodded in the heat.

Ping—peng—peng—pung—pang—pang—paang—paang—paeng—paeng.

Right at last; and Ching threw himself back so that his mouth would open to the widest extent, struck a chord on the three strings, and burst forth with celestial accompaniment into what was in all probability a passionate serenade, full of allusions to nightingales, moonbeams, dew-wet roses, lattice-windows, and beautiful moon-faced maidens, but which sounded to me like—

> "Ti ope I ow wow,
> Ti ope I ow yow,
> Ti ope I ow tow,
> Ti ope I ligh."

The words, I say, sounded like that: the music it would be impossible to give, for the whole blended together into so lamentable a howl, that both Barkins and Smith started up into wakefulness from a deep sleep, and the former looked wildly round, as confused and wondering he exclaimed—

"What's matter?"

As for Smith, he seemed to be still half-asleep, and he sat up, staring blankly at the performer, who kept on howling—I can call it nothing else—in the most doleful of minor keys.

"I say," whispered Barkins, "did you set him to do that?"

I shook my head.

"Because—oh, just look! here are all the people coming out to see what's the matter."

He was right as to the people coming, for in twos and threes, as they finished the refreshment of which they had been partaking, first one path was filled and then another, the people coming slowly up and stopping to listen, while Barkins stared at them in blank astonishment.

"Here Nat—Poet," he whispered, "look at 'em."

"I am looking," I said. "Isn't it just like a picture?"

"It's like an old firescreen," he said; "but I don't mean that. Look! Hang me if the beggars don't seem to like it. Can't you stop him?"

"No, of course not."

"But how long will it be before he has run down?"

"I don't know," I whispered. "But look, aren't those like some of the men we saw by the gates?"

I drew his attention to about half-a-dozen fierce-looking men in showy coats and lacquered hats, who came up to the garden, stared hard at us, and then walked in. Each of them, I noticed, wore a sword, and a kind of dagger stuck in his belt, and this made me at once recall their offensive looks and contemptuous manner towards us, and think of how far we were away from the ship, and unarmed, save for the ornamental dirks which hung from our belts, weapons that would have been, even if we had known how to use them, almost like short laths against the Chinamen's heavy, broad-bladed, and probably sharp swords.

"I say, Gnat," whispered Barkins, "those must be the chaps we saw at the mandarin's gate. Never mind; we'll ask them to have something as soon as old Ching has finished his howling."

But that did not seem likely to be for some time, and I began to think, as I sat there noticing how the men were gradually closing in upon us, that our position was not very safe, right away from the landing-place, and that we had done wrong in stopping so long where we were. I knew that the Chinese were obsequious and humble enough so long as they were face to face with a stronger power, but if they had the upper hand, cruel and merciless to any one not of their own nation, and that it was wiser to give them a wide berth.

Then I began to think that the captain had been too ready to believe in our prestige in giving us leave to go, and that we should have been wiser if we had stayed on board. Finally, I had just come to the conclusion that we ought to stop Ching in his howling or singing, which grew more and more vehement as he saw that his audience was increasing, when Smith jogged my elbow.

"I say," he whispered, "let's get away from here."

"Why?" I said, to get to know what he thought.

"Because I'm afraid those chaps with the swords mean mischief."

"I say, lads," said Barkins, leaning towards us, "aren't those chaps crowding us up rather? What do they mean? Here, I'm senior, and the skipper said I was to take care of you youngsters. We'll go back to the wharf at once."

"What's the good?" said Smith. "The boat won't be there to fetch us off till sundown."

"Never mind, let's get away from here," said Barkins decisively; "we don't want to get in a row with the Chinese, and that's what they want."

"But they're quiet enough," I said, growing nervous all the while.

"Yes, they're quiet enough now," whispered Barkins; "but you look at that big fellow with the yellow belt, he keeps on making faces at us."

"Let him; that will not hurt us."

"I know that, little stupid," he cried, "but what follows may. Look at him now."

I looked up quickly, and saw the man turn away from looking at us, and say something to his fierce-looking companions, who glanced towards us and laughed.

"There," said Barkins, "I'm not going to be laughed at by those jolly old pigtailed heathens. Here, Ching, old chap, we want to go."

As he spoke he gave our guide a sharp nudge, which made him turn round and stare.

"Ti—ope—I—ow!"

"Do you hear? We want to go!"

"Ti—ope—I—ow!" howled Ching, beginning again.

"Yes, we want to go," I said anxiously.

"Ti—ope—I—ow!" he howled again, but as he gave forth his peculiar sounds he suddenly struck—purposely—a false, jarring note, lowered the instrument, seized one of the pegs as if in a passion, and began talking to me in a low, earnest voice, to the accompaniment of the string he tuned.

"Ching see now,"—*peng, peng, peng*—"bad men with swords,"—*pang, peng*—"look velly closs,"—*pang, pong*—"wantee fightee,"—*pang, pang*—"you no wantee fightee,"—*pung, pung*.

"No," I whispered anxiously; "let's go at once."

"No takee notice,"—*pang, peng, peng*. "All flee, walkee walkee round one sidee house,"—*pang, pong*—"Ching go long other sidee,"—*peng, peng*. "No make, hully—walkee velly slow over lit' blidge,"—*ping, ping, ping, ping, pang, pang*.

The little bridge was just behind us, and I grasped all he said—that we were to go slowly over the bridge and walk round the back of the house, while he would go round the front and meet us on the other side.

Bang, jangle, pang, pang, ping, ping, peng, peng, went the instrument, as Ching strummed away with all his might.

"Wait, Ching come show way," he whispered. And as I saw that the mandarin's men were coming nearer and evidently meant mischief, Ching raised his instrument again, and, after a preliminary flourish, began once more, to the delight of the crowd. My messmates and I slowly left our places and walked round the summer-house towards the little bridge over one of the gold-fish tanks, moving as deliberately as we could, while Ching's voice rang out, "Ti—ope—I—ow!" as if nothing were the matter.

The little crowd was between us and the mandarin's retainers, but it was hard work to appear cool and unconcerned. Above all, it took almost a superhuman effort to keep from looking back.

Smith could not resist the desire, and gave a sharp glance round.

"They're coming after us," he whispered. "We shall have to cut and run."

"No, no," said Barkins hoarsely. "They'd overtake us directly. They'd come down like a pack of wolves. We must be cool, lads, and be ready to turn and draw at the last. The beggars are awful cowards after all."

We went on over the bridge, and, in spite of my dread, I made believe to look down at the gold-fish, pointing below at them, but seizing the opportunity to look out for danger.

It was a quick glance, and it showed me that the crowd from the eating-house were taking no notice of us, but listening to Ching, who had left his seat, and, singing with all his might, was walking along one of the paths towards the front of the low building, while we were slowly making for the back, with the result of crowding the mandarin's men back a little, for the whole of the company moved with our guide, carefully making room for him to play, and thus unconsciously they hampered the movements of our enemies.

The distance was not great, of course—fifty yards altogether, perhaps, along winding and doubling walks, for the Chinese are ingenious over making the most of a small garden, but it was long enough to keep us in an intense state of excitement, as from time to time we caught sight of the men following us.

Then we saw that they had stopped to watch which way we went, and directly after we knew that they were only waiting for us to be behind the house to go back and hurry round and meet us.

At last we had passed to the end of the maze-like walk, and were sheltered by the house from the little crowd and our enemies, with the result that all felt relieved.

"I say," said Smith, "isn't this only a scare?"

"Don't know," said Barkins. "P'raps so; but I shan't be sorry to get on board again. They think nothing of cutting a fellow to pieces."

"Let's make haste, then," I said; and, nothing loth, the others hurried on past the back of the house, where the kitchen seemed to be, and plenty of servants were hurrying to and fro, too busy to take any heed of us. Then we turned the corner, and found that we were opposite to a gateway opening upon a very narrow lane, which evidently went along by the backs of the neighbouring houses, parallel with the main street, which was, however, not such a great deal wider than this.

"Here's a way for us to go down, at all events," said Barkins, after we had listened for a few moments for Ching's song, and the wiry notes of his instrument.

"Yes, let's cut down at once," said Smith.

"Where to?" I said excitedly. "We can't find our way without Ching."

"No; and those beggars would hunt us down there at once," said Barkins. "Won't do. I say, though, why don't they give us better tools than these to wear?"

"Hark!" I said; "listen!"

We listened, but there was nothing but the murmur of voices in the house, and not a soul to be seen on our side, till all at once I caught sight of something moving among the shrubs, and made out that it was the gay coat of one of the men from whom we sought to escape.

"Come on!" said Smith excitedly, and he threw open the gate leading into the narrow lane, so that in another moment we should have been in full retreat, had not a door behind us in the side of the house been opened, and Ching appeared.

He did not speak, but made a sign for us to enter, and we were hardly inside and the door thrust to—all but a chink big enough for our guide to use for reconnoitring—when we heard the soft pat-pat of the men's boots, then the rustle of their garments, and the tap given by one of their swords as they passed through the gateway and ran down the narrow lane.

"All gone along, catchee you," whispered Ching. "Come 'long other way."

He stepped out, made us follow, and then carefully closed the door.

"Now, come 'long this way," he said, with his eyes twinkling. "No walkee fast. Allee boy lun after."

We saw the wisdom of his proceedings, and followed him, as he took us by the way our enemies had come, straight out into the main street, down it a little way, and then up a turning, which he followed till we came to another important street parallel to the one by which we had come, and began to follow it downward toward the waterside.

"Muchee flighten?" he said.

"Oh, I don't know," growled Barkins, who had the deepest voice of the three. "It was startling. Did they mean mischief?"

"Mean chop chop. Allee bad wick' men. No catchee now. Ching velly much flighten."

He did not look so, but chatted away with open, smiling face, as he pointed first on one side then on the other to some striking-looking shop or building, though he never paused for a moment, but kept on at a good rate without showing a sign of hurry or excitement.

"How are we to get on board when we get to the river?" I said, as we went on. "There'll be no boat till sundown."

"Ching get one piecee boat low all aboard ship."

"Can't you keep us in your place till our boat comes?"

The man shook his head. "Mandalin boy come burn um down, makee all lun out. So velly hot. No stay. Get boat, low away."

"How far is it, do you think?" asked Smith.

"I don't know," said Barkins. "We seemed to be walking for hours in the hot sun coming up. How far is it, Ching?"

"Velly long way. No look at garden now."

He pointed to one of the handsome gateways about which a party of armed retainers were hanging, and, whispering to us not to take any notice, he walked us steadily along.

But we were not to get by the place without notice, for the loungers saw us coming, and strode out in a swaggering way—three big sturdy fellows in blue and scarlet, and pretty well blocked the way as they stood scowling at us.

"Look out," whispered Barkins, "ready with your toasting-forks, and then if it comes to it we must run."

"You'll stick by us, Gnat," whispered Smith in a hasty whisper.

"I'll try," I said.

"Keep velly close," whispered Ching. "No takee notice. No talkee closs. Ching speakee."

He said something in Chinese to the men, and led us in single file between the two most fierce-looking, our prompt action taking them somewhat by surprise, and, as we gave them no excuse for taking offence, they only turned to gaze after us.

There were plenty of people in the street ready to stand and look at us, and we met with no interruption from them, but I could not help seeing the anxiety in Ching's face, and how from time to time he wiped his streaming brow. But as soon as he saw either of us looking at him he smiled as if there was nothing the matter whatever.

"No velly long now," he said. "Lot bad men to-day. You come walkee walkee 'gain?"

"It's not very tempting, Ching," I said. "Why can't they leave us alone?"

He tightened his lips and shook his head. Then, looking sharply before him, he hurried us along a little more.

"Wish got ten—twenty—piecee soldier man 'longside," he whispered to me, and the next minute he grasped my arm with a spasmodic snatch.

"What's the matter?" I said.

He did not speak, but looked sharply to right and left for a means of escape. For, in spite of the cleverness of our guide, the mandarin's men had been as cunning. They had either divined or been told that we had made for the other street, and had contrived to reach the connecting lane along which we should have to pass. Here they had planted themselves, and just as we were breathing more freely, in the belief that before long we should reach the shore of the great river, we caught sight of them in company with about a dozen more.

We were all on the point of halting, as we saw them about fifty yards in front, but Ching spoke out sharply—

"No stoppee," he said firmly. "Lun away, all come catchee and choppee off head. Go 'long stlaight and flighten 'em. Englis' sailor foleign debil, 'flaid o' nobody."

"There's something in that," said Barkins. "Right. Show a bold front, lads. Let's go straight by them, and if they attack, then out with your swords and let's make a fight for it."

I heard Smith say, "All right," and my heart was beating very fast as I said the same.

Frightened? Of course I was. I don't believe the boy ever lived who would not feel frightened at having to face death. For it was death we had to face then, and in the ugliest shape. But Smith's words sent a thrill through us.

"I say, lads," he said, "we've got to fight this time. If we begged for our lives they'd only serve us worse; so let 'em have it, and recollect that, if they kill us, the old *Teasers'll* come and burn their town about their ears."

"'Fraid, Ching?" I whispered; for he and I were in front.

"No 'flaid now," he whispered back. "Plenty flighten by and by."

He smiled as he spoke, and led us straight on to where the four mandarin's men and the rough-looking fellows with them blocked the road, and if for a moment we had shown any hesitation, I believe they would have rushed at us like wolves. But Ching kept his head up as if proud of acting as guide to three British officers, and when we got close up he nodded smilingly at the men in the mandarin's colours, and then, as if astounded at the little crowd standing fast, he burst out into a furious passion, shouting at them in a wild gabble of words, with the effect of making them give way at once, so that we passed through.

Then I heard him draw a panting breath, and saw that he was ghastly.

"Walkee walkee," he whispered. "Not velly fast. 'Top I say lun, and lun fast alleegether."

At that moment there was a loud shouting behind, then a yell, and, turning my head, I saw that the mandarin's men had their great blades out, and were leading the men after us, shouting to excite themselves and the little mob.

"Now lun!" cried Ching. "I showee way."

"No!" shouted Barkins. "Draw swords and retreat slowly."

We whipped out our weapons and turned to face the enemy, knowing full well that they would sweep over us at the first rush, while a feeling of rage ran through me, as in my despairing fit I determined to make the big fellow opposite to me feel one dig of English steel before he cut me down.

Then they were upon us with a rush, and I saw Ching dart in front and cleverly snatch one of the clumsy swords from the nearest man. The next moment he had whirled it up with both hands, when—

Boom—Crash!

There was the report of a heavy gun, whose concussion made the wooden houses on each side jar and quiver as it literally ran up the narrow street, and, to our astonishment, we saw the little mob turn on the instant and begin to run, showing us, instead of their fierce savage faces, so many black pigtails; the mandarin's men, though, last.

"Hooray!" we yelled after them, and they ran the faster.

"Now, velly quick," panted Ching. "Come back again soon."

We uttered another shout, and hurried along the lane to the principal street, turned at right angles, and began to hurry along pretty rapidly now, Ching marching beside us with the big sword over his shoulder.

But the scare was only temporary, the tremendous report was not repeated, and before a minute had elapsed, our guide, who kept glancing back, cried—

"Now, lun velly fast. Come along catchee catchee, and no big gun go shoot this time."

He was quite right, and we took to our heels, with the yelling mob close at hand, and so many people in front, that we felt certain of being run down long before we could reach the waterside.

"And no chance for us when we do," muttered Barkins from close behind me. "Oh, if a couple of dozen of our lads were only here! Why didn't they send 'em?" he panted, "instead of firing as a signal for us to go back on board."

Chapter Three
Cutting it Close

My messmate uttered these words close to my ears in a despairing tone as we dashed on, and now I saw Ching strike to his right, while I made a cut or two at my left, as men started from the sides and tried to trip us up.

I was growing faint with the heat down in that narrow, breathless street, my clothes stuck to me, and Barkins' heavy telescope banged heavily against my side, making me feel ready to unfasten the strap and let it fall. But I kept on for another fifty yards or so with our enemies yelling in the rear, and the waterside seeming to grow no nearer.

"Keep together, lads," cried Barkins excitedly. "It can't be far now. We'll seize the first boat we come to, and the tide will soon take us out of their reach."

But these words came in a broken, spasmodic way, for, poor fellow, he was as out of breath as any of us.

"Hoolay! Velly lit' way now," cried Ching; and then he finished with a howl of rage, for half-a-dozen armed men suddenly appeared from a gateway below us, and we saw at a glance that they were about to take sides with the rest.

"Lun—lun," yelled Ching, and, flourishing his sword, he led us right at the newcomers, who, startled and astounded by our apparent boldness, gave way, and we panted on, utterly exhausted, for another fifty yards, till Ching suddenly stopped in an angle of the street formed by a projecting house.

"No lun. No, no!" he panted. "Fight—kill."

Following his example, we faced round, and our bold front checked the miserable gang of wretches, who stopped short a dozen yards from us, their numbers swelled by the new party, and waited yelling and howling behind the swordsmen, who stood drawing up their sleeves, and brandishing their heavy weapons, working themselves up for the final rush, in which I knew we should be hacked to pieces.

"Good-bye, old chap," whispered Barkins in a piteous tone, his voice coming in sobs of exhaustion. "Give point when they come on: don't strike. Try and kill one of the cowardly beggars before they finish us."

"Yes," I gasped.

"Chuck that spyglass down," cried Smith; "it's in your way."

Gladly enough I swung the great telescope round, slipped the strap over my head, and as I did so I saw a sudden movement in the crowd.

In an instant the experience we had had upon the river flashed across my brain. I recalled how the crew of the great tea-boat had dropped away from her high stern when Barkins had used the glass, and for the first time I grasped why this had been.

My next actions were in a mad fit of desperate mischief more than anything else. For, recalling that I had a few flaming fusees in my jacket pocket, I snatched out the box, secured one; then, taking off the cap, which hung by a strap, I pulled the brass and leather telescope out to its full extent, presented the large end at the mob, uttered as savage a yell as I could and struck a fusee, which went off with a crack, and flashed and sparkled with plenty of blaze.

The effect was instantaneous. Mistaking the big glass, which had been a burden to me all day, for some terrible new form of gun, the swordsmen uttered a wild yell of horror, and turned and fled, driving the unarmed mob before them, all adding their savage cries of dread.

"Hoor-rah," shouted Barkins. "Now, boys, a Yankee tiger. Waggle the glass well, Gnat. All together. Hurrah—rah—rah—rah—rah!"

We produced as good an imitation of the American cheer as we could, and Ching supplemented it with a hideous crack-voiced yell, while I raised and lowered the glass and struck another match.

As we looked up the street we could see part of the mob still running hard, but the swordsmen had taken refuge to right and left, in doorways, angles, and in side shops, and were peering round at us, watching every movement.

"No' laugh!" said Ching anxiously. "Big fool. Think um bleech-loader. Now, come 'long, walkee walkee blackward. I go first."

It was good advice, and we began our retreat, having the street to ourselves for the first minute. My messmates supported me on either side, and we walked backward with military precision.

"Well done, gun carriage," panted Barkins to me. "I say, Blacksmith, who says the old glass isn't worth a hundred pounds now?"

"Worth a thousand," cried Smith excitedly. "But look out, they're coming out of their holes again."

I made the object-glass end describe a circle in the air as we slowly backed, and the swordsmen darted away to the shelters they had quitted to follow us as they saw us in retreat. But as there was no report, and they saw us escaping, they began to shout one to the other, and ran to and fro, zig-zagging down the street after us, each man darting across to a fresh place of shelter. And as the retreat went on, and no report with a rush of bullets tore up the street, the men gained courage; the mob high up began to gather again. Then there was distant yelling and shouting, and the danger seemed to thicken.

"Is it much farther, Ching?" cried Barkins.

"Yes, velly long way," he replied. "No' got no levolvers?"

"No, I wish I had."

"Fine levolver bull-dog in fancee shop, and plenty cahtlidge. Walkee fast."

We were walking backwards as fast as we could, and the danger increased. In place of running right across now from shelter to shelter, the big swordsmen stopped from time to time on their way to flourish their weapons, yell, indulge in a kind of war-dance, and shout out words we did not understand.

"What do they say, Ching?" asked Smith.

"Say chop all in lit' small piece dilectly."

"Look here," cried Barkins, as the demonstrations increased, and the wretches now began to gather on each side of the street as if threatening a rush, "let's stop and have a shot at 'em."

"No, no," cried Ching, "won't go off blang."

"Never mind, we'll pretend it will. Halt!"

We stopped, so did our enemies, and, in imitation of the big gun practice on board ship, Barkins shouted out order after order, ending with, Fire!

Smith held the flaming fusees now, and at the word struck one with a loud crackle, just as we were beginning to doubt the efficacy of our ruse, for the enemy were watching us keenly; and, though some of them moved uneasily and threatened to run for shelter, the greater part stood firm.

But at the loud crackle and flash of the fusee, and Smith's gesture to lay it close to the eye-piece, they turned and fled yelling once more into the houses on either side, from which now came an addition to the noise, in the shrill howls and shrieks of women, who were evidently resenting the invasion of all these men.

"Now, walkee far," cried Ching. "No good no mo'. Allee fun lun out. No be big fool any longer."

We felt that he was right, and retreated as fast as we could, but still backward, mine being the duty to keep the mouth of our sham cannon to bear upon them as well as the blundering backward through the mudholes of the dirty street would allow.

That street seemed to be endless to us in our excitement, and the feeling that our guide must be taking us wrong began to grow upon me, for I made no allowances for the long distance we had gone over in the morning, while now it grew more and more plain, by the actions of our pursuers, that they were to be cheated no more. The dummy had done its duty, and I felt that I might just as well throw it away and leave myself free, as expect the glass to scare the enemy away again.

"We shall have to make a rush for it," said Barkins at last; "but it is hard now we have got so near to safety. Shall I try the telescope again, Ching?"

"No, no good," said our guide gloomily. "Hi, quick all along here."

'I SAW THE MOB IN FULL FLIGHT.'

He made a dash for the front of a house, which seemed to offer some little refuge for us in the shape of a low fencing, behind which we could protect ourselves; for all at once there was a new development of the attack, the mob having grown during the last few minutes more daring, and now began to throw mud and stones.

Ching's sudden dash had its effect upon them, for when he ran they set up a howl of triumph, and as we dashed after our guide they suddenly altered their tactics, ceased stone-throwing, and, led by the swordsmen, charged down upon us furiously.

"It's all over," groaned Smith, as we leaped over the low fence and faced round.

And so it seemed to be, for the next minute we were stopping and dodging the blows aimed at us. It was all one wild confusion to me, in which I saw through a mist the gleaming eyes and savage faces of the mob. Then, above their howlings, and just as I was staggering back from a heavy blow which I received from a great sword, which was swept round with two hands and caught me with a loud jar on the side, I heard a familiar cheer, and saw the man who had struck me go down backwards, driven over as it were by a broad-bladed spear. As I struggled to my knees, I saw the savage mob in full flight, chased by a dozen blue-jackets, who halted and ran back to where we were, in obedience to a shrill whistle. Then—it was all more misty to me—two strong arms were passed under mine; I saw Smith treated in the same way; and, pursued by the crowd howling like demons, we were trotted at the double down the street to the wharf, which was after all close at hand, and swung down into the boat.

"Push off!" shouted a familiar voice, and the wharf and the crowd began to grow distant, but stones flew after us till the officer in command fired shot after shot from his revolver over the heads of the crowd, which then took to flight.

"What are we to do with the prisoner, sir—chuck him overboard?"

"Prisoner?" cried the officer in charge of the boat.

"Yes, sir, we got him, sword and all. He's the chap as come aboard yesterday."

"Yes," I panted as I sat up, breathing painfully, "it's Ching. He's our friend."

"Yes, flend, evelybody fiend," cried Ching. "Wantee go shore. Fancee shop."

"Go ashore?" said the officer.

"Yes, walkee shore."

"But if I set you ashore amongst that howling mob, they'll cut you to pieces."

"Ching 'flaid so. Allee bad man. Wantee kill young offlicer."

"And he fought for us, Mr Brown, like a brick," said Barkins.

"Then we must take him aboard for the present."

"Yes, go 'board, please," said Ching plaintively. "Not my sword— b'long mandalin man."

"Let's see where you're wounded," said the officer, as the men rowed steadily back towards the *Teaser*.

"I—I don't think I'm wounded," I panted, "but it hurts me rather to breathe."

"Why, I saw one of the brutes cut you down with his big sword," cried Smith.

"Yes," I said, "I felt it, but, but—yes, of course: it hit me here."

"Oh, murder!" cried Smith. "Look here, Tanner. Your glass has got it and no mistake."

It had "got it" and no mistake, for the blow from the keen sword had struck it at a sharp angle, and cut three parts of the way through the thick metal tube, which had been driven with tremendous force against my ribs.

"Oh, Gnat!" cried Barkins, as he saw the mischief, "it's quite spoilt. What a jolly shame!"

"But it saved his life," said Smith, giving him a meaning nod. "I wouldn't have given much for his chance, if he hadn't had that telescope under his arm. I say, Mr Brown, why was the gun fired?"

"To bring you all on board. Captain's got some information. Look, we've weighed anchor, and we're off directly—somewhere."

"But what about Ching?" I said to Barkins.

"Ching! Well, he'll be safe on board and unsafe ashore. I don't suppose we shall be away above a day. I say, Ching, you'll have to stop."

"Me don't mind. Velly hungly once more. Wantee pipe and go sleepee. Velly tire. Too much fightee."

We glided alongside of the gunboat the next minute, where Mr Reardon was waiting for us impatiently.

"Come, young gentlemen," he cried, "you've kept us waiting two hours. Up with you. Good gracious, what a state you're in! Nice addition to a well-dishiplined ship! and—here, what's the meaning of this?" he cried, as the boat rose to the davits. "Who is this Chinese boy?"

"Velly glad get 'board," said the man, smiling at the important officer. "All along big fight. Me Ching."

Chapter Four
Double Allowance

No time was lost in getting out of the mouth of the river, and as soon as the bustle and excitement of the start was over, we three were sent for to the cabin to relate our adventures to the captain, the first lieutenant being present to put in a word now and then.

"The brutes!" the captain kept on muttering from time to time, and Mr Reardon nodded and tightened his lips.

"Well, young gentlemen," he said, when Barkins, who as eldest had been spokesman, finished his recital, "I can do nothing. If you had all three been brutally murdered, of course the Government could have made representations to the authorities, and your families would have secured compensation."

We glanced at one another.

"But as, unfortunately—I mean fortunately—you have neither of you got a scratch, I can do nothing."

"But they were so awfully savage with us, sir," said Smith.

"Yes, Mr Smith, so I suppose. It is their nature; but we cannot punish an unknown mob. We must try and administer the castigation vicariously."

"Please, sir, I don't understand you," said Smith. "Do you mean—"

"Set a vicar to talk to them, Mr Smith? No, I do not. I mean, as we have very good information about three or four piratical junks being in the straits between here and Amoy, we must come down heavily upon them, and administer the punishment there."

Mr Reardon nodded, and rubbed his hands.

"This scrape of yours, though, will be a most severe lesson to me," continued the captain. "It was very weak and easy of me to give you all leave for a run ashore. I ought to have referred you to Mr Reardon. But you may take it for granted that I shall not err again in this way. You can return on deck."

"Oh, what a jolly shame!" grumbled Barkins. "And there was old Reardon chuckling over it, and looking as pleased as Punch. Who'd be a middy? It's like being in a floating prison."

But it was a very pleasant floating prison all the same, I could not help thinking, as we gradually got farther out from the land, over which the sun was sinking fast, and lighting up the mountain-tops with gold, while the valleys rapidly grew dark. Every one on the clean white deck was full of eager excitement, and the look-out most thoroughly on the *qui vive*. For the news that we were going up northward in search of some piratical junks sent a thrill through every breast. It meant work, the showing that we were doing some good on the China station, and possibly prize-money, perhaps promotion for some on board, though of course not for us.

We had been upon the station several months, but it had not been our good fortune to capture any of the piratical scoundrels about whose doings the merchants—Chinese as well as European—were loud in complaint. And with justice, for several cruel massacres of crews had taken place before the ships had been scuttled and burned; besides, quite a dozen had sailed from port never to be heard of more; while the only consolation Captain Thwaites had for his trips here and there, and pursuit of enemies who disappeared like Flying Dutchmen, was that the presence of our gunboat upon the coast no doubt acted as a preventative, for we were told that there used to be three times as many acts of piracy before we came.

And now, as we glided along full sail before a pleasant breeze, with the topgallant sails ruddy in the evening light, there seemed at last some prospect of real business, for it had leaked out that unless Captain Thwaites' information was very delusive, the Chinamen had quite a rendezvous on one of the most out-of-the-way islands off Formosa, from whence they issued, looking like ordinary trading-boats, and that it was due to this nest alone that so much mischief had been done.

A good meal down below, without dog or rat, as Barkins put it, had, in addition to a comfortable wash and change, made us forget a good deal of our weariness; and, as we were still off duty, we three loitered about the deck, picking up all the information we could regarding the way in which the news had been brought, in exchange for accounts of our own adventures, to insure credence in which Barkins carried about the nearly-divided telescope which had stood us in such good stead.

It was rapidly growing dark, when, close under the bulwarks, and in very near neighbourhood to one of our big bow guns, we came upon what looked in the gloom like a heap of clothes.

"What's that?" I said.

"Chine-he, sir," said one of the sailors. "We give him a good tuck-out below, and he come up then for a snooze. Hi, John! The gents want to speak to you."

There was a quick movement, and a partly bald head appeared from beneath two loose sleeves, which had been folded over it like the wings of a flying fox, and Ching's familiar squeaky voice said—

"You wantee me. Go shore?"

"No, no; not to-night," cried Smith. "We shall set you ashore when we come back."

"You go velly far—allee way Gleat Blitain?"

"No, not this time, Ching," cried Barkins, as we all laughed.

"No go allee way London? Ching wantee go London, see Queen Victolia and Plince o' Wales."

"Some other time, Ching," I said. "But I say, how about the fancy shop?"

"Allee light. Ching go back."

"And how are you after our fight to-day?"

"Velly angly. Allee muchee quite 'shame of mandalin men. Big lascal, evely one."

"So they are," said Barkins. "But I say, Ching, are you a good sailor?"

The Chinaman shook his head.

"Ching velly good man, keep fancee shop. Ching not sailor."

"He means, can you go to sea without being sick?" I said, laughing.

He gave us a comical look.

"Don'tee know. Velly nicee now. Big offlicer say jolly sailor take gleat care Ching, and give hammock go to sleep. You got banjo, music—git-tar?"

"One of the chaps has got one," said Smith. "Why?"

"You fetchee for Ching. I play, sing—'ti-ope-I-ow' for captain and jolly sailor. Makee Ching velly happy, and no makee sea-sick like coolie in big boat."

"Not to-night, Ching," said Barkins decisively. "Come along, lads. I'm afraid," he continued, as we strolled right forward, "that some of us would soon be pretty sick of it if he did begin that precious howling. But I say, we ought to look after him well, poor old chap; it's precious rough on him to be taken out to sea like this."

"Yes," I said; "and he behaved like a trump to us to-day."

"That he did," assented Smith, as all three rested our arms on the rail, and looked at the twinkling distant lights of the shore.

"You give Ching flee dollar," said a voice close behind us, and we started round, to find that the object of our conversation had come up silently in his thick, softly-soled boots, in which his tight black trouser bottoms were tucked.

"Three dollars!" cried Smith; "what for?"

"Say all give Ching dollar show way."

"So we did," cried Barkins. "I'd forgotten all about it."

"So had I."

"But you got us nearly killed," protested Smith.

"That was all in the bargain," cried Barkins. "Well, I say he came out well, and I shall give him two dollars, though I am getting precious short."

"Flee dollar," said Ching firmly. Then, shaking his head, he counted upon his fingers, "One, two, flee."

"It's all right, Ching," I said. "Two dollars apiece. Come on, Blacksmith." I took out my two dollars. "Come, Tanner."

"No, no," cried Ching; "tanner tickpence; two dollar tickpence won't do. Flee dollar."

"It's all right," I said, and I held out my hand for my messmates' contributions, afterward placing the six dollars in the Chinaman's hand.

His long-nailed fingers closed over the double amount, and he looked from one to the other as if he did not comprehend. Then he unwillingly divided the sum.

"No light," he said. "Flee dollar."

"The other for the fight," I said, feeling pleased to have met a Chinaman who was not dishonest and grasping.

"You wantee 'nother fight morrow?" he said, looking at me sharply. "Don't know. Not aflaid."

"No, no; you don't understand," I cried, laughing. "We give you six dollars instead of three."

Ching nodded, and the silver money disappeared up his sleeve. Then his body writhed a little, and the arm and hand appeared again in the loose sleeve.

"Sailor boy 'teal Ching dollar?"

"Oh no," I said confidently.

"No pullee tail?"

"Ah, that I can't answer for," I said. "Twist it up tightly."

"To be sure," said Barkins. "It don't do to put temptation in the poor fellows' way. I'm afraid," he continued, "that if I saw that hanging out of a hammock I should be obliged to have a tug."

Ching nodded, and stole away again into the darkness, for night had fallen now, and we were beginning to feel the waves dancing under us.

An hour later I was in my cot fast asleep, and dreaming of fierce-looking Chinamen in showy-patterned coats making cuts at me with big swords, which were too blunt to cut, but which gave me plenty of pain, and this continued more or less all night. In the morning I knew the reason why, my left side was severely bruised, and for the next few days I could not move about without a reminder of the terrible cut the mandarin's retainer had made at me with his sword.

Chapter Five
Ching has Ideas

Week had passed, during which we had cruised here and there, in the hope of falling in with the pirates. Once in the right waters, it did not much signify which course we took, for we were as likely to come across them sailing north as south. So our coal was saved, and we kept steadily along under canvas.

But fortune seemed to be still against us, and though we boarded junk after junk, there was not one of which the slightest suspicion could be entertained; and their masters, as soon as they realised what our mission was, were only too eager to afford us every information they could.

Unfortunately, they could give us none of any value. They could only tell us about divers acts of horrible cruelty committed here and there within the past few months, but could not point out where the pirates were likely to be found.

Ching, in spite of some rough weather, had never been obliged to leave the deck, and had proved to be so valuable an acquisition, that he was informed that he would have a certain rate of pay as interpreter while he stayed on board; and as soon as he was made aware of this, he strutted up to me and told me the news.

"Captain makee interpleter and have lot dollar. Muchee better keepee fancee shop."

This was after, at my suggestion to Mr Reardon, he had been sent out in one of the boats to board a big junk, and from that time it became a matter of course that when a boat was piped away, Ching's pigtail was seen flying out nearly horizontally in his eagerness to be first in the stern-sheets.

But it was always the same. The boat came back with Ching looking disappointed, and his yellow forehead ploughed with parallel lines.

"Ching know," he said to me one evening mysteriously.

"Know what?" I said.

"Plenty pilate boat hide away in island. No come while big ship *Teasler* here."

"Oh, wait a bit," I said; "we shall catch them yet."

"No, catchee," he said despondently. "Pilate velly cunning. See Queen Victolia ship say big gun go bang. 'Top away."

"But where do you think they hide?"

"Evelywhere," he said. "Plentee liver, plenty cleek, plenty hide away."

"Then we shall never catch them?" I said.

"Ching wantee catchee, wantee plenty money; but pilate won't come. Pilate 'flaid."

"And I suppose, as soon as we go away, they'll come out and attack the first merchantman that comes along the coast."

"Yes," said Ching coolly; "cut allee boy float, settee fire junk, burnee ship."

"Then what's to be done?" I said. "It's very disappointing."

"Ching go back fancee shop; no catchee pilate, no plize-money."

"Oh, but we shall drop upon them some day."

"No dlop upon pilate. Ching not captain. Ching catchee."

"How?" I said.

"Take big ship back to liver. Put big gun, put jolly sailor 'board two big junk, and go sail 'bout. Pilate come thinkee catchee plenty silk, plenty tea. Come aboard junk. Jolly sailor chop head off, and no more pilate."

"That sounds well, Ching," I said; "but I don't think we could do that."

"No catchee pilate?" he said. "Ching velly tire. No good, velly hungry; wantee go back fancee shop."

I thought a good deal about what the Chinaman had said, for it was weary, dispiriting work this overhauling every vessel we saw that seemed likely to be our enemy. It was dangerous work, too, for the narrow sea was foul with reefs; but our information had been that it was in the neighbourhood of the many islands off Formosa that the piratical junks had their nest, and the risk had to be run for the sake of the possible capture to be made.

"Ching says he wants to get back to the fancee shop," sad Smith one morning. "So do I, for I'm sick of this dreary work. Why, I'd rather have another of our days ashore."

"Not you," I said. "But I say, look here, I haven't spoke about it before, but Ching says—hi, Tanner, come here!"

"That he doesn't," cried Smith.

"Hallo! what is it?" said Barkins, whom I had hailed, and he came over from the port side of the deck.

"I was going to tell Blacksmith what Ching says. You may as well hear too."

"Don't want to. I know."

"What! has he been saying to you—"

"No, not again."

"What did he say?"

"Ti-ope-I-ow!" cried Barkins, imitating the Chinaman's high falsetto, and then striking imaginary strings of a guitar-like instrument. "*Peng—peng-peng.*"

"I say, don't fool," I cried angrily.

"Gnat!" said Barkins sharply, "you're a miserably-impudent little scrub of a skeeter, and presume upon your size to say insolent things to your elders."

"No, I don't," I said shortly.

"Yes, you do, sir. You called me a fool just now."

"I didn't."

"If you contradict me, I'll punch your miserable little head, sir. No, I won't, I'll make Blacksmith do it; his fists are a size smaller than mine."

"Be quiet, Tanner!" cried Smith; "he knows something. Now, then, Gnat: what does Ching say?"

"That we shall never catch the pirates, because they won't come out when the gunboat is here."

"Well, there's something in that. Tell Mr Reardon."

"Is it worth while? He says we ought to arm a couple of junks, and wait for the pirates to come out and attack us."

"Ching's Christian name ought to be Solomon," said Smith.

"Thanky wisdom teeth," said Barkins sarcastically. "I say, Gnat, he's quite right. They'd be fools if they did come out to be sunk. I daresay they're watching us all the time somewhere or other from one of the little fishing-boats we see put out."

"Well, young gentlemen," said a sharp voice behind us; "this is contrary to dishipline. You can find something better to do than gossiping."

"Beg pardon, sir, we are not gossiping," said Barkins. "We were discussing the point."

"Oh, indeed," said the first lieutenant sarcastically; "then have the goodness to—"

Barkins saw breakers ahead, and hastened to say—

"The Chinaman says, sir—"

"Don't tell me what the Chinaman says, sir!" cried the lieutenant fiercely.

"But it was about the pirates, sir."

"Eh? What?" cried our superior officer, suddenly changing his tone. "Has he some idea?"

"Yes, sir. No, sir."

"Mr Barkins! What do you mean, sir?"

"He thinks we shall never catch them, sir," stammered my messmate, who could see punishment writ large in the lieutenant's face.

"Confound the Chinaman, sir!" roared the lieutenant. "So do I; so does Captain Thwaites."

He spoke so loudly that this gentleman heard him from where he was slowly marching up and down, talking to the marine officer, and he turned and came towards us.

"In trouble, young gentlemen?" he said quietly. "Pray what does Captain Thwaites?" he added, turning to the chief officer.

"I beg your pardon, sir. I was a little exasperated. These young gentlemen, upon my reproving them for idling, have hatched up a cock-and-bull story—at least Mr Barkins has."

"I beg pardon, sir; it was not a—not a—not a—"

"Cock-and-bull story, Mr Herrick," said the captain, smiling at my confusion, for I had rushed into the gap. "Then pray what was it?"

I told him all that Ching had said, and the captain nodded his head again and again as I went on.

"Yes," he said at last, "I'm afraid he is right, Reardon. It is worth thinking about. What do you say to my sending you and Mr Brooke in a couple of junks?"

They walked off together, and we heard no more.

"Oh, how I should like to punch old Dishy's head!" said Barkins between his teeth.

"Don't take any notice," said Smith; "it's only because he can't get a chance to sink a pirate. I don't believe there's one anywhere about the blessed coast."

"Sail ho!" cried the man at the mast-head, and all was excitement on the instant, for after all the strange sail might prove to be a pirate.

"Away on the weather bow, sir, under the land!" cried the man in answer to hails from the deck; and then, before glasses could be adjusted and brought to bear, he shouted—

"She's ashore, sir—a barque—fore—topmast gone, and—she's afire."

The *Teaser's* course was altered directly, and, helped by a favouring breeze, we ran down rapidly towards the wreck, which proved to be sending up a thin column of smoke, and soon after this was visible from the deck.

Chapter Six
My First Horror

I was in a great state of excitement, and stood watching the vessel through my spyglass, longing for the distance to be got over and what promised to be a mystery examined. For a wreck was possible and a fire at sea equally so, but a ship ashore and burning seemed to be such an anomaly that the officers all looked as if they felt that we were on the high road to something exciting at last.

In fact, we had been so long on the station for the purpose of checking piracy, but doing nothing save overhaul inoffensive junks, that we were all heartily sick of our task. For it was not, as Smith said, as if we were always in some port where we could study the manners and customs of the Chinese, but for ever knocking about wild-goose chasing and never getting a goose.

"Plenty on board," cried Barkins. "I say, Gnat, isn't he a humbug? Ha, ha! Study the manners and customs! Stuffing himself with Chinese sweets and hankering after puppy-pie, like the bargees on the Thames."

"Oh, does he?" cried Smith. "Who ate the fricassee of rats?"

"Oh, bother all that!" I said. "Here, Blacksmith, lend me your glass a minute; it's stronger than mine."

"Ho, ho!" laughed Barkins. "His! The wapping whacker! Why, it's a miserable slopshop second-hand thing. You should have had mine. That was something like, before you spoiled it."

"Here you are," said Smith, lending me his glass. "It's worth a dozen of his old blunderbuss."

I took the glass and had a good long inspection of the large barque, which lay heeled over on the outlying reef of one of the many islands, and could distinctly see the fine curl of smoke rising up from the deck somewhere about the forecastle.

"Make out any one on board, Mr Herrick?" said a sharp voice behind me, and I started round, to find that my companions had gone forward, and the first lieutenant was behind me with his spyglass under his arm and his face very eager and stern.

"No, sir; not a soul."

"Nor signals?"

"None."

"No more can I," my lad. "Your eyes are younger and sharper than mine. Look again. Do the bulwarks seem shattered?"

I took a long look.

"No, sir," I said. "Everything seems quite right except the fore-topmast, which has snapped off, and is hanging in a tangle down to the deck."

"But the fire?"

"That only looks, sir, as if they'd got a stove in the forecastle, and had just lit the fire with plenty of smoky coal."

"Hah! That's all I can make out. We've come to something at last, Mr Herrick."

"Think so, sir?" I said respectfully.

"Sure of it, my lad;" and he walked off to join the captain, while just then Ching came up softly and pointed forward.

"Big ship," he said. "Pilate; all afire."

"Think so?"

Ching nodded.

"Hallo, Gnat, what does the first luff say?" asked Barkins, who joined us then.

"Thinks it's a vessel cast ashore by the pirates."

"Maybe. I should say it's one got on the reef from bad seamanship."

"And want of a Tanner on board to set them right," said Smith.

"Skipper's coming," whispered Barkins; and we separated.

For the next hour all was eager watchfulness on board, as we approached very slowly, shortening sail, and with two men in the chains heaving the lead on account of the hidden reefs and shoals off some of the islands. But, as we approached, nothing more could be made out till the man aloft hailed the deck, and announced that he could read the name on the stern, *Dunstaffnage, Glasgow*. Another hour passed, during which the island, a couple of miles beyond, was swept by glass after glass, and tree and hill examined, but there was no sign of signal on tree or hill. All was bare, chilly, and repellent there, and we felt that the crew of the vessel could not have taken refuge ashore.

At last the crew of a boat was piped away, and, as I was gazing longingly at the men getting in under the command of Mr Brooke, a quiet, gentlemanly fellow, our junior lieutenant, Mr Reardon said, as he caught my eye—

"Yes; go."

I did not wait for a second order, you may be sure, but sprang in, and as the *Teaser* was thrown up in the wind with her sails flapping, it being deemed unsafe to go any nearer to the barque, the little wheels chirrupped, and down we went, to sit the next moment lightly upon a good-sized wave which rose up as if to receive us; the falls were cast off, the oars dropped, and the next minute we glided away towards the stranded vessel.

"Quite a treat to get a bit of an adventure, eh Herrick?" said Mr Brooke.

"Yes, sir. Been slow enough lately."

"Oh, you need not grumble, my lad. You did have one good adventure. By the way, how are your sore ribs?"

"My ribs, sir? Oh, I had forgotten all about them. But do you think this is the work of pirates, or that the ship has run ashore?"

"I'm not sure, my lad, but we shall soon know."

We sat watching the fine well-built barque, as the men pulled lustily at their oars, making the water flash and the distance grow shorter. Then all at once my companion said shortly—

"Pirates."

"Where, where?" I said eagerly, and my hand went to my dirk.

Mr Brooke laughed, and I saw all the men showing their teeth.

"No, no, my lad," he said. "I meant this was the work of pirates."

"How do you know, sir?"

"Look at those ropes and sheets hanging loose. They have been cut. The barque has not been in a storm either. She has just gone on to the rocks and the fore-topmast evidently snapped with the shock."

"And the smoke? Is that from the forecastle?"

He shook his head, and stood up in the boat, after handing me the lines, while he remained scanning the vessel attentively.

"Hail her, Jones," he said to the bowman; and the man jumped up, put his hands to his mouth, and roared out, "*Ship ahoy!*"

This again and again, but all was silent; and a curious feeling of awe crept over me as I gazed at the barque lying there on the reef as if it were dead, while the column of smoke, which now looked much bigger, twisted and writhed as it rolled over and over up from just abaft the broken foremast.

"Steady," cried the lieutenant; "the water's getting shoal. Keep a good look-out forward, Jones."

For all at once the water in front of us, from being smooth and oily, suddenly became agitated, and I saw that we had startled and were driving before us a shoal of good-sized fish, some of which, in their eagerness to escape, sprang out of the water and fell back with a splash.

"Plenty yet, sir," said the man in the bows, standing up now with the boat-hook. "Good fathom under us."

"Right. Steady, my lads."

We were only about a hundred yards from the barque now, and the water deepened again, showing that we had been crossing a reef; but the bottom was still visible, as I glanced once over the side, but only for a moment, for there was a peculiar saddening attraction about the silent ship, and I don't know how it was, but I felt as if I was going to see something dreadful.

Under the lieutenant's directions, I steered the boat so that we glided round to the other side, passing under the stern, and then ran alongside, with the bulwarks hanging over towards us, and made out that the vessel had evidently been in fairly deep water close by, and had been run on to the rocks where two reefs met and closed-in a deep channel.

How are we going to get on board? I asked myself, as I looked upward; but I was soon made aware of that, for right forward there was a quantity of the top-hamper of the broken mast with a couple of the square sails awash, so that there was no difficulty about scrambling up.

"I don't think there is any one on board, Herrick," said Mr Brooke, "but sailors should always be on the *qui vive*. Stay in the boat, if you like."

"I don't like, sir," I said, as soon as he had given orders to four men to follow us, and the next minute we were climbing up to stand upon the deck.

"No doubt about it," said Mr Brooke through his teeth. "She has been plundered, and then left to drift ashore or to burn."

For there from the forehold curled up the pillar of smoke we had seen, and a dull crackling noise came up, telling that, though slowly, the fire was steadily burning.

We could not see much below for the smoke, and Mr Brooke led the way forward to the forecastle hatch, which lay open.

"Below! Any one there?" cried my officer, but all was silent as the grave.

One of the men looked at him eagerly.

"Yes, jump down."

The man lowered himself down into the dark forecastle, and made a quick inspection.

"Any one there?"

"No, sir. Place clear and the men's kits all gone."

"Come up."

We went aft, to find the hatches all off and thrown about anyhow, while the cargo had been completely cleared out, save one chest of tea which had been broken and the contents had scattered.

"No mistake about it, Herrick," said Mr Brooke; and he went on to the after-hatch, which was also open and the lading gone.

The next minute we were at the companion-way, and Mr Brooke hailed again, but all was still. Just then the man peering over my shoulder sniffed sharply like some animal.

The sound sent a shudder through me, and Mr Brooke turned to the man sharply—

"Why did you do that?"

"Beg pardon, sir," stammered the man; "I thought that—as if—there was—"

He did not finish.

"Come on," said Mr Brooke sternly, while I shuddered again, and involuntarily my nostrils dilated as I inhaled the air, thinking the while of a butchered captain and officers lying about, but there was not the faintest odour, and I followed my officer, and then for a moment a horrible sickening sensation attacked me, and I shuddered.

But it all passed off, and, myself again directly, I was gazing with the others at the many signs which told us as plainly as if it had been written, that the crew of the unfortunate barque had barricaded themselves in here and made a desperate resistance, for her broken doors lay splintered and full of the marks made by axes and heavy swords. The seats were broken; and bulkheads, cabin windows, and floor were horribly stained here and there with blood, now quite dry and black, but which, after it had been shed, had been smeared about and trampled over; and this in one place was horribly evident, for close up to the side, quite plain, there was the imprint of a bare foot—marked in blood—a great wide-toed foot, that could never have worn a shoe.

"Rather horrid for you, Herrick," said Mr Brooke in a low voice, as if the traces of death made him solemn; "but you must be a man now. Look, my lad, what the devils—the savage devils—have done with our poor Scotch brothers!"

"Yes, I see," I whispered; "they must have killed them all."

"But I mean this—there, I mean."

I looked at him wonderingly as he pointed to the floor, for I did not understand.

The next moment, though, I grasped his meaning, and saw plainly enough what must have happened, for from where we stood to the open stern windows there were long parallel streaks, and I knew that, though they were partially trampled out by naked feet, as if they had been passed over dozens of times since, the savage wretches must have dragged their victims to the stern windows and thrust them out; any doubt thereon being cleared away by the state of the lockers and the sills of the lights.

Just then a peculiar hissing sound came to my ears, and I faced round quickly, as did Mr Brooke, for I felt startled.

For there behind me was one of our men—a fine handsome Yorkshire lad of three or four and twenty—standing glaring and showing his set teeth, and his eyes with the white slightly visible round the iris. His left fist was firmly clenched, and in his right was his bare cutlass, with the blade quivering in his strong hand.

"Put up your cutlass, my lad," said Mr Brooke sternly; and the man started and thrust it back. "Wait a bit—but I don't know how I am to ask you to give quarter to the fiends who did all this. No wonder the place is so silent, Herrick," he added bitterly. "Come away."

He led us out, but not before we had seen that the cabins had been completely stripped.

We did not stay much longer, but our time was long enough to show us that everything of value had been taken, and nothing left in the way of log or papers to tell how the barque had fallen in with the wretches. The crew had probably been surprised, and after a desperate resistance, when driven back into the cabin, fought to the last with the results we had seen.

"But surely they must have killed or wounded some of the pirates?" I said.

"Possibly," replied Mr Brooke; "but there has been rain since; perhaps a heavy sea, too, has washed over the deck and swept away all traces here. Let's hope they made some of them pay dearly for their work."

A short inspection below showed that the barque's planking was crushed in, and that she was hopelessly damaged, even if she could have been got off, so soon after Mr Brooke gave the word to return to the boat.

"I shall not touch the fire," he said. "If the captain has any wishes the boat can return. For my part I should say, let her burn."

The captain listened with his brow contracted to Mr Brooke's recital, when we were back on board; I being close at hand, ready to answer a few questions as well.

"Yes, let her burn," said the captain; and then he turned his back to us, but seemed to recollect himself directly, for he turned again.

"Thank you, Mr Brooke," he said. "Very clear and concise. You could not have done better."

Then turning to the first lieutenant, he said in a low voice—

"Reardon, I'm at my wit's end. The wretches are too cunning for us. What are we to do?"

Chapter Seven
Being Primed

There was a consultation in the cabin that evening, as we lay there about four miles from the stranded barque. It had fallen calm, and, as there was no urgency, the captain preferred to spare the coals, and we waited for a breeze.

I heard afterwards from Mr Brooke all that took place during the discussion, during which the captain heard the principal officers' opinions, and then decided what he would do.

There had been doubts before as to whether we were on the right track for the pirates, who might be carrying on their murderous business elsewhere, but the day's discovery had cleared away the last doubt; it was plain that the information which had sent us up in the neighbourhood of Amoy was perfectly correct, that the wretches were there, and that our presence had kept them quiet till now.

The great difficulty, it was decided, lay in the manner of dealing with people who without doubt had plenty of spies out in native craft, who were passed unnoticed by us, and thus every movement was carefully conveyed to the enemy. As, then, the appearance of the gunboat was sufficient to keep them in hiding, and also as the moment we were out of sight the pirates issued from their lair, only two ways of dealing with the fiends remained to us, and these means, after due consultation, were to be adopted—one or both.

Then it had been arranged that the next morning at daybreak a couple of boats were to be despatched to the Scotch barque, for a more thorough investigation as to whether, in Mr Brooke's rather hurried visit, he had passed over any cargo worthy of salvage, and to collect material for a full report for the authorities and the owners.

This had just been decided upon, when there was a shout from one of the look-out men. It was quite unnecessary, for nearly every one on deck saw the cause of the cry.

We three companions had been watching the wreck with its spiral of smoke, which in the calm air rose up like the trunk of a tall tree, and then all at once spread out nearly flat to right and left, giving it quite the appearance of a gigantic cedar. Then, as one of the witnesses of the horrors on board, I had had to repeat my story again; and, while matters were being discussed below, we in a low tone had our debate on the question, and saw too how the men gathered in knots, and talked in whispers and watched the barque. And to us all one thing was evident, that could our lads only get a chance at the pigtailed, ruffianly scum of the east coast, it would go pretty hard with them.

"I'll bet many of 'em wouldn't go pirating again in a hurry," Barkins said; and we agreed.

Then we fell to wondering how many poor creatures had been murdered by them in their bloodthirsty career, and why it was that there should be such indifference to death, and so horrible a love of cruelty and torture, in the Chinese character. All at once came the shout, and we were gazing at the cause.

For a bright, clear burst of flame suddenly rose from the direction of the ship—not an explosion, but a fierce blaze—and it was evident that the parts around the little fire had grown more and more heated and dry, and that the smouldering had gone on till some part of the cargo beneath, of an inflammable nature, had caught at last, and was burning furiously.

We expected that orders would be given for boats to be lowered, but we had drifted in the current so far away that there was a risky row amongst shoals, so no orders were given, the men gathering on deck to watch the light glow which lit up the cloud of smoke hovering overhead.

We three watched it in silence for some time, with the other officers near, and at last Smith said—

"I don't think I'm a cruel sort of fellow, but I feel as if I should like to kill some one now."

He did not say a Chinese pirate, but he meant it; and I must confess to feeling something of the kind, for I thought how satisfactory it would be to aim one of our big guns at a pirate junk taken in some cruel act, and to send a shot between wind and water that would sink her and rid the seas of some of the fiends.

I quite started the next moment, for Barkins said, in a low, thoughtful voice—

"How do you feel about it, Gnat? Shouldn't you like to kill some of 'em?"

The question was so direct, and appealed to my feelings so strongly, that for some moments I was silent.

"Not he," said Smith; "old Gnat wouldn't stick a pin in a cockroach."

"Of course I wouldn't," I said stoutly, "but I'd crush it under my foot if I found one in the cabin."

"One for you, Blacksmith," said Barkins. "Look here, Gnat, you would like to kill some of the piratical beggars, wouldn't you?"

I remained silent again.

"There," said Smith, "I told you so. If we caught a lot, Gnat would give them a lecture, and tell them they had been very naughty, and that they mustn't do so any more or he would be very angry with them indeed."

"Punch his head, Gnat."

I made no reply to their flippant remarks, for just then I felt very solemn and thoughtful. I hope I was not priggish. No, I am sure I was not; every word I uttered was too sincere, though they chaffed me afterwards, and I have thought since that they felt more seriously than they spoke.

"You chaps didn't go on board that barque," I said quietly; "I did."

"Yes; old Dishy's making a regular favourite of you, Gnat," said Barkins.

But I went on without heeding, my eyes fixed on the burning vessel whose flames shone brightly in the clear air.

"And when I saw the splintered wood and chopped doorway, and the smears and marks of blood, it all seemed to come to me just as it must have been when the poor fellows shut themselves up in the cabin."

"Did they?" said Smith eagerly.

"Yes, that was plain enough," I said; "and they must have fought it out there till the pirates got the upper hand."

"I bet tuppence the beggars pitched stinkpots down through the cabin skylight, and half-smothered them," said Barkins excitedly.

"I daresay they did," I replied thoughtfully, "for I did see one of the lockers all scorched and burned just by the deck. Yes, it all seemed to come to me, and I felt as if I could see all the fighting, with the Chinamen hacking and chopping at them with their long swords, the same as those brutes did at us; and all those poor fellows, who were quietly going about their business, homeward bound with their cargo, must have had friends, wives or mothers or children; and it gets horrible when you think of how they must have been in despair, knowing that those wretches would have no mercy on them."

"Yes, but how it must have made 'em fight," cried Smith. "I think I could have done something at a time like that."

"Yes, it would make any fellow fight; even you, Gnat."

"I suppose so," I said, "for it made me feel as if there wasn't any room in the world for such people."

"There ain't," said Barkins. "Oh, if our chaps could only get a good go at 'em!"

"And then I felt," I went on, "as if it couldn't all be real, and that it was impossible that there could be such wretches on the face of the earth, ready to kill people for the sake of a bit of plunder."

"But it's just precious possible enough," said Smith slowly. "Why, out here in China they do anything."

"Right," said Barkins; "and I hope the skipper will pay them in their own coin. My! how she burns."

"Yes," assented Smith, as the barque, after smouldering so long, now blazed, as if eager to clear away all traces of the horrible tragedy.

"You'll recollect all about that cabin, Gnat, if we do get at the beggars— won't you?"

"Recollect?" I said, with a shiver; "I shall never be able to forget it."

Then we relapsed into silence, and stood resting our arms over the bulwarks, gazing at the distant fire, in which I could picture plainly all the horrors and suggestions of the wrecked cabin. I even seemed to see the yellow-faced wretches, all smeared with blood, dragging their victims to the stern windows. And my imagination then ran riot for a time, as I fancied I saw them seizing men not half-dead, but making a feeble struggle for their lives, and begging in agonising tones for mercy, but only to be struck again, and pitched out into the sea.

I fancy that I must have been growing half hysterical as the scene grew and grew before me, till I had pictured one poor wretch clinging in his despair to the edge of the stern window, and shrieking for help. There was a curious sensation as if a ball was rising in my throat to choke me, and I was forgetting where I stood, when I was brought back to myself by the voice of my messmate Smith, who said in a husky whisper—

"Think we shall come across any of the poor fellows floating about?"

"Not likely," replied Barkins. "Too many sharks in these seas."

My throat felt dry at this horrible suggestion, but I knew how true it was. And then once more there was silence, and, like the rest—officers and men—we stood there watching the burning wreck hour after hour, not a soul on board feeling the slightest disposition to go below.

It must have been quite a couple of hours later, when I started in the darkness, for something touched my arm, and, looking sharply to my right, I could just make out the figure of Ching close to me, while on looking in the other direction I found that I was alone, for Barkins and Smith had gone forward to a group close to the bows.

"You, Ching?" I said, "looking at the mischief your friends have done?"

"Fliends burnee ship? No fliends. Velly bad men. Ching feel allee shame. Velly bad men evelywhere. Killee, get dollar. No velly bad men, London?"

"I'm afraid there are," I said sadly.

"Yes; velly bad men, London. Killee get dollar. You choppee off bad men head?"

"No," I said; "but they kill them if they commit murder."

'WHO'S THAT?'

"Commit murder? You mean killee get dollar?"

"Yes."

"Allee light. Plenty bad men evelywhere. Captain going kill pilate?"

"If we can catch them," I said.

"Yes, velly hard catchee catchee. Captain never catchee in ship. Pilate allee lun away. 'Flaid of big gun. Get two big junk, put plenty sailor boy where pilate can't see. Then pilate come along kill and burnee. Junk steal all along. Jolly sailor jump up and cut allee pilate head off."

"Send that boy forward!" cried a stern voice, which made me jump again. "Who's that?"

"Herrick, sir," I said, touching my cap, for the captain came forward out of the darkness.

"Then you ought to know better, sir. The scoundrel has no business in this part of the ship. What does he want?"

"I beg pardon, sir; he came up to propose a way of trapping the pirates."

"Eh, what?" said the captain eagerly. "Bah! absurd. Send him below; I hate to see the very face of a Chinaman. No; stop! He ought to know something of their tricks. What does he say?"

I told him, and he stood there as if thinking.

"Well, I don't know, Mr Herrick. We might perhaps lure them out of their hiding-places in that way, with a couple of Chinese crews to work the junks. But no; the wretches would be equally strong, and would fight like rats. Too many of my poor lads would be cut down. They would have us at a terrible disadvantage. We must keep to the ship. I can only fight these wretches with guns."

He was turning away, when a thought struck me, and, forgetting my awe of the captain, and the fact that a proposal from a midshipman to such a magnate might be resented as an unheard-of piece of impertinence, I exclaimed excitedly—

"I beg pardon, sir."

"Yes?"

"I think I know how it could be done."

"Eh? You, Mr Herrick! Pooh! Stop," he said sharply, as, feeling completely abashed, I was shrinking away, when he laid his hand kindly on my shoulder. "Let's hear what you mean, my boy. The mouse did help the lion in the fable, didn't he?"

"Yes, sir."

"Not that I consider myself a lion, Mr Herrick," he said good-humouredly, "and I will not insult you by calling you a mouse; but these

Chinese fiends are too much for me, and I really am caught in the net. Here, send that man forward, and come into my cabin."

"Ching, go right up to the forecastle," I said.

"No wantee go s'eep," he said angrily. "Makee Ching bad see ship burned."

"Never mind now; go and wait," I whispered; and he nodded and went off, while I walked hurriedly back to the captain, who led the way to his cabin.

Before I had gone many steps I had to pass Smith, who came quickly up to me.

"Hallo! old chap," he whispered, "what have you been up to now? Wigging from the skipper? I'll go and tell the Tanner, and we'll get clean handkerchiefs for a good cry."

Chapter Eight
My Plan

"Shut the door, Mr Herrick," said the captain, as he threw himself into a chair, and I obeyed and remained standing there.

"Come close up to the table, my lad, and I'll hear what you have to say, for I should be sorry to discourage a young officer who was in earnest about his profession, as I have noted that you seem to be."

"Thank you, sir," I faltered, as I walked forward to where the swinging lamp cast its full light on my face, making my eyes ache, after being so many hours in the darkness, while I noticed that the captain sat in the shade.

"Now, Mr Herrick," he said, "I talked of one fable, let me say a word about another. I hope this is not going to be a case of the mountain in labour, and out crept a mouse."

This put me quite out of heart, my hands grew damp, and I felt a tickling sensation of dew forming upon my temples and at the sides of my nose. My throat felt dry, and my lips parted, but no words came.

"There, there," he said kindly, "don't be afraid. Speak out."

"Yes, sir," I said hastily. "It was only this. I think I read somewhere once, in a paper, about a Malay prahu being taken by the captain of a ship pretending to be helpless, and this made the prahu, which could sail twice as fast as his ship, come close up to attack him."

"Yes; and what then?"

"The captain sunk the prahu, sir."

"Humph!" said Captain Thwaites, frowning and leaning back in his chair. "That's what I should like to do to the piratical junks, Mr Herrick. But—"

He stopped, and I saw that he was watching me keenly. But he had not ordered me out of the cabin, nor called me an impertinent puppy, so I felt better. The plunge had been made, and I waited not quite so nervously for his next words.

"Yes—what I should like to do, Mr Herrick; but I am dealing with cunning Chinese, and not with bold Malays."

"No, sir," I said; "but could not we—you—I mean we—I mean—" I stammered.

"Come, come, Mr Herrick, there is no need for all this tremor. Sit down, my lad."

"Thank you, sir; I would rather stand, please. I think I could talk better."

"Very well, then," he said, smiling; "stand. You have some notion in your head, then?"

"Yes, sir," I said eagerly, for the nervousness all passed away in the excitement I felt. "I thought that if I could do as I liked, I'd take the *Teaser* up some creek where she couldn't be watched, and then I'd close all the ports, send the men over the side to paint out the streak, and I'd paint the funnel another colour, and get yards all anyhow, and hide all the guns. I'd make her look like one of the tea-screws, and get a lot of Chinamen on board for sailors."

I saw that he kept on bowing his head, and I was so excited that I went on.

"No, I know. If you tried to get some Chinese sailors on board, it would be talked about, and perhaps the pirates would get to know, for they must have friends in some of the ports."

"Then down go some of your baits, my lad."

"No, sir. I know. You could make Ching—"

"That Chinese interpreter?"

"Yes, sir. Make him do up some of our lads with pigtails made of blackened oakum, and in duck-frocks they'd do at a distance."

"Heads not shaven?"

"No, sir; but they could have their hair cut very short, and then painted white—I mean yellow, so that the pirates wouldn't know at a distance."

"Humph! anything else?" said the captain drily, but I did not notice it; I was too much taken up by my ideas.

"Yes, sir. Ching could be going about very busily in all directions, showing himself a great deal, and there's no mistake about him."

"No," said the captain, "there is no mistake about him."

"And it wouldn't be a bad plan to be at anchor near the place where you thought they were, sir, with some of the spars down as if you were repairing damages. That would make them feel sure that they were safe of a prize, and they'd come off in their boats to attack."

"And then you would let them board us and find out their mistake?"

"That I wouldn't, sir!" I cried eagerly; and, oddly enough, my side began to ache where I had had that blow. "I wouldn't risk any of our poor fellows being hurt. I'd sink them before they got alongside."

"Humph! Well, you're pretty bloodthirsty for your time of life, young gentleman," said the captain quietly.

"No, sir," I replied in confusion; "but I was with Mr Barkins and Mr Smith, and nearly killed by these people, and yesterday I saw what they had done aboard that barque."

"There? So you did, my lad. Well," he said, "what more have you got to suggest?"

"I think that's all, sir," I said, beginning to grow confused again, for my enthusiasm was dying out before his cool, matter-of-fact way of taking matters.

"Then we will bring this meeting to an end, Mr Herrick."

"Yes, sir," I said dolefully, for I was wishing intensely that I had not said a word. "Shall I go now?"

"If you please, Mr Herrick."

"Good-night, sir."

"Good-night, Mr Herrick; and the sooner you are in your berth the better."

"Yes, sir," I said; and then to myself, as I reached the door, "and I wish I had gone there at once, instead of stopping on deck."

"Stop!"

I turned with the door-handle in my fingers.

"You had better not say anything about the communication you have made to me—I mean to your messmates."

"No, sir, I will not," I replied.

"Nor to any one else, least of all to that Chinaman."

"Oh no, sir, I'll be careful."

He nodded, and I slipped out, feeling, to use an old expression, "horrid."

"Tell anybody about what a stupid donkey I've been," I said angrily— "likely." Then to myself, as soon as I was past the marine sentry, "Why, it would be nuts for Tanner and Blacksmith, and they'd go on cracking them for ever. There was I all red-hot with what I thought was a good thing, and he was just like a cold codfish laughing at me."

I could not help smiling at the absurdity of my idea, for I recalled that I had never seen a cold codfish laughing.

I had no more time for musing then, for I received a sharp slap on the back from Barkins.

"Never mind, Gnat; we all get it some time."

I saw that Smith was hurrying up, for I caught sight of him by the light of one of the swinging lanterns, and had to be on my guard.

I did not want to deceive my messmates nor to be untruthful, but I could not open my heart to them and tell them all that had passed.

"What cheer, messmet?" whispered Smith. "Had a wigging?"

I nodded my head sulkily.

"What had you been up to? Skipper had you into the cabin, didn't he?"

"Let him alone, will you," cried Barkins. "What do you want to worry the poor chap for? The skipper's had him over the coals."

"Well, I know that, Bark. But what for?"

"What's that to you? Let him alone."

"But he might tell."

"Well, he isn't going to tell. If you must know, the Grand Panjandrum came and catched him talking to Squeezums, hanging over the bulwarks together."

"Talking to who?"

"Well then, to Teapot, old Chinese Ching, and snubbed him for having the Yellow-skin so far aft. Didn't he, Gnat?"

"Yes," I said, quite truthfully.

"Then I say it's too bad," cried Smith. "As the snob speakers say, are we—er—serlaves? Besides, 'a man's a man for a' that,' ain't he, Tanner?"

"Chinamen have no business abaft the funnel," said Barkins. "Did he give it to you very warmly, Gnat?"

"Pretty well," I said, glad to escape Smith's examination. "I wasn't sorry to get out of the cabin."

"No, I should think not. Why, what's come to the old boy—taking to bully us himself? I thought he always meant to leave that to Dishy."

"He's getting wild at not catching the pirates, I suppose," said Barkins. "Then all that badger gets bottled up in him, and he lets it off at us. Well, I don't see any fun in watching the fire; I'm going down for a snooze."

"Wish I could," said Smith. "The fellow who invented night-watches ought to have been smothered. I daresay he was a man who had something the matter with him and couldn't sleep. I hate it."

"Pooh!" cried Barkins, laughing. "You haven't got used to it yet, old chap. It's an acquired taste. After a bit you won't care a dump for a regular night's rest, but'll want to get up and take your turn. Won't he, Gnat?"

I laughed.

"I haven't got the right taste yet," I said.

"And never will," grumbled Smith, as we turned to have another look at the burning barque.

"How long will a ship like that be burning, Jecks?" I said to one of the watch.

The man scratched his head, and had a good stare at the glowing object in the distance, as if he were making a careful calculation.

"Well," said Barkins, "out with it, Tom Jecks; we don't want to know to two minutes and a half."

"Well, sir," said the man very deliberately, "I should say as a wessel o' that size—"

"There goes her mainmast!" some one shouted, as a portion of the fire fell off to our left, and lay in the sea.

We stood gazing at this part for a few minutes, during which the light faded slowly out, quenched in the waves.

Then Jecks began again, speaking very oracularly—

"I should say as a wessel o' that size—"

"Yes," said Barkins, imitating him; "a wessel o' that size—"

"Yes, sir—might go on burning till 'bout eight bells."

"Or perhaps a little longer, Tom?"

"Well, yes, sir; little longer, perhaps. 'Morrow night, say."

"Or 'morrow morning, Tom?"

"Well, no, sir; because you see it's 'morrow morning now."

"I meant t'other 'morrow morning, Tom. Nex' day."

"Well, yes, sir; she might last till then."

"Or even next day?"

"Well, sir, I hayve knowed 'em go on mouldering and smouldering for days and days."

"A week, perhaps?"

"Oh yes, sir, quite a week."

"Thankye, Tom," said Barkins, giving me a nudge with his elbow. "I thought you'd know. Nothing like going to a man who has had plenty of experience."

"No, sir, there ain't nothin' like it; and I should say as if you young gen'lemen was to stand here and watch, you'd finally see that there wessel give a bit of a roll to starboard and one to port, and then settle down and go out of sight all to oncet, like putting a stingwisher on a candle; and there! what did I tell yer?"

For all at once the blaze rose quite high, as if it were driven upwards by some explosion below. We saw what looked like tiny sparks falling all around, and some of them floating upon the sea, and then there was the sound as of a puff of wind—heavy and short; and, where the barque had lain blazing and sending up its great waving tongue of fire, there was now darkness, save here and there a few dull specks of light, which went out one by one.

"The last act of a tragedy," said a voice close by us; and Mr Brooke, who had the watch, stood gazing at the dark waters for a few moments. Then in his quiet, decided tones—

"Now, Mr Barkins—Mr Herrick, it is not your watch. You had better go below."

"Yes, sir; good-night, sir."

"Good-morning, you mean," he replied; and we two went down and turned in.

"I say, Gnat," cried Barkins in a sleepy voice; "old Tom Jecks'll be more chuckle-bumptious than ever."

"Yes," I said; "that happened just right for him."

"Yes, that's the luck that kind of bumble-head always gets. He'll set up—now—for—*snore*—set up for—oh, how sleepy I am! What say?"

"I didn't speak," I replied drowsily.

"Who said you did? Oh, I remember now. Tom Jecks'll set up for boss—know—all now. Look here—you help me, and we'll gammon him into—be—believing—he ought to make an alma—alma—nick—nack,"—*snore*.

Barkins was fast asleep, and I was just thinking how suddenly a drowsy person dropped off, when all at once I seemed to be back in the cabin of the burned ship, where I was searching the lockers for pirates, and then some one hauled me out of my berth by one leg, and I raised myself on my elbow to stare wildly at Smith.

Chapter Nine
Preparations

"At last!" he cried. "I began to think your eyelids were sewed up. Dress yourself, sir; do you hear? Do you suppose that the junior officers of the *Teaser* are kept here on purpose to set a bad example to the men?"

"Breakfast ready?" I said, yawning.

"Of course it is, sir. Kidneys and fried soles done to a shade. Fresh water-cresses, hot rolls, and all kinds of don't-you-wish-you-may-get-'ems, waiting. I say, look at old Tanner. Let's rouse him up."

I rose slowly, and, with the customary malignity of one rudely wakened from sleep, began to feel a grim satisfaction in seeing my messmate robbed of his repose in turn.

"Cold pig?" suggested Smith.

"No, no; don't," I said. "It makes the place so wet."

"All right. Come here, then."

I was about to join him, when the peculiar vibration going on made me turn sharply to Smith.

"Hallo!" I said.

"What's the matter?"

"Under steam again?"

"Yes. Orders came soon after daylight, and we're going south with our tail between our legs. Skipper seems to think it's of no use trying any longer; and you mark my words, as soon as we're gone those beggars will come out of their creeks and begin murdering and burning every trading vessel they can catch."

"I am sorry," I said, as I recalled my interview with the captain.

"Sorry! I should think you are. So are we all. It's a shame, that's what it is, Gnat."

"It seems to be a pity, because we might run against them some time."

"Run against them! Why, of course. The scent's hot now. Oh, I only wish I was captain of this ship!"

"Wish you were, Smithy," said Barkins, yawning.

"Oh, you're awake at last, are you?"

"Of course I am. Who's to sleep with you yelping about like that. I say, if you were skipper, we'd share the cabin with you, and have a jolly time of it—eh?"

"Oh, would you?" cried Smith. "We'd see about that. I tell you what, though, if I was skipper, this gunboat shouldn't leave the station while there was a pirate on the east coast."

"Well, there won't be when we've done. I say—oh dear me!—how is it the legs of your trousers will get tangled when you want to put 'em on in a hurry."

"'Cause you put 'em on with your eyes tangled up. Hear that?"

"What, you gabbling?"

"No; the screw at work."

"Eh? Yes. What does it mean?"

"We're going back."

"No!"

"We are—full speed."

"Without yard-arming the beggars who took that ship."

"Yes; ain't it a shame?"

Barkins made no answer, but kept on dressing—snatching on his clothes, so to speak; and when we went on deck that bright, fine morning, there was a lowering look upon every face; and the officers were all snappish, the men discontented, and scowling at the two figures marching up and down the quarter-deck side by side.

I felt disappointed, for we had been looking forward to the exciting moments when we should first overhaul some piratical junk. Of course I knew that there might be some danger, but I foresaw very little: our well-armed ship, with its strong, highly-disciplined crew, would over-ride every opposition offered by the half-savage Chinamen, I felt sure; and, like most people in the service, I felt that, if any one was hurt, it would be some one else. And now there was to be no further search for the pirates. We were going south again, probably to Hong-Kong; and I was sick of hot Hong-Kong, and doing nothing but drill.

I partook, then, of the general feeling of dissatisfaction that morning; and, feeling quite glum and vexed with myself, I leaned over the taffrail and gazed down at the bright, clear water in search of fish.

"I wish I hadn't spoken as I did last night," I said to myself later on; and I was going over the whole scene in the cabin, and thinking of what a noodle I must have looked, when I heard my name uttered in the captain's short, sharp voice.

I turned and saluted, to find that Mr Reardon had gone forward.

"I only want to repeat my caution to you, Mr Herrick," said the captain. "You will not say a word to any one about your visit to me last night."

"No, sir," I said.

"You have not spoken to your messmates?"

"No, sir; not a word."

"But they asked you why I summoned you to my cabin?"

"Yes, sir; but they think it was to snub—reprove me, sir, for making so much of the Chinaman."

"Oh, I see. But snub would have done, Mr Herrick. Reprove sounds pedantic. That will do, but bear in mind my wishes."

"Oh, there you are, Mr Herrick," said the first lieutenant, a few minutes later. "I want you. Find that Chinaman and the ship's tailor, and bring them both to my cabin."

"Yes, sir," I said, wondering; and I hunted them out, told them to follow me, and led the way to Mr Reardon's cabin.

"Shut the door," he said sharply.

I obeyed, and the lieutenant consulted a scrap of paper upon which he had pencilled a few memoranda.

"Now, tailor," he said, "you will have an order for a sufficiency of white duck."

"Yes, sir."

"And by this time to-morrow I want twenty loose frocks cut and made after the fashion of this man's blue cotton blouse thing."

"Couldn't be done, sir, in the time," said the tailor respectfully.

"They must be done, my man. I don't care how roughly they are made, nor how badly sewn, but they must be cut to this pattern. Get as many men as you require to sew, and begin work at once. I'll send this boy to you soon, for you to get the pattern of his garment."

The tailor saluted, and went off wondering; while I wondered no less, as I stood waiting with Ching for what was to come; but for some moments Mr Reardon sat there studying his notes.

All at once he looked up sharply.

"Now, Ching," he said, "can you understand all I say?"

The Chinaman nodded.

"Then look here: I have ordered twenty duck-frocks, as you heard."

"Yes, sir. Velly like Chinaman."

"Exactly. Well, these are for twenty of our men to wear. I want them to look like Chinese."

Ching shook his head.

"Blue flock," he said; "all blue, no white."

"We have no blue, and the white must do."

"Velly well."

"That point is settled, then. Now, then, about their heads."

"Cut hair all off, and glow pigtail."

"That would take years, my man, and I wanted them ready to-morrow."

"How glow pigtail one day?" cried Ching scornfully; and pulling round his own, he held it out, fully four feet in length—a long black plait, with a bit of ribbon tying it at the end.

"Thi'ty yea' long," said Ching. "No one day."

"You must get some oakum, and dye it black. Plait it up, and fasten that on the men's heads."

"With bit o' stling," said Ching, nodding his head. "Go act play—make fleatre 'board ship?"

"Yes, we are going to act a play," said the lieutenant sternly; and I felt the blood come into my face with excitement.

"Shave men's head—shave face; makee look allee same Chinaman."

"Oh, we can manage that," said Mr Reardon, giving me a meaning look. "You can pick out men and boys enough, Mr Herrick, to make twenty smooth-faced ones."

"Yes, sir, I think so," I said.

"Then something must be mixed up, whiting and tallow ought to do it."

"Yes, Ching see; makee head velly white."

"That will do, then."

"No," said Ching sharply. "No tlouser, no boot?"

"That will not matter, my man, so long as they are right in their upper rigging."

"Light in upper ligging!" said Ching. "Ah, you go cheat, gammon pilate?"

Mr Reardon gave him an angry look.

"You go and do— no, stop. You are quite right, my man, but don't talk about it. Get the work done."

"Ching see. Make nineteen twenty men look like Chinese boy. Pilate come along, say, 'Big tea-ship. Come aboard,' and get catchee likee lat in tlap."

"Yes, that's it, my man. Do you think it a good plan, Mr Herrick?" he added drily.

"Oh yes, sir," I cried excitedly. "May we begin at once?"

"Ye–es," said the lieutenant thoughtfully. "I think that's all you can do. Yes," he said decidedly; "take the job in hand, Mr Herrick, and help it along. I want to have twenty men looking like a Chinese crew by to-morrow."

"Come along, Ching."

"Yes," he said. "Do it velly well. Chinese pilate velly cunning fellow. You go gettee two junk, put men on board."

"You go and get the men ready," said Mr Reardon shortly. "That will do."

Directly after I had Ching supplied from the purser's stores with plenty of fine oakum and a couple of bottles of ink. This latter he made boiling hot and poured over the oakum, hanging it to dry by the cook's fire; and while he was doing this I arranged with the cook to have a bucket of tallow and whiting mixed ready for use when required, so that then all necessary would be to warm it up.

I was just going aft again when "Herrick" was shouted, and I turned, to see Barkins and Smith coming after me. But Mr Reardon heard the hail, and came striding after us.

"You leave Mr Herrick to the business he is on, young gentlemen, and attend to your own," he cried. "Go on, Mr Herrick. This is no time for gossiping."

I hurried off, and began my next task, that of selecting twenty men without beards; and there was no difficulty, for I soon picked sixteen and four big lads, upon whose heads the ship's barber was set to work to cut the hair pretty short, the men submitting with an excellent grace, Jack being ready enough to engage in anything fresh, and such as would relieve the monotony of shipboard life.

They were ready enough to ask questions, but I had nothing to tell; and the preparations went merrily on, but not without my having learned that we were steaming right away out of sight of land.

But long before we had reached this pitch, I found that orders had been given, and the men were busy up aloft, lowering down the main-topgallant mast, and then laying the maintop mast all askew, as if it were snapped off at the top. After which the yards were altered from their perfect symmetry to hang anyhow, as if the ship were commanded by a careless captain. The engine was set to work to squirt water thickened with cutch, and the beautiful white sails were stained in patches, and then roughly furled.

Towards evening, when the sea appeared to be without a sail in sight, we lay-to; platforms were got over the side, and men hung over with their paint-pots and brushes, working with all their might to paint out the streak, while others smeared over the gilding and name at the stern, but with a thin water-colour which would easily wash off.

Then came the turn of the great funnel, which was painted of a dirty black. The bright brass rails were dulled, ropes hung loosely, and in every way possible the trim gunboat was disfigured and altered, so that at a short distance even it would have been impossible to recognise her as the smart vessel that had started from the neighbourhood of the burned ship so short a time before.

But even then Mr Reardon did not seem to be satisfied, for he set the men to work hauling water casks from the hold, and make a pile of them amidships. Lastly, a couple of the boats were turned bottom upward on improvised chocks placed over the deck-house and galley.

I have not mentioned the guns, though. These were completely hidden, the lesser pieces being drawn back, and spare sails thrown over the two big guns forward.

"There," said Mr Reardon quietly to me; "what do you say to that, Mr Herrick? Think this will deceive them?"

"There's one more thing I should do, sir," I said, as I looked aloft.

"One more? Nonsense; there is nothing more to be done."

"Yes, sir," I said, smiling; "I'd have some shirts and trousers hung up in the rigging to dry, just as if the men had been having a wash."

"To be sure," he cried. "What else?"

"It wouldn't be bad if we could catch a few big fish, and let them be hanging over the stern rail as if to keep them fresh."

"I'll set Mr Barkins and Mr Smith to try and catch some," he said eagerly. "The idea's splendid, my lad; and if it turns out to be successful, I'll—there, I don't know what I won't do for you."

Soon after, I had the pleasure of seeing a lot of the men's garments hung on a couple of lines in the rigging, and Barkins and Smith hard at work fishing, in which they were so wonderfully successful that I longed to go and join them; but I was too busy over my task of disguising the twenty sailors, and consequently my two messmates had all the sport to themselves, dragging in, every few minutes, an abundance of good-sized fishes, which were at last strung upon a piece of stout line and hung over the stern rail.

That night the crew were all in an intense state of excitement, and roars of laughter saluted my party of sham Chinamen, some of whom were paraded in the newly-made frocks, two being in the full dress of whitened head and pigtail, and looked so exactly like the real thing at a short distance that no doubt was felt as to the success of this part of the proceedings.

Officers and men had been a little puzzled at first, but in a very short time they were all talking about the cleverness of the "captain's dodge," as they called it; and the low spirits of the morning gave place to eager talk about the adventures which all felt sure must come now.

The ship's head had been turned and laid for the islands we had so lately left; but our progress was purposely made exceedingly slow, the screw just revolving, and the water parting with a gentle ripple to right and left.

Meanwhile the tailor and his mates were hard at work by the light of the swinging lanterns, and, upon my being sent by Mr Reardon to make inquiries, the tailor answered that he should be up to time with the twenty Chinee gownds, and went on stitching again as if for his very life.

I was on the watch that night, and stood listening for long enough to the yarns of one of the men, who had not been in Chinese waters before, but "knowed a chap as had;" and he had some blood-curdling tales to tell of the cruelties perpetrated by the desperate gangs who haunted the coast in fast-sailing junks.

"But they're an awfully cowardly lot, arn't they, Billy?" said another.

"Well," said the man, "it's like this, messmet; they is and they arn't, if you can make that out. They'll scuttle away like rats if they can; but if they can't, they'll fight that savage that nothing's like it; and if it is to come to a fight, all I've got to say is, as the chap as hasn't got his cutlash as sharp as ever it can be made 'll be very sorry for it."

"Oh, I don't know," said another; "there won't be much cutlashing; 'tain't like it used to was in the old days. Most everything's done with the big guns now; and if they do get alongside to board, why, a man's cutlash is always stuck at the end of his rifle, just as if it was a jolly's bag'net growed out o' knowledge, and then it's all spick and spike."

"Maybe," said the man; "but you mark my words, they're a nasty lot when they gets wild, and you'll have to look pretty sharp if you don't want to get hurt."

It was not cheering, after a very wearying day and a very short night before, to listen to such talk, and I began to wonder whether the captain would take sufficient precautions to keep the Chinese off, for I felt that to properly carry out the plan, the fighting men must be kept well out of sight till the very last; but I soon came to the conclusion that I need not worry about that, from the spirited way in which everything possible to disguise the ship had been done.

Then, as I leaned over the side looking over the black water, in which a faint star could be seen from time to time, I began to smile to myself at the quiet, dry way in which my ideas had been taken up; but I frowned directly after, as I thought of what a little credit I was getting for it all, and that the captain or Mr Reardon might have said an encouraging word or two to show that they appreciated my efforts.

It was laughable, too, the way in which I had heard the captain's dodge discussed by Barkins and Smith, who never once associated my summons to the cabin with all that had been done.

The time was going along slowly, and I was beginning to feel very drowsy, so I had a walk up and down a few times, and then came suddenly upon something like a big bundle under the weather bulwark.

"Why, Ching," I said, "you here?"

"Yes; velly hot down below, no sleepee sleepee. Come on deck, nicee cool. You have fightee morrow?"

"I hope so," I said; but asked myself the next moment whether I really did hope so.

"Velly bad fightee, bad pilates come, and captain killee whole lot. Allee velly bad man, killee evelybody."

"Do you think they will come out of hiding?"

"Ching don'tee know. Ching thinkee muchee so. Now go sleepee. Velly much tire."

He curled himself up, drawing his tail round out of the way, and seemed to go off directly; while I rejoined the officer of the watch, who happened to be Mr Brooke, and we walked right forward to the bows, and saw that the men were keeping a bright look-out.

"Well, Herrick," he said, "got your dirk sharp?"

"No," I said. "Don't laugh at me, please, Mr Brooke."

"Oh no, I will not laugh at you, my lad," he said; "but as it is quite likely that we may have a bit of a scrimmage to-morrow, if the scoundrels are lured out of their holes, and grow desperate on finding that they have made a mistake, you had better keep out of the way."

"But—"

"Oh yes, I know what you are going to say; but you are very young yet, and what chance would you have against a great strong savage Chinaman— for there are plenty of powerful fellows among these scoundrels. You must wait a bit before you take to fighting."

I felt uncomfortable. He seemed to be looking down upon me so, in spite of my being an officer; but I could not boast of my strength, and remained silent for a time.

"Do you think they are likely to get on board, sir?"

"Oh no," he said. "We shall not give them a chance. Once the captain is sure that they are the pirates, if we are lucky enough to lure them well out from the shore, the men will be ordered up to the guns, and we shall give them a few broadsides, and sink them."

"It sounds horrid, sir," I said. "Then they'll never have a chance to fight us?"

"Not if we can help it, my lad. But, as you say, it does sound horrid, and rather cowardly; but what would you do with a poisonous snake? You would not give it a chance to strike at you first, if you met it and had a loaded gun in your hands?"

"Of course not, sir," I said quickly.

"Well, these wretches are as dangerous as venomous serpents, and, after what you saw on board that barque, you do not think we need be squeamish about ridding the earth of such monsters?"

"No, sir, not a bit," I said quickly.

"Neither do I, Herrick. I should like to aim the gun that sends a shot through them between wind and water."

"Light on the port bow!" announced the look-out forward; and, upon using his night-glass, Mr Brooke made out the vessel, which showed the light to be a large junk, with her enormous matting-sails spread, and gliding along faster than we were, and in the same direction.

As we watched the light, it gradually grew fainter, and finally disappeared, while all through our watch the screw kept on its slow motion, just sending the gunboat onward.

Toward what? I asked myself several times; and, in spite of my determination to acquit myself manfully if we did go into action, I could not help hoping that the next night would find us all as safe as we were then. But all the same the thoughts of our preparations were well in my mind, and never once did I hope that we should not encounter the enemy.

All the same, though, when my watch was at an end and I went below, perhaps it was owing to its being so hot, as Ching said, for it was a long time before I could get off to sleep.

Chapter Ten
The Enemy

"Oh, I say, do wake up and come on deck. It's such a lark."

"What is?" I said, rolling out of the berth, with my head feeling all confused and strange, to stare at Barkins.

"Why, everything. You never saw such a miserable old rag-bag of a ship in your life."

I hurriedly dressed and went on deck, to find the preparations complete, and I could not help thinking that, if the pirates mistook the *Teaser* for a man-of-war now, they must be clever indeed.

For on the previous day I had only seen the alterations in bits, so to speak, but now everything was done, even to having a quantity of coal on deck, and the clean white planks besmirched with the same black fuel. The paint-pots had altered everything; the figure-head was hidden with tarpaulin; the rigging, instead of being all ataunto, was what Smith called "nine bobble square," and one sail had been taken down and replaced by an old one very much tattered, so that up aloft we looked as if we had been having a taste of one of the typhoons which visit the Chinese seas. These preparations, with the men's clothes hanging to dry, the boats badly hauled up to the davits, and the fish hanging over the stern (after the fashion practised in west-country fishing-boats), completely altered the aspect of everything. Then I found that the officers were all in tweeds, with yachting or shooting caps; the bulk of the crew below, and my twenty men and lads all carefully got up with painted heads and pigtails complete, under the charge of Ching, who was bustling about importantly, and he came to me at once and began whispering—

"Captain say, Ching takee care allee men, and show himself evelywhere."

"Yes, of course," I said. "Yes. You wanted to say something?"

"Yes, Ching want say something."

"Well, what is it? Quick, I must go."

"Ching want you tell sailor boy be velly careful. Take care of Ching when pilate come."

"All right," I said; "but they haven't come yet."

"Think big junk pilate."

"Which one? where?" I said.

He pointed forward to where, about five miles off the lee-bow, a great junk was slowly sailing in the same direction as we were.

"Is that the one which passed us in the night?" I said.

"Yes."

"Why do you think she is a pirate?"

"Ching tink why she no sail light away and not stop while man-o'-war clawl along velly slow. You tellee captain."

I nodded, and found that there was no need, for the captain was carefully observing the junk from where he was hidden by a pile of casks, and Mr Reardon was with him.

"Here, Mr Herrick," he cried, "your eyes are young. Have a look at that junk. Take your uniform cap off, my lad, and, as soon as you have done, take off your jacket and put on a coloured suit."

I had a good look through the glass at the junk, and made my report.

"I think it's only a big trader, sir," I said. "Looks like the boats we saw at Amoy, and as if she were going up to Wanghai."

"Yes, that's it, I think," said Captain Thwaites to Mr Reardon. Then he sharply turned to me and gave me a dry look. "Well, Mr Herrick, you see I have taken your advice, and put my ship in this disgraceful state."

"Yes, sir," I said eagerly; "and I hope it will prove successful."

"So do I," he said drily. "That will do, Herrick. Now, Mr Reardon, I think we will keep on just as we are, just about four knots an hour. It gives the idea of our being in trouble; and if we keep on close outside the islands, it may draw the scoundrels—that is, if they are there."

"Yes, sir, if they are there," said the lieutenant.

"How long do you reckon it will take us to get abreast of the reef where that barque lay?"

"We ought to be there by noon, sir, I should say."

"That will do. We shall seem to be making for Wanghai."

I heard no more, but went below, and directly after breakfast reappeared in white flannels and a cricketing cap, a transformation which satisfied the first lieutenant, but displeased Barkins and Smith, who had orders to keep below in uniform.

"I hate so much favouritism," grumbled Barkins. "Who are you, Gnat? You're our junior; and here are we kept below, and my lord you parading about the deck, and seeing everything."

"Why, you're in the reserve," I said banteringly, "and will have all the fighting to do."

"Who wants all the fighting to do?" cried Smith. "I don't. I suppose if we do take a lot of pirate junks, you'll be promoted, and we shan't get a word."

"Stuff!" I said. "How can I get promoted?"

"But I want to know why you're to be picked out," cried Barkins.

"Go and ask the skipper," I said. "Now, look here both of you; if you're not civil, I won't come and report everything. If you are, I'll come down as often as I can to tell you all that is going on."

"Oh then, I suppose we must be civil, Smithy," said Barkins sourly, "but we'll serve the beggar out afterwards."

I went up on deck again to find that our speed had been slightly increased, but we drew no nearer to the junk, which sailed on exactly in the same course as we were taking, and that seemed strange; but beyond watching her through the telescopes, and seeing that she had only about a dozen men on board—all blue-frocked Chinamen—no further notice was taken of her.

Ching was seated right forward, with his blue frock showing well up against the grey white of one of the hanging-down sails, and he had been furnished with a pipe, which he smoked slowly and thoughtfully; half-a-dozen men were in the fore-rigging, making believe to repair damages up aloft; and soon after four more were sent up to begin tinkering at the topmast, which they made great efforts to lower down on deck, but of course got no further.

They had orders from the first lieutenant to take it coolly, and coolly they took it, looking like a lazy, loafing set of Chinese sailors, whose intentions were to do as little as they could for their pay.

Mr Reardon, in a shooting-suit and straw hat, went about giving orders, and the captain and Mr Brooke had cane seats on the quarter-deck, with a bottle and glasses, and sat sipping beer and smoking cigars, as if they were passengers.

Then came long hours of patient—I should say impatient—crawling along over the same course as we had followed the previous day, with no sail in sight but the big junk, which took not the slightest notice of us, nor we of it.

There was no doubt whatever, though, of her actions. She kept sailing on at about the same rate as we steamed, evidently for the sake of being in company, and to have a European vessel close at hand to close up to in case of danger from the shores of the mainland, or one of the islands we should pass, for it was an established fact that the pirates seldom attacked ships that were in company.

All through the early part of the morning the novelty of the affair interested the men, and there was a constant burst of eager conversation going on, but as noon came, and matters were in the same position, and we still far away from the spot where the barque had been burned, every one grew weary, and I fidgeted myself into a state of perspiration.

"It will all turn out wrong," I thought, "and then they will blame me."

With these fancies to worry me, I kept away from my messmates as much as I could; and when by accident I encountered either of my superiors, I saw that they looked—or I fancied they did—very stern.

"All these preparations for nothing," I said to myself, as I saw the guns all ready, but covered over with tarpaulins, cartridges and shells waiting, and the crews armed and impatient.

Dinner had been long over, and I need hardly say that I did not enjoy mine. Some of the men were having a nap, and the heat below must have been very great, for it was scorching on deck.

At last we were abreast of the rocky islands dotted here and there, and upon the reef I could just make out a few pieces of the burned vessel.

But as I swept the rocky islets and channels and then the horizon, I could not make out a sail, only our companion the junk, with her bows and stern high out of the water, sailing easily along that fine afternoon.

Another hour passed, and there were rocky islands on our starboard bow and two astern, but not a sign of inhabitant, only high bluffs, rugged cliffs, and narrow channels between reefs whitened by the constant breaking upon them of a heavy swell.

"Rather slow work, Reardon," said the captain, as they two came by where I was at the bulwark, using a small glass. "See anything, Mr Herrick?"

"No, sir," I said.

"No, sir, indeed; of course you don't," cried the captain impatiently. "Nice trick you've played me, sir. Made me dress up my men and the ship in this tomfool way. There you are using your glass. What have you got to say for yourself, eh?"

I could not tell whether he was speaking banteringly or really angrily, and, keeping my glass to my eye in the hope of seeing something to report, I mumbled out some excuse about meaning it for the best.

"Best, indeed!" he said pettishly. "Nice objects we look. What do you think the First Lords of the Admiralty would say to me if they could see Her Majesty's gunboat—the finest clipper in the service—in this state? Eh? Why don't you answer, sir?"

"I suppose, sir," I cried desperately, "that they would say you were doing your best for the sake of trying to catch the pirates."

"Humph! do you, indeed? Well? Anything to report? What's the use of holding that glass to your eye if you can't see anything? Anything to report, I say?"

"Yes, sir," I cried breathlessly, and with my heart throbbing heavily, "the junk has run up a little pennon to her mast-head."

"She has?" cried Mr Reardon excitedly, and he raised his own glass. "Yes, you're right. Well done, Herrick! There, sir, I told you the lad was right."

"Right? when they are signalling to us for water or a bag of rice."

"When they have only to heave-to and let us overhaul them, sir," cried Mr Reardon, swinging his glass round and narrowly missing my head. "No, sir, they're signalling to the shore; and before long we shall see another junk come swooping out from behind one of those headlands, to take us in the rear. If they don't, I'm a Dutchman."

"Then Dutchman you are, Reardon," said the captain, smiling. "I only wish they would."

"Here they come, sir," I cried excitedly— "one—two—yes, there are three."

"What? Where?"

"You can only see the tops of their sails, sir, over that flat, low island this side of the big cliffs."

"Eh! yes."

Only those two words, as the captain sighted the slowly-moving objects just indistinctly seen, but they were enough to send a thrill all through the ship.

For there was no mistaking the matter. The junk that had been hanging by us all night was a pirate after all, and she had signalled to companions on shore. I could see, too, that she was slightly altering her course.

The enemy was at last in sight.

Chapter Eleven
The Fight

"Oh, if I only dared hooray!" I said to myself; and then a flush of pride rose to my cheeks, for the captain gave me a smart clap on the shoulder.

"Bravo, Herrick!" he said in quite a whisper. "I thought you were right, my lad, or I shouldn't have done all this. Mr Reardon and I will make a fine officer of you before we have done."

"Shall I pass the word down for the men to be on the *qui vive*?" said the lieutenant.

The captain laughed, and nodded his head in the direction of the hatches, which were black with peeping heads.

"No need, Mr Reardon; there is not a soul on board who does not know. It is no time for making fresh arrangements. We'll keep exactly to our plans. Don't let a man show on deck, for depend upon it they will have a look-out aloft ready to give warning of danger, and we must not give them an excuse for signalling to their confederates to sheer off."

"Keep steadily on, then, sir?"

"Yes, steadily and stupidly. Let the men go on as before up aloft, and let the rest of the men show their white heads and pigtails at the bulwarks as if they were wondering who the strangers were. Good pressure of steam below?"

"Yes, sir, almost too much," said the lieutenant, after communication with the engine-room.

"Not a bit," said the captain, rubbing his hands. "We shall want it soon."

My heart began to beat as they passed on, and I wondered what would be the first steps taken. But I did not forget my promise. My duties were about nil, and as soon as I had seen the men staring over the bulwarks, and noted that the sham repairs to the rigging were steadily going on, I ran down the companion-way, and breathlessly told Barkins and Smith.

"Then there are four of them, Smithy," cried Barkins. "Look here, Gnat; he stuck out that there were only three. But well done, old chap, you are a good one to come and tell us. Here, don't go yet; I want to—"

I never heard what he wanted to, for there was too much exciting attraction on the deck, to which, being as it were licensed, I at once returned.

The captain and Mr Reardon were on the quarter-deck, conscious that savages as the Chinese or Formosan pirates were, they probably did not despise the barbarian instruments known as telescopes, and that most likely every movement on board the *Teaser* was being watched. Any suspicious act would be quite sufficient to make them sheer off, and consequently the strictest orders were given to the men to play their parts carefully, and make no movement that was not required.

Dressed as I was in flannels, my appearance was thoroughly in keeping with the assumed peaceful character of the ship, and hence I heard and saw nearly everything.

Just as I went on the quarter-deck the captain was saying to the first lieutenant—

"Don't be so excitable, man. When I ask you a question, or give an order, take it deliberately, and dawdle off to see it done."

"Right through, sir?" said Mr Reardon petulantly.

"No," said the captain quietly. "When I give the order, 'Full speed ahead,' then you can act. Till then you are mate or passenger, whichever you like, of this dirty-looking trader. Ah, those three low junks, or whatever they are, can creep through the water pretty quickly."

"Yes; and the big junk too," said Mr Reardon, using his glass. "It is astonishing how rapidly those great heavily-sailed craft can go. She's full of men, sir," he continued; "I can see more and more beginning to show themselves. Not much appearance of dishipline, though."

"So much the better for us," muttered Captain Thwaites, turning in his cane arm-chair, and looking in the direction of the islands again, from which the three smaller vessels were coming on rapidly. "Yes,"—he said, as if to himself, "a head keeps showing here and there; they are full of men too."

I was not experienced, of course, that only being my third voyage, but I knew enough of navigating tactics to grasp the fact that the four vessels were carefully timing themselves so as to reach us together, and this evidently was their customary mode of procedure, and no doubt accounted for ship after ship being taken and plundered. I felt startled, too, as I realised the strength of the crews, and what a simultaneous attempt to board might mean. With an ordinary merchantman, even with a strong crew, undoubtedly death and destruction, while even with our well-armed men and guns I began to have doubts. A slip in the manoeuvres, ever so slight a mistake on Captain Thwaites' part, or a blunder in the carrying out of his orders, might give one vessel the chance to make fast, and while we were arresting their onslaught there would be time for the others to get close in and throw their scores of bloodthirsty savages upon our decks.

Mr Reardon had strolled forward, and returned just as the captain said to me—

"You may as well fetch me my sword and cap from the cabin, Mr Herrick."

"Yes, sir," I said quickly, and I was off, but he stopped me.

"Not now, boy," he cried impatiently; "when the first gun is fired will be time enough. Well, Reardon, men all ready?"

"Ready, sir? they want wiring down. I'm only afraid of one thing."

"What is that?"

"That they will jam one another in the hatches in their excitement."

"Give fresh stringent orders, sir," said the captain sternly; "every man is to go quickly and silently to his post, as if on an ordinary drill. By George! they are coming on quickly; we shall have it all over by daylight."

"And they'll plunder the ship by lamplight, eh?" said Mr Reardon drily.

"Of course. I think there is no need to feel any doubt now as to these being the men we want?"

"I don't know, sir," said the lieutenant quietly; "but there is no doubt about their meaning to try and take this peaceful merchantman. Look, they feel sure of us, sir, and are showing themselves. Why, they swarm with men."

"Poor wretches!" said the captain gravely. "I don't like shedding blood, but we must do it now, to the last drop."

The enemy were now less than a mile away, and coming on rapidly, the smaller vessels helping their progress with long, heavy sweeps; and as I stood behind the captain's chair, and looked round the deck from the wheel, where one of our sham Chinamen stood, with another seated under the bulwarks apparently asleep, but ready to spring up and join his messmate at a word; round by the bulwarks where four or five stood stupidly looking over the side; and then up aloft to the men making believe to work very hard at the damaged spar—all looked peaceful enough to tempt the wretches, without counting the most prominent figure of all, Ching, as he sat high up, smoking placidly, and looking as calm and contemplative as a figure of Buddha.

"The men ought to be called up now, and the guns set to work," I said to myself, as every pulse throbbed with excitement, and in imagination I saw, from the captain's neglect or dilatoriness, our deck running with blood.

But I had to master these thoughts.

"They know better than I do when to begin," I said to myself, and, after a sharp glance at the coming vessels, I began to pity my two messmates who were cooped up below, and I thought of how excited they must be. Then I thought of Mr Brooke, and hoped he would not be hurt; and shuddered a little as I remembered the doctor, who would be all ready below, waiting to attend upon the first wounded man.

"See that, sir?" said Mr Reardon quickly.

"What?" said Captain Thwaites in the most unmoved way.

"That smoke on board two of them."

"On board all," said the captain. "I noticed it a minute ago. They are getting the stinkpots ready for us, I suppose."

"Yes, that's it, sir. Do you think it necessary to have the hose ready in case of fire?"

"No; if any come on board, the firemen can be called up from the stokehole with their shovels. I think we'll go now upon the bridge. You can come too, Mr Herrick. I may want you to take an order or two."

And as he walked quietly towards the bridge, where the speaking-tubes and signals joined with the engine-room were, he was as calm and deliberate as if there was not the slightest danger menacing the *Teaser*; while for my part I could not help feeling that the position there upon the bridge was a highly-exposed one, and that I should have been much safer in the shelter of the bulwarks, or down below.

All this time we were gently forging ahead, and the junk was quietly manoeuvring so that we should pass her so close that she could just avoid our prow, and then close and grapple with us, for they were busy on her starboard quarter, and through my glass I could make out great hooks.

"Won't they think we are taking it too coolly, and grow suspicious, sir?" whispered Mr Reardon excitedly.

"I hope not," said the captain. "Perhaps one might show fight now, but I am trusting to their believing that we are stupid, for I want to get them all, Reardon, if I can. Now, silence, if you please."

Mr Reardon drew back a step or two and waited during those terrible minutes which followed, and I gave quite a start, for the enemy suddenly threw off all reserve as a yell came from the junk, which was answered from the other vessels, and, with their decks crowded with savage-looking desperadoes, they swept down upon us literally from both sides, bow and stern.

But still the captain did not make a sign; and, in the midst of the horrible silence on board, I saw the dressed-up men turning their heads to gaze at us anxiously, as if the suspense was greater than they could bear, and their eyes implored their commander to give the word before the wretches began swarming on board.

I glanced at Mr Reardon, whose face was white, and the great drops of perspiration stood upon his cheeks, while his eyes, which were fixed upon the captain between us, looked full of agony; for the great junk with its wild crew was apparently only a hundred yards ahead, and the others not much farther, coming rapidly on.

"It's all over," I thought, in my horror, "he will be too late;" and that I was not alone in my thoughts obtained confirmation, for, though the crew to a man stood fast, I saw Ching suddenly drop from his perch and look round for a place of retreat.

At the same moment the captain moved his hand; there was a sharp tinging of the gong in the engine-room, which meant full speed ahead; and, as the vibration rapidly increased, he then gave a sharp order or two, and in an instant almost the men came pouring up from the various hatches upon deck, but so quickly and quietly that the transformation was almost magical.

I don't think my eyes are peculiarly made, but I saw the various crews muster round the guns, and the marines range up, and the men with their rifles at their various posts, with each officer in his place, although all the time I was standing with my gaze fixed upon the great junk.

I saw, too, my twenty pigtailed men come sliding down the ropes from above, and snatch up the cutlasses and rifles laid ready beneath a tarpaulin; but all the time I was seeing, in obedience to orders, two parties of the crew going forward at the double, and I knew that the captain was communicating with the two men at the wheel.

Quick as lightning there was another order as we began to leave the three low vessels behind, and I involuntarily grasped the rail before me as all the men on board lay down—crews of the guns, marines, and those who had doubled forward under the command of Mr Brooke.

Hardly was the evolution performed, when there, right before us, were the lowering mat-sails of the great junk, and then, crash! there was a wild despairing yell, and we were into her amidships, the ponderous gunboat literally cutting her down and going right over her; while at a second command every man sprang up again, and for the next minute or two bayonet and cutlass were flashing in the evening sunlight as the wretches who climbed on board were driven back.

While this was going on, the bell in the engine-room rang out again and again, and we began to move astern to meet the three low junks, which, undismayed by the fate of their comrade, came at us with their crews yelling savagely.

Then there was a deep roar as the first gun belched forth its flame and smoke, with the huge shell hurtling through the air, dipping once in the calm sea, and crashing through one of the junks, to explode with a report like the echo of the first, far beyond.

'CRASH!'

Captain Thwaites turned quietly and looked at me.

"Yes, sir?" I stammered.

"I said when the first gun was fired you could fetch my cap and sword, Mr Herrick," he said quietly, and I ran down just as the second big gun bellowed, but I did not see with what result. I heard the sharp, short order, though, and another gun roared, and another, and another, as the junks came well into sight; for each gun I heard the crash of the shell hitting too, and the fierce yells of the men, as I dashed into the cabin, seized cap and sword, and then ran back to the bridge, eager to see the fight, and in my excitement forgetting to feel afraid.

But a heavy smoke was gathering over us and the junks,—two were indistinct, though they were close aboard of us. Then, as the *Teaser* glided astern, I saw that the third was smoking, while crash, crash, the others struck our sides, and their crews grappled, hurled their stinkpots on board, and began to swarm over the bulwarks.

But the guns were being steadily served with terrible effect; the few poor wretches who reached the deck were bayoneted, and in how long or how short a time I cannot tell, for everything seemed to be swept away in the excitement; we steamed away out of the smoke into the ruddy sunset, and there I saw in one place a mass of tangled bamboo and matting, with men clustering upon it, and crowding one over the other like bees in a swarm. There was another mass about a quarter of a mile away, and I looked in vain for the third junk; but a number of her crew clinging to bamboos, sweeps, spars, and what looked to be wicker crates, showed where she had been. The last of the four, with her great matting-sails hauled up to the fullest extent, was sailing away toward the nearest island, and on either side they had sweeps over with two or three men to each, tugging away with all their might to help their vessel along.

"The brutes!" I thought to myself, as I watched the glint of the ruddy sun upon their shiny heads and faces, with their pig tails swinging behind, as they hung back straining at the great oars. For their sole idea seemed to be escape, and not the slightest effort was made to pick up any of their comrades struggling in the water.

It was wonderful how quickly they went, and I began to think that the junk would escape. Three miles would be enough to place her all amongst the reefs and shoals, where the gunboat dare not follow; and I was thinking, as we glided rapidly in her wake, that the *Teaser* would chase her swiftly for about half the distance, and then lower the boats to continue the pursuit, but I was wrong; I saw that the captain gave Mr Reardon some order, then the gong rang in the engine-room, the way of the *Teaser* was checked, a turn of the wheel made her describe a curve, and she slowly came to a standstill broadside on to the flying junk.

The next minute the crews were piped away to the boats with their complement of marines to each; and as they were lowered down a steady fire was maintained with shell upon the junk.

I stood watching the shots, and saw the first of the broadside from one heavy and three smaller guns strike the water close to the junk's hull, fly up, dip again, and then burst over the cliffs.

The second went wide to the left, while the third also missed; and I saw the captain stamp impatiently as the fourth went right over her.

"She'll get away," I thought; and it seemed a pity for this junk to escape and form a nucleus for another strong pirate gang.

The firing continued, another broadside being directed at the flying pirates, who seemed to be certain now of escape, for the junk was end-on to us, and moving rapidly, forming a very difficult object for our marksmen; the gunboat, of course, rising and falling all the time upon the heaving sea.

In the intervals between the shots I had caught a glimpse of Barkins and Smith climbing into two of the boats, but it was only a glimpse; and then I was watching the effects of the fire again, as the boats pushed off to go to the help of the floating men.

Shot after shot had been fired most ineffectively, and I heard expostulations and angry words used to the captains of the guns; while at every ineffective shell that burst far away a derisive yell rose from the crowded junk — the shouts increasing each time.

"Another broadside, Reardon," cried the captain; "and then we must run in as far as we dare. Pick out half-a-dozen of the best men with the rifle to place on the bows to pick off the steersman."

"Ay, ay, sir," cried Mr Reardon; then directly, "All gone in the boats, sir."

Just then, as I was thinking that the junk must escape, one of our big guns was fired with a crash which made the deck vibrate. There was a tremendous puff of smoke, which was drawn toward us so that I could not see the effect, but the shell seemed to burst almost directly with a peculiar dull crash, and another yell arose from the distant vessel. Only it was not a derisive cry like the last, but a faint startling chorus of long-continued shrieks, despairing and wild.

"That's got her, sir," cried Mr Reardon; and we waited impatiently for the smoke to float by. But it still shut out the junk from where we stood, while it passed away from the men forward at the gun, and they gave us the first endorsement of Mr Reardon's words by bursting out into a hearty cheer, which was taken up by the crews of the other guns. Then we were clear of the smoke, looking landward to see a crowd of men struggling in the water, swimming about to reach planks and pieces of the junk, which had been blown almost to pieces by our great shell, and had sunk at once, while yet quite a mile from the nearest rocks.

"Ha!" ejaculated the captain, "a good evening's work! Now, Reardon, down with the other two boats, and save every poor wretch you can."

"Only one left, sir," cried Mr Reardon; and in a few minutes, fully manned, she was about to be lowered down, when I looked quickly at the captain, and he read my meaning.

"Want to go?" he said, and then nodded sharply.

I dashed down, climbed upon the bulwark, seized the falls just as they were about to be cast off, and slid down into the stern to take my place. Then the oars fell with a splash, and away we went over the ruddy sea to try and save all we could of the wretches upon whom so terrible a retribution had come.

One of the warrant officers was in command; he gave me a grim nod.

"Want to see the fun?" he said.

"I want to see the men saved," I replied; "I don't know where the fun comes in."

"You soon will," he said. "Look out for yourself, my lad; and don't be too eager to help them."

"Why?"

"You'll soon see," he said gruffly. Then turning to the four marines in the stern-sheets—"fix bayonets, and keep a sharp look-out."

I looked at him wonderingly, for fixed bayonets did not seem very suitable things for saving drowning men. But I said nothing, only sheltered my eyes from the level rays of the sun as we rowed swiftly on, and gazed across the water at the despairing wretches fighting for their lives upon the blood-red surface of the water.

It was very horrible after a time, for, as I looked with my heart feeling contracted, I saw a man, who had been swimming hard, suddenly throw up his hands and sink.

It was too much for me.

"Row, my lads, row," I cried; "we may catch him as he comes up."

"No," said the warrant officer grimly, "we shall never see him again."

"But try, try!" I cried.

"Yes, we'll try our best," said the officer sternly; "but it's their turn now. Many a poor wretch have they seen drown, I know, and laughed at when he cried for help."

I knew it was true; but all the same there was only one thought besides in my breast, and that was to save all the poor wretches who were clinging to the pieces of wreck.

As we drew nearer, we came upon the first of quite thirty, clinging to a sweep which was under his left arm; while, to my horror, I had seen three more swimming without support go down without a cry, and not one rise again.

"Easy there," said the officer; "ready there, coxswain; can you reach him with the hook?"

The man who was standing in the bows reached out to hook the pirate, but just then the end of the floating sweep touched our boat, and turned right off, so that the coxswain missed his stroke, and the result was that the pirate glided aft.

The officer by my side leaned over, reached out, and, to my intense satisfaction, caught the Chinaman by his left sleeve to draw him to the boat; but in an instant the wretch threw his right arm out of the water, and I saw the flash of a long knife in his fingers, as, with his teeth grinning, he struck at my companion with all his might.

I was so taken by surprise that I sat as if paralysed; but I was conscious of a quick movement from behind, something red passed over me, and, all instantaneously, there was the flash of another blade, a horrible thud—the pirate was driven under water; and I wrenched, as it were, my eyes round from him to look up over my shoulder at the marine, who with a dexterous twist of his rifle withdrew his bayonet from the savage's chest.

"Hurt, sir?" he said.

"No thankye, marine. Very quick and well done of you. There, Mr Herrick; now you see why I told you to look out."

"The brutes!" I cried excitedly; "they're not worth trying to save."

"No," he said; "but we must do it. I suppose they don't believe much in the mercy they'll get from us; so there's no wonder. Look at that!"

I turned my head in the direction in which he pointed, and saw what he meant. Five men were clinging to a piece of floating wreck about fifty yards away, and three more left the plank to which they had been clinging as we approached, and swam to join them.

I looked at the first group, fully expecting to see them hold out their hands to help their comrades; but in place thereof, I saw one wretch, who occupied the best position on the floating mass of wreck, raise a heavy piece of bamboo with both hands, and bring it down with a crash upon the head of the first man who swam up.

"Yah, you cowardly beggar!" roared one of the boat's crew. "I've marked you."

"Nice wild-beasts to save, Mr Herrick," said the warrant officer. "I feel as if I should like to open fire on them with my revolver."

"It's too horrible," I panted. "Look, look, Mr Grey!"

"I'm looking, my lad," said my companion. "Give way, my boys; let's stop it somehow."

For there was a desperate fight going on at the piece of wreck; three men, knife in hand, were trying to get upon the floating wood, and those upon it stabbing at them to keep them off.

But, in their despair, the swimmers made a dash together, regardless of the blows, climbed on, and a terrible struggle began.

"Starn all!" roared Mr Grey; and the boat's progress was checked. We were backed away just in time, for the pirates were all now on one side of the piece of wreck, thinking of nothing but destroying each other's lives, and heaped together in what looked like a knot, when the side they were on slowly sank, the far portion rose up and completely turned over upon them, forcing them beneath the water, which eddied and boiled as the struggle still went on below the surface.

"Give way, my lads," said the officer sternly; "let's try and save some of the others."

"Ay, ay," cried the man who had shouted before. "These here arn't worth saving."

The boat swept round in a curve, and we pulled off for another group, kneeling and crouching upon what seemed to be a yard and a mass of matting-sail.

Mr Grey stood up.

"Now, my lads," he shouted, "surrender."

For answer they bared their knives and defied us to come on, yelling and striking at us with them.

Mr Grey looked round at me half-laughingly.

"Cheerful sort of prisoners to make. If we go close in, some of us will get knifed."

"You can't go close," I said.

"If I don't they'll drown," he cried; "and the captain will ask me what I've been about."

"Hadn't you better let the jollies put 'em out of their misery, Mr Grey, sir?" cried one of the men. "They arn't fit to live."

"No," cried another fiercely. "They arn't men; they're tigers."

"Silence!" said the officer sternly. "There is a man yonder about to sink; give way," he cried.

This man had left a barrel, to which he had vainly tried to cling, but it kept on turning round; and at last, in his despair, he had left it to try and swim to the nearest rocks.

His strength was failing, though, and he began to paddle like a dog, too much frightened to try and swim.

A few strokes of the oar took us within reach, and this time the coxswain succeeded in hooking his loose cotton jacket, and drawing him to the side.

Hands seized him directly, and he was hauled in to lie down trembling, and looking wildly from one to the other.

"Come; he's a quiet one," said the coxswain. "Mind, sir!"

"Mind! look out!" roared the boatswain.

But he was too late. One moment the Chinaman crouched, limp and helpless, in the bottom of the boat forward, with his hands hidden in his wet sleeves, the next he had made a frog-like leap at the coxswain, driven a sharp knife in the muscles of his back, and leaped overboard. Not into safety, though; for one of the men stood ready, and, as the wretch rose, brought down the blade of his oar with a tremendous chop across the head, and the pirate went down to rise no more.

I heard the boatswain utter a low fierce growl as he crept forward, and I followed to try and help, for the injured man had sunk upon his knees, with the boat-hook across the bows, and began to wipe the perspiration from his forehead.

"Much hurt, my lad?" cried Mr Grey.

"Tidy, sir, tidy; makes one feel a bit sicky-like. Any one like to have the next turn with the boat-hook? I'm going to miche a bit.—Do it bleed?"

All thought of saving the pirates was given up till the wound, which bled sharply, was carefully bandaged, and the man laid down in the bottom of the boat. Then the crew looked at their officer.

"Hadn't we better polish 'em off, sir?" growled one of the men.

"The captain's orders were to pick up all the drowning men we could," said the boatswain sternly.

"But they won't be picked up, sir."

"Give way."

The men rowed to another floating group of four, and I stood up and called to them to surrender.

For answer they sprang into the water, and began to swim to some of their comrades on the next piece of wreck.

"This is a puzzling job, Mr Herrick," said the boatswain. "I'm not a brute; I'd jump overboard to save any of the wretches, but it would be like giving my life, or the lives of any of the crew, to set them the job. Those wretches will begin upon their mates, you'll see."

He was quite right, for the possessors of the next floating piece of wreck yelled to their comrades to keep off, and, as they still swam on, a fresh fight began of the most bloodthirsty nature, and one of our men said drily—

"Take it coolly, sir. If we lay on our oars a bit, there won't be none to fish up."

The feeling of horror and pity for the drowning men began to wear off, and I was glad when Mr Grey suddenly ordered the men to row hard, and I saw him steer shoreward to cut off a little party of four, who, with a thick bamboo yard between them, were swimming for the rocks.

"They must be saved as prisoners or not at all," he said sternly; "not a man of them must land."

As soon as this last party saw us coming, we noticed that they drew their knives to keep us off, but energetic measures were taken this time. We got between them and the shore; and then a rope was made ready, one of the men stood up and dexterously threw it right over a pirate's head, snatched it tightly to him, dragged him from his hold, and he was at last drawn to the side half-drowned, hauled aboard, and his hands and feet tied.

This successful plan was followed out with the others, with the result that we had four prisoners lying safely in the bottom, and then turned to capture some more in the same way.

But we had been so excited and taken up by this work that we had not seen what was going on seaward, where a gun was fired for our recall.

"Where's the next of them?" said Mr Grey.

I did not answer, as I stood up looking round to see a few fragments of wreck floating here and there, but there was not another pirate left to save.

Chapter Twelve
Repairing Damages

For some moments I could not believe it true, and I stood on the thwart and gazed carefully round, scanning every fragment of the wreck in the expectation of seeing some trick to deceive us—men lying flat with only their faces above the surface of the water, and holding on by sweep or bamboo with one hand. But in a very short time we were all certain that not a living being was near; of the dead there were several, as we found on rowing here and there. One, as he was turned over, seemed to be perfectly uninjured, but the others displayed ghastly wounds in face, neck, and breast, showing how horribly fierce had been the encounter in which they had been engaged.

Satisfied at last that our task was at an end, the word was given, and the men began to row back to the *Teaser*, which still lay so transformed in appearance, as seen from a distance, that I was thinking that it was no wonder that the pirates had been deceived, when one of the men, forgetful of all the horrors through which we had passed, of his wounded comrade, and the dangerous prisoners under his feet, burst out into a merry fit of laughter.

"Say, lads," he cried, "we shall have a nice job to-morrow, to wash the old girl's face."

The rest of the crew laughed in chorus, till the boatswain sternly bade them give way.

"I doubt it," he said in a low voice to me. "I should say that the captain will do a little more to make her less ship-shape, ready for the next lot."

"But you don't think there are any more pirates, do you?"

"More!" he said, looking at me in surprise. "Why, my lad, the coast swarms with them. We never hear a hundredth part of the attacks they make. It is not only European vessels they seize, but anything that comes in their way. It strikes me, Mr Herrick, that we have only just begun what may turn out a very successful cruise."

Ten minutes later we were nearing the *Teaser*, and I saw the reason why we could not see either of the other boats. They were swinging to the davits, and we were therefore the last.

Just then Mr Reardon hailed us.

"How many men hurt?" he shouted between his hands.

"Only one, sir; Barr—coxswain."

"Badly?"

"Oh no, sir," shouted the sufferer. "Bit of a scrat on the back."

"How many prisoners?"

"Four, sir."

Then we were alongside, the boat was run up, and, after our wounded man had been lifted out, I stepped on board, eager to know the result of the action on the part of the other boats, and to learn this I went below, and found Barkins alone.

"Well," I cried, "how many prisoners?"

"Round dozen," he cried.

"Any one hurt?"

"Round dozen."

"I know, twelve prisoners," I said impatiently. "I asked you how many were hurt."

"And I told you, stupid," he replied, "a round dozen."

"What! a man wounded for every prisoner?"

"That's it; and we shouldn't have taken any, the beggars were game for fighting to the last, if Mr Brooke hadn't given the word for them to be knocked on the head first with the thick end of the oars."

"To stun them?"

"Yes; and our lads got so savage after seeing their mates stabbed when trying to save the brutes' lives, that they hit as hard as they could. They killed two of 'em, or we should have had fourteen."

"How horrid!"

"Horrid? Why, I enjoyed it," said my messmate. "When I saw poor old Blacksmith—"

"What!" I cried excitedly, "he isn't hurt?"

"Not hurt? why, one yellow-faced savage, when poor old Smithy held out his hand to pull him aboard, took hold of his wrist, and then reached up and stuck his knife right through the poor old chap's arm, and left it there."

"Poor old Smithy!" I cried huskily, and a choking sensation rose in my throat. "I must go and see him."

"No, you mustn't. I've just been, and they sent me away."

"But where is he?"

"Doctor's got him, and been mending him up. He has gone to sleep now."

"Was he very bad?"

"Stick a stocking-needle through your arm, and then square it, cube it, add decimal nine, eight, seven, six, five, four, three, two, one, and then see how you feel."

"Poor old boy!" I said; "I am sorry."

"Well, so am I," said Barkins sourly; "but I don't keep on howling."

"Did they take the blackguard prisoner?"

"Well, they did, and hauled him aboard, but he was no good, and they pitched him overboard again."

"Why?" I said wonderingly.

"Why! because he was dead. Bob Saunders, that red-haired chap, was in the stern-sheets helping to catch the beggars with hitches, and as soon as he saw the big yellow-faced wretch stick his knife into poor old Blacksmith, he let drive at the brute with the boat-hook, twisted it in his frock, and held him under water. He didn't mean to, but he was savage at what he had seen, for the lads like Smithy, and he held the beggar under water too long."

I shuddered, and thought of the man being bayoneted from our boat, and Mr Grey's narrow escape.

"Your fellows behaved better, I s'pose?" said Barkins.

"Not a bit," I said. "We've got a man stabbed just in the same way—" and I told him of our adventures.

"They're nice ones," said Barkins sourly. "I don't think our chaps will want to take many prisoners next time. But I say, what a crusher for them—all four junks, and not a man to go back and tell the tale."

"It's glorious," I cried, forgetting the horrors in our triumph.

"For you," said Barkins sourly.

"Why for me? You and poor old Smith did your part. Don't be so jolly envious."

"Envious? Come, I like that," he cried. "If you felt as if something red-hot was being stuck in your leg you'd feel envious too. You're the luckiest beggar that ever was, and never get hurt or anything."

"No more do you," I said, laughing.

"Oh, don't I? What do you call that, then?" he cried, swinging his legs round, for he was sitting with one of them under the table.

To my horror and astonishment, I saw that his leg was bandaged, and a red stain was showing through.

"Why, Tanner, old chap," I cried, catching his hand as my eyes were blurred; "I didn't know you were hurt."

He looked quite pleased at my weakness, and the emotion I showed.

"Oh, it ain't much," he said, smiling and holding on to my hand very tightly; "but it pringles and sticks a bit, I mean stingles—no, I don't! My tongue's getting all in a knot, it tingles and pricks a bit. I say, Gnat, old chap, you don't think those chaps carry poisoned knives, do you?"

"What, like the Malays? Oh no."

"I'm glad of that, because it made me feel a bit funky. I thought this stinging might mean the poison spreading."

"Oh no, don't think that," I cried; "and some one told me a Malay prince said it was all nonsense about the knives being poisoned."

"He did?"

"Yes; he laughed, and said there was no need to poison them, they were quite sharp enough to kill a man without."

"That depends on where you put it in," said Barkins grimly.

"Yes," I said; "but what did the doctor say?"

"What about?"

"Your leg."

"He hasn't seen it yet."

"Why, Tanner," I cried, "you haven't had it properly bandaged."

"No; I felt so sick when I got on board, that I sneaked off here to lie down a bit. Besides, he had poor old Blacksmith to see to, and the other chaps."

"But didn't he see the bandage when you went there?"

"No; there was no bandage then. It's only a bit of a scratch; I tied it up myself."

"How was it?"

"I don't hardly know. It was done in a scuffle somehow, when we had got the first prisoner in hand. He began laying about him with a knife, and gave it to two of our lads badly, and just caught me in the leg. It was so little that I didn't like to make a fuss about it. Here, stop, don't leave a chap. I want to talk to you."

"Back directly," I cried, and I hurried on deck so quickly that I nearly blundered up against Mr Reardon.

"Manners, midshipman!" he said sharply. "Stop, sir. Where are you going?"

"Doctor, sir."

"What, are you hurt, my lad?" he cried anxiously.

"No, sir, but poor Barkins is."

"Bless my soul, how unfortunate! Mr Smith down too! Where is he?"

I told him, and he hurried with me to the doctor, who was putting on his coat, after finishing the last dressing of the injured men.

"Here, doctor," cried Mr Reardon sharply, "I've another man down— boy, I mean."

"What, young Smith? I've dressed his wound."

"No, no; Barkins has been touched too."

"Tut, tut!" cried the doctor, taking up a roll of bandage. "Are they bringing him?"

"No, sir; he's sitting by his berth. He tied up the wound himself."

Without another word the doctor started off, and we followed to where Barkins sat by the table with his back leaning against the side of his berth, and as soon as he caught sight of us he darted a reproachful look at me.

"Oh, I say, Gnat," he whispered, "this is too bad." For the doctor had raised the leg, and, after taking off the handkerchief, roughly tied round just above the knee, made no scruple about slitting up the lad's trousers with an ugly-looking knife, having a hooky kind of blade.

"Bad?" said Mr Reardon anxiously.

"Oh dear, no," replied the doctor. "Nice clean cut. Sponge and water, youngster. Ha, yes," he continued, as he applied the cool, soft sponge to the bleeding wound, "avoided all the vessels nicely."

"Gnat, old chap," whispered Barkins, as I half supported him, "pinch me, there's a good fellow."

"What for?" I whispered back.

AS IF HE ENJOYED HIS TASK.'

"Feel sicky and queer. Don't let me faint before him."

"Here, hallo! Barkins, don't turn like a great girl over a scratch—lower his head down, boy. That's the way. He'll soon come round. Ever see a wound dressed before?"

"No, sir," I said, repressing a shudder.

"Don't tease the boys, doctor," said Mr Reardon sharply; "get the wound dressed."

"Well, I am dressing it, arn't I?" said the doctor cheerily, and as if he enjoyed his task. "I must draw the edges together first."

He had taken what seemed to be a pocket-book from his breast and laid it open, and as I looked on, feeling sick myself, I saw him really put in three or four stitches, and then strap up and bandage the wound, just as Barkins came to and looked about wonderingly.

"I didn't faint, did I?" he said anxiously.

The doctor laughed.

"There, lie down in your berth," he said. "Let me help you."

He assisted my messmate gently enough, and then said laughingly—

"One can dress your wound without having three men to hold you. I say, Reardon, isn't it waste of good surgical skill for me to be dressing the prisoners' wounds, if you folk are going to hang them?"

"I don't know that we are going to hang them," said the lieutenant quietly. "Perhaps we shall deliver them over to the Chinese authorities at Wanghai."

"What? My dear fellow, go and beg the captain to hang 'em at once out of their misery. It will be a kindness. Do you know what a Chinese prison is?"

"No."

"Then I do. It would be a mercy to kill them."

"The Chinese authorities may wish to make an example of them so as to repress piracy."

"Let 'em make an example of some one else. Eh? Bandage too tight, my lad?"

"No, sir," said Barkins rather faintly. "The wound hurts a good deal."

"Good sign; 'tis its nature to," said the doctor jocosely.

"But—er—you don't think, sir—"

"'That you may die after it,' as we used to say over cut fingers at school. Bah! it's a nice clean honest cut, made with a sharp knife. Heal up like anything with your healthy young flesh."

"But don't these savage people sometimes poison their blades, sir?"

"Don't people who are wounded for the first time get all kinds of cock-and-bull notions into their heads, sir? There, go to sleep and forget all about it. Healthy smarting is what you feel. Why, you'll be able to limp about the deck with a stick to-morrow."

"Do you mean it, sir?"

"Of course."

Barkins gave him a grateful look, and Mr Reardon shook hands, nodded, and left us to ourselves for a moment, then the doctor thrust in his head again.

"Here, lads," he said, "Smith's all right, I've made a capital job of his arm. Your turn next, Herrick. Good-bye."

This time we were left alone.

Chapter Thirteen
A Wild-Beasts' Cage

All doubts as to our next destination were set at rest the next morning, for it was generally known that we were making for Tsin-Tsin, at the mouth of the Great Fo river, where the prisoners were to be delivered over to the Chinese authorities.

I had been pretty busy all the morning with Barkins and Smith, going from one to the other, to sit with them and give them what news I could, both looking rather glum when I went away, for they were feverish and fretful from their wounds. But I promised to return soon with news of the men, who were all together in a cool, well-ventilated part of the 'tween-decks, seeming restful and patient, the doctor having been round, and, in his short, decisive way, given them a few words of encouragement.

I saw their faces light up as I went down between the two rows in which they were laid, and stopped for a chat with those I knew best, about the way in which they had received their wounds, the coxswain of our boat being the most talkative.

"They all got it 'bout the same way, sir," he said. "It all comes of trying to do the beggars a good turn. Who'd ever have thought it, eh, sir? Trying to save a fellow from drownding, and knives yer!"

They were all very eager to know what was to become of the prisoners, and upon my telling the poor fellows what I knew, I heard them giving their opinions to one another in a lying-down debate.

"Seems a pity," said one of the men. "Takes all that there trouble, we does; captivates 'em; and then, 'stead o' having the right to hang 'em all decently at the yard-arm, we has to give 'em up to the teapots."

"How are you going to hang 'em decently?" said another voice.

"Reg'lar way, o' course, matey."

"Yah, who's going to do it? British sailors don't want turning into Jack Ketches."

"'Course not," said a third. "Shooting or cutting a fellow down in fair fight's one thing; taking prisoners and hanging on 'em arterwards, quite another pair o' shoes. I says as the skipper's right."

"Hear, hear!" rose in chorus, and it seemed to be pretty generally agreed that we should be very glad to get rid of the savage brutes.

I was on my way back to where Smith lay, when I encountered the doctor, who gave me a friendly nod.

"At your service, Mr Herrick," he said, "when you want me; and, by the way, my lad, your messmate Barkins has got that idea in his head still, about the poisoned blade. Try and laugh him out of it. Thoughts like that hinder progress, and it is all nonsense. His is a good, clean, healthy wound."

He passed on, looking very business-like, and his dresser followed, while I went on to see Smith.

"Good, clean, healthy wound!" I said to myself; "I believe he takes delight in such things."

I turned back to look after him, but he was gone.

"Why, he has been to attend to the prisoners," I thought, and this set me thinking about them. To think about them was to begin wishing to have a look at them, and to begin wishing was with me to walk forward to where they were confined, with a couple of marines on duty with loaded rifles and fixed bayonets.

The men challenged as I marched up.

"It's all right," I said. "I only want to have a look at them."

"Can't pass, sir, without orders," said the man.

"But I'm an officer," I said testily. "I'm not going to help them escape."

The marine grinned.

"No, sir, 'tain't likely; but we has strict orders. You ask my mate, sir."

"Yes, sir; that's it, sir," said the other respectfully.

"What a bother!" I cried impatiently. "I only wanted to see how they looked."

"'Tain't my fault, sir; strict orders. And they ain't very pretty to look at, sir, and it'd be 'most as safe to go in and see a box o' wild-beasts. Doctor's been in this last hour doin' on 'em up, with depitty, and two on us inside at the 'present' all the time. They'd think nothing o' flying at him, and all the time he was taking as much pains with them as if they were some of our chaps. They have give it to one another awful."

"Well, I am sorry," I said. "I should have liked to see them."

"So'm I sorry, sir; I'd have let you in a minute, but you don't want to get me in a row, sir."

"Oh no, of course not," I said.

"My mate here says, sir—"

"Get out! Hold your row," growled the other, protesting.

"Yes, what does he say?" I cried eagerly.

"That if we was to shut 'em up close in the dark and not go anigh, sir, till to-morrow morning, there wouldn't be nothing left but one o' their tails."

"Like the Kilkenny cats, eh?" I said, laughing; and I went back on deck with the desire to see the prisoners stronger than ever.

Captain Thwaites was on the quarter-deck, marching up and down, and the men were hard at work cleaning up, squaring the yards, and repainting. The spars were up in their places again, and the *Teaser* was rapidly resuming her old aspect, when I saw Mr Reardon go up to the captain.

"I'll ask leave," I said. "He has been pretty civil;" and I made up my mind to wait till the lieutenant came away.

"No, I won't," I said. "I'll go and ask the captain when he has gone."

The next moment I felt that this would not do, for Mr Reardon would be sure to know, and feel vexed because I had not asked him.

"I'll go and ask leave while they are both together," I said to myself. "That's the way."

But I knew it wasn't, and took a turn up and down till I saw Mr Reardon salute and come away, looking very intent and busy.

I waited till he was pretty close, and then started to intercept him.

His keen eye was on me in an instant.

"Bless my soul, Mr Herrick!" he cried, "what are you doing? Surely your duty does not bring you here?"

"No, sir," I said, saluting. "I beg your pardon, sir; I've been going backward and forward to Mr Barkins and Mr Smith."

"Ho! Pair of young noodles; what did they want in the boats? Getting hurt like that. Well?"

"Beg pardon, sir; would you mind giving me permission to see the prisoners?"

"What! why?"

"I wanted to see them, sir, and go back and tell my messmates about how they looked."

"Humbug!" he cried. "Look here, sir, do you think I have nothing else to do but act as a wild-beast showman, to gratify your impertinent curiosity? Let the miserable wretches be."

"Yes, sir."

"And be off to your cabin and study your navigation, sir. Your ignorance of the simplest matters is fearful. At your age you ought to be as well able to use a sextant as I am."

"Beg pardon, sir, I am trying."

"Then be off and try more, and let me see some results."

I touched my cap, drew back, and the lieutenant marched on.

"Jolly old bear!" I muttered, looking exceedingly crestfallen.

"Herrick!" came sharply, and I ran up, for he was walking on, and I had to keep up with him.

"Yes, sir."

"You behaved very well yesterday. I'm horribly busy. Here, this way."

"Thank you, sir," I said, wondering what he was going to set me to do, and thinking that he might have given me the permission I asked.

"Now then, quick," he said; and, to my surprise, he led the way to the hatchway, went down, and then forward to where the two marines were on duty, ready to present arms to the officer who always seemed of far more importance in the ship than the captain.

"Let Mr Herrick pass in, marines," he said. "Keep a sharp eye on your prisoners."

I gave him a look of thanks, and then felt disappointed again.

"Stop," he said; "fetch up two more men and a lantern, Herrick."

I gladly obeyed; and then the door was opened. After a look in through the grating, and followed closely by three of the marines with their rifles ready, we walked in to where the prisoners were squatted upon their heels all round close up against the bulkheads, bandaged terribly about the faces and necks, and with their fierce eyes glowering at us.

I had expected to find them lying about like wounded men, but, bad as several were, they all occupied this sitting position, and glared at us in a way that told us very plainly how unsafe it would be to trust our lives in their keeping even for a minute.

"Beg pardon, sir," whispered the corporal of marines, who was carrying a lantern; "better be on the look-out."

"Oh yes," said Mr Reardon. "We shall not stay. I only wanted a look round. Look sharp, Mr Herrick, and see what you want of them."

"Doctor was dressing that farthest chap's head, sir," whispered the corporal to me; "and as soon as he was about done, the fellow watched his chance and fixed his teeth in the dresser's arm, and wouldn't let go till—"

"Well? Till what?" said Mr Reardon, gazing fixedly at the brutal countenance of one of the men right before us.

"We had to persuade him to let go."

"Humph!" ejaculated the lieutenant. "Wild-beast."

"How did you persuade him?" I whispered.

"With the butt-end of a rifle, sir; and then we had to wrench his teeth open with bayonets."

'ON THE LIEUTENANT'S BACK.'

I looked round from face to face, all ghastly from their wounds, to see in every one a fierce pair of eyes glaring at me with undying hatred, and I was wondering how it was that people could think of the Chinese as being a calm, bland, good-humoured Eastern race, when Mr Reardon said to me—

"Nearly ready, Herrick? The sight of these men completely takes away all compunction as to the way we treat them."

"Yes, sir; and it makes one feel glad that they are not armed."

"Ready to come away?"

"Yes, sir," I said; "quite."

"Come along, then."

He took a step towards the door, when the corporal said, "Beg pardon, sir; better back out."

"Eh? oh, nonsense!" said the lieutenant, without changing his position, while I, though I began to feel impressed with the glaring eyes, and to feel that the sooner we were out of the place the pleasanter it would be, thought that it would be rather undignified on the part of officers to show the wretches that we were afraid of them.

Just then Mr Reardon glanced sidewise to where one of the men on our left crouched near the door, and said quickly—

"The surgeon saw all these men this morning?"

"Yes, sir," said the corporal, "not half an hour ago."

"He must be fetched to that man. The poor wretch is ready to faint."

"Yes, sir; he shall be fetched."

Mr Reardon bent down to look at the prisoner more closely.

"Hold the lantern nearer," he said.

The corporal lowered the light, which shone on the pirate's glassy eyes, and there was a fixed look in his savage features which was very horrible.

"Get some water for him," said Mr Reardon.

But hardly had the words left his lips when I was conscious of a rushing sound behind me. I was dashed sidewise, and one of the prisoners, who had made a tremendous spring, alighted on the lieutenant's back, driving him forward as I heard the sound of a blow; the corporal was driven sidewise too, and the lantern fell from his hand. Then came a terrible shriek, and a scuffling, struggling sound, a part of which I helped to make, for I had been driven against one of the prisoners, who seized me, and as I wrestled with him I felt his hot breath upon my face, and his hands scuffling about to get a tight grip of my throat.

Chapter Fourteen
The Sequel

If ever I was active it was at that moment. I struck out with my clenched fists, throwing all the power I possessed into my blows, and fortunately for me—a mere boy in the grasp of a heavily-built man—he was comparatively, powerless from loss of blood consequent upon his wounds, so that I was able to wrest myself free, and stand erect.

At that moment the corporal recovered the lantern, and held it up, showing that fully half the prisoners had left the spots where they were crouching the minute before, and were making an effort to join in the fray initiated by one of the savages of whom we had been warned.

It is all very horrible to write of, but I am telling a simple story in this log of what takes place in warfare, when men of our army and navy contend with the uncivilised enemies of other lands. In this case we were encountering a gang of bloodthirsty wretches, whose whole career had been one of rapine and destruction. The desire seemed to be innate to kill, and this man, a prisoner, who since he had been taken had received nothing but kindness and attention, had been patiently watching for the opportunity which came at last. Just as Mr Reardon was stooping to attend to his fellow-prisoner, he had made a tremendous cat-like bound, driving me sidewise as he alighted on Mr Reardon's back, making at the same time a would-be deadly stroke with a small knife he had managed to keep hidden in the folds of his cotton jacket.

As I rose up I could see the knife sticking in the lieutenant's shoulder, apparently driven sidewise into his neck, while he was standing with his eyes dilated, looking in horror at his assailant, who now lay back, quivering in the agonies of death, literally pinned down to the deck.

My brain swam, and for a few moments everything looked misty, but that horrid sight forced itself upon me, and I felt as if I must stare hard at the pirate, where he lay bayoneted and held down at the end of the rifle by the strong arms of the marine sentry, who was pressing with all his might upon the stock.

The struggling went on for a few moments, then grew less and less violent, while a low hissing sound came from the prisoners around. Then the quivering entirely ceased, and the marine gave his bayonet a twist, and dragged it out of the wretch's chest, throwing himself back into position to strike again, should it be necessary. But the last breath had passed the pirate's lips; and, while the sentry drew back to his place by one side of the door and stood ready, his comrade fell back to the other, and the corporal and the fourth man seized the pirate, and rapidly drew him forth through the doorway; we followed, the place was closed and fastened, and I stood panting, as if I had been running hard, and could not recover my breath.

The next moment I was clinging to Mr Reardon, trying to hold him up, but he misinterpreted my action, and seized and gave me a rough shake.

"Don't, boy," he cried in an angry, excited tone. "Stand up; be a man."

"Yes, yes," I gasped; "but quick, corporal! never mind—that wretch—run—the doctor—fetch Mr Price."

"Bah!" cried Mr Reardon roughly, and trying to hide his own agitation, "the man's dead."

I stared at him in horror.

"He don't know!" I gasped. "Mr Reardon—sit—lie—lay him down, my lads. Don't you know you are badly hurt?"

"I! hurt?" he cried. "No; I felt him hit me, but it was nothing."

I reached up my trembling hand, but he caught it as it touched his shoulder, and was in the act of snatching it away, when his own came in contact with the handle of the knife.

"Great heavens!" he ejaculated, as he drew it forth from where it was sticking through the stiff collar of his coat; "right through from side to side—what a narrow escape!"

"I—I thought he had killed you," I cried faintly, and a deathly sensation made me feel for the moment as if I must fall.

"No, not a scratch," he said firmly now. "A little memento," he muttered, as he took out his handkerchief and wrapped it round the blade before thrusting the knife in his breast-pocket. "I must keep that for my private museum, Herrick. Here, my lads, throw something over that wretch. Sentry, I'll talk to you later on. You saved my life."

"Officer's orders, sir," said the man, looking uncomfortable and stiff as he drew himself up.

"What, to save my life?" said Mr Reardon, smiling, and trying to look as if everything had been part of the ordinary business of life.

"No, sir; to keep my eye on the Chinees. I had mine on that chap, for he looked ugly at you, and I see him pull himself together, shuffle in his blue jacket, and then make a jump at you, just like a cat at a rat."

"What?"

"Beg pardon, sir," said the man awkwardly; "I don't mean to say as you looked like a rat."

"I hope not, my lad."

"I meant him jumping like a cat."

"Yes; and you saw him springing at me?"

"Yes, sir."

"Well, what then?"

"Only bayonet practice, sir—point from guard, and he came right on it."

"Yes?"

"Then I held him down, sir."

I saw Mr Reardon shudder slightly.

"That will do, sentry," he said shortly. "I will see you another time. Come, Mr Herrick."

I followed him on deck, and saw him take off his cap and wipe his forehead, but he turned consciously to see if I was looking.

"Rather warm below," he said drily. "I'd better have kept to my first answer to you, my lad. You see it's dangerous to go into a wild-beasts' cage."

"Yes, sir, I'm very sorry," I said; then, anxiously, "But you are sure you are not hurt, sir?"

"Tut, tut! I told you no, boy. There, there, I don't mean that. Not even scratched, Mr Herrick. You can go to your messmates now with an adventure to tell them," he added, smiling; "only don't dress it up into a highly-coloured story, about how your superior officer relaxed the strict rules of dishipline; do you hear?"

"Yes, sir, I hear," I said, and I left him going to join the captain, while I went down and told Barkins what had been going on, but I had not been talking to him five minutes before I heard a heavy splash as if something had been thrown over the side.

"What's that?" said Barkins, turning pale.

I did not answer.

"Sounds like burying some one," he whispered. "Don't say poor old Blacksmith has gone?"

"No no," I said. "I know what it is. Wait till I've told you all I have to tell, and then you'll know too."

He looked at me wonderingly, and I completed my account of the scene in the black-hole place.

"Oh, I see," he cried; "it was the Chinaman?"

I nodded carelessly, but I felt more serious than ever before in my life, at this horrible sequel to a fearful scene.

Chapter Fifteen
A Disappointment

"Very jolly for you," said Barkins, as we cast anchor off Tsin-Tsin a couple of mornings later. "You'll be going ashore and enjoying yourself, while I'm condemned to hobble on deck with a stick."

"I say, don't grumble," I cried. "Look how beautiful the place seems in the sunshine."

"Oh yes, it looks right enough; but wait till you go along the narrow streets, and get some of the smells."

"Hear that, Smithy?" I said to our comrade, who was lying in his berth. "Grumbles because he can't go ashore, and then begins making out how bad it is. How about the fox and the grapes?"

"If you call me fox, my lad, I'll give you sour grapes when I get better. Where's your glass?"

I took down my telescope, adjusted it for him, and pushed his seat nearer to the open window, so that he could examine the bright-looking city, with the blue plum-bloom tinted mountains behind covered with dense forest, and at the shipping of all nations lying at the mouth of the river.

"S'pose that tower's made of crockery, isn't it?" said Barkins, whose eye was at the end of the telescope.

I looked at the beautiful object, with its pagoda-like terraces and hanging bells, and then at the various temples nestling high up on the sides of the hills beyond.

"I say," said Smith, "can't you tell Mr Reardon—no, get the doctor to tell him—that I ought to be taken ashore for a bit to do me good?"

"I'll ask him to let you go," I said; but Smith shook his head, and then screwed up his white face with a horrible look of disgust.

"Oh, what a shame!" he cried. "He gets all the luck;" for a message came for me to be ready directly to go ashore with the captain in the longboat.

It meant best uniform, for the weather was fine, and I knew that he would be going to pay a visit to some grand mandarin.

I was quite right; for, when I reached the deck a few minutes later, there was Mr Brooke with the boat's crew, all picked men, and a strong guard of marines in full plumage for his escort.

The captain came out of his cabin soon after, with cocked hat and gold lace glistening, and away we went for the shore soon after; the last things I saw on the *Teaser* being the two disconsolate faces of my messmates at the cabin window, and Ching perched up on the hammock-rail watching our departure.

I anticipated plenty of excitement that day, but was doomed to disappointment. I thought I should go with the escort to the mandarin's palace, but Mr Brooke was considered to be more attractive, I suppose, and I had the mortification of seeing the captain and his escort of marines and Jacks land, while I had to stay with the boat-keepers to broil in the sunshine and make the best of it, watching the busy traffic on the great river.

Distance lends enchantment to the view of a Chinese city undoubtedly, and before long we were quite satiated with the narrow limits of our close-in view, as well as with the near presence of the crowd of rough-looking fellows who hung about and stared, as I thought, rather contemptuously at the junior officer in Her Majesty's service, who was feeling the thwarts of the boat and the hilt of his dirk most uncomfortably hot.

"Like me to go ashore, sir, to that Chinesy sweetstuff shop, to get you one o' their sweet cool drinks, sir?" said one of the men, after we had sat there roasting for some time.

"No, thank you, Tom Jecks," I said, in as sarcastic a tone as I could assume. "Mr Barkins says you are such a forgetful fellow, and you mightn't come back before the captain."

There was a low chuckling laugh at this, and then came a loud rap.

"What's that?" I said sharply.

"This here, sir," said another of the men. "Some 'un's been kind enough to send it. Shall I give it him back?"

"No, no!" I cried, looking uneasily shoreward; and at that moment a stone, as large as the one previously sent, struck me a sharp blow on the leg.

"They're a-making cockshies of us, sir," said Tom Jecks; "better let two of us go ashore and chivvy 'em off."

"Sit still, man, and —"

Whop!

"Oh, scissors!" cried a sailor; "who's to sit still, sir, when he gets a squad on the back like that? Why, I shall have a bruise as big as a hen's egg."

"Oars! push off!" I said shortly, as half-a-dozen stones came rattling into the boat; and as we began to move away from the wharf quite a burst of triumphant yells accompanied a shower of stones and refuse.

"That's their way o' showing how werry much obliged they are to us for sinking the pirates," growled Tom Jecks. "Oh, don't I wish we had orders to bombard this blessed town! Go it! That didn't hit you, did it, sir?"

"No, it only brushed my cap," I said, as the stones began to come more thickly, and the shouting told of the keen delight the mob enjoyed in making the English retreat. "Pull away, my lads, and throw the grapnel over as soon as we are out of reach."

"But we don't want to pull away, sir. They thinks we're fear'd on 'em. There's about a hundred on 'em—dirty yaller-faced beggars, and there's four o' us, without counting you. Just you give the word, sir, and we'll row back in spite o' their stones, and make the whole gang on 'em run. Eh, mates?"

"Ay, ay!" said the others, lying on their oars.

"Pull!" I cried sharply, and they began rowing again; for though I should have liked to give the word, I knew that it would not only have been madness, but disobedience of orders. My duty was to take care of the boat, and this I was doing by having it rowed out beyond stone-throwing reach, with the Union Jack waving astern; and as soon as the stones fell short, and only splashed the water yards away, I had the grapnel dropped overboard, and we swung to it, waiting for the captain's return.

The men sat chewing their tobacco, lolling in the sun, and I lay back watching the crowd at the edge of the water, wondering how long the captain and his escort would be, and whether the prisoners would be given up.

"Hope none o' them pigtailed varmint won't shy mud at the skipper," said one of the men, yawning.

"I hope they will," said Tom Jecks.

"Why, mate?"

"'Cause he'll order the jollies to fix bayonets and feel some o' their backs with the p'ints."

The conversation interested me, and I forgot my dignity as an officer, and joined in.

"Bayonets make bad wounds, Jecks," I said.

"Yes, sir, they do; nasty three-side wounds, as is bad to get healed up again. They aren't half such a nice honest weapon as a cutlash. But I should like to see them beggars get a prod or two."

"It might mean trouble, Jecks, and a big rising of the people against the English merchants and residents."

"Well, sir, that would be unpleasant for the time, but look at the good it would do! The British consul would send off to the *Teaser*, the skipper would land a lot on us—Jacks and jollies; we should give these warmint a good sharp dressing-down; and they'd know as we wouldn't stand any of their nonsense, and leave off chucking stones and mud at us. Now, what had we done that we couldn't be 'lowed to lie alongside o' the wharf yonder? We didn't say nothing to them. Fact is, sir, they hates the British, and thinks they're a sooperior kind o' people altogether. Do you hear, mates?—sooperior kind o' people; and there ain't one as could use a knife and fork like a Chrishtian."

"And goes birds'-nestin' when they wants soup," said another.

"Well, I don't fall foul o' that, matey," said Jecks; "'cause where there's nests there's eggs, and a good noo-laid egg ain't bad meat. It's the nastiness o' their natur' that comes in there, and makes 'em eat the nest as well. What I do holler at, is their cooking dog."

"And cat," said another.

"And rat," cried the third.

"Yes, all on 'em," said Jecks; "and I don't want to use strong language afore one's orficer, who's a young gent as is allers thoughtful about his men, and who's beginning to think now, that with the sun so precious hot he'll be obliged to order us ashore soon for a drop o' suthin' to drink."

I laughed, and Tom Jecks chuckled.

"But what I do say about their eatin' and cookin' is this, and I stands by what I says, it's beastly, that's what it is—it's beastly!"

"Ay, ay," was chorussed, "so it is;" and then there was silence, while we all sat uneasily in the broiling sun.

"Wish I was a gal," growled one of the men at last.

"Ain't good-looking enough, matey," said Jecks. "Why?"

"'Cause then I s'ould have a sunshade to put up."

"Ay, 'tis warm—brylin', as you may say. Any on you know whether the Chinese is cannibals? You know, sir?"

"I have heard that they cook very strange things now and then," I said, laughing.

"Then they is," said Jecks; "and that being so, they'll have a fine chance to-day. Hadn't you better send word to some on 'em to lay the cloth, sir?"

"What for?"

"'Cause I'm nearly done, sir; and Billy Wakes looks quite. Billy ought to eat nice and joocy, messmates."

"And old Tom Jecks tough as leather," cried Wakes.

"That's so, matey," growled Jecks, who began to pass his tongue over his lips, and to make a smacking sound with his mouth.

"My hye, matey, you do seem hungry," said one of the others. "Look out, Billy, or he won't leave John Chinaman a taste."

"Get out!" growled Jecks; "that don't mean hungry, messmate—that means dry. Beg pardon, sir, we won't none on us try to slope off; but a good drink o' suthin', if it was on'y water, would be a blessin' in disguise just now."

"Yes, Jecks, I'm thirsty too," I said.

"Then why not let us pull ashore, sir, and get a drink at one o' them Chinee imitation grog-shops yonder?"

"Because it would be a breach of discipline, my man," I said, trying to speak very sternly. "I should look nice if the captain came back and found me with the boat and no men."

"Hark at that now!" cried Jecks. "Just as if we'd be the chaps to get a good-natured kind young orficer into a scrape. Look here, sir, put Billy Wakes ashore to go and fetch some drink. My hye, what we would give for half-a-gallon o' real good cool solid old English beer."

"Ha!" came in a deep sigh, and I could not help feeling that a glass just then would be very nice.

"Will you give the order, sir?" said Jecks insinuatingly. "Billy Wakes is a werry trustworthy sort of chap."

"Yes," I said; "but he'd forget to come back, and then I should have to send you to find him, and then the others to find you. I know. There, you can light your pipes if you like."

"And werry thankful for small mussies," said the old sailor, taking out his pipe. "You won't want no matches, lads. Fill up and hold the bowls in the sun."

They lit up, and began smoking, while I watched the long narrow street down which the captain and his escort must come.

"Think we shall have to land the prisoners, sir?" said Jecks, after a smoky silence.

"I suppose so," I replied. "I expect that is what the captain has gone ashore about."

"Don't seem much good, that, sir. We takes 'em, and they'll let 'em go, to start a fresh lot o' plundering junks."

"Thundering junks, matey?" said Billy Wakes.

"I said plundering, Billy, and meant it. Your eddication ain't what it oughter be."

"No, Jecks," I said; "if the pirates are given up, they'll be executed for certain."

"Who says so, sir?"

"First lieutenant," I said.

"Well, he ought to know, sir. Been on the Chinee station afore. P'raps it's best, but I don't want 'em to be hung."

"Don't hang 'em here, Tommy," growled one of the two silent men.

"What do they do, then, old know-all?"

"Chops their heads off, I've heerd."

"Oh, well, I don't want 'em to have their heads chopped off. How should we like it if we was took prisoners?"

"Oh, but we arn't Chinees," growled Billy Wakes.

"Nor arn't likely to be, mate; but we've got heads all the same. I know how I should like to be executed if it was to-day."

The others looked up, and I could not help turning my head at the strangely-expressed desire.

"I'll tell yer," said Jecks, looking hard at me. "I should like it to be same as they did that young chap as we reads of in history. They drowned him in a big tub o' wine."

"Grog would do for me," said Billy Wakes.

"Or beer," cried the others.

"Ask the captain to let you have some tea," I cried, "Quick, haul up the grapnel! Here they come!"

Pipes were knocked out on the instant, the grapnel hauled up, and oars seized; but, in spite of urging on the men, I saw to my vexation that the captain had reached the landing-place first, and I kept him waiting nearly five minutes in the broiling sun.

He did not say anything, only glared at me as he stepped in, followed by his escort. The oars were dropped, and, as we began to row back to the *Teaser*, I saw that his face was scarlet with the heat, and he looked in a regular temper.

"I shall catch it," I thought to myself; but the very next moment my attention was taken to the shore, where a yell of derision arose from the crowd gathered to see the officers embark.

"Brutes!" muttered the captain; and then he sprang up in a rage, for a shower of stones came pattering into the boat, and splashing up the water all round.

He was so enraged by the insult, that he ordered the marines to load, and a volley of twelve rifles was fired over the people's heads.

The result was that they all ran helter-skelter, tumbling over each other, and by the time they returned and began throwing again we were out of their reach, but they kept on hurling stones and refuse all the same, and shouting "Foreign devils!" in their own tongue.

Chapter Sixteen
An Interview

"Mr Herrick! Come to my cabin," said the captain as he stepped on deck, and I followed him.

"You stupid fellow," whispered Mr Brooke as I passed him, "why didn't you keep the boat by the wharf?"

I gave him a comical look, and followed the captain; but I was kept waiting for a few moments at the door while the servant was summoned, and when I did go in my officer was lying back in his chair, with ice on the table, and a great glass of what seemed to be soda-water and brandy before him, but which proved by the decanter to be sherry.

"Oh," he cried angrily, "there you are, sir! Why didn't you come at once, sir?"

"I did, sir; but was kept waiting till you were ready."

"Well, sir, don't answer in that pert way. It sounds like insolence. That will not do, Mr Herrick, if you wish to get on in your profession. Now, sir, your orders were to stop by the landing-place, with the boat in charge, ready for my return, were they not?"

"Yes, sir; but—"

"Silence, sir! How dare you interrupt me? I go up through the broiling heat to have an interview with that wretched, stolid, obstinate mandarin, with his confounded button and peacock-feather; and when I do get back, perfectly exhausted by the heat, half-dead, I find no boat."

"No, sir; but—"

"Silence, sir! Will you let me speak? The consequence is that, because you choose to disobey orders, and take the men off to indulge in some of the disgusting drinks of this wretched country—"

"I beg pardon, sir," I cried; "I—"

"Mr Herrick! am I to place you under arrest? Be silent, sir. I say, I return with my escort from an important diplomatic visit, arranged so as to impress the people, and when I return, almost fainting with the heat, there is no boat, because you have allowed the men to impose upon you; and you are away drinking with them, I suppose?"

"No, sir; I—"

"Mr Herrick!" he roared, "I will not bear it. I say there was no boat; and not only am I forced to submit to the indignity of waiting, and listening to the gibes of the low-class Chinese, and to see their scowls, but our delay there—through you, sir—results, I say results, in the miserable wretches taking advantage thereof, and, thinking me helpless, working themselves up to an attack. When at last you do come crawling up with those four men, they are purple-faced from drinking, every one threatened by apoplexy— why, your own face is crimson, sir; and I could smell the men when I stepped on board."

"No, sir—the dirty harbour, sir," I said. "Smells horrid."

"You are under arrest, sir. Go! No; stop and hear me out first, sir. I say that, through your delay, I am kept there on that wretched wharf; and when I do push off, I have—I, Her Majesty's representative, in the sight of these Chinese scoundrels—I have, I say, to suffer from the insult and contumely of being pelted, stoned, of having filth thrown at me. Look at my nearly new uniform coat, sir. Do you see this spot on the sleeve? A mark that will never come out. That was a blow, sir, made by a disgusting rotten fish's head, sir. Loathsome—loathsome! While the insult to Her Majesty's flag called upon me to fire upon the mob. Do you know what that means, sir?"

"Yes, sir; a good lesson. They won't be so saucy again."

"You ignorant young puppy!" he cried; "it may mean a serious international trouble—a diplomatic breach, and all through you. There, I was hot and bad enough before, now you have made me worse."

He stretched out his hand for the glass, but did not drink; and the sight of the cool liquid half-maddened me, for the heat and emotion had made my throat very dry.

"Now, sir," he cried, "I am your commanding officer, and no one on board Her Majesty's cruiser shall ever say that I am not just. Now then, speak out; what have you to say? How came you to let the men go away to drink?"

"I didn't, sir," I said huskily. "They wanted to go, for they were choking nearly, but I wouldn't let them."

"What? Don't seek refuge in a lie, boy. That's making your fault ten times worse. Didn't I see you returning to the wharf?"

"Yes, sir," I cried indignantly; "but the men had not been to drink."

"Then how dared you disobey my orders, and go away?" he roared, furious at being proved wrong.

"I went, sir, because it was my duty."

"What!"

"We stayed till the stone-throwing grew dangerous for us, and then I had the boat rowed out and anchored."

"Oh!"

"But I kept watch till you came in sight, sir; and we were as quick as we could be."

"The mob pelted you too, Mr Herrick?"

"Yes, sir," I said; "and we couldn't fire over their heads, nor yet row right away."

He looked at me angrily, and then his countenance changed.

"Pert, Mr Herrick," he said, "but very apt. You have me there on the hop. Dear me! I've made a great mistake, eh?"

"Yes, sir," I said hoarsely.

"And you sat out there in the broiling sun, and the miserable savages pelted you as they did me?"

"Yes, sir."

"Tut, tut, tut! and the heat was maddening. Terribly irritating, too; I felt excessively angry. I really—dear me, Mr Herrick, I'm afraid I spoke very unjustly to you, and—I—ought a captain to apologise to a midshipman?"

"I really don't know, sir," I said, feeling quite mollified by his tone.

"Well, I think I do," he said, smiling. "Decidedly not. As Mr Reardon would say, it would be totally subversive of discipline. It couldn't be done. But one gentleman can of course apologise to another, and I do so most heartily. My dear Mr Herrick, I beg your pardon for being so unjust."

"Pray don't say any more about it, sir," I cried.

"Well, no, I will not. But all the same I am very sorry—as a gentleman—that I—as your superior officer—spoke to you as I did."

"Thank you, sir."

"And, dear me, my lad, you look terribly hot and exhausted. Let me prescribe, as Mr Price would say."

He quickly placed a lump of ice in a tumbler, and, after pouring in a little sherry, filled it up with soda-water.

I grasped the glass, and drank with avidity the cool, refreshing draught to the last drop.

"Humph! you were thirsty."

"I was choking, sir," I said, with a sigh, as I placed the glass upon the table.

"And now, Mr Herrick, perhaps it would be as well not to talk about this little interview," he said quietly. "I rely upon you as a gentleman."

"Of course, sir," I replied; and feeling, in spite of the severe wigging I had had, that I never liked the captain half so well before, I backed out and hurried to my own cabin.

Chapter Seventeen
We lose our Prisoners

"Here he is," cried Barkins, who was resting his leg; while Smith was sitting by the open window so as to catch all the air he could. "Got your promotion?"

"Got my what?" I cried.

"Promotion. I never saw such favouritism. Always being sent for to the skipper's cabin. I wonder Reardon stands it."

"Don't talk nonsense," I cried. "Phew, isn't it hot?"

"Yes, for us. Regular prisoners, while you have all the fun—"

"Of being roasted, and then stoned by the Chinese."

"That's right," said Smith sulkily, "make as little as you can of it. Did the skipper consult you about our next movement?"

"He gave me a good bullying for not having the boat ready when he wanted to come on board."

"Was that why you went in the cabin?" cried Barkins.

"Of course."

"Oh then, if that's the case, we'll let you off. Eh, Blacksmith?"

"Well, I suppose so."

"Let me off what?"

"We had been discussing the matter," said Barkins, "Smithy and I, and come to the conclusion that as you were such a swell you were too good for us, and we were going to expel you; but, under the circumstances, I think we'll let you off this time. Oh!"

"What's the matter?"

"My leg! There's that horrible tingling and aching again. I'm sure that knife was poisoned."

"Hi! look here," cried Smith just then; "here are two big row-boats coming out to us."

We both made for the window, and there, in the bright sunshine, were two large barges, gay with gilding and showy ensigns, coming pretty swiftly in our direction, while, as they drew nearer, we could see that their occupants were in brilliant costumes and fully-armed, swords and spears flashing, and gold and silver embroidery lending their glow to the general effect.

"Why, those must be all the big pots of the city," said Barkins—"these in the first boat."

"And the second is full of soldiers."

"I know," I cried; "they're coming to fetch the prisoners. I must go on deck."

"And we shall see nothing of the fun again," cried Barkins.

"Why not?" I said; "I'll help you on deck."

"Come on, then," cried Barkins eagerly. "Oh, hang this wound!"

He caught hold of my shoulder, and with a little pulling and hauling I got him on deck, hurting him a good deal, I'm afraid, but he bore it like a martyr, till I had him seated upon a place near the starboard gangway.

I then turned to go and help up Smith, but found he had called in the aid of a couple of the sailors, and the next minute he too was seated by Barkins.

Meanwhile the drum had called the men to quarters, the officers were on deck in uniform, and the marines drawn-up to form a guard of honour, sufficiently smart and warlike, with the white-ducked Jacks, and big guns bright as hands could make them, to impress the barbaric party coming on board.

The boats were rowing very near now, and the captain came on deck, to stand under the awning which had been stretched out since the *Teaser* had been restored to order. Then the gangway was opened, the steps were lowered, and half-a-dozen Jacks descended to help the visitors to mount, while the marines stood at attention.

The boatmen managed to fall foul of the side, and nearly upset the barge, but our lads saved them from that disaster; and the mandarin and his suite, who had come off, soon mounted to the deck, to stand haughtily returning the salutes of the officers.

Then there was an awkward pause, for our officers only knew a few words of Chinese, while the mandarin's party, although they had had Englishmen in their city for nearly a hundred years, could not speak a word of our tongue, and they had brought no interpreter.

There was an awkward pause, broken by a high-pitched voice just outside the gorgeous-looking throng.

"You wantee Ching?"

"Yes," cried the captain; "tell these gentlemen that they are heartily welcome on board Her Majesty's ship."

Ching nodded, and, bowing down humbly, gazed at the white deck, and squeaked out a long speech to the contemptuous-looking Chinese official, who stood in front of his attendants, each in his long, stiff, embroidered silk dressing-gown; and what seemed the most comically effeminate was that the gorgeous officers, with rat-tail moustachios and armed with monstrous swords, each carried a fan, which he used constantly.

"He's putting an awful lot of fat in the captain's speech," whispered Barkins, who was just behind me.

Then the chief of the party said a few words, without condescending to notice the interpreter, and Ching backed away, to turn to the captain.

"His most noble excellency the big-buttoned mandalin has come on board the gleat fine ship with his genelals, and blavest of the blave, to fetch the most wicked and double-bad plisoners whom the gleat sea captain of the foleign devils—"

"Eh! what?" said Captain Thwaites. "Did he say that?"

"Yes. Come fetch allee bad bad plisoners velly much all together."

"Very well," said the captain; "tell him he can have them, and welcome."

Ching approached the mandarin again, in his former humble form, and made another long speech; after which the great official turned to one of his attendants and said something; this gorgeous being turned and spoke to another; and he went to the gangway and stood fanning himself as he squeaked out something to the soldiers in the second boat.

Then an order was given, and in a curious shambling way about forty soldiers came up the steps, and ranged themselves in a double row, something after the fashion of our drilling.

I was watching these men with their heavy swords and clumsy spears, when there was a clanking sound, and a dozen more men came on deck with quite a load of heavy chains, which at a word of command they banged down with a crash upon the deck, and then stood waiting.

At the same moment the captain gave an order, and our marine officer marched off with a strong detachment of his men right forward; and after a pause, during which Englishmen and Chinamen stood staring at each other and the grandees used their fans, the first prisoner was brought forward by a couple of marines, strolling along in a heavy, careless way till he was abreast of his fellow-countrymen.

Then at a word from an officer four soldiers seized the unfortunate wretch and threw him heavily down upon his face; two knelt upon him, and in a trice heavy chains were fitted to his legs and wrists, the latter being dragged behind his back. Then, by one consent, the four Chinamen leaped up, and waited for the prisoner to follow their example, but he lay still.

"If he has any gumption he won't move," whispered Barkins, who like myself was an interested spectator.

Mr Reardon walked to us.

"Silence, young gentlemen," he said sternly. "Let us show these barbarians what dishipline is. — Brute!"

This last applied to one of the Chinamen, who said something to the prisoner, who merely wagged his tail, and then received a tremendous kick in the ribs.

He sprang up then like a wild-beast, but he was seized by as many as could get a grip of him, bundled to the gangway, and almost thrown down into the barge, where other men seized him and dragged him forward to where some spearmen stood ready on guard.

By this time another had been thrown down and chained. He made no scruple about rising and walking to the side to be bundled down.

Another followed, and another, the grandees hardly glancing at what was going on, but standing coolly indifferent and fanning away, now and then making some remark about the ship, the guns, or the crew.

Seven had been chained, and the eighth was brought forward by two marines, seized, thrown down, and fettered. Then, instead of allowing himself to be bundled into the boat as apathetically as the others, he gazed fiercely to right and left, and I saw that something was coming.

So did the indifferent-looking Chinese, for one of the most gorgeously dressed of the party whipped out a heavy curved sword, whose blade was broader at the end than near the hilt, and made for him; but, active as a cat, and in spite of the weight of his chains, the man made a series of bounds, knocked over two of the soldiers, and leaped at the gangway behind them, reached the top, and fell more than jumped over, to go down into the water with a heavy splash.

Half-a-dozen of the men leaped on to the rail, and stood looking down, before the captain could give an order; while a few words were shouted from the barge below.

The officer returned his sword, and began fanning himself again; the soldiers seized the next prisoner and began chaining him, but no one stirred to save the man overboard, and we all grasped the reason why,—twenty pounds of iron fetters took him to the bottom like a stone.

I saw the captain frown as he said something to Mr Reardon, who merely shook his head.

"Ain't they going to lower a boat, sir?" I whispered to Mr Brooke.

"We could do no good," he said. "There are twenty fathoms of water out there, Herrick, and the man could not rise."

The incident did not seem to discompose the Chinese, who disposed of the next prisoner. And then I saw that the marines had charge of another, who suddenly made an attempt to escape, and our men only having one hand, at liberty, the other holding a rifle, he would have succeeded, had not six or seven of the soldiers rushed at and seized him, dragging him to the lessening heap of chains, when he suddenly threw up his hands and dropped upon his knees, throwing them off their guard by making believe to resign himself to his fate.

'A RUSH AT THE MANDARIN.'

But before the first fetter could be dragged to where he knelt, he sprang up with the fire of fury in his eyes, and made a rush at the mandarin, seized him, and it would have gone ill with his gaudy costume, had not a couple of the officers dragged out their swords.

What followed took only a moment or two. I saw the blades flash, heard a sickening sound, and saw the prisoner stagger away, while the second of the two officers followed him, delivering chop after chop with his heavy blade, till the unfortunate wretch dropped upon the deck, where he was at once seized and pitched overboard without the slightest compunction.

"Here, interpreter, tell the chief I cannot have my deck turned into a butcher's shamble like this," cried the captain angrily.

Ching shuffled forward, and advanced towards the mandarin, spoke at length; the mandarin replied with a haughty smile, and Ching backed away again.

"Gleat big-button mandalin say he velly much 'blige captain big fine ship, and he allee light, no hurtee 'tall by killee badee bad men."

"Bah!" ejaculated the captain, turning angrily away; and I saw Mr Reardon's face grow fixed, as if carved in wood, in his efforts to keep from smiling.

The last of the prisoners had been brought out of confinement, thrown down, chained, and bundled into the barge, half the soldiers followed, orders were given, and the second barge pushed off, when the captain once more had recourse to Ching's help.

"Ask the mandarin if he will come into the cabin and take a glass of wine."

But this was declined, and Ching communicated the fact that the great man "would not eatee dlinkee, but wantee velly much see ship."

He was taken round, the whole following keeping at his heels, and his officers and soldiers scowling fiercely, or looking about with supreme contempt, as they made a great display of their weapons, and acted generally as if they were condescending to look round, so as to be civil to the Western barbarians.

At last they went over the side, and the gorgeous barge was rowed away.

"Thank goodness, Reardon," I heard the captain say; and directly after, as I was passing, Tom Jecks' voice was heard in the midst of a group of the Jacks.

"Say, messmate," he said, "fancy, stripped and fists only, how many Chinese could you polish off?"

"Dunno," said a voice, which I knew to be that of Billy Wakes, a big manly-looking young Plymouth fellow. "'Course I could do one, and I think I could doctor two on 'em; I'd have a try at three; and I'm blest if I'd run away from four. That is about as fair as I can put it, messmate."

I was helping Barkins to the companion-way, and Smith was walking very slowly by us. But as we heard this we stopped to laugh, just as Mr Brooke came up and asked what amused us. We told him, and he laughed too.

"That means one of our fellows would try at four Chinamen. He's too modest. Four to one, lads! why, if it came to real righting, ten of them would follow me against a hundred of the enemy. Ten to one.—News for you."

"News, sir; what?" I said.

"We sail again directly. There is another gang at work south, and we have a hint of the whereabouts of their nest."

Chapter Eighteen
In a Trap

"Ever feel at all uncomfortable about—that—Chinaman, Morris?" I said one day, after we had been coasting along the shore southward for about a week. I had not encountered that marine sentry alone since the terrible scene in the place where the prisoners were confined; and now, as soon as I saw him, the whole affair came back with all its shuddering horrors, and I felt quite a morbid desire to talk to him about it.

"What, bayoneting him, sir?" said the man quietly. "Well, no, sir, it's very odd, but I never have much. I was so excited when I see him with his knife ashining by the light o' the corporal's lantern, that all the bayonet practice come to me quite natural like, and, as you know, I give point from the guard, and he jumped right on it, and I held him down after as you would a savage kind of tiger thing, and felt quite pleased like at having saved the first luff's life. After you'd gone all the lads got talking about it, and I felt as proud as a peacock with ten tails. And I got wondering, too, about what Mr Reardon would do, for he said he would see me again. It was all very well then, but that night when I turned in I felt quite sick, and I couldn't sleep a wink. The more I turned about in my hammock, the hotter and worser I got. There it all was before me, I could see myself holding that pirate chap pinned down, and there was his eyes rolling and his teeth snapping as he twisted about. Ugh! it was horrid, sir; and I felt as I was in for it, and began to understand what one has read about chaps as commits murder always being haunted like with thoughts of what they've done, and never being happy no more. Then it got worse and worse, and I says to myself, 'If it was as bad as that for just doing your duty, and saving your officer's life, what must it be when you kills a man out o' sheer wickedness to get his money?'"

The man stopped then, and looked round to see if any one was within hearing, but we were quite alone, and he went on quietly—

"You won't laugh at me, sir, will you?"

"Laugh?" I cried wonderingly. "It's too horrible to laugh about."

"Yes, sir; but I meant, feel ready to chaff about it, and tell the other young gentlemen, and get thinking me soft."

"Of course not, Morris."

"No, sir, you ain't that sort. You've got a mother, too, ain't you?"

"Yes; but I shouldn't have liked her to see all we saw that day."

"No, sir, you wouldn't. I haven't got no mother now, sir, but I did have one once."

I felt ready to smile, but I kept my countenance.

"Seems rum of a big ugly fellow like me talking about his mother, sir; but, Lor' bless you! all us chaps has got a bit of a soft spot somewhere insides us for our old woman, even them as never talks about it; and do you know, sir, that night just when I felt worst as I rolled about in my hammock, and was going to get out and find the bucket of water for a drink, I got thinking about my old mother, and how she used to come and tuck me up in bed of a night, and kiss me and say, Gawd bless me, and then of how she used to talk to me and tell me always to do what was right, and, no matter what happened, I should feel at rest. And then I got thinking as I must have done very wrong in killing that Chinee, to feel as bad as I did. And I got arguing it over first one way and then the other for a minute or two, and the next thing I remember is it being tumble-up time, and till you spoke to me about it just now, I've never hardly thought about it since. It was doing my duty, sir, of course; now, warn't it?"

"Of course, Morris," I said importantly; and the man nodded, looked satisfied, and then glanced to right and left again before unbuttoning his jacket and cautiously pulling out an old-fashioned gold watch.

"Why, hallo, Morris!" I cried.

"Hush, sir; keep it quiet. Mr Reardon give it to me the day afore yesterday, and said I wasn't to talk about it, for it was just between ourselves."

"It's a fine old watch," I said, feeling glad that the man we lads looked upon as such a stem tyrant could show so warm and generous a side to his nature.

"Said, sir, he gave it to me for attending so well to dishipline, as he called it, for he said if I had not attended well to my drill, there would have been no first lieutenant to give me a watch out of gratitude for saving his life."

"You must take care of that, Morris," I said.

"Yes, sir," he said dolefully. "That's the worst of it. Gold watch is an orkard thing for a marine, but I mean to try."

"And be very careful to wind it up regularly every night."

He looked at me with his face all wrinkled up.

"Would you, sir—would you wind it up?"

"Why, of course; what's a watch for?"

"Well, that depends, sir. It's all right for a gentleman, but don't seem no good to me. We allus knows how many bells it is, and the sergeants takes good care that we're in time for everything. It's rather in my way, too. Look here, sir; s'pose you took care of it for me to the end of the voyage?"

"Oh no, Morris. You'll soon get used to having a watch," I said. "Take care of it yourself."

He shook his head.

"I don't know as I can, sir," he said. "If it had been a silliver one, I shouldn't so much have minded. I was thinking of sewing it up in the padding of my jacket."

"No, no; keep it in your pocket and never part with it," I said. "It's a watch to be proud of, for it was earned in a noble way."

"Thankye, sir," he cried, as I stood wondering at my own words; "that's done me good;" and he buttoned his jacket up with an intense look of satisfaction.

"I'm beginning to think the doctor was right, Gnat," said Barkins one morning.

"What about?" I said.

"My wound; I don't think the knife was poisoned."

"Why, of course it wasn't; you fancied it all."

"Well, I couldn't help that, could I? You wait till you get your wound, and then see how you'll begin to fancy all sorts of things. I say, though, Smithy's getting right pretty quick. The doctor's pitched him over. I should have sent him back to his duty before, if I'd been old Physic. He was all right yesterday."

"How do you know?"

"Because he was so nasty tempered. Nothing was good enough for him."

"Oh, come, I like that," cried Smith, who overheard him. "Why, I was as patient as could be; I appeal to the Poet. Did I ever go fussing about telling people I was wounded by a poisoned knife?"

"No," I said; "you were both magnificent specimens of brave young midshipmen, and behaved splendidly."

"Oh, did we?" cried Barkins. "Look here, Blacksmith, we'll remember this, and as soon as we're strong enough we'll punch his head."

"Agreed. He's been growing as cocky as a bantam since we've been ill. We must take him down."

"Why, what for?" I cried.

"Making game of your betters. Sarce, as Tom Jecks calls it."

We had something else to think of three days later, and in the excitement both my messmates forgot their wounds, save when some quick movement gave them a reminder that even the healing of a clean cut in healthy flesh takes time.

For we overhauled a suspicious-looking, fast-sailing junk, which paid no heed to our signals, but was brought to after a long chase, and every man on board was chuckling and thinking about prize-money.

But when she was boarded, with Ching duly established as interpreter, and all notion of returning to the "fancee shop" put aside for the present, the junk turned out to be a peaceful trader trying to make her escape from the pursuit of pirates, as we were considered to be.

Ching soon learned the cause of the captain's alarm. The day before he had come upon a junk similar to his own, with the crew lying murdered on board, and, judging from appearances, the wretches who had plundered her could not have gone long.

Mr Brooke was the officer in charge of the boat, and he told Ching to ask the master of the junk whether he had seen any signs of the pirates.

The man eagerly replied that he had seen three fast boats entering the Ayshong river, some thirty miles north of where we then were, and as soon as he found that we really were the boat's crew of a ship working for the protection of the shipping trade, his joy and excitement were without bounds, and showed itself in presents,—a chest of tea for the crew, and pieces of silk for Mr Brooke and myself; parting with us afterwards in the most friendly way, and, as Ching afterwards told me, saying that we were the nicest foreign devils he ever met.

Our news when we went on board made the captain change our course. We were bound for a river a hundred miles lower down, but it was deemed advisable to go back and proceed as far up the Ayshong, as a fresh nest of the desperadoes might be discovered there.

By night we were off the muddy stream, one which appeared to be of no great width, but a vast body of water rushed out from between the rocky gates, and from the desolate, uninhabited look of the shores it seemed probable that we might find those we sought up there.

It was too near night to do much, so the captain contented himself with getting close in after the boat sent to take soundings, and at dark we were anchored right in the mouth, with the watch doubled and a boat out as well to patrol the river from side to side, to make sure that the enemy, if within, did not pass us in the darkness.

All lights were out and perfect silence was maintained, while, excited by the prospect of another encounter, not a man displayed the slightest disposition to go to his hammock.

It was one of those soft, warm, moist nights suggestive of a coming storm, the possibility of which was soon shown by the faint quivering of the lightning in the distance.

"Storm before morning," whispered Barkins.

"Yes," said Smith; "storm of the wrong sort. I want to hear our guns going, not thunder."

From time to time the boat which was on the patrol duty came alongside to report itself, but there was no news; in fact, none was expected, for such a dark night was not one that would be chosen by vessels wishing to put to sea.

I had been disposed to ask for permission to go in the boat, but Mr Reardon's countenance looked rather stormy, so I had given up the idea, and contented myself with stopping on board with my two messmates, to watch the dark mouth of the river.

It soon grew very monotonous, having nothing to see but the shapes of the distant clouds, which stood out now and then like dimly-seen mountains high up above the land. But by degrees the distant flickering of the lightning grew nearer, and went on slowly growing brighter, till from time to time, as we leaned over the bulwarks, listening to the faint rushing sound of the river, sweeping past the chain cable, and dividing again upon our sharp bows, we obtained a glimpse of the shore on either side. Then it glimmered on the black, dirty-looking stream, and left us in greater darkness than ever.

Once we made out our boat quite plainly, and at last there came so vivid a flash that we saw the river upward for quite a mile, and I made out the low shores, but could see no sign of house or vessel moored anywhere near where we lay.

Another hour must have passed, during which we made out that the country on either side was flat and marshy, but we could see no sign of human habitation. As far as could be made out, the river was about three hundred yards broad, and about this time we became aware that it must be very nearly low tide, for the stream which passed us was growing more and more sluggish, till at last it ceased ebbing, and the *Teaser* began to swing slowly round, a sufficient indication that the tide had turned.

We had swung to our anchor till we were right across the stream, when from higher up a shot was fired, and, as if caused by the report, a dazzling flash cut right across the heavens, lighting up the river with its muddy sides, and there, not five hundred yards away, we made out two large junks that had come down with the tide, which had now failed them, just as they were close to the mouth.

All had been perfectly silent so far, but as the intense darkness succeeded the brilliant flash, there was a loud gabbling and shouting from the direction of the junks, then came the splashing of great oars, followed by their regular beating, and, as we swung further round with the men hurrying to their quarters, the boat came alongside, and was hoisted.

"Well, Mr Brooke?"

"Two large junks, sir; come down with the tide; they've put about, sir, and are going back."

"Sure?"

"Yes, sir, certain. Hark!"

The hissing sound of the tide had recommenced, and above it we could hear the splash, splash of great sweeps, sounding hurried and irregular, as if the men at them were making all the haste they could. Every now and then, too, came a curious creaking sound, as wood was strained against wood.

"Tide's setting in very hard, sir," said Mr Brooke.

"Yes," said the captain. "Come on board; ha!"

There was another vivid flash, and we distinctly saw the great matting-sails of two junks for a moment, and again all was black.

"Come on board, Mr Brooke; they could not sweep those great craft out against such a tide as this, and there is no wind to help them even if they wished."

Then the falls were hooked on, after the coxswain had with some difficulty drawn the cutter up to where the light of a lantern was thrown down for his guidance, the men stamped along the deck, and the cutter rose to the davits for the men to spring on board.

Daylight found us lying head to sea, with the tide rushing up, a beautifully verdant country spreading out on either side, but no habitation in sight, and our men in great glee, for it was pretty evident that unless the junks should prove to be merchantmen, we had come upon a little-known river, up which we had trapped the pirates, who had been to land plunder at their nest, and were about to make their way again to sea.

Chapter Nineteen
Up the River

The threatening of a storm had passed away, and the sun rose upon us, showing distant mountains of a delicious blue, and the river winding inland broader than at its mouth, and, as far as could be seen, free of additional entrances through which an enemy could escape to sea.

Steam was got up, the *Teaser's* head swung round, and, after the lead had shown great depth and a muddy bottom, we began to glide steadily up with the tide.

Our progress was very slow, for, as you will easily understand, and must have noted scores of times in connection with some wreck, a ship is of immense weight, and, even if moving ever so slowly, touching a rock at the bottom means a tremendous grinding crash, and either the vessel fixed, perhaps without the possibility of removal, or a hole made which will soon cause it to sink. Navigation, then, is beset with dangers for a captain. If he is in well-known waters, matters are simple enough; every rock will be marked upon his chart, every mile near shore will have been sounded, and he will know to a foot or two how much water is beneath his keel. But as soon as he ventures up some strange creek or river, paradoxically speaking, "he is at sea." In other words, he would be journeying haphazard, if the greatest precautions were not taken.

These precautions were soon taken, a couple of boats being sent on ahead with a man in each taking soundings, while we had this advantage — we were journeying with a rising tide, and the river naturally grew deeper and deeper.

But we encountered no difficulty; we steamed on just fast enough to give the vessel steerage way, while the boats went on, the leads were heaved, and the result was always the same; plenty of water, and so soft and muddy a bottom, that even if we had gone aground, all that would have happened would have been a little delay while we waited for the tide to lift us off.

The course of the river was so winding that we could not see far ahead. Hence it was that a careful look-out was kept as we rounded each bend, expecting at every turn to see a kind of port to which the piratical junks resorted, and with a village, if not a town, upon the shore. But we went on and on without success, the river, if anything, growing wider, till all at once, as we were slowly gliding round a bend, leaving a thick track of black smoke in the misty morning air, one of the men in the top hailed the deck.

"Sail ho, sir!"

"Where away?"

"Dead astern, sir!"

"What?"

"Dead astern, sir!"

Two of the men near me burst into a laugh, which they tried to hide as the first lieutenant looked sharply round. But there, sure enough, were the tops of the junk's masts dead astern, for the course of the river proved to be just there almost exactly like that piece of twisted flat wire which ladies fasten on the backs of their dresses, and call an eye; the great stream forming first a small circle, and then going right away to form the large loop of the eye, while the junks were lying at the far side of the loop, so that to reach them where they lay, right across an open plain about two miles in width, we had to sail for some distance right away, apparently leaving them right behind.

A little use of the telescope soon showed that we were going quite right, though, and we went steadily on with the boats ahead sounding, and the men waiting to be called to quarters.

"I don't believe it's going to be a fight, Gnat!" cried Smith.

"Why not?"

"Can't smell anything like prize-money in it. They're only a couple of big trading junks."

"Then why did they run away from us as they did?"

"Same reason as the one did last time. Thought we meant mischief. How stupid it is taking all this trouble to crawl up a muddy river."

"What's he talking about?" said Barkins, stepping over to our side for a moment before every one would have to be in his place, and unable to stir.

"Says they're trading junks."

"Then it's all up. He knows. Either his wound or the doctoring has made him go better. He's awfully sharp now. I'll go and tell the skipper to turn back."

"That's right; chaff away," cried Smith. "Look at the place we're in! There isn't a sign of a town. What would bring pirates up here?"

"Pirates don't want towns, do they, stupid?" cried Barkins; "they want a place to lay up their ships in, and here it is. I'll bet anything those are pirates, but we shan't catch 'em."

"Why?" I asked. "Think they'll go up higher where we can't follow?"

"Could follow 'em in the boats, couldn't we, clever? Hi! look! they're on the move! They're pirates, and are going up higher because they see us. But we shan't catch 'em. If they are getting the worst of it, they'll run themselves aground, and get ashore to make a dash for it."

Barkins was right; they were on the move, as we could distinctly see now, and my messmate said again—

"Yes, it's all over; they'll follow this river right away to the other side, and come out in the Black Sea, or somewhere else. We draw too much water to follow them farther."

But we did follow them a great deal farther, and found that on the whole, in spite of our careful progress, we gained upon the junks, getting so near them once from their position across a bend of the river that a discussion took place as to whether it would not be advisable to open fire at long range.

But no gun spoke, and we kept on slowly, carried by the tide, and with the screw revolving just sufficiently for steering purposes, till once more the course of the river grew pretty straight, and the junks were in full view, our glasses showing the men toiling away at the long sweeps, and that the decks were crowded.

This last was intensely satisfactory, for it swept away the last doubts as to the character of the vessels. Up to this point it was possible that they might have been trading junks whose skippers had taken alarm, but no mercantile junks would have carried such crews as we could see, with their bald heads shining in the sun.

Just about that time Smith and I passed Tom Jecks, who gave me a peculiar look.

"What is it?" I said, stopping to speak.

"Can't you put in a word to the skipper, sir, and get him to stir up the engyneers?"

"What for, Tom?"

"To go faster, sir. It's horrid, this here. Why, I could go and ketch 'em in the dinghy."

"Do you want the *Teaser* stuck in the mud?" I said.

"No, sir, o' course not; but I say, sir, do you think it's all right?"

"What do you mean, Jecks?"

"This here river, sir. I ayve read in a book about Chinee Tartars and magicians and conjurors. There was that chap in 'Aladdin' as left the boy shut up down below. He were a Chinee, wasn't he?"

"I think so, Tom; but what have the *Arabian Nights* got to do with our hunting these pirates?"

"Well, that's what I want to know, sir. If there was magic in them days in China, mayn't there be some left now?"

"No, Tom," I said. "We've got more magic on board the *Teaser* in the shape of steam, than there is of the old kind in all China."

"Well, sir, you've had more schooling than ever I've had, but if it ain't a bit magicky about them boats, I should like to know what it is."

"What's he talking about?" said Smith. "What do you mean?"

"They're will-o'-the-wispy sort o' boats, sir," replied Jecks. "Don't you see how they keep dodging on us? Just now they was in easy shot, now they're two mile away. What does that mean?"

"Physical conformation of the road," said Smith importantly.

"Oh, is it, sir?" said Jecks, scratching his head, with a dry smile on his face. "Well, I shouldn't have thought as physic had anything to do with that, but I daresay you're right, sir. Wish we could give them junks physic."

"I don't believe we shall get near enough to give them a dose," said Smith discontentedly. "If I were the skipper, I'd—"

Smith did not say what he would, for just then there was a shout from the boat, the man with the lead giving such shallow soundings that we heard the gongs sound in the engine-room, and the clank of the machinery as it was stopped and reversed.

Then orders were given for soundings to be taken right across the river, but the result was always the same; the stream had suddenly shallowed, and it was at first supposed to be a bar; but sounding higher up proved that the shoal water was continuous, and though the lighter-draft junks had gone on, they had now come to a standstill, which suggested that they too had been stopped.

"Told you so," grumbled Barkins, joining us. "All this trouble for nothing. Why didn't the skipper open fire and blow 'em out of the water when he had a chance?"

"Go and ask him, Mr Barkins," said Mr Brooke, who overheard his remark. "And if I were you, I'd ask him at the same time why it is amateurs can always manage better than the leader."

Mr Brooke nodded, and I saw that he looked very serious as he walked aft, and a minute later I knew why.

"Bah!" growled Smith, as soon as he was out of hearing. "Shouldn't have listened."

"No," said Barkins. "It isn't quite manly to play the spy. Talk about snubbing, why is it officers should think it so precious fine to be always dropping on to their juniors? Now, then, look out! there's orders coming. The old *Teaser's* going to waggle her tail between her legs, and we're going back again. More waste of Her Majesty's coals."

"If we don't lie-to till the tide turns," I said. "Oh, I say, you two look sharp and get quite well again; I didn't know that having wounds would make fellows so sour."

"Who's sour. Here, let's get aft; quick, or we shall be out of the fun."

For the whistles were going, and the men springing to the boats, three of which were manned, and the one lying alongside being filled with a strong, well-armed crew.

We all three did press forward, in the full hope of being sent as well, and made ourselves so prominent that I saw Mr Reardon frown. But no orders came; and at last, in a great state of excitement, Barkins seized the opportunity to speak.

"May I go in the longboat, sir?"

"You—lame still from your wound, sir? Absurd! No, nor you neither, Mr Smith."

He caught my eye just then, but turned away, and I could not help feeling disappointed, though I knew well enough that the risk would have been great.

"Oh, I do call it a shame," grumbled Barkins, as the order was given, the men cheered, and, under the command of Mr Brooke, the four boats pushed off, the oars dropped, the oily water splashed in the bright sunshine, and each boat with its colours trailing astern glided rapidly up-stream.

"Yes, it's too bad," grumbled Smith in turn, who unconsciously began nursing his arm as if it pained him.

"Why, it's worse for me," I cried. "I'm quite strong and well. I ought to have gone."

Barkins exploded with silent laughter, laid his hand on Smith's shoulder, and said huskily, as if he were choking with mirth—

"I say, hark at him! What for? There'll be plenty of mosquitoes up there to sting the poor fellows; they don't want a gnat to tickle them and make them fight."

"No," said Smith. "Never mind, little boy, be good, and we'll take you on an expedition some day."

"All right," I replied; "I don't mind your chaff, only you needn't be so nasty because you are disappointed."

"Mr Herrick! Where's Mr Herrick?" cried the first lieutenant.

"Here, sir," I shouted; and I could not help giving my companions a look full of triumph as I dashed aft.

"Oh, there you are, sir. Now look here, I'm going to mast-head you. Got your glass?"

"Yes, sir."

"Then up with you, right to the main-topgallant cross-trees. Notice everything you can."

My heart began to beat before I reached the main shrouds, and it beat more heavily as I toiled up the rattlins, reached the top, and then went on again, too much excited to think of there being any danger of falling, my mind being partly occupied with thoughts of what Barkins and Smith were saying about my being favoured in this way.

"Just as if they could have come up," I said half-laughing; "one with a game leg, the other with a game arm."

My thoughts ran, too, as much upon what I was about to see, so that beyond taking a tight hold, and keeping my spyglass buttoned up in my jacket, I paid little heed to the height I was getting, I reached the head of the topmast, and then began to mount the rattlins of the main-topgallant mast, whose cross-trees seemed to be a tremendous height above my head.

But I was soon there, and settled myself as comfortably as I could, sitting with an arm well round a stay, and one leg twisted in another for safety; but the wood did not feel at all soft, and there was a peculiar rap, rap, rap against the tapering spar which ran up above my head to the round big wooden bun on the top of all, which we knew as the truck.

For a moment or two I couldn't make out what the sound was. Then I saw it was caused by the halyards, the thin line which ran up through the truck and down again to the deck, for hoisting our colours. This doubled line, swayed by the breeze, was beating against the tall pole, but I checked the noise by putting my arm round it and holding the thin halyard tight.

I looked down for a moment or two at the deck which lay beneath, giving me a bird's-eye view through the rigging of the white decks dotted with officers and men, and the guns glistening in the sunshine. There were several faces staring up at me, and I made out Barkins and Smith, and waved my hand. But these were only momentary glances; I had too much to see of far more importance. For there, spread out round me, was a grand view of the low, flat, marshy country, through which the river wound like a silver snake. Far away in the distance I could see villages, and what seemed to be a tower of some size. Beyond it, cultivated land and patches of forest; behind me, and to right and left, the shimmering sea, and straight in front the two junks; while almost at my feet, in spite of their hard rowing, there were our four boats, with the oars dipping with glorious regularity, and making the water flash and glitter, but not so brightly as did the bayonets of the few marines in each, as they sat in the stern-sheets with their rifles upright between their legs, and the keen triangular blades at the tops of the barrels twinkling at every movement of the boats.

It was a sight to make any one's heart throb, and in spite of my splendid position for seeing everything I could not help wishing I was there to help make a part of the picture I saw, with the men in their white ducks and straw hats, the marines glowing like so many patches of poppies, and the officers with their dark blue coats faintly showing a lace or two of gold.

How I longed to be with them bound upon such an exciting trip, and all the time how glad I was to be up there in so commanding a position, as, after watching the progress of the boats for a few moments, I opened and focussed my glass, rested it against a rope, and fixed it upon the junks.

The first thing I noticed was that one of them lay a little over to port, as if from being too heavily laden on one side; while, as I gazed, the other was evidently settling in the other direction.

I wondered what they were doing to them, and whether it meant changing heavy guns over to one side, when I grasped the fact,—they had gone as high up-stream as they could, and then run aground, and were fixed in the sticky mud of which the bottom of the river was composed.

"Ahoy! there aloft," shouted Mr Reardon. "What do you make out?"

I did not take the glass from my eye, but shouted down to him—

"Both junks fast aground, sir. Chinese crews running backwards and forwards, trying to work them off, sir."

An eager conversation ensued between Mr Reardon and the captain, during which I carefully scanned the two Chinese vessels, and could see the men swarming here and there, as if in an intense state of agitation, but they soon ceased trying to rock the junks, and, as I judged, they were waiting for the tide to rise higher and float them off.

There was nothing between to hinder my having a thoroughly good view of where they lay, just round a slight bend, but I felt certain that they could not see our boats, and I had proof that this was the case, on noticing that a group of men had landed, and were running towards a clump of tall trees, where they disappeared amongst the growth.

"Cowards!" I said to myself, for I felt that they were deserters, and, after watching for their reappearance, I was about to turn the glass upon the junks again, when I noticed a peculiar agitation of the branches of one tree, which stood up far above the others.

"Well, Mr Herrick, I am waiting for your reports," cried the first lieutenant.

"Yes, sir," I shouted. "Half-a-dozen men landed from one of the junks, and ran across to a patch of wood."

"Deserters? Any more leaving the ship?"

"No, sir."

"Ah, they saw the boats coming, I suppose?"

"No, sir, but they soon will. One of them is climbing a big tree, much higher than the junk's masts."

"For a look-out, eh?"

"Yes, sir, I think so," I shouted; and then to myself, "Oh, bother! It's hard work talking from up here. There he is, sir, right up at the top. You could see him from the deck."

"No, I can see nothing from here. Well, what is he doing?"

"Making signals with his hands, sir, and now he's coming down again."

"Then you think he has seen the boats?"

"No, sir; they are following one another close in under the bank."

"Then they can't see them," cried Mr Reardon, "and Mr Brooke will take them by surprise."

He did not shout this, but said it to the captain. Still the words rose to where I sat watching, till the Chinamen ran out from among the bushes at the foot of the trees, and I saw them making for the junks again.

I could not see them climb on board, but I felt that they must have jumped into a boat and rowed off to their friends, and, fixing my glass upon the deck of first one and then the other, I began to make out more and more clearly the actions of the crews, and, judging from the glittering, I saw some kind of arms were being distributed.

I announced this at first as a supposition, telling Mr Reardon what I thought it was.

"Yes, very likely," he replied; and a few minutes after I saw something else, and hailed.

"Yes," he said, "what now?" and I saw that, though he did not speak, the captain was listening attentively.

"They're burning something, sir."

"Confound them! Not setting fire to the junks?"

"I don't know, sir; I think so," I replied, still watching intently; and, as I gazed through my glass, I saw black smoke rising in little coils from both junks, at first very thick and spreading, then growing smaller.

"I think, sir, they've set fire to the junks in several places," I said.

He asked me why, and I told him.

"Watch attentively for a few minutes."

I did so, and felt puzzled, for it seemed so strange that the fire should grow smaller.

"Well," he said, "are the junks burning?"

"The little curls of smoke are rising still, sir."

"Have the men left the decks?"

"Oh no, sir! They're running here and there, and seem very busy still."

"Then they have not set fire to the vessels," he cried decisively. "Pirates, without a doubt. Those are stink-pots that they have been getting ready. Go on watching, and report anything else."

A noise below, familiar enough, with its rattle and splash, told me that an anchor had been dropped from the bows; and as the *Teaser* slowly swung round from the force of the tide, I also had to turn, so as to keep the telescope fixed upon the enemy, who were as busy as ever, though what they were doing I could not make out. The flashes of light came more frequently, though, as the sun played upon their weapons; and now I had something else to report—that they had both assumed a different position, being lifted by the tide and floated upon an even keel.

My first idea was, that now they would sail on beyond our reach; in fact, one moved a good deal, but the other stopped in its place, so that at last they were so close together that they seemed to touch.

"Make out the boats?" came from the deck.

"No, sir; they're close under the bank." Yes, I caught a glimpse of the marines' bayonets just then.

"How far are they away from the junks, do you think?"

"I can't tell, sir; about a quarter of a mile, I think."

Mr Reardon was silent while I gazed intently at a patch of open water just beyond a curve of the bank, hoping to see the boats there, though I felt that as soon as they reached that spot, if the enemy had not seen them before, they would be certain to then, for beyond that the junks lay clearly to be seen from where I sat.

"Well? See the boats?" came from the deck.

"No, sir, not yet."

I glanced down to answer, and could see that every one who possessed a glass was gazing anxiously aft, the only face directed up to me being the first lieutenant's. Then my eye was at the glass again.

"More smoke from the junks, sir," I cried; but there was no sign of fire, and I felt that Mr Reardon must be right, for if they had set a light to the inflammable wood of the vessels, they would have blazed up directly.

"Can't you see the boats yet?" cried the first lieutenant impatiently, and his voice sounded as if he were blaming me.

"No, sir, but the junks are more out in the middle of the stream. I can see them quite clearly now, away from the trees. They are crowded with men, and—"

"The boats—the boats?"

"No, sir;—yes, hurrah! There they go, sir, all abreast, straight for the junks."

"Ha!" came in one long heavy breath from below, as if all left on board had suddenly given vent to their pent-up feelings.

"How far are they away from the junks?" cried Mr Reardon.

'MY HANDS WHICH HELD THE TELESCOPE WERE QUITE WET WITH EXCITEMENT.'

"About two hundred yards, sir; you'll see them directly."

"Yes, I see them now, sir," cried Barkins, who was a little way up the mizzen-shrouds, where I had not seen him before.

"Silence!" cried the captain sternly. "Go on, Mr Herrick; report."

"Smoke from the junks, sir—white," I cried, and the words were hardly out of my mouth when there came the report of guns—first one and then another; then two together; and I fancied that I could see the water splashing up round about the boats, but I could not be sure.

"Boats separating," I shouted.

"Go on."

"Pulling hard for the junks."

"Yes, go on; report everything."

I needed no orders, for I was only too eager to tell everything I saw.

"Two boats have gone to the right; two to the left.—More firing from the junks.—Boats separating more.—Two going round behind.—Both out of sight."

By this time, in addition to the sharp reports of the small guns on board the junks, the sharper crackle of matchlocks and muskets had begun; but so far I had not seen a puff of smoke from our boats.

"Are our men firing?"

"No, sir; the two boats I can see are pulling straight now for the junks.— Now the water splashes all about them."

"Yes? Hit?"

"Don't think so, sir.—Now.—Ah!"

"What—what is it, boy?"

"Can't see anything, sir; they've rowed right into the smoke."

My hands which held the telescope were quite wet now with the excitement of the scene I had tried to describe to my superior officer, and I thrust the glass under my left arm, and rubbed them quickly on my handkerchief, as I gazed at the distant smoke, and listened to the crackle of musketry alone, for the guns had now ceased from fire.

This I felt must be on account of the boats coming to closer quarters, and then to the men boarding. But I could see nothing but the smoke, and I raised the glass to my eye again.

Still nothing but smoke. I fancied, though, that the firing was different— quicker and sharper—as if our men must have begun too.

"Well, Mr Herrick?" now came from below. "Surely you can see how the fight is going on?"

"No, sir, nothing but smoke,—Yes," I cried excitedly, "it's lifting now, and floating away to the left. I can see close up to the junks. Yes; now the decks. Our right boat is empty, and there is a great fight going on upon the junk."

"And the other?"

"There are two boats close up, and our men are firing. There is black smoke coming out of one boat. Now the men are climbing up, and—now, the smoke is too thick there."

"Go on, boy; go on," shouted the first lieutenant, stamping about, while the captain stood perfectly still, gazing at the rising smoke, from the bridge.

"They seem to be fighting very hard, sir," I said, trembling now like a leaf. "I can see quite a crowd, and that some of the people are in white."

"But who is getting the best of it?"

"I can't see, sir," I said sadly.

"Then for goodness' sake come down, and let some one else come up," roared Mr Reardon.

"Yes, sir."

"No, no; stay where you are, boy. But use your glass—use your glass."

I tried my best, but I could only make out a blurred mass of men on board both junks. They seemed to be swaying to and fro, and the smoke, instead of passing off, once more grew thicker, and in place of being white and steamy, it now looked to be of a dirty inky black, completely enveloping the vessels and our boats.

This I reported.

"They surely cannot have set them on fire?" said Mr Reardon.

"I can't see any flames, sir."

Silence again; and we found that the firing had ceased, all but a sharp crack from time to time, sounds evidently made by rifles. But there was nothing more to see, and, in spite of the angry appeals of the lieutenant, I could report no more than that the black smoke was growing thicker, and hanging down over the water, hiding everything, to the bushes and trees upon the bank.

And now, as I gave one glance down, I saw that the captain was walking to and fro upon the bridge, evidently in a great state of excitement, for there was not a sound now; the firing had quite ceased; the black cloud seemed to have swallowed up our four boats and men; and a chilly feeling of despair began to attack me, as I wondered whether it was possible that our poor fellows had been beaten, and the boats burned by the stink-pots the pirates had thrown in.

The thought was almost too horrible to bear, and I stared hard through the glass again, trying to make out the junks beyond the smoke, and whether it was really our boats which where burning, and raising the black cloud which hid all view.

"I can see a boat now, sir," I cried excitedly, as one of them seemed to glide out of the end of the cloud; but my heart sank as I made the announcement, for I saw only that which confirmed my fears.

"Well, go on, lad," cried Mr Reardon, stamping with impatience, "what are they doing in her?"

"She's empty, sir, and floating away, with a cloud of black smoke rising from her."

"Ah!" he exclaimed, with quite a savage snarl, and I saw the captain stop short and raise his glass again, though I knew that from where he stood he could see nothing.

"We're beaten," I said to myself. "Oh, our poor lads—our poor lads!"

A mist rose before my eyes, and I nearly dropped the glass, but I passed my hand across my face and looked again, sweeping the telescope from the left side, where the boat was gliding up-stream smoking more than ever, to the right and the shore.

"Hooray!" I yelled.

"Yes! what?" roared the captain and Mr Reardon together.

"Chinese running in a regular stream away from the shore; making for the woods. One down—another down."

At the same moment almost came a couple of volleys, then several men went down, and the crackle of firing commenced again.

"Go on, Herrick!" cried Mr Reardon.

"Our fellows ashore, and running Jacks and jollies together, sir. Stopping to fire. Running again."

"And the enemy?"

"Running like deer, sir. More of them down. Making for the wood."

"One man stopped, sir, and returning."

"Yes, yes, that's good. What now?"

"Boat out from the smoke, rowing after the other one, sir. They've got it. Yes, I can see. They're throwing something out that smokes—now something more."

"Bah! stink-pots!" roared Mr Reardon. "Now then, quick!—quick! Don't, go to sleep, sir. What next?"

"I'll shy the spyglass at you directly," I muttered; and then aloud, "Fire, sir; both junks blazing."

"Hurrah!" came from the deck as the rest of the crew set up a tremendous cheer, for the smoke had suddenly grown less dense; and the junks gradually grew visible as it floated away; while even in the bright sunlight the flames were visible, and I could now make out that they were two floating furnaces with the great tongues of fire licking the broad matting-sails: and, best news of all, there, quite plainly, were our four boats, with the men just visible above their sides.

I reported this, and cheer after cheer rose again. After which there was dead silence once more, so that my reports could be heard.

"Now, Mr Herrick, what now?" cried Mr Reardon.

"Two boats lying in mid-stream, sir; the others are rowing to the side."

"To pick up the men who were sent ashore, I suppose. Good."

"Junks burning very fast, sir; and they're floating across to the other side. The wind's taking them straight, for the smoke floats that way."

"Very likely," said Mr Reardon; and there was a long pause.

"One junk has taken the ground, sir," I said, "and—"

"Yes, well, what?"

"Her masts and sails have fallen over the side."

"And our boats?"

"Lying-to, sir, doing nothing."

But that was as far as I could see, for they were doing a good deal, as we afterwards heard.

"Other junk has floated over, sir, nearly to the same place."

"Good; burning still?"

"Oh yes, sir—very fast."

He need not have asked; for, as Barkins told me afterwards, they could see the flames from the deck, though our boats were invisible.

"Well, what now?" cried Mr Reardon, as I saw the captain quietly pacing to and fro on the bridge.

"Other two boats pushed off from the shore, sir."

"Ha! that's right. See anything of the Chinamen?"

"No, sir; the forest goes right away for miles. There isn't one to be seen."

"And the boats?"

"All rowing back, sir, close under the left bank."

"Can you see them?"

"Only three of them, sir," I replied. "Now another is out of sight."

"Then, as soon as they are all invisible, you can come down," cried Mr Reardon.

"Yes, sir; all out of sight now."

"Then come down."

"Thankye for nothing," I muttered; and then aloud, "Yes, sir;" and I closed my glass, and wiped my wet forehead, feeling stiff and sore, as if I had been exerting myself with all my might.

"I suppose I'm very stupid," I said to myself, as I began to descend slowly, "but I did try my best. What a height it seems up here! If a fellow slipped and fell, he would never have another hour up at the mast-head."

I went on downward, with my legs feeling more and more stiff, and a sense of heavy weariness growing upon me. My head ached too, and I felt a pain at the back of my neck, while mentally I was as miserable and dissatisfied as ever I remember being in my life.

"I hope he'll send old Barkins up next time," I thought. "He wouldn't feel so precious jealous then. Nice job, squinting through that glass till one's almost blind, and nothing but bullying for the result."

It seemed to be a very long way down to the deck, but I reached the remaining few rattlins at last, and I was nearly down to the bulwarks, meaning to go below and bathe my head, if I could leave the deck, when I was stopped short, just in my most gloomy and despondent moments, by the captain's voice, his words sounding so strange that I could hardly believe my ears.

For, as I held on to the shrouds, and looked sharply aft at the mention of my name, he said—

"Thank you, Mr Herrick; very good indeed;" while, as I reached the deck, Mr Reardon came up—

"Yes, capital, Mr Herrick. A very arduous task, and you have done it well."

Chapter Twenty
After the Fight

"Bravo, Gnat! Well done, little 'un!" whispered Barkins the next minute, as I walked aft, feeling quite confused, while my headache and sensation of misery passed off as if by magic. "Blacksmith would have done it better, of course; wouldn't you, Smithy?"

"Done it as well as you would," said my messmate sulkily; and there was a heavy frown on his brow; but, as he met my eyes, it cleared off, and he smiled frankly. "I say: Well done our side!" he whispered. "What would they do without midshipmen!"

"I say, though," said Barkins, "we've given John Pirate another dressing-down; but what about the plunder?"

"Ah, of course," said Smith. "Junks both burned, and no swag. What about our prize-money? Eh, Gnat?"

"I wasn't thinking about that, but about our poor lads. They must have had a sharp fight. I hope no one is hurt."

My companion were silent for a moment or two. Then Barkins said quietly—

"I thought it would be only the teapots that were broken. Think our chaps were hurt? You couldn't see?"

"I could see that there was a big fight going on; and look here!"

I nodded in the direction of one of the companion-ways, from which the doctor suddenly appeared with his glasses on, and an eager, expectant look in his eyes as he bustled up to us.

"I'm all ready," he said. "Boats in sight yet?" I shuddered, and I noticed that Smith looked white. "Well, why don't you answer? What's the matter, my lads? Oh, I see." He laughed.

"Horrible sort of person the doctor, eh? But you didn't look like that when I tackled your wounds the other day. But if you people will fight, the surgeon must be ready. Oh, let's see: you were up at the cross-trees, Mr

Herrick, with your glass, and saw all. Will there be much work for me to do?"

"I don't know, sir," I said, trying hard to speak quietly. "I couldn't see much for the smoke. I hope not."

"So do I, boy, heartily. I don't mind the wounds so long as they're not too bad. It's painful to have fine strong lads like ours slip through one's fingers. But we must do our best. Any Chinese prisoners? Sure to be, I suppose."

"I should think so, sir."

"And wounded. Well, if there are, you three lads ought to come and be my body-guard with your dirks. Like to see the operations, I daresay?"

"Ugh!" I said, with a shudder.

"Bah! Don't act like a great girl, Herrick," said the doctor scornfully. "You would never have done for a doctor, sir. I never shudder at the worst cases."

"But then you are hardened, sir," said Barkins.

"Hardened be hanged, sir!" cried the doctor indignantly. "A clever surgeon gets more and more softened every time he operates, more delicate in his touches, more exact in his efforts to save a limb, or arrange an injury so that it will heal quickly. Hardened, indeed! Why, to judge from your faces, any one would think surgery was horrible, instead of one of the greatest pleasures in life."

"What, cutting and bandaging wounds, and fishing for bullets?" blurted out Smith; "why, sir, I think it's hideous."

"And I think you are an impertinent young coxcomb, sir," cried the doctor indignantly. "Hideous, indeed! Why it's grand."

He looked round at us as if seeking for confirmation of his words, but neither spoke.

"Hideous? horrible?" he said, taking off his glasses and thrusting his hand into his pocket for his handkerchief to wipe them, but bringing out something soft and white, which proved to be a piece of lint. "Oh, I do call it cool. If there's anything hideous it's your acts, sir; having those thundering guns fired, to send huge shells shivering and shattering human beings to pieces for the doctor to try and mend; your horrible chops given with cutlasses and the gilt-handled swords you are all so proud of wearing—insolent, bragging, showy tools that are not to be compared with my neat set of amputating knives in their mahogany case. These are to do good, while yours are to do evil. Then, too, your nasty, insidious, cruel bayonets, which make a worse wound than a bullet. Oh, it's too fine to call my work horrible, when I try to put straight all your mischief."

"Here they are," cried Barkins excitedly, as a hail came from the top.

We ran aft to see the first boat come steadily along close in shore, which was being hugged so as to avoid the full rush of the tide.

Directly after the others came in sight, and glasses were all in use from the bridge and quarter-deck.

I adjusted mine directly, and saw at the first glance that there was plenty of work for Dr Price, for men were lying in the stern-sheets with rough bandages on limbs and heads, while several of those who were rowing had handkerchiefs tied round their foreheads, and others had horrible marks upon their white duck-frocks, which told tales of injury to them as well as to their enemies.

The third boat was given up to men lying down or sitting up together, leaving only just room for the rowers, while the fourth and largest boat was being towed; the thwarts, that in an ordinary way would have been occupied by rowers, now holding the marines, who sat with their rifles ready, and fixed bayonets, while the stern-sheets were filled with Chinamen, seated in three groups, and all in the most uncomfortable-looking way. I could see that their hands were tied behind their backs, and it was horribly plain that several of them were wounded; but why they should have formed these three groups, and sat there with their heads laid close together, was what puzzled me.

A loud cheer rose from our deck as the boats came near; and this was taken up directly by the returning party, the men rowing harder as they shouted, and the little triumphant procession reached the side.

The first hail came from the captain.

"Mr Brooke—where's Mr Brooke?"

"Here, sir," cried that officer, standing up with a stained handkerchief about his head, and his uniform all black and scorched.

"Any fatalities?"

"No, sir; not one."

I saw the captain's lips move, but no one heard him speak. I guessed, though, what he said, and I felt it.

Then as quickly as possible the boats were run up to the davits, and the uninjured men leaped on deck. Next the wounded, such as could stir, descended from the boats, one poor fellow staggering and nearly falling as soon as he reached the deck. After which the badly wounded were carefully lifted out and carried below, to be laid in a row to wait the doctor and his assistant make their first rapid examination, to apply tourniquets and bandaged pads to the most serious injuries.

"Good heavens, Mr Brooke, what a condition you are in! The doctor must take you first."

"Oh no, sir," said the young lieutenant quietly. "I'm not very bad; a cut from a heavy sword through my cap. It has stopped bleeding. My hands are a little bruised."

"But how was this?"

"As we advanced to board, they threw quite a volley of stink-pots fizzing away into us. I burned myself a little with them."

"Chucking 'em overboard, sir," cried the boatswain. "Splendid it was."

"Nonsense!" cried Mr Brooke. "You threw ever so many. But it was hot work, sir."

"Hot! it is horrible. How many prisoners have you there?"

"Eighteen, sir; the survivors escaped."

"But you shouldn't have fired the junks, man," said the captain testily. "There may have been wounded on board."

"Yes, sir," said Mr Brooke, with his brow puckering; "wounded and dead there were, I daresay, thirty; but the enemy set fire to their vessels themselves before they leaped overboard, and it was impossible to save them: they burned like resin. We saved all we could."

"I beg your pardon; I might have known," cried the captain warmly. "Come to my cabin. Mr Reardon, be careful with those prisoners; they are savage brutes."

"Enough to make 'em, Gnat. Look! What a shame!"

I looked, but I could not see any reason for Smith's remark.

"Beg pardon, sir," growled one of the men, who had a bandage round his arm; "you wouldn't ha' said so if you'd been there. They was all alike. The junk we took was burning like fat in a frying-pan, and me and my mate see one o' them chaps going to be roasted, and made a run for it and hauled him away—singed my beard, it did; look, sir."

Half of his beard was burned off, and his cheek scorched.

"Then my mate gets hold of his legs, and I was stooping to get my fists under his chest, when he whips his knife into my arm 'fore I knowed what he was up to. But we saved him all the same."

"Here," cried Mr Reardon, as the marines descended from the third boat, and stood at attention in two parties facing each other; "who was answerable for this? Why, it is an outrage. Brutal!"

"S'pose it was my doing, sir," said the boatswain, touching his cap; "but I asked leave of Mr Brooke first, and he said yes."

"What, to tie the poor wretches up like that, sir, and half of them wounded!"

"Beg pardon, sir; there was no other way handy. We lashed their arms behind 'em to keep 'em from knifing us, and then they kept on jumping overboard, and trying to drown themselves. We haven't hurt them."

"Cast them loose at once."

"Yes, sir; I should like half-a-dozen strong chaps in the boat, though."

"Well, take them," said Mr Reardon, who was speaking less severely now. "I'll have the uninjured men in irons this time. Be careful."

'THE FIRST LIEUTENANT HAD RETURNED.'

"And if I'd my way, I'd have 'em all in iron boxes, 'cept their hands."

The boatswain said this to me, with a nod, as the first lieutenant turned away, and, unable to control my curiosity, I sprang up on the bulwark to look into the boat.

"Let's have a look too," cried Smith, and he jumped up to gain a position much closer than mine, but quitted his hold and dropped back on deck, lost his footing, and came down sitting; for, as he leaned over the boat's gunnel, one of the prisoners made a sudden snap at him, after the fashion of an angry dog, and the marines burst into a roar of laughter.

Smith got up scowling and indignant.

"My hands slipped," he said to me aloud. And then, to carry off his confusion, "How many are there, Herrick?"

"Three lots of six," I said, as I now saw plainly enough how it was that the prisoners were in such a strange position. For they had been dragged together and their pigtails lashed into a tight knot, a process admirably suited to the object in hand—to render them perfectly helpless; and their aspect certainly did not excite my anger.

Meanwhile the boatswain had stepped into the swinging boat, and he turned to me, but looked at Smith as he spoke.

"Like to try whether either of the others will bite, Mr Herrick?" he said.

Smith coloured and frowned.

"No, thank you," I replied; "I'm satisfied."

"Now then, you two," said the boatswain, "stand by with your bayonets; and you, my lads, be ready as we cast them loose. Get a good grip of each fellow by the tail; he'll be helpless then."

I stood looking on at the curious scene, and the next minute was conscious of the fact that the first lieutenant had returned to supervise the putting of the prisoners in irons himself; and, as the tails were unlashed, he took note of the men who were injured, and had them lifted out and laid on deck.

The others made no attempt to escape, for they were too firmly held; but, as the armourer fitted on the irons, I could see their wild-beast-like eyes rolling in different directions, and then become fixed with a look of savage hate on our men, who were certainly none too tender with a set of wretches who only waited an opportunity to destroy life without the slightest compunction.

At last they were all lying on the deck—nine with serious wounds, the other half for the most part injured, but only to a very slight extent, and these were soon after taken one by one between a file of marines to the place in the hold appointed once more for their prison.

Then the doctor came up for ten minutes, and, after a few words with the sergeant of marines, examined the nine prisoners, passing over six to the sergeant with orders, and having three laid aside for his own ministrations.

We three lads stood watching the sergeant, who had evidently had some practice in ambulance work, and skilfully enough he set to work sponging and bandaging injuries. But all the time a couple of marines stood, one on either side, ready to hold the prisoners down, for each seemed to look upon the dressing of his wounds as a form of torture which he was bound to resist with all his might.

"Nice boys, Mr Herrick," said the boatswain drily. "Do you know why we are taking all this pains?"

"To save their lives and give them up to the authorities at Tsin-Tsin, I suppose."

"Yes, sir."

"For them to be put on their trial for piracy on the high seas."

"Yes, sir, that's it; but it would be a greater kindness to let the wretches die out of their misery."

"But some of them mayn't be guilty," I said.

The boatswain laughed.

"I don't think there's much doubt about that, sir," he said. Just then, as the last man was treated by the sergeant, the doctor came on deck with his assistants, both in white aprons and sleeves—well, I'm a little incorrect there—in aprons and sleeves that had been white.

"I've no business here," said the doctor hurriedly; "but these men cannot be left. Keep an eye on them, my men, and don't let them do me any mischief. I can't be spared just now."

The next moment he was down on his knees by the side of one of the prisoners, who, in his eyes for a few minutes, was neither enemy nor piratical Chinaman, but a patient to whom he devoted himself to the full extent of his skill, performing what was needful, and leaving his assistant to finish the bandaging while he went on to the next.

In another ten minutes he had finished, and rose from his knees.

"There, Mr Herrick," he said; "do you call that horrible? because I call it grand. If those three ill-looking scoundrels had been left another hour they would have died. Now, with their hardy constitutions, they will rapidly get well, perhaps escape and begin pirating again. Possibly, when we give them up—oh my knees! how hard that deck is!—the authorities will—"

"Chop off all head. Velly bad men—velly bad men indeed."

The doctor laughed, and hurried away while the last prisoner was carried down below.

"There," said the boatswain, when all was over, "that job's done, Mr Herrick. Nice fellows your countrymen, Ching."

"Not allee nice fellow," replied Ching seriously. "Pilate velly bad man. No use. Why captain save him up?"

"Ah, that's a question you had better ask him. But I say, Ching, those fellows came up here with cargo, didn't they?"

"Calgo?" said Ching.

"Yes; plunder out of the ships they took."

"Yes," said Ching.

"Then where is it? There was none on board the junks."

"Ching know," said the interpreter, laying his finger to the side of his nose. "You likee Ching show?"

"Yes, of course. Prize-money, and you'd share."

"Ching likee plize-money. You bling ship along, and Ching show."

Chapter Twenty One
In the Creek

Ching's announcement cleared up what had been somewhat of a mystery. It had appeared strange to everybody that the junks had been up this river apparently for no purpose, and more strange that they should have been light, and not laden with the plunder of the vessels they had taken. And now, as without any need for taking soundings the *Teaser* slowly steamed back, Ching pointed out a kind of landing-place in a little creek hidden amongst dense growth, so that it had been passed unnoticed on our way up.

The country here on both sides of the river was wild, and no trace of a dwelling could be seen; but about half a mile from the shore there was a low ridge, round one end of which the creek wound, and toward this ridge Ching pointed, screwing his eyes up into narrow slits, and wrinkling up his face in all directions.

"Velly bad man live along-along there. Plenty plize-money; plenty tea, lice, silk; plenty evelyting. Come and see."

The *Teaser* was moored, and a couple of boats manned with well-armed crews, Ching looking on the while and cunningly shaking his head.

"No wantee big piecee sword gun. Pilate all lun away and hide."

"Never mind," said Mr Reardon, who was going in command of the expedition; "we may find somebody there disposed to fight."

"Takee all along big empty boat; cally tea, silk, lice, plize-money?"

"Better see first," said the captain; "there may not be anything worth carriage. Go with them," he said to Ching. "They may want an interpleter."

"Yes, Ching interpleter. Talk velly nice Inglis."

"You can come if you like in my boat, Mr Herrick," said the lieutenant; and I jumped at the opportunity, but before I reached the side I turned, and saw Barkins and Smith looking gloomily on.

"Well, what are you waiting for?" said Mr Reardon.

"Beg pardon, sir," I said; "I was only thinking that Mr Barkins and Mr Smith would be very glad to go ashore."

"Of course they would, but I suppose you don't want to give up your place to them?"

"No, sir," I said; "but I will."

"Oh, very well. Here, Mr Barkins, Mr Smith; do you feel well enough to go in my boat?"

"Yes, sir," they cried together eagerly.

"Jump in, then."

"Thank you, sir," cried Smith, and he mounted into the first boat; but Barkins hesitated a moment.

"Thank you, old chap," he whispered, "but I don't like to go."

"Off with you," I said, and I hurried him forward. "Shall I give you a leg up?" I added, for he limped a good deal still.

"No, no; I don't want to let them see I'm lame. But I say, Gnat, you go."

"Be off," I whispered. "Quick!" and I helped him in.

"Here, Ching, you had better go in the second boat," said Mr Reardon sharply; and, as the Chinaman rolled out of the first boat, blinking and smiling, orders were given to lower away, and the first boat kissed the water.

I was looking down at my two messmates, feeling a little disappointed, but glad that they had a chance at last, when Mr Reardon looked up.

"Here, Mr Herrick," he cried. "You had better come on in the other boat, and take charge of the interpreter. Look sharp."

I did look sharp, and a few minutes later I was sitting in the stern-sheets, being rowed ashore.

"Plenty loom in littlee liver," said Ching, pointing to the creek. "Pilate take allee plize-money in sampan up littlee liver."

"Ching thinks the boats could go up the creek, sir, and that the pirates go that way."

"Try, then; go first, Mr Grey," cried the first lieutenant; and, ordering his boat's crew to lie on their oars, he waited till we had passed, and then followed.

"Ching going showee way," whispered the Chinaman to me.

"But how do you know there is a place up there?" I said. "Have you ever been?"

Ching shook his head till his black tail quivered, and closed his eyes in a tight smile.

"Ching interpleter," he said, with a cunning look. "Ching know evelyting 'bout Chinaman. Talkee Chinee—talkee Inglis—velly nicee."

"But talking English velly nicee doesn't make you understand about the pirates."

"Yes; know velly much allee 'bout pilate," he said. "Velly bad men—velly stupid, allee same. Pilate get big junk, swordee, gun, plenty powder; go killee evelybody, and hide tea, silk, lice up liver. One pilate—twenty pilate—allee do same. Hide up liver."

"Perhaps he's right," said Mr Grey, who sat back with the tiller in his hand, listening. "They do imitate one another. What one gang does, another does. They're stupid enough to have no fresh plans of their own."

By this time we were in the creek, which was just wide enough for the men to dip their oars from time to time, and the tide being still running up we glided along between the muddy banks and under the overhanging trees, which were thick enough to shade as from the hot sun.

The ride was very interesting, and made me long to get ashore and watch the birds and butterflies, and collect the novel kinds of flowers blooming here and there in the more open parts, the lilies close in to the side being beautiful.

But we had sterner business on hand, besides having the first lieutenant in the following boat, so I contented myself with looking straight ahead as far as I could for the maze-like wanderings of the creek, and I was just thinking how easily we could run into an ambuscade, and be shot at from the dense shrubby growth on the bank, when Mr Reardon called to us from his boat.

"Let your marines be ready, Mr Grey," he said, "in case of a trap. If the enemy shows and attacks, on shore at once and charge them. Don't wait to give more than one volley."

"Ay, ay, sir," said the boatswain; and the marines seized their pieces, and I looked forward more sharply than ever.

But Ching shook his head.

"No pilate," he whispered to me. "Allee too velly much flighten, and lun away from foleign devil sailor and maline."

"But they might have come down to their place here," I said.

Ching smiled contemptuously.

"Pilate velly blave man, fight gleat deal when allee one side, and know sailor can't fightee. When plenty sailor can fightee, pilate lun away velly fast, and no come back."

"Can you understand him, Mr Grey?" I said.

"Oh yes, I understand him, and I daresay he's right, but there's no harm in being on the look-out;" and, to show his intention of following out his words, the boatswain took his revolver from its case, and laid it ready upon his knees.

"How much farther is this village, or whatever it is?" said Mr Reardon from behind.

"Do you hear, Ching?" I said.

"Ching hear; Ching don'tee know; not velly far," was the unsatisfactory reply.

"I'm afraid we've come on a cock-and-bull hunt," said the boatswain, looking to right and left as he stood up in the boat, for the creek now grew so narrow that the men had to lay in their oars, and the coxswain also stood up and drew the boat onward by hooking the overhanging boughs.

"Do you think they do come up here, Ching?" I said.

He nodded, and looked sharply about him.

"There can be no big traffic up here, Mr Grey," said the lieutenant. "What does the interpreter say?"

"Do you hear, Ching?" I whispered; "what do you say?"

"Allee light," he replied. "Pilate come along in littlee sampan; cally silk, tea, lice."

"Oh, bother!" I said. Then aloud to Mr Reardon, whose boat was half hidden by the growth overhead, "He seems quite sure they do come up here, sir."

"Well, then, go a little farther, but I feel far from sure. Push right in at the next place where there's room for the boat, and climb up the bank."

"Yes, sir," I cried; and we went on again for another hundred yards, when all at once I caught sight of an opening where I could land, and pointed it out to Mr Grey.

"Yes," said Ching, "allee light. That place where pilate land allee plize-money."

I laughed, and Mr Grey told the coxswain to draw the boat close to the bank, when, to my intense surprise, I found there was a broadly-trampled path, beaten into soft steps, and I turned in my glee and shouted—

"Here's the place, sir."

The boat glided rustling in; two men sprang out, and then we followed. The second boat came alongside, and five minutes later our sturdy little force was tramping along through a dense patch of wood by a well-beaten path, and in about ten minutes more were out at the foot of a low ridge which hid the river from our sight, and in face of a couple of dozen or so low bamboo huts, two of which were of pretty good size.

"Steady! halt! form up!" cried the lieutenant, and skirmishers were sent forward to feel our way, for no one was visible; but open doors and windows, suggested the possibility of danger in ambush.

A few minutes settled all doubts on that score, and the word to advance was given. We went up to the front of the huts at the double, and examination proved that the places must have been occupied within a few hours, for the fire in one hut was still smouldering; but the people had fled, and we were in possession of the tiny village so cunningly hidden from the river.

Our men were pretty quick, but Ching surpassed them.

"Look at him running!" cried Barkins, as, with his tail flying, Ching ran from hut to hut, and finally stopped before the two more pretentious places, which were closely shut.

"Hong—warehouse," he cried to me, and an attempt was made to enter, but the doors of both were quite fast.

"Steady!" said Mr Reardon; "there may be some of the enemy inside;" and our men were so placed that when the door was burst in, any fire which we drew would prove harmless.

One of the sailors came forward then with a heavy flat stone, which looked as if it had been used to crush some kind of grain upon it, and, receiving a nod from the lieutenant, he raised it above his head, dashed it against the fastening, and the door flew open with a crash, while the sailor darted aside.

But no shot issued from within, and Mr Reardon stepped forward, looked in, and uttered an ejaculation.

"Look here, Grey," he cried; and the boatswain stepped to his side. Then my turn came, and there was no doubt about Ching's idea being correct, for the place was literally packed with stores. Chests, bales, boxes, and packages of all kinds were piled-up on one side; bags, evidently of rice, on the other; while at the end were articles of all kinds, and crates which seemed to be full of china.

"Sentry here," said the lieutenant sternly; and, leaving a marine on guard, he led the way to the other store, whose door was burst in, and upon our entering, without hesitation now, this place proved to be choked with the cargo of different junks which the pirates had rifled, for everything of value had been packed in tightly, and the pirates' treasure-houses were no doubt waiting for some favourable opportunity for disposing of the loot.

"Sentry here," cried Mr Reardon again; and the man having been planted, we stood together in one of the huts, while the lieutenant made his plans.

"You wantee big empty boat?" said Ching suddenly.

"Yes, my man, and I wish we had brought one." Then, after a few minutes' consideration, Mr Reardon decided what to do.

"Now, Mr Herrick," he said, "take a marine and one man with the signal flags, and go up to the ridge yonder. Place your marine where he can command the plain, and he will fire if he sees the enemy approaching. The man is to signal for two more boats."

I started for the ridge after getting my two men, which was about two hundred yards away, the ground rising in a slope; and, as we went off at the double, I heard orders being given, while, by the time we were up on the top, I looked back to see our men going in a regular stream down to the boats, laden with bales of silk, the white frocks of the Jacks showing through the thick growth from time to time.

My sentry was soon posted in a position where he could command the plain for miles, and the Jack hard at work waving flags till his signal was answered from the ship, which seemed from where we stood to be lying close at hand.

Then we two returned, to find that one boat was already packed as full as it would hold; and Barkins and Mr Grey went off with it back to the river, while the second was rapidly laden, and in half an hour followed the first. Then Smith and I followed the lieutenant into the store, with its low reed-thatched roof, and gazed about wonderingly at the richness of the loot upon which we had come.

"I say, Gnat, we shan't go home without prize-money this voyage," whispered Smith; and then, nothing more being possible, the sentries—four, posted at different distances—were visited, and we all sat down in the shade to rest, and partake of the refreshments in the men's haversacks.

Chapter Twenty Two
Fresh Danger

"They're a long time sending those boats, Herrick," said the lieutenant to me soon after we had finished our meal.

"It's rather a long way, sir," I ventured to suggest.

"Oh yes, it's a long way; but with the state of dishipline to which I have brought the *Teaser* they ought to have been here by now. Suppose we were surrounded by the enemy, and waiting for their help to save us!"

"We should think it longer than we do now, sir." Mr Reardon turned to me sharply, and looked as if in doubt whether he should treat my remark as humorous or impertinent. Fortunately he took the former view, and smiled pleasantly.

"So we should, Herrick, so we should. But if they knew it was to fetch all this loot on board, they'd make a little more haste."

"They know it by this time, sir," I said. "They must have met the first boat."

"Oh, I don't know," he said rather sourly. "The men are very slow when I am not there."

"Here they are, sir!" I cried; for the marine sentry down by the river challenged, and then there was a loud cheering, and soon after Mr Brooke appeared, followed by a long train of fully-armed Jacks.

"Why, I thought when we started that we had come to fight," cried Mr Brooke as he reached us. "We met the two loaded boats. Is there much more?"

"Come and look," said Mr Reardon; and we went first into one and then the other store, while our party of Jacks communicated our luck to the newcomers, the result being that, as we came out of the second long hut, the men cheered again lustily.

Then no time was lost; and the way in which the crew attacked those two stores of loot was a sight to see. It was tremendously hot, but they laughed and cheered each other as those returning met the laden ones going down to the boats. They would have liked to make a race of it to see which crew could load up their boat first, but Mr Reardon stopped that; and the strength of all was put to work to load one boat and get it off, so that there were two streams of men going and coming; and the first boat was deeply laden in an incredibly short space of time, the men leaving themselves no room to row, but placing the chests amidships to form a platform, and two smaller ones in the bow and stern.

They would have laden the boat more deeply still but for Mr Brooke, who superintended at the side of the creek, while Mr Reardon was at the stores.

Then the first of the boats Mr Brooke had brought was sent off, and by the time the next was loaded one of those we had previously sent off returned.

"Velly plime lot of plize-money," Ching said to me every time we met; and he toiled away with the rest, his face shining, and while our men grew red he grew more and more yellow. But, in spite of the tremendously hard work of carrying down those loads, the men took it all as a party of pleasure; and when, later on in the day, after boatload after boatload had gone down the creek for hours, I had to go up to Mr Reardon with a message from Mr Brooke, I was astonished to see how the contents of the stores had disappeared.

It was getting close upon sundown when the last load was packed into the longboat. Silk bale, tea-chest, rice-bag, crate, and box, with an enormous amount of indescribable loot, including all kinds of weapons, had been taken aboard; and the men who had come up for fresh burdens began cheering like mad as they found the task was done.

"That will do, my lads; steady—steady!" cried Mr Reardon. "Fall in."

Bang!

It was not a loud report, only that of the rifle fired by the sentry on the ridge; and immediately the men stood to their arms, and were ready for what promised to be an interruption.

"See the sentry, Mr Herrick?" cried the lieutenant.

"Yes, sir," I said; "he's running in fast."

The next minute the man came up, breathless.

"Strong body of John Chinamans, sir, coming across from over yonder."

"Time we were off, then," said Mr Reardon; and, giving the word, we started away at the "double" from before the empty stores and huts, toward the creek.

Our run through the wood, though, was soon brought to a walk, for we overtook the last laden men, and had to accommodate our pace to theirs. But they hurried on pretty quickly, reached the boat just as another empty one returned; the loading was finished, and as soon as the boat was ready, an addition was made to her freight in the shape of a dozen Jacks and marines, and she pushed off just as a loud yelling was heard from the direction of the empty stores.

"They'll be down on us directly," muttered Mr Reardon; and we all crowded into the empty boat and pushed off after the loaded one, but had not descended the creek far before we were stopped by the loaded boat, and had to arrange our pace by hers.

"Now for a slow crawl," I thought, "and they'll be after us directly."

A loud bang behind us told that I was right, and the handful of rough slugs in the heavy matchlock flew spattering amongst the leaves overhead, cutting off twigs which fell into the boat.

"Lie down all who can," cried the lieutenant; and we waited for the next shot, which, to be rather Irish, was half-a-dozen in a scattered volley.

But though the twigs and leaves came showering down, no one was hit; and the coxswain steadily poled us along as fast as the progress of the other boat would allow.

I saw that Mr Reardon was on the *qui vive* to order a return of the fire; but so far we could not see from whence it came, and it seemed as if nothing could be done but keep steadily on with our retreat.

"They might have given us another half-hour, Herrick," he said. "I should like to get the boys on board unhurt."

"Think they can get on ahead, sir?" I whispered.

"I hope not. The forest on each side is so dense that I don't fancy they can get along any faster than we do. Make haste, my lads, make haste," he said, almost in a whisper; "we shall have it dark here under these trees before long."

Crash came another volley, accompanied by a savage yelling, but we were so low down between the muddy banks that again the slugs went pattering over our heads.

"Would you mind passing the word to the other boat, messmate," said a familiar voice. "Tell 'em not to hurry themselves, as we're very comfortable."

"Who's that? Silence!" cried Mr Reardon.

No reply came to his question, but I could hear the men chuckling.

The next minute they were serious enough, for there was a burst of voices from very near at hand.

"Aim low, my lads," said Mr Reardon. "You six in the stern-sheets, as near to where the shooting is as you can."

The rifles were levelled, three of the barrels being passed over our shoulders. Then came the usual orders, and the pieces went off like one.

This silenced our pursuers for a few minutes, during which we continued our progress, snail-like at the best, for the boat in front looked like a slug.

"I'd give the order to them to draw aside and let us pass, Herrick," whispered the lieutenant, who now, in this time of peril, grew very warm and friendly; "but—ah, that's getting dangerous."

For another volley from very near at hand rattled over us, and was answered by our men.

"What was I going to say?" continued the lieutenant coolly, "Oh, I remember! If we tried to get by them they might take the ground with all that load, and be stuck."

"And it would be a pity to have to leave that load, sir," I said.

"Velly best load—allee best silk!" cried Ching excitedly, "Good, velly good plize-money!"

There was a roar of laughter at this, and Mr Reardon cried—

"Silence!"

Then, sharply, "Fire, my lads, if you see any one following."

"Ay, ay, sir."

"Yes, it would be a pity," said the lieutenant thoughtfully; "but it's tempting. If we could get in front, Herrick, we could tow the load, and it would shelter us all from the firing."

"Unless they got to be level with us, sir," I said.

"And—quick! right and left, my lads. Fire!" cried the lieutenant; for there was the breaking of undergrowth close at hand on either side, and a savage yelling commenced as our pursuers forced their way through.

The men, who had been like hounds held back by the leash, were only too glad to get their orders; and in an instant there was quite a blaze of fire from both sides of the boat, the bullets cutting and whistling through the thick trees and undergrowth; and the movement on the banks, with the cracking and rustling of the bushes and tufts of bamboo, stopped as if by magic.

"Cease firing!" cried Mr Reardon; and then, as if to himself, "Every shot is wasted."

I did not think so, for it had checked the enemy, who allowed us to go on slowly another hundred yards or so.

"Allee velly dleadful," whispered Ching to me, as he crouched in the bottom of the boat. "You tinkee hit Ching?"

"I hope not," I said. "Oh no; we shall get out into the river directly."

"No," he said; "velly long way yet."

"But who are these?" I said—"some village people?"

"Pilate," he cried. "Allee come home not kill, and findee plize-money gone. Makee velly angly. Wantee chop off sailor head."

"Like to catch 'em at it," growled Tom Jecks, who had been very silent for some time.

"Silence there!" cried Mr Reardon sternly. Then to me, "We seem to have checked them, Herrick."

At that moment there was a sudden stoppage in front, and our coxswain growled—

"Starn all!"

"What is it?" cried Mr Reardon, rising.

There was a rattle of matchlocks from our right, and Mr Reardon fell sidewise on to me.

"Hurt, sir?" I cried in agony.

"Yes, badly—no—I don't know," he cried, struggling up with his hand to his head. "Here! why has that boat stopped?"

His voice was drowned by the reports of our men's rifles, as they fired in the direction from which the shots had come; and just then a voice from the laden boat came through the semi-darkness—

"Ahoy!"

"Yes; what is it?" I said, as I saw that a man had crawled over the stack-like load.

"There's a gang in front, sir; and we're aground."

"And the tide falling," muttered Mr Reardon. "Herrick, I'm a bit hurt; get our boat close up; half the men are to come astern here, and check the enemy; the other half to help unload and get enough into our boat to lighten the other."

"Yes, sir," I said; and I gave the orders as quickly and decisively as I could.

The men responded with a cheer; and, with scarcely any confusion, our boat's head was made fast to the other's stern, and the men swarmed on to the top of the load, and began to pass down the bales rapidly from hand to hand.

Crash came a ragged volley from right ahead now; but this was answered by three rifles in the stern of the laden boat, and repeated again and again, while the strong party in the stern of ours kept up a fierce fire for a few minutes.

It was a perilous time, for we knew that if the enemy pushed forward boldly we should be at their mercy. They could come right to the edge of the bank unseen, so dense was the cover; and, working as our men were at such a disadvantage in the gloom, which was rapidly growing deeper, there was no knowing how long it would be before the first boat was sufficiently lightened to float again; it even seemed to be possible that we might not keep pace with the fall of the tide, and then perhaps we should also be aground.

"Hurt much, sir?" I said to Mr Reardon, who was now seated resting his head upon his hand.

"Don't take any notice of me, my lad," he said, pressing my hand. "Hit by a bullet. Not very bad; but I'm half stunned and confused. The men and boats, Herrick; save them."

"If I can," I thought, as I hurried forward again, and gave orders to the men to pass the silk bales that were nearest to the bows.

"Ay, ay, sir," they shouted, as readily as if I had been the captain.

From here I went back to the stern, where I found that Mr Reardon was seated now in the bottom of the boat, supported by Ching, while the men were keeping up a steady fire at every spot from which a shot or yell came.

"We're hard at it, sir," said Tom Jecks, who was handling his rifle as coolly as if it had been a capstan bar; "but I don't think we're hitting any of 'em. How's the first luff seem?"

"I don't know," I said excitedly.

"Well, sir, we're all right," said the man, "and are doing our best. You needn't stop if you can hurry the boys on forward."

It was a fact; I could do no good at all, so I hurried forward again. But even here I could do nothing; the men had their task to do of lightening the first boat, and they were working as hard as if they had been lying down in the shade all day, and just as coolly, though every now and then the rough slugs the pirates fired from their clumsy matchlocks went spattering through the trees overhead and sent down fresh showers of leaves and twigs.

But I was obliged to say something, and I shouted first one order and then another.

"That's your sort, lads," cried a cheery voice. "Down with 'em, and I'll stow. It's like bricklaying with big bricks."

"Who's that?" I said sharply, for the man's back was towards me, and it was getting quite dark where we were.

"Me it is, sir—Bob Saunders, sir. Beg pardon, sir."

"Yes; what is it?"

"Tide's going down very fast, sir, arn't it?"

"Yes; why?"

"'Cause we don't seem to get no forrarder. Hi! steady there! D'yer want to bury yer orficer?"

"Never mind me, man. Stow away; she must soon be lightened enough to make her float."

"Then we'll lighten her, sir; but don't you go and give orders for any of the stuff to be chucked overboard. It's too vallerble for that."

"Only as a last resource, Bob," I replied.

"Beg pardon, sir."

"Don't," I cried to the man who touched me. "Never mind ceremony now; go on firing."

"Yes, sir; but Tom Jecks says, sir, would you like six on us to land and have a go at the beggars?"

"No," I cried. "Keep together; we may be afloat at any moment."

"Right, sir; on'y we're all willing, if you give the word."

"I know that," I cried. "But be careful, my lads. It's a terrible position, with our chief officer down like this."

"So it is, sir," said the man, taking careful aim at a part of the bank where he thought that he saw a movement. Then, almost simultaneously, there was a flash from the place, and another from his rifle muzzle.

"Either on us hit?" he said coolly, as I clapped my hand to my ear, which felt as if a jet of cold air had touched it. "Don't think I touched him, sir, but he has cut off. I can hear him going. Not hurt, are you, sir?"

"No; a bullet must have gone close to my ear," I said.

"Oh yes; I felt that, sir. It went between us. But it's no use to take no notice o' misses."

"Well?" I said; for one of the men behind me now touched my arm, and I found it was Bob Saunders.

"We're getting dead down at the head, sir; hadn't we better begin stowing aft?"

"Yes, yes, of course," I said excitedly, and feeling annoyed that I had not thought of this myself.

"Then, if you'll make the lads ease off to starboard and port, sir, we'll soon pack a row of these here little bales between 'em. Or look here, sir! how would it be to bring 'em a bit amidships, and let us begin right astern, and build up a sort o' bulwark o' bales? They could fire from behind it when we'd done."

"Yes, capital!" I cried, once more annoyed with myself because I, a mere boy, had not the foresight of an experienced man.

'WE COULD HEAR THEM CREEPING NEARER THROUGH THE BUSHES ON OUR RIGHT.'

"No, no," I cried the next moment. "How could we get at the tiller?"

"You won't want no tiller, sir; we can row aboard easy enough, once we get out o' this fiddling little drain."

"You are right, Saunders," I said. "Go on."

All the while the men astern were keeping up a steady fire, which certainly had one effect, that of checking the enemy's advance. And now Saunders came aft with a bale on his head, keeping his balance wonderfully as he stepped over the thwarts.

"Mind yer eye, Pigtail," he cried.

"Keep back! Where are you coming?" growled a man who was loading.

"Here, matey," cried Saunders; and he plumped the bale down right across the stern.

"Hooroar!" cried Tom Jecks, stepping behind it, and resting his rifle on the top.

No more was said, the men easing off out of the way as bale after bale was brought and planted in threes, so that when six had been placed there was a fine breast-work, which formed a splendid protection for those in the stern, and this was added to, until we were fairly safe from enemies behind. But once more we could hear them creeping nearer through the bushes on our right; the firing grew more dangerous, and there was nothing for it, I felt, but to order every man in the two boats to take his piece, shelter himself behind the bales, and help to beat the enemy back.

It was a sad necessity, for I knew that the tide was falling very fast, and that before long we should be immovable; but to have kept on shifting the load and allow the enemy to get close in over our heads on the densely-clothed sides of the stream would, I knew, be madness; and the men showed how they appreciated the common-sense of the order by getting at once under cover, and then the sharp rattle of our fire was more than doubled.

But, enraged by their defeat, and doubly mortified to find that we had discovered their treasure, the pirates seemed now to have cast aside their cowardice, and were creeping in nearer and nearer, yelling to each other by way of encouragement; and, in addition to keeping up an irregular fire, they strove, I suppose, to intimidate us by beating and making a deafening noise on gongs.

"They will be too much for us," I thought, when we seemed to have been keeping up the struggle for hours, though minutes would have been a more correct definition; and, with the longing for help and counsel growing more and more intense, I was about to kneel down and speak to Mr Reardon, and ask him to try and save himself.

But I started to my feet, for there was a louder yelling than ever, and the pirates made quite a rush, which brought them abreast of us.

"Cutlasses!" I cried; and there was the rattle made in fixing them, bayonet fashion, on the rifles, when—*boom!*—*thud!*—came the roar of a heavy gun; there was a whistling shrieking in the air, and then somewhere overhead an ear-splitting crash, followed by the breaking of bushes and trampling down of grass and bamboo.

Then perfect silence, followed by a cheer from our men.

"Well done, *Teaser!*" shouted Tom Jecks.

It was a diversion which, I believe, saved us, for the enemy fled for some distance, and gave us time to go on lightening the foremost boat.

But before we had been at work many minutes there was a cheer from close at hand, and upon our answering it, another and another, with splashing of oars, and the next minute I heard Mr Brooke's voice from beyond the first boat.

Chapter Twenty Three
Saved

"Look sharp, sir," I said, after going forward, and in a few words explaining our position.

"Right, my lad. Get your men together in the stern of your boat, and keep up the fire, while we make fast and try and tow you off. Hi! quick there!" he roared; and a cheer told us that another boat was close at hand.

But my work was cut out, the men placed well under cover, and we waited listening for the first sounds of the returning enemy, while from time to time Mr Brooke's clear, short orders came out of the darkness behind us, and we knew that he had sent a party into the fixed boat to rock it from side to side. Then came a cheer, as the water rolled hissing and whispering among the reeds; there was the simultaneous plash of oars, and a creaking sound.

Then another sound from the bank of the creek, which I knew well enough.

"Say when, sir," whispered Tom Jecks. "They're a-coming on." To our astonishment, for the enemy had crept forward so silently that we had hardly heard a sound, there was a hideous yell, and a crashing volley, the bullets hissing over our heads again, and once more the gong-beating began.

"Fire!" I said.

"Yes, fire, my lads, steady—where you see the flashes of their matchlocks."

The voice came from close to my ear.

"Mr Reardon!" I cried in astonishment.

"Yes, Herrick; that bullet quite stunned me for a minute or two. I'm better now. But hasn't it grown dark rather suddenly?"

"Yes, sir," I said; for I felt in my excitement as if it would be impossible to enter into explanations then.

"But we're in motion."

"Hooray!"

Every one took up that cheer; for the combined efforts of the men who rowed the laden craft, and the tugging of two boats' crews of men straining with all their might at their stout ashen blades, had the required effect. We were indeed in motion, and going steadily down the stream.

"Ahoy, there: Mr Reardon!"

"Answer him, Herrick," said Mr Reardon; and I hailed again.

"Can you keep them off with your fire?"

"Say, yes."

"Yes; all right," I cried.

"Then we'll tow you out as fast as we can."

"Thank Heaven," I heard Mr Reardon whisper, as he crouched there, listening to the yelling, gong-beating, and firing, and with our men replying from time to time whenever there seemed a chance.

And now the bullets from the matchlocks began to patter upon the bales; for the banks were growing lower and lower, and the trees more open, but not a man was hit; and after another quarter of an hour's sharp replying we heard fresh cheering, the overshadowing trees on the banks suddenly began to grow distant. Then it became lighter still, with the stars twinkling over head and the lights of the *Teaser* apparently close at hand.

But the enemy, enraged at our escape, now crowded down to the bank and began to fire rapidly, while the men replied till the *crack crack* and *ping ping* of the rifles was silenced,—the men stopping as if by mutual consent. For there was a flash from the side of the *Teaser* right in front of us, a shell whistled over our heads and crashed in among the trees where the petty firing of the matchlocks was kept up. Then—*crash!* the shell sent shrieking amongst them exploded, and all was still but the steady beating of our oars.

"Are you much hurt, sir?" I said to Mr Reardon; but Ching took the inquiry to himself.

"Velly stiff; velly hungly," he said.

"I wasn't speaking to you," I cried angrily; for my temper seemed to have suddenly grown painfully acid, and a titter rose from among the men.

"No, Mr Herrick, scarcely at all. The bullet struck my cap-band, just above my temple, and glanced off. I can think more clearly now. How many men are hurt in this boat?"

There was no reply; and as we at the same moment glided alongside, the question seemed to be echoed from the *Teaser's* side high above our heads.

Still no reply, and the captain said sharply—

"Who is below there, Mr Reardon—Mr Brooke?"

"Ay, ay, sir," cried the latter.

"How many men did you find they had lost?"

"None, sir."

"Brought all off safely?"

"Yes, sir."

A tremendous cheer arose from the deck.

"I felt too giddy to speak just then, Herrick," said Mr Reardon. "Not one man injured except myself. It is marvellous, my lad. But there; we had plenty of poor fellows wounded aboard."

Ten minutes later two of the boats were swinging at the davits, and our two were being towed astern, as the head of the *Teaser* once more swung round, and we went down with the tide. We anchored off the mouth of the muddy river till morning, to which time was put off the hoisting on deck of the rest of the loot, the account of whose amount and probable value did more, they said, toward helping on the wounded than any of Dr Price's ministrations.

But he had serious work with two of the wounded men, who tried very hard, as he put it, to go out of hand; but he wouldn't let them. Two of the pirates did die, though, and were cast overboard, sewn up decently in hammocks, and with shot at their heels.

Seven days later we came to an anchor again off Tsin-Tsin, by which time Mr Reardon's right eye and temple were horribly discoloured, but in other respects he was quite well, and was present at what he called our second gaol delivery, for he came on deck to see the prisoners, wounded and sound, handed over to the Chinese authorities; but there was no such display of pomp as on the first occasion, one row-boat only coming alongside, with a very business-like officer, who superintended the chaining of the pirates, and bundled them down.

"Just as if they had been so many sacks," Barkins said; and he was very apt in his comparison.

I only said one word in allusion to the Chinese soldiery and their officers. That word was—

"Brutes!"

Chapter Twenty Four
A Surprise

I don't think the Chinese authorities were very grateful to us of the *Teaser*, — there, you see, I say *us*, for I did do something to help in routing out and destroying two nests of pirates; but the merchants, both Chinese and English, fêted us most gloriously, and if it had not been for Mr Reardon we three middies might have always been ashore at dinners and dances.

"But," cried Barkins, "so sure as one gets an invitation he puts his foot down."

"Yes," said Smith; "and it is such a foot."

"But it's such a pity," grumbled Barkins; "for Tsin-Tsin is after all rather a jolly place. Mr Brooke says the ball at the consul's last night was glorious, no end of Chinese swells there, and the music and dancing was fine."

"Don't be so jolly envious, Tanner," sneered Smith. "You couldn't have danced if you had gone."

"Dance better than you could," cried Barkins hotly.

"No, you couldn't. Fancy asking a young lady to waltz, and then going dot-and-go-one round the room with your game leg."

"You've a deal to talk about, Smithy; why, if you asked a lady to dance you couldn't lift your right arm to put round her waist."

"Couldn't I?" cried Smith. "Look here."

He swung his arm round me, took three steps, and dropped on to the locker, turning quite white with pain.

"Told you so," cried Barkins, springing up. "Waltz? I should just think! — oh, murder!"

He sat down suddenly to hold his leg tightly with both hands, giving Smith a dismal look.

"Oh dear!" he groaned; "what a long time it does take a wound to get well in this plaguey country. I know that knife was poisoned."

"Nonsense!" I cried, unable to restrain my mirth. "Why, you are both getting on famously."

"But Dishy might have let us go to the ball last night."

"Play fair," I said; "we've been out to seven entertainments."

"Well, what of that? They've been to a dozen. It's all old Dishy's way of showing his authority. I'm sure we all work hard when we're on duty, and run risks enough."

"Go on, you old grumbler. Aren't we to go up the river shooting on Thursday with Mr Brooke and the doctor?"

"Yes, that's right enough; but we shall be off again soon on another cruise, and get no more fun for long enough."

"I say, let's ask for a run ashore to-day."

"And get chivvied by the pigtails, same as we did down at that other place."

"Oh, but perhaps they'll be more civil here," I said.

Smith burst out laughing.

"Why, didn't they pelt you, and shy mud at the skipper?"

"Oh, if you're afraid, you can stop," I said. "Tanner and I can go."

"Afraid!" cried Smith, doubling his fist and holding it within an inch of my nose. "Say afraid again, you miserable insect, and I'll flatten you."

"Couldn't with that hand," I said, and I caught his wrist.

"Oh, don't! Murder!" he roared. "I say, you shouldn't. It's like touching one's arm with red-hot iron."

"Then be civil," I said.

"Ah, only wait. I say, Tanner, our day's coming. As soon as we're both quite strong he has got to pay for all this, hasn't he?"

"Oh, bother! I say, the skipper and Dishy are both going ashore to-day with an escort of Jacks and marines."

"Are they?" I said eagerly.

"Yes; there's some game or another on. Let's ask leave, and take old Ching with us."

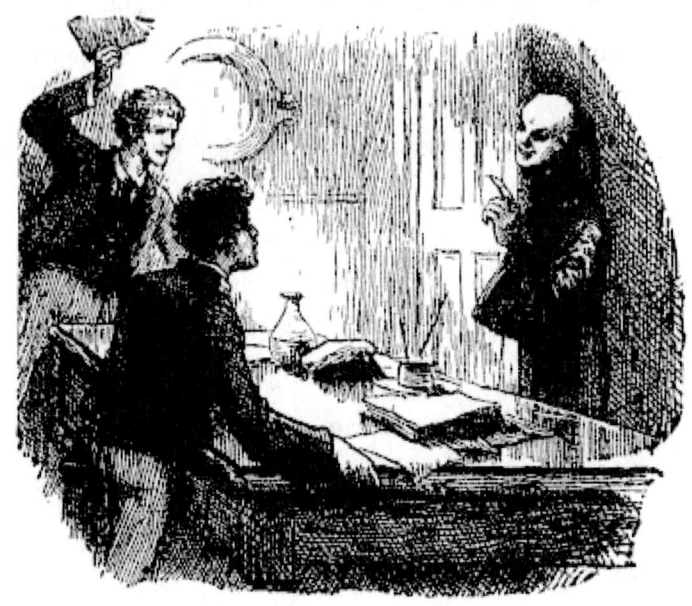

'SOMETHING TO THROW.'

"Want to try puppy-pie again?" said Smith, grinning.

"I want to do something for a change. I know! I'll go and see the doctor, and tell him we want a walk in the country to collect flowers, and ask him if he'll name them."

"Well, he can't give us leave."

"No; but he'll ask Dishy to let us off."

"Bravo!" cried Smith. "Off you go. I say, though, we must have old Ching too. You see if he don't come out in his new gown!"

"What new gown?" I said.

"Hallo! didn't you know? He went ashore yesterday and bought himself a new blue coat. Not a cotton one, but silk, real silk, my boy, and beckoned me to come and see it,—beckoned with one of his long claws. He's letting his fingernails grow now, and getting to be quite a swell."

"Oh yes; old Ching's getting quite the gentleman. He says he wrote home to his broker to sell the fancee shop. What do you think he said, Gnat?"

"How should I know?" I replied.

"That it wasn't proper for a gentleman in Queen Victolia's service to keep a fancee shop."

"Murder! Look at that!" cried Smith. "Why, you yellow-skinned old Celestial, you were listening!"

Barkins and I picked up each something to throw at the round, smooth, smiling face thrust in at the door, which was held close to the neck, so that we saw a head and nothing more.

"No flow thing at Ching," the Chinaman said softly. "Offlicer don't flow thing. Ching come in?"

"Yes," said Barkins, "come in. What is it?"

Ching entered looking very important, and gave his head a shake to make his tail fall neatly between his shoulders, and drew the long blue sleeves of his gown over the backs of his hands till only the tips of his fingers, with their very long nails, were visible.

He advanced smiling at us each in turn, and bowing his round head like a china mandarin.

"You all velly good boy?" he said softly.

"Oh yes; beauties," said Barkins. "What's up?"

"You likee ask leave go for bit walkee walkee?"

"Don't!" roared Smith. "Don't talk like a nurse to us. Why don't you speak plain English?"

"Yes; Ching speak ploper Inglis. No speakee pigeon Englis. All ploper. Interpleter. You likee go shore for walkee, see something?"

"You beggar, you were listening," cried Barkins. "How long had you been there?"

"Ching just come ask young genelman likee walkee walkee."

"Yes, allee likee walkee walkee velly much," said Barkins, imitating the Chinaman's squeak. "Why? Can you give us leave?"

Ching shook his head.

"Go ask offlicer. Go for walkee walkee, take Ching; you likee see something velly nice ploper?"

"Yes," I cried eagerly. "Can you take us to see a Chinese theatre?"

Ching closed his eyes and nodded.

"You come 'long o' Ching, I showee something velly nice ploper."

"All right," I cried. "Now, Tanner, go and try it on with the doctor."

"No, no. Ask offlicer. Doctor only give flizzick. Velly nastee. Ugh!"

Ching's round face was a study as he screwed it up to show his disgust with the doctor's preparations.

Barkins went off and returned directly.

"Well," we cried; "seen Price?" and Ching, who was squatted on the floor, looked up smiling.

"No."

"Not seen him?"

"No; I ran against Dishy, and thought I'd ask him plump."

"And you did?"

"Yes."

"What did he say?"

"I know," cried Smith; "that we were always going out."

"That's it exactly."

"And he won't let us go?" I said in a disappointed tone.

"Who says so?" cried Barkins, changing his manner. "The old chap was in splendid fettle, and he smiled,—now, now, don't both of you be so jolly full of doubts. On my honour as an officer and a gentleman, he smiled and clapped me on the shoulder."

"Yes, my lad, of course," he said. "We shall be off again soon, and then it will be all work and no play again, and we mustn't make Jack a dull boy, must we?"

"He's going off his head," said Smith.

"Let him go, then," I cried, "if it makes him like this."

"Don't chatter so, Gnat," cried Smith. "I say, did he really say we might go?"

"Yes; and that we ought to start at once before the day grew hotter, and that we were to take great care of ourselves."

"Hurra!"

"And be sure and wash our faces and our hands before we started," added Barkins.

"Get out; I can see where it joins," I cried. "But did he say any more?"

"Only that we were to mind and not get into any trouble with the people, and that we had better take Ching."

"Yes," said that individual gravely. "Much better take Ching. Velly useful take care."

"To be sure," I cried, full of excitement at the idea of a run through the mazes of the quaint town, and the prospect of seeing a Chinese performance. "I say, Ching," I cried, striking an attitude, "take us where you can give us a tune, 'Ti—ope—I—ow.'"

"Yes; velly nicee music," he said, nodding and smiling. "Ching takee see something velly good. You leady?"

"In five minutes," cried Barkins. "Gnat, go and tell them to have the boat ready. Mr Reardon said we were to be rowed ashore."

"Ching leady in five minutes," said the interpreter, running towards the door.

"Eh? Why, you are ready," said Smith.

"No. Go put on new blue silk flock. Leady dilectly."

Ten minutes later we were being rowed ashore, to be landed at the wharf where we met with so unpleasant an attack a short time before. But there was no mob of idlers there now, and we stepped ashore, leaving the good-natured-looking crew smiling at us, and giving the shops many a longing look, as they pushed off and began to row back at once.

"Plenty time," said Ching. "You likee fust go lestaulant—eatee, dlinkee, spend plize-money?"

"Can't spend what we haven't yet got, Ching," said Barkins. "What do you say, lads? I'm hungry again, aren't you?"

Smith sighed.

"I'm always hungry," he said.

"Of course you are. I believe he's hollow all through, Gnat. How do you feel?"

"As if I haven't had any breakfast," I said earnestly.

Ching smiled.

"Velly much nicee bleakfast all along o' Ching."

He led the way in and out among the narrow streets, apparently again as much at home as in his own city; and it was hard work to keep from stopping to gaze at the hundreds of objects which attracted and set me longing to make purchases to take home for curiosities. But Ching bustled us along.

"No time now. Come along get good bleakfast. Wantee good bleakfast before go to see gland show."

"Here, what is it you are going to take us to see, Ching?" cried Barkins— "all right; I wasn't talking to you," he added, as a couple of Chinamen turned round to gaze at the young outer barbarian.

"You waitee," cried Ching, smiling; "all velly ploper gland. You likee see the show."

"Oh, all right. Where's the restaurant?"

"Nex' stleet," said Ching; and after a few minutes he turned into a showy-looking eating-house, where his blue silk gown and long nails seemed to command the most profound respect from the attendants; and where, after laying down the law very stringently to Ching, that we were to have neither dog, cat, nor rat, we resigned ourselves to our fate, and ate birds'-nest soup, shark-fin, and a variety of what Barkins called messes, with midshipmen appetites.

Ching smiled, and seemed to be very proud of our performance.

"You all eat dlink velly much," he said, as we gave up, defeated. "You all velly quite full?" he said, rubbing his hands carefully, so as not to injure his long nails.

"Yes, full up, and the hatches battened down," cried Barkins. "Now then, ask for the bill. How much apiece?"

Ching smiled and nodded his head.

"You come have bleakfast 'long o' Ching. Ching velly glad to see you; Ching pay."

"What? nonsense!" cried Smith, while we others stared.

"Yes; Ching plenty money. Captain gave Ching plenty plize-money; make him velly happy to see young offlicer to bleakfast."

"Oh, but we can't let him pay for us, Smithy," cried Barkins.

"No, of course not," we chorussed.

"Ching velly much hurt you want to pay," he said, with dignity.

"But—" I cried.

"You ask Ching bleakfast like Chinese genelman another time, make Ching velly glad. Come along, makee haste, see gland show."

"But the bill isn't paid," I cried.

"Ching pay long time 'go," he said, rising; and there was nothing for it but to follow him out and along three or four streets to where there was a dense crowd in front of a gateway in a high mud wall.

There were some soldiers there too, and Ching walked up full of importance, showed them some kind of paper, when one, who appeared to be their officer, spoke to those under him, and they cleared a way for us to pass to the gate.

Here Ching knocked loudly, and the gate was opened by another soldier; the paper was shown; and an important-looking official came up, looked at us, and made way for us to enter.

"It's all right," said Smith. "Ching knows the manager. It will be a private box."

The official pointed to our left, and Ching led the way behind a kind of barricade where there were seats erected, and, selecting a place, he smilingly made us sit down.

"Ching know gleat mandalin," he said. "Askee let come see gland show."

"But what's it going to be?" I asked, as I looked curiously round the square enclosure surrounded by a high wall, and with seats and pens on three sides. "I thought we were coming to a theatre!"

"No," said Ching, smiling. "Velly gland show; wait."

We waited, and saw that the space in front of us was neatly sanded, that posts stood up here and there. In other places there were cross bars, and in two there were ropes hanging.

"I know!" cried Barkins; "he needn't make such a jolly mystery of it. It's Chinese athletic sports. Look, there's the band coming."

He pointed to a military-looking party marching in with drums, gongs, and divers other instruments; and almost at the same time quite a crowd of well-dressed people entered, and began to take the different places reserved behind the barriers.

Then a body of soldiers, with clumsy spears and shields, marched in and formed up opposite the band, the place filling up till only the best places, which were exactly opposite to us, remained empty.

"You're right, Tanner," said Smith just then; "but they're military athletic sports. I say, here come the grandees."

For in procession about twenty gorgeously-arrayed officials came marching in, and the next moment I gave Barkins a dig in the ribs.

"Look," I said.

"All right; I see. Well, we needn't mind. But I say, what a game if we hadn't got leave!"

"I say," whispered Smith, "look over there. The skipper and old Dishy! This was where they were coming, then; they'll see us directly."

"Let 'em," said Barkins, as the party settled themselves. "Now then, we're all here. All in to begin. We ought to have a programme. Here, Ching, what's the first thing they do?"

"Ching no quite sure; p'laps lichi."

"Lichi?" I said.

"You don't know? You see velly gland—velly ploper for bad, bad man."

He turned away to speak to a Chinese officer close at hand, while we began to feel wondering and suspicious, and gazed at each other with the same question on our lips.

Ching turned to us again, and I being nearest whispered—

"I say, what place is this? What are they going to do?"

"Bring out allee wicked men. Choppee off head."

Chapter Twenty Five
The Entertainment

I felt as it were a sudden jar run through me when I heard Ching's words. It was as if I had been awakened by a sudden revelation. This, then, was the grand show he had contrived for us as a treat! It was all clear enough: our officers had been invited to the execution of the pirates we had taken, and conceiving, with all a Chinaman's indifference to death, that we three lads, who had been present at their capture, would consider it as a great treat to be witnesses of the punishment awarded by the Government, Ching had contrived to get permission for us to be present.

I glanced at the Tanner, who had grasped the situation, and was screwing his face up so as to look perfectly unconcerned; but it was a dismal failure, for I could see a peculiar twitching going on at the corners of his eyes, and he passed his tongue rapidly over his lips and went through the action of swallowing as if his mouth and throat were dry.

I next looked at Smithy, whose eyes showed more white than usual, and whose complexion was of a sickly-green, just as I had seen it during some very rough weather we had going down the Channel on first starting for this voyage.

How I looked I have only Barkins' word for, and he told me afterwards that I seemed as if I was waiting for my turn to suffer with the pirates.

After the sharp glance I gave at my fellows neither of us stirred, but sat there as if petrified. I was horror-stricken, and there was a strong impulse upon me to jump up and run out, but shame and the dread of being considered cowardly kept me in my place. In fact, as after-confessions made clear, we were absolutely stunned, and I don't think we could have stirred had we made up our minds to go.

Then I felt dizzy, and the brilliant group of officials and military magnates and judges opposite to where we sat grew blurred and strange-looking in the bright sunshine.

At last I felt as if I must argue out the question, and with my teeth set firm, and my eyes fixed upon the sandy ground of the enclosure, some such thoughts as these ran through my brain— "It is only just that these men should suffer for their horrible crimes, for they are more dangerous than venomous serpents, and I suppose that Captain Thwaites and Lieutenant Reardon are obliged to come as a kind of duty; but we three came under the idea that we were to see some kind of exhibition, and old Ching did it out of kindness, not knowing of what kind of stuff we were made. I shan't stop."

There I paused to fight with other ideas.

"Tanner and Blacksmith will laugh at me and think I am a coward. Well, let them," I said to myself at last. "It isn't cowardice not to wish to see such a horror as this. I didn't feel cowardly when they were shooting at us down in the creek, and it would be far more cowardly to sit here against my will without speaking. I will tell them I want to go."

I should think that every lad of the age I then was, will pretty well understand my feelings, and what a bitter thing it was to turn and confess what they would jeer at and call "funk." It was hard work indeed.

"I don't care," I muttered. "I know they'll protest and say they don't want to come, but be very glad to come away all the time. I will speak."

Just then that horrible Chinaman turned to me with his round fat face, all smiling and delighted.

"You velly glad you come?" he said. "You feel velly happy?"

My mind was made up at this, and I spoke out.

"No," I said in a husky whisper. "I didn't know we had come to see this. I shall go."

"What?" said Barkins, with a forced laugh. "Look here, Blacksmith, he's showing the white feather."

"Ho! ho!" laughed Smith. "Come, Gnat, I thought you had a little more spirit in you. Serve the beggars right."

"Yes, I know that," I said firmly enough now, as I looked at their faces, which, in spite of the masks they had assumed, looked ghastly; "and I daresay I haven't pluck enough to sit it out. But I don't care for your grins; I'm not ashamed to say that I shall go."

"Oh, well, if you feel that it would upset you," said Barkins, in a tone of voice full of protest, "I suppose that we had better see you off, and go somewhere else."

"Poof!" ejaculated Smith in a low tone. "Look at him, Gnat; he's in just as much of a stew as you are. Well, it's too bad of you both, but if you must go, why, I suppose we must."

"You beggar!" snarled Barkins angrily. "Why, you're worse than I am. Look at him, Gnat! There, I will own it. I felt sick as soon as I knew what was going to happen, but I won't be such a bumptious, bragging sneak as he is. Look at his face. It's green and yellow. He wants to go worse than we do."

Smith did not seem to be listening, for his starting eyes were fixed upon the far right-hand gate, over which there was a kind of pagoda, and he rose from his seat.

"Come on at once," he whispered, "they're going to begin."

"Confessed!" whispered Barkins, pinching my knee. "Come on then quick, Gnat, old man; it's too horrid."

We all rose together, and were in the act of turning when a low hoarse murmur rose from behind, and we saw that a crowd of angry faces were gazing at us, and that they were nearly all armed men.

But before we had recovered from our surprise, Ching had caught my arm and pressed me to my seat.

"No go now," he whispered, with a look of alarm in his face, and he leaned over me and dragged my companions down in turn. "No can go now. Allee gate fasten. Makee blave velly angly and dlaw sword; fightee fightee. Ching velly solly. Must stop now."

There was a low hissing noise all about us, and threatening looks, while a fierce man in embroidered silk said something in his own tongue to Ching, who answered humbly, and then tamed to us and whispered—

"Small-button mandalin say make big-button peacock-feather mandalin velly angly. You no sit still. Sh! sh!"

"We must sit it out, boys," I said, with a shudder; "but we need not look."

My words were quite correct to a certain extent, but as my companions, who now looked more ghastly than ever, sank back in their seats, I felt compelled to gaze across to where I could now see a red table exactly facing me. Then a movement to the right caught my attention, and through the far gateway, and lowering it a little as he passed under the archway, rode an officer with a yellow silk banner, upon which were large black Chinese characters. Behind him came some more showily-dressed officials; and then, in a kind of sedan chair, one whom I at once saw to be the chief mandarin, for whom we had been waiting.

He was carried across to the front, where he alighted and walked slowly across to the red table, followed by sword, spear, and matchlock men, who, as he took his place at the table, ranged themselves on either side facing us, and completing a spectacle that, seen there in the bright light, strongly suggested the opening of some grand pantomime.

I remember thinking this, and then shuddering at the horrible thought, and at the same time I began wondering at the intense interest I could not help taking in what was going on.

Two more grandees in chairs of state followed, and then there was a pause. I could see that our officers were politely saluted, and that care was taken that no one should be in front of them. And now came the more exciting part of the terrible exhibition.

Suddenly there was the loud booming of a gong, and the head of an escort of spearmen marched through the gateway, followed by a group of men in twos, each pair bearing a long bamboo pole, from which, hanging in each case like a scale, was a large basket, and heavily chained in each basket was a man, whom we knew at once to be one of the pirates we had captured, without Ching whispering to us—

"Velly bad men, killee evelybody. They killee now."

My eyes would not close. They were fascinated by the horrible procession; and I now saw, just in front of the bearers, a tall-looking bare-headed man carrying a large bright sword, curved in the fashion we see in old pictures of the Turkish scimitar, a blade which increases in width from the hilt nearly to the end, where it is suddenly cut off diagonally to form a sharp point.

Behind this man marched five more, the procession moving right to the front between us and the brilliant party whose centre was the principal mandarin.

I now saw, too, that every one of the miserable culprits was ticketed or labelled, a bamboo upon which a piece of paper was stuck being attached to his neck and head.

A low murmur ran round among the spectators, as, at a signal from the man with the great sword, who I saw now must be the executioner, the bearers stopped, and with a jerk threw the poles off their shoulders into their hands, bumped the baskets heavily down upon the ground, and shot the malefactors out as unceremoniously as if they had been so much earth.

I heard Barkins draw a deep breath, and saw Smith leaning forward and gazing wildly at the scene, while I felt my heart go *throb throb* heavily, and found myself wishing that I had not shared in the capture of the wretched men.

The chief mandarin then turned to the officer on horseback, who carried the imperial yellow flag, said a few words in a low tone, and he in turn pushed his horse a little forward to where the executioner was waiting, and evidently conveyed the mandarin's orders.

Then suddenly the pirates, as if moved by one consent, struggled to their feet and began shouting.

Ching placed his lips close to my ear—

"Say, please no choppee off head. Velly bad men, killee lot always; velly bad."

And now I felt that the time had come to close my eyes, but they remained fixed. I could not avert my gaze from a scene which was made more horrible by a struggle which took place between the first pirate of the long row in which they stood and the executioner.

The man shouted out some words angrily, and Ching interpreted them in my ear, his explanation being in company with a strange surging noise—

'THE SWORD FLASHED.'

"Say he come back and killee him if he choppee off head. Oh, he velly bad man."

But quickly, as if quite accustomed to the task, two of the executioner's assistants rushed at the pirate; one of them forced him down into a kneeling position; they then seized his long tail, drew it over his head and hung back, thus holding the pirate's neck outstretched; lastly, I saw the executioner draw back, the sword flashed, I heard a dull thud—the head fell, and the body rolled over on one side.

Before I could drag my eyes from the horror there was the same terrible sound again, and another head fell upon the ground, while, with a rapidity that was astounding, the assistants passed from one culprit to the other in the long row, the miserable wretches making not the slightest resistance, but kneeling patiently in the position in which they were thrust, while *whish, whish, whish,* the executioner lopped off their heads at one blow.

"Allee done," said Ching. "Execution man have velly much plactice."

He said this to me, but I made no reply, for the whole place seemed to be going round and round.

"You thinkee they all come back again and have junk? Go kill shoot evelybody, pilate ghost-man?"

"No," I said hoarsely; "can we go now?"

"Velly soon. Gleat clowd all along gate. Lookee, Mis' Tanner go s'eep."

These words roused me, and I turned to Barkins, who was lying back with his eyes nearly closed and looking ghastly, while Smith sat staring straight before him, with his hands grasping the seat on either side, in a stiff, awkward position.

"Here, Smithy," I said, "quick, Tanner has fainted;" but he took no notice, and I whispered to him angrily—

"Get up. It's all over now. Come and help me. Don't let these horrible people see Tanner like this."

He turned to me then, and let his eyes fall on our messmate.

"Can you get me a drink of water, Ching?" he murmured.

"Yes, d'leckly; wait lit' bit. Po' Mr Barki' Tanner leg velly bad, makee sick. You' alm velly bad still?"

"Very bad; it throbs," murmured Smith.

"Ah, yes! Wait lit' bit and no clowd. Ching take you have cup flesh tea, and quite well d'leckly. You not likee execution?"

I shook my head.

"Velly good job cut allee head off. No go killee killee, burn ship no more."

"We're not used to seeing such things," I said weakly, as I supported Barkins to keep him from slipping to the ground.

"You no go see execution when Queen Victolia cut off bad men's head?"

I shook my head.

"Ah, I see," said Ching. "Me tink you have velly gleat tleat. But I see, not used to see. Velly blave boy, not mind littlee bit next time."

"What's the matter? Don't, doctor. It's getting well now."

It was Barkins who spoke, and his hands went suddenly to his injured leg, and held it, as he bent over towards it and rocked himself to and fro.

"Throbs and burns," he said, drawing in his breath as if in pain. "I—I—"

He looked round wildly.

"I remember now," he said faintly. "Don't laugh at me, you chaps. I turned sick as a dog as soon as that butchering was over. I never felt like this over the fighting. I say, Gnat, did I faint right away?"

"Yes, dead!" I said; "I was nearly as bad."

"Enough to make you. But oh, my leg, how it does sting! I say, isn't it queer that it should come on now? Did the fainting do it?"

"I dunno," said Smith hastily, "but my arm aches horribly. I say, do let's get away from here, or I shall be obliged to look over yonder again."

"Yes, I'm all right again now," said Barkins quietly. "Let's get away. I say, lads, it's of no use to be humbugs; we did all feel precious bad, eh?"

We looked at each other dolefully.

"Yes, let's get away," I said. "I thought we were coming out for a jolly day."

Barkins shuddered and now stood up.

"Yes," he said; "I hope the skipper liked it. Can you see him now?"

"Skipper? Cap'n?" said Ching, whose ears were always sharp enough to catch our words. "Gone along, Mr Leardon. Make gland plocession all away back to palace. You go sail, soon catch more pilate."

"I hope, if we do," said Smith, "that we shall not bring back any prisoners."

The enclosure was thinning fast now, as we walked toward the gateway by which we had entered, where a strong body of soldiers had been on guard over the barricades, in case of an attempt being made by the pirates' friends to rescue them, and we saw plainly enough that had we wanted there would have been no getting away.

"You likee go in and see plison?" said Ching insinuatingly. "Plenty bad men lock up safe."

"No, thank you," I said eagerly. "Let's get out of this, and go and have some tea."

"Yes, plenty tea. Ching show way."

The Chinese soldiers stared at us haughtily as we walked by, and I drew myself up, hoping that no one there had witnessed our weakness, for if they had I knew that they could not feel much respect for the blue-jackets who hunted down the scoundrels that infested their seas.

Both Barkins and Smith must have felt something after the fashion that I did, for they too drew themselves up, returned the haughty stares, and Barkins stopped short to look one truculent savage fellow over from head to foot, especially gazing at his weapons, and then, turning coolly to me, he said, with a nod in the man's direction—

"Tidy sort of stuff to make soldiers off, Gnat, but too heavy."

The man's eyes flashed and his hand stole toward his sword hilt.

"'Tention!" roared Barkins with a fierce stamp, and though the order was new to the guard, he took it to be a military command and stepped back to remain stiff and motionless.

"Ha! that's better," cried Barkins, and he nodded and then passed on with us after Ching, whose eyes bespoke the agony of terror he felt.

"Come long quickee," he whispered excitedly. "Very big blave that fellow. Killee—fightee man. You no 'flaid of him?"

"Afraid? No," said Barkins shortly. "There, let's have this tea."

Ching glanced round once, and we were about to imitate his example, but he said excitedly—

"No, no, don't lookee. Big blave talkee talkee soldier, and tink Inglis offlicer 'flaid. Walkee past."

He led us as quickly as he could get us to go towards the tea-house he sought, and I must own that I was only too anxious about the Chinese guards to help feeling in a good deal of perturbation lest they should feel that they had been insulted, and follow us so as to take revenge. Hence I was glad enough to get within the tea-house's hospitable walls, and sat there quite content to go on sipping the fragrant infusion for long enough.

I suppose we were there quite an hour and a half drinking tea, until we were satisfied, and then passing a look round to draw attention to our interpreter, who sat back with his eyes half closed, sipping away cupful after cupful, till Smith whispered to me that he thought he had kept correct account.

"How many do you think Ching has had?" he whispered.

"Don't know; nearly a dozen?"

"Fifty-three, or thereabouts," whispered Smith.

But I did not believe him, and I do not think he believed himself.

"Now, you likee go 'long see somethin' else?" said Ching, when he had really drunk tea enough.

"Yes," said Barkins, "I feel ready. What do you say to going to see the *Teaser*, lads?" he continued.

"I'm willing," said Smith. "I want to lie down."

"You ready, Gnat?"

"Oh yes," I replied. "I don't feel as if I could enjoy anything to-day."

"Right, then. No, Ching; back on board ship."

"You go velly soon? Now?"

"Yes, directly."

Ching smiled—he had a habit of smiling at everything nearly, and we paid our reckoning and followed him down to the landing-place, to arrive there just in time to see the barge with the captain and his escort gliding rapidly away toward the ship.

"Too soon findee boat," said Ching. "Tellee man come when sun go out of sight."

"Yes, and that means two hours good," said Barkins. "Look here, Ching, hire a boat cheap. Get a fellow with a sailing-boat, if you can."

"Yes," said the Chinaman, nodding his head in a satisfied way, "Good boat—velly nice boat—boat with velly big sail fly over water, eh?"

"Yes, that's it," said Barkins. "And look sharp, for there are a lot of low blackguardly-looking fellows coming up, and we don't want another row."

Barkins was quite right, for, as in our own seaports, there were plenty of roughs about, and whether in blue frocks and pith boots or British rags, the loafer is much the same. Ching saw at a glance that the sooner we were off the better, and hurried us a little way along the wharf till he saw a boat that seemed suitable.

"You all get in velly quick," he said.

"But we must make a bargain with the man."

"Plesently," he replied, as we hurried in, and he ordered the man in charge to put off.

The man began to protest volubly, but Ching rose up, and with a fierce look rustled his new coat and sat down again, with the result that the man loosened the rope which held his boat to the side, and the swift tide began to bear us away directly, the man hoisting up a small matting-sail and then meekly thrusting an oar over, with which to steer.

"Why, what did you say to him, Ching?" I asked; and the interpreter smiled, and wrinkled up his eyes till he resembled a piece of old china on a chimney-piece.

"Ching say velly lit' bit; only shake his new coat till common man see it silk. He feel velly much flighten all a same, as if big-button mandalin get in him boat."

"And what shall we have to pay him?"

"P'laps nothing 'tall."

"Oh, nonsense!" I said. "We must pay him the proper fare."

"Velly well, pay him ploper money."

I anticipated trouble, but when we got to the side and a dollar was handed to the man, his heavy round face lit up with pleasure, and he said something aloud.

"What does he say, Ching?" I asked.

"Say velly glad, and didn't tink he get anything 'tall."

We made the best of our way below, fully expecting that, if the captain and Mr Reardon saw us, they would take us to task for being at the execution, and ask; us how we dared to follow them there. But, as luck had it, they had been too much occupied by the horrible affair in progress, and our presence had escaped them. But it was a long while before I could get the scene out of my head or think of our trip ashore that day as anything but a horrible mistake.

Chapter Twenty Six
"Man Overboard"

It was a great relief to us all to find that our visit to the Chinese prison had not been noticed. We of course kept silence about it, not even telling Mr Brooke, who was the most friendly of our officers, and we had the satisfaction of finding that Ching obeyed our orders, and kept his peace.

I used to be rather sorry for him, his position being so solitary on board. For he could not make himself at home with the sailors in the forecastle, and though as frank, good-hearted fellows as ever lived, they seemed to look upon him only in one way, that of being a butt for their sharp witticisms, an object upon whom they were to play practical jokes.

Consequently I used often, when I found him standing alone by the bulwarks watching the shore, to edge up to him, and stop to talk; our conversation being directed by me toward some little unpleasantry in the forecastle, which if he had complained about to the first lieutenant, there would have been a severe reprimand.

I remember one of these occasions, when Ching came flying up out of the hatch, followed by a roar of laughter, and as he reached the deck, *clang-clang* went something against the sides of the hatch; but Ching paid no heed, running forward till he was right up by the side of the bowsprit.

I followed quickly, feeling angry on the man's behalf.

"What's the matter?" I cried. "What have they been doing?"

"No know," he said rather pitifully, as he stood there trembling. "Done something. Thlow tin-kettle after."

"But what for? What were you doing?"

"Doing? fass 'sleep, dleam 'bout big fly come and bite leg. Jump up and lun. Then thlow kettle after."

"Here, let's look," I said; for as he shook his head there was the same hollow sound again, just like that made by a tin sheep-bell.

"Why, they've tied it to you," I said sharply.

"Tie to Ching flock? Don't matter. Not bess blue silkee."

"Here, let me see," I cried. "Turn round."

He turned sharply, and something banged against the bulwark.

"What a shame!" I cried. "They've tied the old canister to your tail."

"Tie canny all along Ching tow-chang?" he cried.

"Yes, and it's a rascally shame."

"Yes, allee lascally shame," he said, nodding his head. "Not hurt velly. Only flighten velly much, makee lun fass."

"Stand still, and I'll soon have it off," I cried, whipping out my knife.

"No, no," he cried, dragging the long plait from my hand; "mightee cut tow-chang, and that velly dleadful. Take long time glow."

"Very well, then. I'll unfasten it, and show it to Mr Reardon."

"What for? make Mis' Leardon velly angly, scold jolly sailor boy. Then they not like Ching 'tall."

"But it's too bad; treating you just as if you were a dog."

"Jolly sailor boy tie tin-pot dog tow-chang? No. Mr Hellick make laugh. Dog not got tow-chang."

"No," I said, trying very hard to get the pot off, "but dogs have got tails."

"Yes, got tails. Don't tellee, make no good. Didn't hurt Ching."

"But it's an insult to you," I said. "Any one would think they were a pack of boys."

"Yes, jolly sailor boy. You no makee come off?"

"No," I said. "They've made a big hole through the bottom of the canister, pushed the end of the tail—"

"Tow-chang."

"Well, tow-chang, if you like to call it so—through into the inside, and then hammered the tin back round it and made it as fast as fast. Here, I shall have to cut it, Ching."

"No, no," he cried, seizing the canister. "No cuttee piece of tow-chang."

"Then how are we to get it off?"

"Don't know, Mr Hellick; look velly bad?"

"Horrible—absurd; every one will laugh at you."

"Yes, velly bad. Ching put it in pocket."

"Oh, you're there, are you?" I cried, as Tom Jecks came cautiously on deck. "I should have thought that a man of your years would have known better than to help torment this poor Chinaman."

"Not velly poor," he whispered. "Ching got fancee shop. Plenty plize-money now."

"Didn't have nought to do with it," growled Tom Jecks.

"Then who did, sir?"

"Dunno, sir; some o' the boys. I was caulking till they wakened me wi' laughing."

"But you saw it done?"

"No, sir; it was all done aforehand. They'd turned his tail into a bull-roarer, and if you was to swing it round now like a windmill, it would make no end of a row."

"Silence, sir," I cried. "It's disgraceful."

"Lor', sir, they on'y meant it for a bit of a lark."

"Then they should lark among themselves, and not take advantage of a poor foreigner whom they ought to protect."

"Yes, sir, that's right enough. But he were asleep, and it didn't hurt him till one on 'em stuck a pin in his leg to waken him up."

"Ah!" I cried. "Who did?"

"Well, sir," said Tom Jecks. "Now you do puzzle me above a bit. It was one o' the lads, because the pin must have gone into his leg, for he squeaked out and then run up the ladder with the tin-pot banging about right and left, but who it was stuck that pin in, it were so dark that I couldn't say."

"You mean that you won't say, Tom?"

"Well, sir, you're orficer, and I'm on'y AB, and I shan't contradict you; have it that way if you like."

"I shall say no more, but we'll see what Mr Reardon says when he hears about it."

"Why, Mr Herrick, sir, yo' wouldn't go and tell upon the poor lads, would you? It were on'y a bit of a game, were it, Mr Ching?"

"No, only bit game," said the Chinaman.

"There, you hear, sir. There wasn't no bones broke."

"Hold your tongue, sir."

"Cert'n'y, sir."

"And come here."

Tom Jecks stepped forward obsequiously.

"Look, the tin sticks all round fast into the tail as if it were a rabbit trap."

"Ay, sir, it do; and if I might say so, they managed it very cleverly."

"Cleverly?"

"Yes, sir. If I'd been doing it, I should on'y have thought of tying it on with a bit o' spun-yarn; but this here tin holds it wonderful tight."

"How are we to get it off?"

"Oh, I can soon get it off," cried Tom Jecks, who seemed to be imbued with the same notion as Alexander of old, who unsheathed his sword to cut the Gordian knot. For he hauled out his knife by the lanyard, opened the blade with his teeth, and took a step forward, but Ching held the canister behind him and dodged round me.

"Steady, my lad," growled Tom Jecks, "it arn't a operation. Stand by."

"No, no, no!" shrieked Ching.

"Steady, my lad, I'll soon have it off. I won't cut down to the bone."

"No, no!" cried Ching, who was excited and alarmed, and who now began chattering in his own tongue, all *pang ang nong wong ong*, and a series of guttural sounds, while I could do nothing for laughing, but had to stand like a post for Ching to dodge behind.

"Why don't you stand by, messmate?" growled Tom Jecks. "You can't go through life with that there tin-kettle tied to your tail. Fust one as see yer will be calling, 'Mad dog.'"

By this time the watch had come to see what was going on, and I now began to feel sorry for the Chinaman.

"Here, Ching," I said. "Come down below."

But he was too much alarmed for the moment to listen to my words, expecting every moment as he was that some one would make a snatch at his tail, to obviate which accident he was now holding the canister tightly beneath his arm, and looking wildly round for a way to escape.

"Hadn't we better have it took off, sir?" said Tom Jecks, and there was a roar of laughter. "Let's ketch him and take him to the doctor."

"No, no!" cried Ching, dodging round me again, for Tom Jecks, to the delight of the others, made a snatch at him.

"You'll be a deal more comfortable, messmate—you know you will. Here, let's have it?"

Tom Jecks made another snatch at him, but Ching avoided it, and to save him from further annoyance I too made a snatch.

Poor fellow, interpreter though he was, he misinterpreted my intentions. He tore away from my grasp and made a rush forward, but several men were coming in that direction, and he dashed back to find himself faced by Tom Jecks again. In his desperation he charged right at the sailor, lowering his head as he did so, and striking him with so much force that Tom Jecks went down sprawling, and Ching leaped over him.

There was no way open to him for escape, as it seemed, and he made a rush for the side, leaped up, was on the bulwarks in an instant, and made a snatch at the foremast shrouds as if to climb up into the rigging, when either his foot slipped or his long loose cotton jacket caught in something, I don't know how it was, but one moment I saw him staggering, the next there was the terrible cry of "Man overboard" raised as I rushed toward the side, heard the splash, and got upon the bulwark in time to see the agitated water.

That was all.

It was rapidly getting dark, the tide was running swiftly seaward, and even if the Chinaman could swim it seemed very doubtful whether he could maintain himself long, hampered as he was by his loose clinging clothes.

But at the raising of the cry, "Man overboard," there is not much time lost on board a man-of-war. A crew leaped into the boat; the falls were seized; and in a minute the keel touched the water, and I found myself, as I stood on the bulwark holding on by a rope, called upon to direct those who had gone.

"Which way, sir? See him?"

I could only answer no, and then reply to Mr Reardon, who came up panting.

"Who is it?" he cried. "Mr Herrick?"

"No, sir, I'm here," I shouted. "It's the interpreter."

"And what business had he up on the hammock-rail?" roared the lieutenant as he climbed up there himself. "Steady, my lads, he can't be far."

At that moment there was a flash, and a brilliant blue-light burst out on the surface of the black water, sending a glare all round from where it floated on the trigger life-buoy, which had been detached and glided away astern, while directly after a second blue-light blazed out from the stern of the boat, showing the men dipping their oars lightly, and two forward and two astern shading their eyes and scanning the flashing and sparkling water.

"Can't you see him?" roared the lieutenant.

"No, sir."

We leaped downward, hurried right aft where the captain and the other officers were now gathered, and the orders were given for a second boat to be lowered and help to save the poor fellow.

"He ought to float, sir," said Mr Reardon in answer to some remark from the captain. "He's fat enough."

Then he began shouting orders to the men to row to and fro; and my heart sank as I vainly searched the lit-up water, for there was no sign of the unfortunate Chinaman.

"What a horrible ending to a practical joke!" I thought, and a bitter feeling of disappointment assailed me, as I asked myself why I had not gone in the second boat to help save the poor fellow.

Perhaps it was vanity, but in those exciting moments I felt that if I had been there I might have seen him, for it never occurred to me that I had a far better chance of seeing him from my post of vantage high up on that quarter-deck rail.

"See him yet?"

"No, sir!" — "No, sir!"

The first hail loudly from close by, the other from far away where the blue-lights shone.

"Bless my soul!" cried Mr Reardon, with an angry stamp. "I can't understand it. He must have come up again."

"Unless his pockets were heavily laden," said the captain, going to where Mr Reardon stood. "These men carry a great deal about them under their long loose clothes. Some heavy copper money, perhaps. A very little would be enough to keep a struggling man down."

"Ha!" ejaculated Mr Reardon, while I shivered at the idea of poor old Ching coming to so terrible an end.

"A glass here!" cried Mr Reardon, and one was handed up to him.

"Try the life-buoy," cried the captain.

"Bless me, sir, I was going to," retorted the lieutenant irritably; "but the idiot who uses this glass ought to be turned out of the service for being short-sighted. I shall never get it to the right focus."

The captain gave a dry cough, and I turned round sharply, expecting to hear some angry exclamation.

"No," cried Mr Reardon, "he is not clinging to the life-buoy. I wouldn't for anything that it should have happened. Poor fellow! Poor fellow!"

"Ay, poor fellow!" muttered Captain Thwaites. "Any use to lower another boat, Reardon?"

"No, sir, no," cried the lieutenant, "or I would have had one down. Ahoy there!" he roared. "Light another blue!"

"Ay, ay, sir!" came from far away, for the tide ran hissing by our sides in full rush for the sea, and the third blue-light which blazed out looked smaller and smaller, while those of the first boat and the life-buoy began to show faint, and then all at once that on the buoy seemed to go out.

"That blue-light ought to have burned longer on the buoy," cried Mr Reardon.

"They've picked up the buoy and laid it across the bows of the boat," said Mr Brooke, who was watching through his night-glass, and at that moment the light blazed out again like a star.

And still the halos shed by the lights grew fainter and fainter. Then one light burned out, and the lieutenant stamped with anger, but there was no cause for his irritation. Another flashed out directly.

The boats were too far away now for us to see much of what was going on, the heads of the men growing blurred, but we saw that they were zig-zagging across the tide, and we listened in vain for the hail and the cheer that should accompany the words—

"Got him, sir!"

The buzz of conversation among the men, who clustered on deck, in the shrouds and tops, grew fainter, and I was thinking whether I was very much to blame, and if I could in any way have saved the poor fellow. Then I began thinking of the men in the forecastle, and their punishment for being the cause, in their boyish way of playing tricks, of the poor Chinaman's death.

I wouldn't be Tom Jecks for all the world, I muttered, and then I turned cold and shuddered, as the hope, faint though it was, of Ching being picked up went out like one of the lights that now disappeared; for Captain Thwaites said sadly—

"I'm afraid we must recall the boats, Mr Reardon."

"Yes, sir," said the lieutenant in a husky voice. "I don't think any one is to blame about the attempt to save the poor fellow, sir. The life-buoy was let go, and the boat lowered promptly; the dishipline of the men was good."

"Excellent, Mr Reardon. I have nothing to say there. It would have been better perhaps to have lowered down the second boat sooner. But I think we have done our best. Can you make them hear from this distance?"

"Yes, I think so; a voice will travel far over the smooth water on a still night like this. Shall I recall them?"

Captain Thwaites was silent for a full minute, and we all stood gazing aft at the faint stars on the black water, while to right and left were those that were more dim and distant, being the paper lanterns of the house-boats moored a short distance from the bank.

Then the captain spoke again, and his words re-illumined the parting light of hope which flashed up like an expiring flame.

"Do you think he has struck out straight for the shore?"

"He may have done so, sir," replied Mr Reardon, as we all stood in a knot together on the quarter-deck, "but he could never have reached it."

"Not in this mill-race of a tide!" said Captain Thwaites. "Recall the boats."

But Mr Reardon made no sign. He stood there gazing through the night-glass for some moments, and the captain spoke again.

"Recall the boats, Mr Reardon."

"I beg your pardon, sir," said the lieutenant, with quite a start. "Aloft there! Who's in the foretop?"

"Ay, ay, sir; Jecks, sir."

I shivered.

"Hail the boats to come back."

The man did not answer for a moment, and Mr Reardon made an angry gesture, but just then Tom Jecks, with his hands to his mouth, sent forth a hoarse deep-toned roar.

Then there was a pause and a faintly-heard hail came from far away, the zig-zagging movement of the boats ceased, and we saw one of them, that is to say one of the lights, glide slowly toward the other, till one was apparently only a short distance in front, and the other following.

"Let me know when the boats come alongside, Mr Reardon," said the captain quietly.

"Yes, sir."

"And, by the way, I'll trouble you for my night-glass."

Mr Reardon gave a violent start.

"Your night-glass, sir?" he said.

"Yes, mine; you borrowed it."

The lieutenant handed the telescope without a word, and at another time we should all have had to turn away to smother the desire to burst out laughing, as we recalled the irritable remarks about the idiot to whom the glass belonged, and the wretchedness of his eyesight, coupled with an opinion that he ought to be dismissed the service.

But it was not a time for mirth: we were all too sad, and Barkins contented himself with whispering—

"I say, I'm jolly glad it wasn't I who said that. Don't the skipper take it coolly now? But he'll give old Dishy a talking-to for it when he gets him alone."

Mr Reardon's face was not visible to us, but we could see his movements, which were, so to speak, fidgety, for he began to walk up and down hastily, and once or twice I heard him mutter—

"How could I be such a fool?"

A dead chill had settled down upon the ship, and I felt as I stood there as if eight or nine years had suddenly dropped away from me—that I was a little child again, and that I should like to creep below somewhere out of sight, or sit down and cry and sob.

For it was such a horrible lesson to me of the nearness of death, and I felt as if it was impossible for it all to be true—that it must be some terrible dream.

And now for the first time it dawned upon me that I had a liking for the strange, simple-hearted Chinaman, who had always shown himself to be frank, honest, and brave in our service. He had been comic and peculiar, but always devoted to me as a faithful servant; and now, just too as I was joining in the mirth against him, instead of being indignant on behalf of one who had been insulted by the men's horseplay, he was as it were snatched from life to death.

I was brought back to the present by a voice at my ear—

"Poor old Ching! I am sorry, Gnat."

"Yes, and so am I."

I had not seen my messmates all through the trouble, and now they appeared close to me in the darkness in a way which made me start.

I turned to them, and I don't know how it was, but as we three stood there in the darkness, which was hardly relieved by a lantern here and there, Barkins held out his hand and shook mine, holding it tightly without letting go. Directly after, Smith took my other hand to give it a warm, strong pressure; and then we three parted without a word more, Barkins going one way, Smith another, while I went to the stern rail and leaned my arms upon it, and then rested my chin upon my arms to gaze out over the rushing water at the two blue stars.

But they were not there now. They had burned out some time before, and I could see nothing, only take it for granted that the boats were being slowly rowed back against the heavy tide, our anchor-lights acting as their guide.

"Is it possible that they have found him after all?" I thought, and for a minute I was hopeful. But once more the hope died out, for I knew well enough that if they had picked the poor fellow up they would have cheered.

Chapter Twenty Seven
A Surprise

That night had set in very dark. The clouds were heavy overhead, and the river now looked intensely black, but toward the shore there were the dull lights of the Chinese town glimmering in the water, while from some building, whether on account of a religious ceremony or a festival, a great gong was being beaten heavily, its deep, sonorous, quivering tones floating over the place, and reaching my ears like the tolling of a church bell.

It only wanted that depressing sound to make my spirits at the lowest ebb, and set me thinking of home, the perils of the career in which I was engaged, and wondering whether I should ever see England again.

The watch had been set, and from time to time Mr Reardon came aft to look anxiously astern.

The last time Mr Brooke was with him, and they stopped near where I was standing.

"But they ought to be back by now," Mr Reardon said.

"It's a long pull," Mr Brooke replied, "and the tide is terribly sharp at this time."

"Yes, yes—it is; but I want to see them back. Who's that?"

"Herrick, sir."

"Oh! Looking out for the boats?"

"Yes, sir."

"That's right. I like to see a young officer take an interest in the men."

They moved away to walk forward, while my face burned, for I did not deserve the praise, and my words had not been quite so honest as I could have wished.

. once, from out of the blackness astern, I heard the regular dip of
.d at the same moment one of the watch challenged and received an
.er. A minute later they were close up, and I shouted—

"Found him?"

"No, sir; not a sign of him anywhere."

I uttered a low groan, and the boats separated, one going to starboard
and the other to port, to be hauled up to their quarters, and there was the
customary trampling of the men going to their positions to run them up.

"Poor old Ching!" I said aloud; and then I started back as if I had
received a stroke, for my name was uttered from below in a sharp whisper.

"Mister Hellick! Mister Hellick!"

"Ching!" I cried, leaning over as far as I could reach, and gazing down
at the water. "Help!—help!" I shouted. "Here he is!"

Mr Brooke ran to me.

"What do you mean, my lad?"

"He's down here," I cried, "clinging to the chains."

"Nonsense! the boats would have seen him."

"But he is," I cried. "He has just called me. Below there! Ching!"

"Yes; help! Velly cold," came up in a piteous wail.

"Hold hard there!" shouted Mr Brooke. "Port boat back here under the
counter."

The falls were unhooked, and the boat drawn back by the coxswain till
she passed round close to the rudder.

"Any one there?" cried Mr Brooke.

"Ay, ay, sir!" and a cheer broke out from the men hurrying aft.

"Help! help!" came in a sharp wail. "No cut tow-chang! No cut tow-
chang!"

"Nobody's going to cut it, my lad. All right, we've got you," came up
from close under the stern windows, where even if it had been light we
could not have seen.

"Found him?" cried the captain, who now came up.

"Ay, ay, sir! Will you lower us down a lantern, sir? He's tied up somehow to the chain and a ring-bolt. We can't quite lee."

'HE'S ALL TWISSEN.'

The next minute, as I stood there longing to lower myself down into the boat, a lantern was swung over to them; while the men came swarming up the hatchway, for the news had soon spread, and they came running as far aft as they dared.

"Now then, steady," came from beneath us. "Let go; we've got you, I say."

"No cuttee tow-chang! No cuttee tow-chang!"

"Then he must have caught at the rudder-chains as he was swept along the side," said the captain. "Why didn't the fellow hail us, instead of letting the boats go on such a fool's errand?"

"Too much scared, sir," replied Mr Reardon. "Below there! Got him in the boat?"

"Got him, sir, and we can't get him," said one of the men. "He's all twissen up round the chain in a knot somehow."

"What?"

"He's tied hisself up somehow."

"Well, then, cut him loose, man," cried Mr Reardon.

"No cuttee tow-chang! No cuttee tow-chang!" cried Ching in a piteous wail.

"Not cut his toe?" said the captain in a tone full of disgust. "What does he mean? He can't have tied his foot to the chain."

"Hold still, will yer!" growled a deep voice; "I'm only untwisten on it. Nobody wants to cut yer pigtail."

"Oh, no cuttee tow-chang!" wailed Ching piteously.

"Tow-chang?" said the captain.

"Yes, sir; his tail," I said.

"Oh, I see! They're very proud of the length."

"Well, I'm blessed if ever I see such a snarl," cried the man below. "That's it. There you are. Here, cut this hankychy thing."

"Got him now?"

"Ay, ay, sir! all right," came from the boat; and at this the men burst out cheering again like mad, while the boat was drawn along the side with difficulty till the falls were reached, hooked on, and with a stamp and a run she was hauled up, and I was close up to the side as she was swung in, and Ching lifted out dripping, and sank down in a heap as soon as the men tried to set him on his feet.

"Here, let me have a look at him," said the doctor.

"But first of all, why did you cling there instead of calling for help?" cried Mr Reardon angrily.

"Bah! don't worry the man, sir," said the doctor sharply. "He's nearly insensible. What's this canister doing at the end of his tail?"

"Bah!" ejaculated the captain angrily, and he said something to Mr Reardon, and then went down to the cabin.

"Look here," cried the lieutenant angrily, "I want the names of the men who played this blackguardly trick upon the poor fellow."

"Yes, afterwards," said the doctor. "He's insensible, poor fellow. Here, one of you, a knife?"

Half-a-dozen jack-knives were opened and presented to the doctor, but I sprang forward.

"Don't do that, sir, please!" I cried excitedly.

"Eh? Not cut off this absurd thing?"

"No, sir. The poor fellow went overboard to escape having the pigtail cut, and it would break his heart."

Mr Reardon turned upon me sharply, and I anticipated a severe reproof, but he only gave me a nod.

"Carry him below," he said. And I walked beside the men to save the poor fellow from any fresh indignity, while half-an-hour later he had had a good rubbing and was lying in hot blankets fast asleep, partly from exhaustion, partly consequent upon having had a tumbler of mixture, steaming and odorous, which the doctor had administered with his own hands.

"Not to be taken every three hours, Herrick," he said, with a curious dry smile. "Fine mixture that, in its proper place. Know what it was?"

"It smelt like grog, sir," I replied.

"Oh, did it? Now, do you for a moment suppose that when a carefully-trained medical man of great experience is called in to a patient suffering from shock and a long immersion he would prescribe and exhibit such a commonplace remedy as grog?"

"Don't know, sir," I said. "But I should."

"Then, my good lad, as soon as you get back from this unpleasant voyage, the best thing you can do will be to go straight to your father and tell him that you have made a mistake in your vocation, and that he had better enter you for a series of terms at one of the universities, and then as a student at one of the hospitals."

"But I'm going to be a sailor, sir."

"Yes, a bad one, I daresay, my lad, when you might become a good doctor or surgeon."

"But I don't want to be one," I replied, laughing.

"Of course not, when it is the grandest profession in the world."

"But do you think he will come round all right, sir?" I said anxiously.

"Oh yes, of course. But you are not going to let that absurd thing stop on the end of his tail?"

"No, sir," I replied. "I'm going to try and get it off directly."

"How?"

"Lay it on a stool and stamp upon it."

"Good! that will flatten it and make the opening gape."

It did, after the exercise of a fair amount of pressure; and then, by the help of Tom Jecks, who was wonderfully penitent now, and eager to help with a tool he brought—to wit, a marlinespike—the star-like points of tin were one by one forced out, and the tail withdrawn uninjured, except that the silk ribbon at the end was a good deal frayed.

"Ha!" ejaculated Tom. "We've made an end of it at last. My word, Mr Herrick, sir, it's truly-thankful-Amen I am that the poor chap's all right again."

"And so am I, Tom Jecks," I replied.

"O' course you is, sir; I never meant to cut his tail, only to frighten him a bit; but, poor heathen, he took it all as serious as seas. Shall I go and chuck the tin-can overboard?"

"No; leave it here for him to find when he wakes up."

"Right it is, sir. But what a fuss for a man to make about a bit o' hair. He never howls about having his head shaved."

"No," I said; "but you see he would have given anything sooner than have his tail touched."

"And most got drownded, sir. Well, that all come o' the lads skylarking. If ever I'm skipper of a ship, no skylarking then. I s'pose there'll be a reglar hooroar in the morning, and Mr Reardon wanting to know who started the game."

"And you'll tell him, Tom?" I said.

"O' course, sir," he replied, with a solemn wink. "I'm just the man to go and split upon my messmates."

"But you'll be punished if you don't tell. You can't get out of it, because it's known that you were teasing him; and it wouldn't be fair for you to be punished and for them to escape."

"No, sir, it wouldn't; but sech is life. Wrong chap generally gets the kick as some one else ought to have ketched, but 'tarn't your fault, and it's no use to grumble."

"But it is your fault, if you know who were the offenders and will not tell."

"Is it? Humph! S'pose it is, sir. You're right. That's where you gents as is scholards gets over the like of me. I see it now; you are right, sir. What a wonderful head you've got for arguing, sewerly!"

"Then you'll tell Mr Reardon in the morning?"

"I didn't say as I would, sir."

"No; but you will?"

"No, sir, but I won't!" he said emphatically. "But I say, sir, do you think if I was to go overboard, and then hitch myself on to the rudder-chains till I was took aboard, the doctor'd give me a dose of that same physic as he give him?"

"Very likely, Tom," I said. "But you'd rather be without, wouldn't you?"

He smiled.

"But it was physic?"

"Oh yes, sir, it was physic. But then you see there's physic as he takes out of one of his little bottles with stoppers, and there's physic as he makes out of the ship's rum, hot with sugar. I could take a dose now easy, and it would do me good."

"Nonsense!" I said, after a glance at the sleeping Chinaman. "But I say, Jecks, how did he manage?"

"Oh, easy enough, sir. Tide would suck him right along the side, and he'd catch the chains."

"But how did he get in such a tangle?"

"Tied hisself on, sir, with a handkerchy round his left arm, to the chain; and then Dick Spurling says he twissened his tow-chang, as he called it, round and round, and tucked the canister in at the neck of his frock and buttoned it. Dick had no end of a job, as you know, to get him undone."

"Yes," I said thoughtfully, "I know that; but a man couldn't hang by his hair."

Tom Jecks laughed softly.

"Oh yes, he could, sir. There's no knowing how little a man can hang by when he's obliged. Why, ain't you heard how we men hangs on to the yards when we're aloft?"

"Oh yes, I've heard," I said; "by your eyelids."

"That's it, sir," he said, with a dry grin; "and that's harder than a man hanging on by his hair."

Ching was still sleeping heavily, and our conversation did not disturb him, and after a few moments' thought I said—

"But I don't feel at all sure why he did not hail the boats when they were going off."

"Oh, I do, sir," replied Tom Jecks. "I wouldn't ha' thought it possible, but the poor fellow was regularly scared, and wouldn't speak at first, because he thought that if he was hoisted on board the first thing we would do would be to go for his tail."

"Yes," I said, "that sounds likely; but he did hail after all."

"And enough to make him, sir; poor chap. Do you know why?"

"Well, not exactly," I said.

"A'cause the first fright had gone, and the bigger one had come. At first he was all in a squirm about losing his tail, but after a bit he got wacken up to the fact that if he didn't get took aboard he'd precious soon lose his life."

Chapter Twenty Eight
Ching has a Note

I suppose that Mr Reardon thought better of his threat, or probably he came to the conclusion that the expectation of punishment would prove as effective as the punishment itself. At all events nothing was said, and the routine of the ship went on as usual. The decks were scrubbed, the guns polished, and the marines drilled, till, as Barkins said, they could walk up to the top of a ladder and down the other side without touching.

The Jacks, too, had their gun drill and sword exercise, till their cutlasses flashed about with an exactness that promised to shave a head without cutting off an ear—promised: the performance might have been another thing.

As soon as I had an opportunity I started to go below and see Ching, but before I was half-way there I ran against Smith.

"Where are you going in such a hurry?"

"To see how Ching's getting on."

"Did you put on a clean shirt?"

"No," I said innocently. "I can't stand one every day."

"Oh, come, this won't do!" cried Smith. "Here, hi, Barkins!"

"What's the row?" said our messmate, coming up.

"Row enough. Look here, this won't do. The Gnat's going below to see His Excellency Ching Baron fancee shop, and Knight of the Tow-chang, without putting on a clean shirt."

"Go and report him to the captain. Why, worse and worse, he hasn't shaved!"

"No, that he hasn't."

"Well, I haven't got any razors like you fellows have," I retorted. "I say, Tanner, have you stropped yours up lately? Smithy's are getting rusty with the sea air."

"You're getting rusty with the sea air," grumbled Smith, who was very proud of the possession of a pair of razors with Sunday and Monday etched on the blades. He had once or twice shown them to me, saying that they were a present from his father, who was going to leave him the other five, which completed the days of the week, in his will.

I remember how I offended him at the time by saying—

"Well, that will be quite as soon as you want them."

"Look here," said Smith rather haughtily, after a look at Barkins; "we've been talking this business over, and it is time it was stopped."

"What do you mean?" I said.

"Oh, you know well enough. You came on board the *Teaser* to take your place as an officer and a gentleman, and we your seniors received you in a gentlemanly way."

"Yes, you were right enough," I said. "A bit cocky and bounceable at first, till you found that I wouldn't stand it, and then you were both civil."

"Well, I *am* blessed!" cried Barkins, blowing out his cheeks and looking down at me. "Of all the impudent little cockboats of boys you are about the most cheeky. Pretty strong turn that for a Gnat, Smithy."

"Yes; we shall have to put him down, and the sooner the better. Will you speak to him, or shall I?"

"Oh, I'm just in the humour for it," said Barkins; "so I'll give him his dose at once. Look here, young fellow: as aforesaid, when you interrupted, we received you as gentlemen should, and have taken great care of you, and tried to smooth you down into something like a budding officer."

"Thank you," I said humbly; "I'm so grateful."

"And so you ought to be, sir. But look here, what in the name of thunder do you mean by forsaking us and taking to bad company?"

"Who does?"

"Why, you do, sir. Smithy and I talked it over last night, and we both agreed that you're never happy unless you're along with the forecastle Jacks, or sneaking about with old Ching."

"Get out!" I said indignantly.

"None of your impudence, sir, because that won't do. It's come to this: either you've got to give up low society, or high."

"Which is which?" I said.

"What?"

"I said which is which? Do you mean you two fellows are high society?"

"Do you hear this beggar, Smithy?"

"Oh yes, I hear him. Isn't it awful to find so much depravity in such a small body? But keep him to it, and make him speak. He has got to choose."

"Yes, you've got to choose, Gnat. We can't have a brother officer always associating with the low Chinee."

"Do you mean that I oughtn't to go and see the poor fellow now he's below ill?"

"Something of the sort: you're not a doctor. Of course he ought to visit the men."

"So ought an officer when his men are in trouble."

"Yes; but not to make friends of them. It won't do, Gnat, and we've made up our minds not to stand it. That will do now. You have heard what I had to say, and I hope you will profit by it."

I burst out into a roar of laughter, for Barkins' assumption of dignity was comic.

"What do you mean by that, sir?" he cried in an offended tone.

"Second-hand captain's rowing!" I cried. "Why, I heard him say those very words to you."

"Hi! stop!" cried Smith, as Barkins turned red with annoyance. "Where are you going, sir?"

"Down below to see Ching," I replied coolly; and I descended the companion-ladder to where the man lay.

He was looking very yellow and gloomy, but as soon as he caught sight of me his face lit up.

"You come along see Ching?" he said in his high voice; and upon my nodding— "Velly glad. Doctor say stop along, velly much, not gettee up to-day."

"But you are ever so much better?"

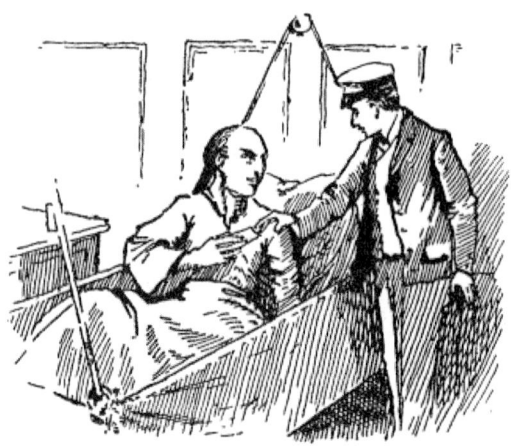

"Yes, quite well. Not velly wet now. Captain velly closs Ching tumb' overboard?"

"No, he hasn't said anything."

"Ching velly glad. You go tell captain something?"

"What about?" I said.

"Ching get lettee flom fliend."

"That's right," I said. "How is he?"

"Velly glad you catchee pilate."

"Oh, he is, is he?"

"Yes, velly muchee glad, and send lettee."

"Yes, you said so."

"Allee 'bout pilates."

He took a piece of paper from somewhere and handed it to me.

"You no lead lettee?"

I shook my head as I glanced at the queer Chinese characters.

"No; what does he say about the pirates?"

"Say two muchee big junk in river going to sail, catchee tea-ship, lice-ship, silkee-ship."

"Going to sail from here?" I cried.

"Yes."

"But how does he know?"

"Know evelyting. Muchee big man. Wantee catchee more pilate."

"But do you mean your friend knows of these junks sailing?"

"Yes."

"When did you get the letter?"

"Chinese coolie bling lettee in flesh-vegetable boat."

"What, this morning?"

"Yes, bling lettee."

"When are the junks going to sail?"

"No know. Keepee watchee and catchee."

I sat thinking for a few moments, and I made up my mind to go and tell the first lieutenant, but found the Chinaman looking at me smiling the while.

"You likee this?" he said, holding out a tiny thin stoppered bottle, covered with Chinese characters.

"Like it? No. What for?"

"Velly good. Headache: lub lit' dlop here. Toothache: lub lit' dlop there. Got pain anywhere, lub lit' dlop."

I took out the stopper and smelt it.

"Smell velly good; all nicee."

"Why, it smells of peppermint drops," I said carelessly.

"Yes, smell beautiful, all peppimint. Velly gleat stlong. Muchee lit' dlop, so."

He took the bottle, drew out the stopper, and covered the neck with one finger, turned the vial upside down, and then rubbed the tiny drop of moisture upon his temples, replaced the stopper, and gave it back to me.

"Thank you, Ching," I said, placing it in my pocket, but without valuing the gift in the slightest degree. "I'm going now to tell the first lieutenant what you say."

"Yes, tell Mr Leardon watchee watchee, killee allee pilate."

"Yes," I said; and I hurried away, muttering, "Watchee watchee, killee. What stuff they do talk! Any one would think they were all big babies, who had been taught to speak English by a nurse."

As I reached the deck I saw Barkins and Smith standing by the first lieutenant, and he was nodding his head.

"Why, they've been telling him about me," I thought as I went aft. "No; they wouldn't be such sneaks."

But all doubt was at an end directly, for they came down to meet me, and Smith cried—

"Mr Reardon wants to speak to you directly, Herrick;" while, as I looked up and caught Barkins' eye, he coloured a little, and hurriedly avoided my gaze.

"Thank you, tale-bearer," I said to Smith.

"Don't you be insolent, sir, unless you wish me to give you a severe thrashing."

"With fists?" I said.

"Yes, sir, with fists. I suppose the rules of the service will not allow us to use such weapons as officers are accustomed to."

"Do you mean officers like you?" I said contemptuously.

"Yes, sir; officers like me."

"Oh, you mean knives and forks, then," I said carelessly. "I say, Barkins, I didn't think you could have been such a jerry sneak."

He turned upon me with an apologetic look, but his lips began to bluster.

"What do you mean, sir?"

"Oh, nothing; I am not going to quarrel with old Barkins. He wouldn't have done this, if it had not been for Blacksmith."

"Go and obey the first lieutenant's orders, sir," said Smith haughtily. "We will talk to you later on."

"You go and show Doctor Price your arms and legs," I said contemptuously and spitefully; for, to use a common phrase, my monkey was up. "Fight? With fists? Where are your muscles? Why, I could upset you both with a swab."

I hurried aft, and ran up the steps to the quarter-deck in time to encounter the first lieutenant, who was coming from the wheel with an angry look upon his face.

Chapter Twenty Nine
A Queer Quarrel

"I sent a message to you, Mr Herrick," he cried angrily, and I could then guess that he had been coming to see why I had delayed. "I have something to say to you, sir, respecting the company you keep, and the society you affect, which I am given to understand is not that which conduces to good dishipline."

"Oh, that's what Mr Smith thinks, sir," I said coolly.

"Oh, indeed!" he cried sarcastically.

"Yes, sir; he said something about it to me this morning, but he does not know."

"Indeed!" he cried, growing black as a thundercloud; "then I am to take it, sir, that you do?"

"I hope so, sir; I try to know."

"Then you know, sir, possibly why it was that when I sent you a summons I am kept waiting?"

"Yes, sir; I was delayed a little—"

"Oh, thank you. I am glad to hear that, Mr Herrick. Perhaps you have something else of importance to communicate?"

"Yes, sir, very."

"Thank you. I am sorry I cannot ask you to sit down."

"Don't name it, sir," I said quietly, while he began to breathe very hard.

"I was down with Ching the interpreter, sir, this morning—"

"Were you really, Mr Herrick?" he said sarcastically. "Dear me, I hope he is much better?"

"Yes, sir, he's nearly all right. I was coming to you when I met Mr Barkins, and Smith." I couldn't say Mr Smith, I felt so exasperated against him.

"What a curious coincidence, Mr Herrick! If I had known I might have spared myself the trouble of sending."

"Yes, sir."

"And pray, may I know for what reason I was to be honoured?"

"Of course, sir," I said coolly enough, for I was enjoying the way in which he was working himself up for an explosion to fall upon my unfortunate head. "The fact is, sir—"

"Oh, it is a fact, is it?"

"Yes, sir—Ching has friends ashore."

"And wants leave of absence? Are you his envoy?"

"Oh no, sir. One of his friends sent him an important letter this morning by the vegetable boat."

"Eh? letter?" said Mr Reardon, beginning to grow interested.

"Yes, sir. This friend is a kind of a merchant or something; and he has news of two big junks—piratical junks—lying in this very river."

"The dickens he has! Here, Herrick, come down to my cabin."

He took my arm and marched me quickly to the ladder and down to his cabin. On the way I caught sight of Barkins and Smith watching us, and I gave them a nod.

"Now, my lad, sit down," cried Mr Reardon excitedly. "Let's hear."

I sat down, and he walked to and fro—two steps and turn.

"There's very little more to tell you, sir," I said; "but there are two very large junks assuming to be merchantmen. They are anchored close by here somewhere."

"You don't know which two?"

"No, sir; but we shall know them by their sailing at once, and I should say by boats coming off to them with extra men directly after."

"Yes, that's good, Herrick—very good. But you have no other information about them?"

"Only, sir, that they are just off on a cruise, and if we could catch them—"

"We will catch them, my lad. But is that all?"

"Yes, sir, that's all; I thought it rather big news."

"So it is, Herrick—very big news. Just what we wanted. It's time we made another capture. And to Ching has a friend on shore who sent this information?"

"Yes, sir."

"Not a trap, is it—to get us away?"

"Oh no, sir; Ching is as honest as the day."

"Humph, yes," said Mr Reardon, with his fingers to his lips. "I think he is, for he seems to have taken to us and to be working hard in our service. But he may have been deceived. He is cunning enough; but so are his countrymen, and they would glory in tricking the man who has taken up with the English. I don't know what to say to it, Herrick."

"But suppose we see two big junks setting sail, watch them with a boat, sir, and find that they take others on board, there could be no mistake then."

"Oh yes, there could, my boy. We might follow these junks, seize them, and spend a long time in their capture and bringing back into port. Then we should apply to the authorities, and find that we had got into sad trouble, for we had seized two vessels which the occupants could prove were intended for peaceable pursuits. We could not contradict them possibly, and all the time the scoundrels we wanted to take had sailed off upon a piratical expedition, consequent upon our absence. Now, sir, what do you say to that?"

I shook my head.

"I think Ching ought to know best," I said.

"Perhaps so," he replied. "We shall see. Come on now to the captain."

He opened the door, and I followed. I had forgotten all about Barkins and Smith for the time, but now all that had passed occurred to my mind, and I felt certain that they would be waiting somewhere to meet me and make sport of the tremendous setting-down which I had had.

I was not wrong: they were talking together amidships, just where they could command the companion-way, and as soon as we appeared I saw Smith's features expand into a malicious grin, while Barkins remained perfectly stolid.

As we passed to the ladder Smith looked after us wonderingly, and I saw him turn and whisper something, which I felt sure was—

"Taking him to the skipper."

For the captain was not in his cabin, but walking up and down the quarter-deck with his hands clasped behind him, and the telescope which had made Mr Reardon so angry under his left arm.

As we reached the deck he was going aft, so we followed him, and timed our pace so that when he turned we had only a step or two to take to be facing him.

"Yes, Mr Reardon," he said in response to our salute, "anything fresh?"

"Yes, sir, something very fresh. Will you listen to what Mr Herrick has to say?"

"Certainly," he replied, and he made room for me on his right Mr Reardon placed himself on my right, and as I narrated all I had said before as nearly as I could, they marched me up and down between them, from the binnacle to the end of the quarter-deck, turned and marched me back again.

As we approached the rail I could see Barkins and Smith watching us with all their eyes, and as we came in sight again they were still watching intently, evidently in the full belief that I was being, as we should have called it, wigged tremendously. And certainly they had some excuse for this idea, for I had been summoned by the first lieutenant, taken into his cabin, talked to, and then marched off to the captain. It almost looked like being dismissed from the ship in their eyes, and now I could see them scanning my features with intense interest for sight of my breaking down.

The captain heard me out, and then listened to Mr Reardon's objections.

"Yes," he said quietly at last, "that's very true, Mr Reardon, but we must not let an opportunity slip. I was intending to sail to-morrow for the north; now we will sail which way the junks lead. That will do for the present, Mr Herrick, and I thank you for your diligence in Her Majesty's service."

I touched my cap and went to the ladder, and as I descended there were my two messmates coming towards me.

Trying to make my face as mobile as possible, I stretched it here and there into wrinkles, and was walking straight along the deck looking the image of despair, when they stopped me.

"Serve you right!" said Smith exultantly. "There, be off below, and don't let the men all see what a setting-down you have had."

I gave each of them a piteous look, turned as they had suggested, and hurried down to our cabin to have a good laugh all to myself.

To my surprise, though, they followed me, Barkins to seat himself on the table, and Smith to lean up against the door.

"Well, Skeeter," said the latter, "you've had it pretty hot. Serve you right for being sarcy; you'll behave better next time."

"I hope so," I said meekly.

"Dishy gave you his lecture, then, and walked you off to the skipper, eh?"

"Yes," I said.

"Well, it's of no use for you to be grumpy. You've had your lesson, and now you've got to behave yourself."

"Yes."

"And I am very glad to see you are so humble. Aren't you, Tanner?"

"Yes," said Barkins gruffly.

"You see it won't do for a little gnat of a fellow to think he is going to do what he likes on board one of Her Majesty's ships. It was quite time you were taken down a few pegs—wasn't it, Tanner?"

"I suppose so," said Barkins.

"Then I don't see that it's any use for us to jump upon him, and show bad blood."

"No, not a bit," cried Barkins, with more animation. "We won't."

"No, I said we wouldn't; so look here, youngster: we're going to forgive you, if you promise to behave better and do as you're bid. This isn't school, you know, where a boy can set himself up against his elders, but the Queen's service, where every one has his place, and has to keep it too—mind that. There, that's all I've got to say."

"And very nicely said too," I replied.

He looked at me sharply, but my face was like marble, and he concluded that I had spoken seriously, for he turned to Barkins—

"There, Tanner, I've done; now it's your turn."

"What for?"

"To give him a few words."

"Oh, I don't think I want to say anything," said Barkins slowly. "I'm sorry the poor little beggar got into such a row."

"It'll do him good."

"I hope so," said Barkins slowly and reluctantly, and there was rather a mournful look in his eyes as he spoke.

"You'd better give him a few words of advice," said Smith in an off-hand tone.

"Oh no, he's had enough jawing. I shan't say anything."

"Thank you, Tanner," I said.

"Oh, all right," he cried, and he held out his hand and shook mine, brightening up the next moment, and looking as pleased as if he had just got a great trouble off his mind.

"You needn't be in such a jolly hurry to forgive him," said Smith in a remonstrant tone; "he has been a cheeky little beggar, and deserved all he got."

"But it isn't nice to be wigged, all the same," said Barkins sharply.

"No, but it don't matter if you deserved it. Now then, Gnat, tell us what Dishy said."

"What about?" I asked innocently.

"What about? Why, your associating with Ching so much."

"Oh, that!" I cried.

"Oh, that!" he said, mocking my way of speaking. "Why, what did you think I meant?"

"I don't know."

"Well, what did he say?"

"Nothing at all."

"What! no lies now."

"Who's telling lies? He didn't say a word about it. We had something of more consequence to talk about."

"Now, Tanner, hark at that. Did you ever hear such a miserable cheeky little beggar in your life? It's of no use; we must give him a regular good towelling."

"Better tell us what the luff said, Gnat," growled Barkins, in so strange an accession of gruffness that I began to laugh.

"Why, what's the matter with you?" I said. "Don't gruff and grow hoarse like that."

"Can't help it; got a cold, I s'pose," he cried. "But I say, stop it now; we want to be friends. Tell us what the luff said."

"Precious little," I replied. "I did all the speaking till we went up on the quarter-deck."

"Don't listen to him," cried Smith, growing wroth with me. "I never saw such cheek. One tries to be friends with him, but it's of no use; directly you open your mouth he jumps down your throat."

"Then you shouldn't have such a big mouth, Smithy," I said sharply, and then the storm burst.

Tanner roared with laughter, for the width of Smith's mouth had often been food for our mirth; and, as Barkins afterwards said, my remark came out so pat.

"Look here," cried Smith, "I'm not going to stand this sort of thing. You may be fool enough to put up with it, but I won't."

"If you call me a fool I'll punch your head, Smithy," growled Barkins.

"No, you won't," was the retort; "and that's the way you take sides against me, and encourage the miserable little beggar in his impudent ways? Now then, you Herrick, you've got to go down on your knees and beg my pardon, and then tell me everything the skipper and the first luff said."

"When?" I asked coolly.

"When? Why, now, directly," cried Smith fiercely. "Now then, no nonsense," he cried, seizing me by the collar; but I wrested myself away, and in the slight struggle sent him staggering against Barkins.

"Now then, keep off me, please," growled Barkins.

"Keep off yourself; why don't you get out of the way?"

"How was I to know that a blundering idiot was coming up against me?"

"It'll tell you when I've done with the Gnat," said Smith angrily; for I had unintentionally hurt his arm. "Now you, Skeeter."

"Let him alone," said Barkins gruffly.

"When I've done with him," said Smith; "you could have had first go at him if you had liked."

"I don't want to hit the little fellow, I'm not overbearing like you are. Let him alone, I say."

"I shall let him alone when I choose," retorted Smith fiercely. "I'm not going to let our junior ride roughshod over me, if you're fool enough to."

"I shall be fool enough to kick you out of the cabin if you touch him," cried Barkins angrily. "I won't have him bullied; and it was a mean sneaking thing to go telling tales as you did to old Dishy."

"Look here," cried Smith, "if any one is a sneak it's you, for harking back and taking the miserable little beggar's side."

"Never mind about that; you let him alone."

"Oh, I say, Tanner," I said, "don't quarrel with him about me. What he said did no harm. Mr Reardon was as friendly as could be."

"That's a cracker," cried Smith sharply.

At that moment a marine came to the door.

"First lieutenant wants to see Mr Herrick directly."

"Yes; where is he?" I said, smiling—purposely, of course.

"With the cap'n, sir, on the quarter-deck."

"All right; I'll be there directly."

The man saluted and marched off, while I followed to the door, where I turned, thrust in my head, and said banteringly—

"Now be good boys and don't fight while I'm gone."

Bang!

A book off the table, flung by Smith, struck the door which I was holding half open, for I saw the missile coming, and dodged it. Then I popped my head in again.

"Don't take any notice of him, Tanner," I cried; "he's bilious. Thankye for sticking up for me. Can I say a word for you to the captain?"

"Here, get up," cried Smith, with a snarl. "Touch your hat to him. He's promoted; and they'll send poor old Brooke a step lower. All hail, Lieutenant Skeeter!"

"All right!" I cried, and I hurried away, leaving Barkins looking as if he could not believe his ears.

The next minute I was facing the captain and Mr Reardon.

Chapter Thirty
A Fresh Start

"Mr Herrick," said the captain, as I saluted, "I have decided that, as you know so much about this business, you shall go with Mr Brooke in one of the boats; but I wish you to observe what I say: the success of our expedition depends a great deal upon secrecy, so do not chatter anything about your mission in the hearing of the men."

"No, sir, certainly not," I said, wondering what the mission might be, and whether we were going to cut out the junks.

"That's right; you had better take the interpreter with you."

"To search for the junks, sir?"

"Hush; guard your tongue, sir. You are ostensibly going up the river with Mr Brooke upon a little shooting expedition for wild-fowl, so get rid of your uniform. I daresay we can lend him a gun, Mr Reardon?"

"If he'll take care of it, he can have mine, sir," said Mr Reardon.

"Then off with you, my lad, and be as observant as you can. Mr Brooke will tell you, I daresay, all about his instructions."

I saluted, and darted away in time to see that Smith had been watching me, for he drew back as I approached, and I found him standing by where Barkins sat, looking exceedingly glum.

I daresay it was very petty, but Smith had been so malicious, and had so often made himself disagreeable, that I could not help feeling a delicious sensation of triumph as I bustled into the cabin and rushed to my locker, without taking any notice whatever of Smith, while I felt sorry for big burly Barkins, who I felt would not say an unkind word if it were not for Smith's influence.

I remember Charles Dickens saying in one of his tales something about it being hard enough to live with any one who had a bad temper in a large house, but to be shut up with the said person in a cart or travelling van was terrible. Of course I am not giving his exact words, only making the allusion to illustrate the fact that it is quite as bad to exist with an ill-tempered person in the small cabin of a vessel at sea. For you may depend upon it there is no better—or worse—way of finding out a companion's peculiarities than that.

I acted pettily, but then I was only a boy; and now I am a man, getting on in years, I don't know that I am much better. But it was very comic all the same to see those two fellows try to ignore my proceedings, poor old Barkins following Blacksmith's lead once more. They did not want to know what I was going to do—not a bit. And I laughed to myself as I hurriedly kicked off my shoes and put on a pair of strong boots, carefully took off my uniform jacket and replaced it by a thin tweed Norfolk, after which I extricated a pith helmet from its box, having to turn it upside down, for it was full of odds and ends.

Smith had taken up a book and pretended to read, while Barkins sat back on a locker with his hands in his pockets, and his lips thrust out and screwed as if he were whistling, but no sound came, and he stared hard at the bulkhead facing him.

But try how he would he could not keep his eyes fixed there—they would follow my movements; and twice over I caught Smith peeping round the side of the book with which he was screening his face.

I began to whistle as I rapidly made my preparations, and at last Smith could bear it no longer.

"What's the idiot dressing himself up for?" he cried contemptuously.

That started Barkins, and he burst out with—

"What's up, Gnat? Shore leave?"

"Eh! Didn't you know?" I said coolly. "Shooting."

"What!" they exclaimed in a breath, and Smith's eyes were more wide open than I had ever seen them.

"Shooting," I said coolly. "Brooke and I are going after ducks."

"Gammon!" cried Barkins. "Why, you have no gun."

"No," I said. "Reardon is going to lend me his double breech-loader, central fire, number twelve."

Barkins gave his leg a sharp slap.

"We're going up the river; plenty of sport up there among the marshes."

"Going to walk?" said Barkins.

"Oh no; we're to have a crew and one of the cutters."

"Don't you believe him, Barkins, it's all gammon. The little humbug can't deceive me."

"All right, call it gammon," I said, stooping to tighten my boot-laces. "Roast duck for dinner, Tanner, to-morrow."

Barkins rushed on deck, leaving me with Smith, and the next minute he was back again.

"It's all right, Smithy," he cried; "and they're shoving in a basket of prog for the beggars."

"What!" yelled Smith. "Do you mean to say that Brooke and this—this—thing are going off wasting Her Majesty's time shooting?"

"Yes; I saw Brooke, and he said it was so."

"Then I shall resign. Hang me if I'll stop in a service where such beastly favouritism is shown. Profession for gentlemen's sons, is it? I call it a mockery!"

"Oh, don't be so snaggy, Smithums," I said banteringly; "wait till his poor old wing's all right again, and he shall go a shooting too."

That was too much. He made a rush at me, but Barkins flung an arm round his waist, and as they struggled together I dodged to the other side of the table and escaped from the cabin, but popped my head in again.

"Don't hit him, Tanner," I cried; "he ain't got no friends. Good-bye, old chap, I wish you were coming too."

Our eyes met, and I suppose my tone and the look I gave him seemed sincere, for, as he held Smith, his arms tightly round him from behind, and his chin resting upon our messmate's shoulder, he gave me a friendly nod.

"All right, old chap," he said; "I hope you'll enjoy yourself."

"And I hope the John Teapots 'll get hold of you, you miserable little cad!" cried Smith. "I shan't be there to help you this time."

I burst out laughing and ran on deck, to find the men mustered ready, and Mr Brooke standing there in sun helmet and gaiters, looking as unlike a naval officer as he could be.

"Oh, there you are, Herrick," he said, giving me a look over. "Yes, that will do."

"But the men," I whispered. "Oughtn't they to be armed?"

"All right, my lad; plenty of tackle in the boat under the thwarts."

"But my gun—I mean Mr Reardon's?"

"In the stern-sheets, with plenty of cartridges. Where's Ching?"

"I don't—down below, I suppose."

"Fetch him up; we're off at once."

There was no need, for the interpreter appeared smiling and happy, looking as if he had not passed through such a terrible ordeal a short time before.

The captain and Mr Reardon came up then.

"Ready, Mr Brooke?"

"Yes, sir."

"Order the crew into the boat, Mr Reardon."

As the men sprang in, the captain came close to us.

"You'll keep up the appearance of a sporting expedition, Mr Brooke," he said in a low voice. "I expect you'll find the junks in the river off some village. The rest I must leave to you."

"Take them, sir, if I feel pretty certain?"

Captain Thwaites knit his brows, and stood as if thinking for a few moments.

"No," he said at last; "but that I leave all to your discretion. Don't risk your men, if they are strong. I'm afraid some of these mandarins are mixed up with the piratical expeditions, and share in the plunder, and I am certain that every movement we make is watched. There, off with you; don't let Mr Herrick get hurt. I trust you to do your best."

We sprang into the boat, which was lowered down; the falls were unhooked; and as Tom Jecks, who was coxswain, gave us a shove off, the tide, which was running up, bore us right aft; then the oars dropped with a splash, the rudder lines were seized, and away we went up-stream on as glorious a day as ever made a dirty Chinese city look lovely.

I looked back, and there were Barkins and Smith leaning over the side watching us, but I hardly noticed them, for something else caught my eye.

"Why, they're getting up steam, Mr Brooke!" I said.

"Yes, my lad, they're getting up steam, and I hope your information may mean some good active service for us. Here, Ching," he whispered, "you have not told the men anything about our business?"

Ching shut his eyes and shook his head solemnly.

"Velly muchee keepee mouf shut," he said, with the addition now of a few nods of the head. "Nobody but Ching an' officer know."

Chapter Thirty One
Getting Warm

The men were in high glee, and, had they not been checked, would have sent the boat spinning up the river, in their delight to escape from the monotony of harbour-life, and the natural love there is in Englishmen for a bit of sport.

"Steady, my lads," said Mr Brooke quietly. "Just give her headway, and back water the moment I speak."

I did not hear what one of the men whispered to his messmate, but I saw his face as he leaned forward, and it certainly suggested to me that he said—

"They mean some of the tame ducks to make sure."

"No, we do not, my man," said Mr Brooke, and I stared at him in astonishment, that he should have taken the same idea as I had.

The man coloured through his tan, and Mr Brooke; said in a low voice to me—

"Our work's cut out, Herrick; how are we to pick out the right two junks from all this crowd?"

"I don't know, sir," I said. "But I don't fancy they would be down here where other people might talk about them. I should think they would be up the river."

"Well, we must find them, my lad, so use our brains as much as you can, and if you see a junk with a very evil-looking lot aboard, just give me a hint as we pass."

"I'll ask Ching what he thinks, sir."

Mr Brooke nodded, and I turned to the interpreter, who was squatting in the bottom of the boat right aft, his eyes half shut, and apparently taking no heed of anything.

"How are we to know which are the junks we want, Ching?" I said.

"Oh, velly soon find," he said. "Ching look along. Not these. Pilate boat big and tall. Empty. No got big calgo aboard. Stand high up now. Velly full and low down when full of plize-money."

"Then you don't think they are down here?"

He shook his head as he glanced at the various forms of trading-boat moored off the town, from the tiny sampan to the heavy, clumsy mat-sailed vessel, whose stern towered up, and whose great bamboo yards looked as if they must be perfectly unmanageable.

"What do you think we had better do, then—row about here and watch?"

"No good," he said; "makee men low fast light up liver, findee, pilate junk."

"But suppose we pass them?" I said.

"No pass pilate boat: Ching here."

"And so you think you will know them?"

The Chinaman screwed his face up into a curiously comic smile.

"Ching know pilate when he see him."

"And you think it better to go right up the river?" said Mr Brooke, turning suddenly to join in the conversation.

"Yes; pilate junk long way."

"How do you know?"

He gave a cunning smile at us both, his little eyes twinkling in a singularly sly manner.

"You see vegetable boat come along mo'ning?"

"Yes, I saw the boat come alongside."

"Blought Ching 'nothee lettee, allee same fliend. Say pilate boat long way uppee liver in big cleek, waitee come down along lunning water in the dalk."

"Then you pretty well know where they are?" said Mr Brooke.

"No; far uppee liver; in cleek."

"I suppose this is right?" said Mr Brooke to me.

"Yes, quite light. Ching likee see Queen Victolia ship killee catch pilate."

"Give way, my men," said Mr Brooke, and the boat shot forward, while, relieved for the moment from the task of scanning the different boats, I sat gazing at the beautiful panorama of quaint houses, narrow streets debouching on the river, and the house-boats all along the edge of the river, while smaller boats were swinging here and there wherever there was room.

It was a wonderfully interesting sight, for, in addition to the curious shapes of the buildings, there was plenty of brilliant colour, and every now and then patches of brightest blue and vivid scarlet were heightened by the glistening gilding which ornamented some particular building. Then there were temples dotted about amongst the patches of forest, which fringed the high ground at the back of the city, and away beyond them the steep scarps of rugged and jagged mountains, which stood up looking of so lovely a pinky-blue, that I could for the moment hardly believe they were natural, and was ready to ask whether it was not some wonderful piece of painting.

The house-boats took my fancy greatly, for, in endless cases, they were of a variety of bright colours, pretty in shape, and decorated with showy flowers in pots and tubs; some had cages containing brightly-plumaged birds, and in most of them quaint bald-headed little children were playing about or fishing.

Higher up we saw men busy with nets which were attached to the end of a great bamboo pole, balanced upon a strong upright post fixed in the river's bottom, and by means of this balanced pole the net was let down into the depths of the river, and hoisted from time to time, sometimes with a few glittering little fish within the meshes, sometimes having nothing but weed.

"Yes, catchee fish; catchee velly big fish some time."

About ten minutes after, Ching pulled my sleeve and pointed to the other side of the river, where I caught sight of a very familiar old friend sitting in his boat, just as I had seen him in an old picture-book at home.

There he sat with a big umbrella-like sunshade fixed up over him on a bamboo pole, in front of him a kind of platform spread across the front of his moored boat, and upon it sat perched eight or nine of my old friends the cormorants, one of which dived into the river from time to time, and soon after emerged and made its way back to the boat with a fish in its beak.

"See that, Mr Brooke?" I cried eagerly. "I suppose we can't stop to watch them?"

"Not when on Her Majesty's service, Herrick," he said, with a smile, and we glided rapidly on, till the houses, which had long been growing scattered, finally disappeared, and we were following the windings of the river in company with a few small junks and sampans, which seemed bound for one of the cities higher up the great waterway.

"Shoot bird now," said Ching, in answer to an inquiring look from Mr Brooke.

"Yes; but do you think the junks are up here?"

"Oh yes, velly quite su'e. Plenty eye in boat watchee see what Queen Victolia offlicer going to do uppee river."

"What does he mean?" said Mr Brooke, who was puzzled by this last rather enigmatical speech. "Of course we have watchful eyes in our boat, but I don't see anything yet worth watching."

"He means that very likely there are friends of the pirates in one of these boats, and that we had better begin shooting, so as to take off attention from our real purpose."

"Yes, allee same; p'laps pilate fliend in lit' boat go and tell Queen Victolia foleign devil sailor boy come catchee."

"Oh, I see," said Mr Brooke. Then, turning to me, "You do understand a little French, don't you?"

"Well, sir, I used to learn some at school," I replied, feeling very doubtful about my proficiency.

"I daresay you can understand my Stratford-atte-Bow French," said Mr Brooke, laughing.

"I'll try, sir," I said; and he said to me directly in excellent French—

"I feel doubtful about this man. You have seen more of him than I have. Do you think he is honest, or leading us into a trap?"

"Honest, sir," I said, "I feel certain."

"Well, then, we will trust him fully; but if he betrays us, and I can get a last shot—well, then—"

"He'll be sorry for it, sir," I said, for Mr Brooke did not finish his remark.

"Exactly; get out your gun and put on your cartridge belt."

I followed his example, and Ching smiled.

"Velly good thing," he said. "Now pilate fliend, see jolly sailor boy, and say—Come killee duck-bird, goose-bird to make nicee dinner, not come catchee catchee pilate."

"You hear what this man says, my lads?" said the young lieutenant, addressing the men.

"Ay, ay, sir."

"Then you understand now that we have not only come up to shoot?"

"Ay, ay, sir."

"Keep your rifles and cutlasses quite handy in case they are wanted. No confusion, mind, but at the word be ready."

Mr Brooke's words seemed to send a thrill through the men, who pulled on now with a more vigorous stroke, while, with our guns charged, and the butts resting on our knees, we gave place to the coxswain, who took the tiller.

"We'll go forward, Herrick," said my companion; and he stepped over the thwarts into the coxswain's place, and I sat by him, watching alternately for birds, junks, and creeks, up which the latter might lie.

"Begin shootee soon," said Ching rather anxiously.

"Why?"

"Velly muchee sail boat behind think why we come."

"There goes something, Herrick," said Mr Brooke just then, and I looked up and saw a bird flying over the river at a tremendous rate.

I raised my piece quickly, fired, and as soon as I was a little clear of the smoke, fired again.

"You hit him, sir!" said our stroke-oar. "I see him wag his tail."

"It was a miss," I said quietly.

"Velly good," whispered Ching. "Allee men in other boat look see;" while I replaced the cartridges in my gun, and looked shoreward, to see that the land was level for miles, and that little flocks of duck or other birds were flying here and there. Soon after a wisp of about a dozen came right over head, and as they approached the men rested upon their oars till Mr Brooke had fired, without result.

He looked at me and smiled, while the men pulled again, and we went merrily along, getting a shot now and then, but the result for the game-bag was very meagre indeed, at which I was not surprised on my own account, but I fully expected Mr Brooke to have done some good.

'I TOOK AIM AND FIRED BOTH BARRELS QUICKLY.'

And still we went on along the great river, with the country, save for the distant mountains, looking wonderfully English, and making it hard to believe that we were in China. In places where we were close to the shore I could see forms of growth different to our own, but at a little distance the trees, shrubs, and reeds looked much the same as those we should have encountered at home, and I confess to feeling a little disappointed. Then all at once, as if he too were suffering from the same sensation, Mr Brooke spoke.

"They will laugh at us when we get back, Herrick," he said, "as far as our birds are concerned, but I am beginning to think that we shall find the pirate junks are somewhere up here."

"You think so, sir? Look, a flock coming this way!"

"Of pirate junks?" he said drily.

"No, sir, ducks."

"Give it them, then, my lad—both barrels."

I took aim and fired both barrels quickly one after the other, but as I drew trigger I felt that I had done wrong, for I had aimed right in front of the swiftly-flying flock.

"Umbrellas up!" shouted one of the men. "Rains geese!" and there was a cheer and a roar of laughter, as one by one five geese fell with a splash in the river, two to lie perfectly still while they were retrieved—the others, poor birds, to make desperate efforts to swim broken-winged away, but to be shot one by one by Mr Brooke, and after a sharp row dragged into the boat.

"Velly nicee," said Ching, smiling.

"Yes, I must take lessons in shooting from you, Mr Herrick," said the young lieutenant, smiling. "It's my turn next."

I felt hot and uncomfortable, for my success seemed to be the result of pure accident, and I said so, but Mr Brooke laughed and shook his head.

"Never mind the birds, Herrick," he said; "I feel sure our other game is close by somewhere."

"Yes, up cleek somewhere," said Ching.

"Why do you say that?"

"No pointee—no look. I tell you," said the Chinaman, taking up and pretending to examine the mottled brown wing of the goose he opened out. "Boat come behind, pilate fliend come see which way we go."

"Yes, I'm sure you are right," said Mr Brooke, taking up another of the birds; "and if I'm not very much mistaken, that other boat you see ahead has his eye upon us."

"Ching not velly sure, p'laps; only see one man look over side thlee times."

"There's a bit of a river runs off here, sir, to the right," said one of the men, nodding to his left, where there was an opening in a patch of forest which came down to the river, with fine timber trees overhanging the muddy banks, and their branches every here and there showing dead grass and reeds caked with mud, as if at times this part of the country was deeply flooded.

"Yes," said Ching very quietly; "p'laps plenty mud up there. Go see."

"And while we are up a side branch of the river, they may come down the main stream and escape."

Ching shook his head.

"Fliend say pilate junk hide up liver in cleek."

"Yes, but—"

"Wait lit' bit," said Ching, with a cunning look. "Go up lit' way, shoot birds, and no lit' boat come after, no pilate fliend. If come after, plenty muchee pilate fliend, and junk not vellee far."

"He's right, Herrick," said Mr Brooke, nodding. "Turn up the side branch, my lads. Keep up the comedy of the shooting, and have a shot at something."

"But there's nothing to shoot at, sir," I said, feeling rather doubtful of the accuracy of Ching's ideas.

But as we turned up the narrow branch of the river—a creek not much wider than an English canal, I caught sight of a black-looking bird, which rose from the water and flew away paddling the surface with its feet.

I fired and dropped the bird, but it flapped along, and the men cheered and pulled in chase for two or three hundred yards before it was retrieved.

"It's a sort of moor-hen," I said, as I looked up from my captive.

"One of the pirate's hens, perhaps, Herrick," said Mr Brooke, smiling.

"Well, Ching, had we better go on?"

"Yes, go 'long," said the Chinaman rather huskily. "Velly good place."

We rowed on for another three or four hundred yards, the branch winding a great deal, so that we seemed to be in a succession of lakes, while the trees on either side completely shut us in.

"Stream runs very fast," I said.

"Yes, velly fast," said Ching.

"There, I think we had better turn back now," said Mr Brooke, but Ching smiled in a curious way.

"What go turnee back? Pilate fliend both come in cleek after, to see what Queen Victolia jolly sailor boy go to do."

"Are you sure?" said Mr Brooke excitedly.

"Yes, sir, I see the top of one of their sails," said Tom Jecks.

"Then, by George, we are in the right track," cried Mr Brooke, and, as my heart began to beat rapidly, "Give way, my lads," he cried, "give way."

Chapter Thirty Two
A Startling

"What are we going to do?" I said, with my heart beating fast.

"Afraid?" said Mr Brooke in a whisper.

"I don't know, sir—a little," I replied.

"We're not going to fight, Herrick. I shall go on and find the junks so as to know them again—take their portraits in our minds—and then go back for help. They can't escape out of the river, and once we know them, our boats can soon follow and bring them to book."

The men pulled as if their hearts were in their work, and upon rounding a bend, there, about a quarter of a mile away, lay two large vessels, moored close up to the trees.

"We'll keep up the idea that we are shooting," said Mr Brooke. "No, there is no need now. We have kept it up long enough. We must reconnoitre and go back. They will think still that we are a shooting-party, and not know that we are making for them."

"Of course not," I said thoughtfully. "How could they know we had heard?"

We rowed steadily on for a minute or two, and then Ching said quietly—

"One boat—two boat come behind."

We glanced back, and there, sure enough, were the sailing craft, which had been hanging about in front and aft, coming steadily along in our wake. A moment or two later Ching spoke again—

"Look over boat side, see jolly sailor boy."

"Never mind those boats," said Mr Brooke impatiently.

"Steady, my lads, hold hard now; that's right," he continued, as the oars were held, and checked the boat's progress. "Now, Mr Herrick, take a good look at them. Do you think we should know them again if you saw them coming down the river?"

"Yes, sir," I said; "the stern of this one and bows of the other would be unmistakable. I don't think I could make a blunder."

"No; almost impossible; pull starboard, back water, port side. Now, we'll just turn and row gently back. I don't see any men on board."

"All lie down flat," said Ching sharply. "Plenty men aboard."

"Ah, well, it does not matter. I'm not going to run risks by attacking the savages. Lift your gun and look about, Herrick. Let them keep in the same mind."

I stood up in the boat at this, and noted how rapidly the tide was running up as Mr Brooke gave the word to pull again.

The movement of the boat brought me in full view of the two sampans which had followed us, each with a man and boy aboard; and now, as I looked, I was surprised to see a yellow head raised and begin watching us. Then another; and Ching said quickly—"Lot men in both boats."

I don't know how they had stowed themselves, but now, to our intense astonishment, head after head appeared, till Mr Brooke exclaimed—

"Why, the boats are packed full of men."

"Yes, and the junks too," I whispered hastily; for their decks, which a few moments before had appeared to be bare, were now crowded.

"Trapped, Herrick!" said Mr Brooke through his set teeth. "Is this a trick on the part of Mr Ching?"

The men were looking hard at us, and they did not have long to wait.

"Arms ready, my lads?"

"Ay, ay, sir."

"That's right. Now then, lay your backs to it, and row with all your might."

"Ay, ay, sir."

"What are you going to do?" I said huskily.

"Run for it. The junks can't follow against this tide. We must row out into the river. Keep your fire till I give orders. They may not try to stop us. If they do, I shall try and ram one. We have four barrels for the other, without troubling the men."

"You don't think it's a false alarm?"

"No," he said sternly; "the falsity lies somewhere else."

"He means Ching," I said, but there was no time for much thought, not even to see a great deal. The men grasped the situation as soon as the boat's head was straight, and Mr Brooke took the tiller in his left hand, his gun in his right, and cocked it, while I followed suit.

Then I felt disposed to laugh as Ching made a dive down, and began to crawl under the thwarts among the men's legs, but the laugh changed to a serious grin as Mr Brooke steered to pass between the two boats, when the course of one was changed so as to throw her right athwart our way, and quite a dozen men rose up in each, armed with clumsy swords, yelling at us, and dancing about as they gesticulated and seemed to be trying to frighten us back.

"Very well, if you will have it," said Mr Brooke between his teeth. "Be ready, my lads. Cutlasses, if they try to board."

A sound like the exhaustion of a heavy breath escaped from the men, and Mr Brooke roared at them to pull, while I sat with my finger on the first trigger and the gun lowered a little, gazing wildly at the savage crew before us.

Those moments were like long minutes, but I could make out that, instead of frightening us, the men in the boat which crossed us were now frightened themselves, and they made an effort to give us room.

But there were too many of them—they got in each other's way. Then there was a wild shriek, a crash, and the head of our fast cutter crashed into them, driving their bows round, partly forcing them under water, and the flimsily-built boat began rapidly to fill.

The second party held a little aloof, too much startled by the boldness of our manoeuvre to attempt to help their companions, so that we had only the first boat to tackle, as such of the men as could trampled over one another in their struggle to get on board us.

But the moment the crash had come our lads sprang up with a cheer, and, forgetting their proper weapons, let go at the enemy with their oars, using them as spears and two-handed swords, and with such effect that in less than a minute the wretches were driven back or beaten into the water, to swim to and cling to their half-sunken boat, whose light bamboos refused to go right down.

"Now pull—down with you—pull!" roared Mr Brooke, and, thanks to Mr Reardon's grand "dishipline," every man dropped into his place, and the boat, which had come to a standstill, now began to move forward, while the tide carried the enemy towards their junks, from whence came now as savage a yelling as that from the boats.

"Without firing a shot," cried Mr Brooke exultantly. "Pull, boys. Now, a cheer! they can't follow us against this tide."

The men sent up a triumphant shout, and, as we swept round the next bend, we lost sight of the junks, and directly after of the two boats, the last I saw of them being that the crew of the second were dragging their companions of the first out of the water, and loading their own down to the gunwale edge.

"Now," cried Mr Brooke, "who's hurt?"

There was no answer for a moment or two. Then one of the men said, with a grin—

"I arn't drownded, sir; but I shall ketch cold if something arn't done— my feet's wet."

"Yes, so velly wet," cried a plaintive voice, and Ching struggled up from the bottom of the boat, and stood up, showing his blue cotton garments to be drenched with water.

"What, have we sprung a leak?" cried Mr Brooke.

"Yes, sir," said Tom Jecks, "she's got a hole in her skin here forrard; but if I might be so bold, sir, if you was to send Mr Ching to lean up agin it, we shouldn't hurt much."

"Pull—pull steady," cried Mr Brooke. "Here, take the tiller, Mr Herrick."

He laid his gun behind us and handed me the rudder, before going right forward to the coxswain, while I sat envying the men their coolness as they sat pulling away nonchalantly enough, though the water was rising fast and nearly covered their bare feet and ankles, while it soon invaded the grating upon which my own boot-covered feet were placed.

"Much injured, sir?" I shouted; and Mr Brooke gave me back poor Mercutio's answer to his friend, in *Romeo and Juliet*—

"'Tis not so deep as a well, nor so wide as a church door: but 'tis enough; 'twill serve."

"Here, my lads, one of you; I must have a frock."

"Right, sir, mine'll do," said the coxswain, unfastening and dragging his white duck garment over his head.

This was soaked and wrung out to make it softer, and then thrust into the hole in our bows.

"There, you must sit forward here, and plant both feet against it, my lad," said Mr Brooke.

"Ay, ay, sir. Men never knows what he may come to. Fancy my toots being used to caulk a leak!"

He, laughing, sat down on the forward thwart, and pressed his feet against the jacket.

"Now then, a man to bale," cried Mr Brooke, and the coxswain fished the tin baler out of the locker forward. "No; pass it here," continued our leader. "Pull away, my lads, and Mr Herrick and I will take it in turns to bale. We must get out of this narrow creek as soon as we can."

"Me balee water out," squeaked Ching, who looked very wet and miserable.

"No, thank you," said Mr Brooke coldly.

"Beg pardon, sir; I've got nothin' to do but sit here like a himage," said the coxswain; "I can reach down and bale."

"Without shifting your feet?"

"Yes, sir; look here."

The man took the baler, and began to send the water, which still came in but slowly, over the side; while, after satisfying myself that we should not be obliged to run our boat ashore and tramp back to the city, I kept on directing anxious glances backward to see if we were pursued.

"We shan't sink, Herrick," said Mr Brooke, returning to my side; while, after glancing at my very serious, and at the young lieutenant's stern countenance, Ching crept forward under the oars to where the coxswain was baling, and, getting a second tin from the locker, he seated himself, tucked his loose things out of the way, and began meekly to toss out the water as fast as he could scoop it up.

"That fellow's a traitor," said Mr Brooke to me in a low voice, after a glance back by Ching.

"Oh no, I hope not, sir," I said.

"I wish I could hope so too, my lad. There's a deal of cunning in his plans, and he tried hard to make it seem that he was all the time working upon our side; but I feel as if he has led us into a trap, and we were very nearly coming to our end in it without a man left to tell the tale."

"But why, sir? What object could he have?"

"Plunder, for one thing; our boat, and weapons such as they cannot get. Yes, I believe that he is in league with those pirates."

"Oh, I can't think it, Mr Brooke," I cried. "He has served us so well."

"Yes, to gain his own ends."

"But surely he wouldn't do such a base thing for the sake of getting a paltry share in these rifles and cutlasses?"

"He would have the satisfaction of seeing us massacred."

"But what satisfaction could that be, sir?" I cried. "We have always been his friends."

"The Chinese hate the outer barbarians and foreign devils, as they call us, my lad. They are obliged to tolerate our presence, but the common people, as you know well, would feel an intense pleasure in murdering every European they came across."

"All the same, sir," I said, "I don't believe poor old Ching would do anything that was against us."

"Well, we shall see. But what an escape, my lad! What a trap we were in!"

"And how capital to get out of it without having a man hurt."

"It's splendid, my lad. The captain will be delighted at that, and forgive me about the boat."

"But we had to run away, sir," I said.

"Rather strange running away to charge that boat as we did! But don't you take it into your head, my lad, that it is cowardly to retreat at the proper time. It is madness to go throwing away the lives of your men when you can do no good by fighting. It might sound very grand and heroic for us to have fought both those boats, and then tried to capture the junks; but we must have been cut to pieces in the attempt, and what then—"

"We should have been able to say that we did not turn tail upon our enemies."

"No, we should not, my boy, because there would not have been a soul left to tell the story. There, my lad, don't indulge in romance. He is the best commander who gains victories at the smallest cost of blood to his country.—Ha, at last! how much longer the creek seems coming back than it did going up."

"Running against the tide, too," I cried; and the next minute we glided out into the big stream, crossed the river, and settled down to a quiet, steady row on the far side, where the eddy enabled us to make a very fine rate of speed.

But our rate did not satisfy Mr Brooke, who kept on looking at his watch as the time went on, and we found that the swift tide had carried us much farther than we thought for.

"We shall never get back at this rate," said Mr Brooke, "and it can't be very long before the tide turns, and then those scoundrels will come sailing down, perhaps pass us before we can get to the *Teaser.*"

"Hardly," I ventured to observe.

"Well, no; you are right," he said. "I am too impatient. We have a good start, and must get to the gunboat long before they can."

Meanwhile Tom Jecks sat fast, pressing his feet against the jacket placed over the hole, and kept baling, while Ching took his time from him, and used his baler with enough skill to help get rid of a great deal of water, so that the boat was freed to an extent which set aside all danger of our sinking; but with all their efforts they never got beyond a certain point, for the water oozed in pretty constantly through and round the extempore plug.

At last, faint with heat and nearly exhausted, we came in sight of the first straggling houses, then they grew more close together, and fields and gardens gave place to the closely-packed habitations. For we had reached the town, though even then we had quite a long row before we could reach the *Teaser.*

The final stretch came at last—just about a quarter of a mile to traverse, and then we should be alongside.

"Thank goodness!" said Mr Brooke, drawing a deep breath; "I don't know when I have felt so anxious. Now, my lads, only another five minutes—a long pull and a strong pull, and all together."

The men cheered and pulled, sending the boat merrily along now, for the tide was close upon its highest point, and for some little time it grew more and more sluggish before the coxswain cried out—

"She's swung round, sir; tide's with us."

"Ha!" ejaculated Mr Brooke. "Then we shall get to the *Teaser* in time. They couldn't start from the creek with those light junks till now."

"How much farther is it, sir?" I said, as he stood up and shaded his eyes with his hand.

"It can't be many hundred yards," he replied. "It must be just beyond that head where the boats lie so thick. Yes, off that temple there up on the hill."

The men gave a cheer, and the boat sped on fast now, feeling the push given by the falling tide, and the short distance that lay between us; and the spot where we had lain at anchor so many days was soon traversed—the latter part in perfect silence, with Mr Brooke standing in the stern-sheets gazing straight ahead, and turning his eyes from side to side of the busy water thoroughfare.

"She has shifted her moorings," he said at last.

"Has she, sir?" I replied, as I recalled how the furnace fires were going and the *Teaser* was getting up steam when we started.

"Yes; how tiresome!" he muttered. "Just, too, when we want to communicate at once."

"But you can see her, sir?"

"No, my lad, no," he cried. "How can I see her if she is not here?"

"But I thought you said she had shifted her moorings, sir?"

"Yes, and gone down the river somewhere. Hang it all, she can't have sailed without us."

"They wouldn't do that, sir," I cried, feeling quite startled at the idea of the ship leaving us with our small boat in the midst of strangers. "Why, she must have had news of some other junks, sir, and gone in pursuit, or is it a mistake? We can't have come far enough. No; this is the spot."

The men were looking at me inquiringly, just as men accustomed to be led lean on their superiors for orders, even if one of those superiors be a mere boy, while I, acting in precisely the same spirit, looked up to Mr Brooke, and listened excitedly for what he would say next.

It seemed to be a long time before he spoke, and then it was between his teeth and with angry vehemence, as he dropped down into his seat.

"After all this hard struggle to get back with our news," he muttered, in so low a tone that I only heard his words, while the men sat with their oars balanced gazing forward to see if they could make out the *Teaser's* funnel and tall spars. "They ought not to have stirred; it's playing at dog and the shadow. Here have we brought the substance, and they are snapping at the reflection."

"Mr Brooke!" I said in a whisper.

"All right, my boy; don't be down-hearted. It's the fortune of sea life. Here we are, tired, hungry, and hot, with a badly leaking boat, and a far from friendly place to land in and get her repaired."

"But they can't have gone far," I said.

"I don't know, my lad. Had some news of pirates, perhaps. All I know now is that they've left us in the lurch."

Chapter Thirty Three
An Exchange

"Now then," said Mr Brooke, after a few minutes' pause, "what's the first thing, Herrick? We can't keep watch for the junks in this boat."

"The first thing is to get her mended, sir."

"Yes; but how?"

"Let's ask Ching."

"Ching!" said Mr Brooke angrily.

"You wantee Ching?" came in the familiar highly-pitched voice from forward. "You wantee Ching go buy new boatee?"

He came hurrying aft, nearly tumbling once; while, left to his own power alone, the coxswain redoubled his efforts to keep down the water, and the tin baler went *scoop scroop, scoop scroop,* and *splash splash,* as he sent the water flying.

But the dark, angry expression of Mr Brooke's countenance repelled the Chinaman, and he stopped short and looked from one to the other in a pleading, deprecating way, ending by saying piteously—

"You no wantee Ching?"

Mr Brooke shook his head, and our interpreter went back over the thwarts, reseated himself, and began to bale again, with his head bent down very low.

"Give way, my lads," said Mr Brooke, bearing hard on the tiller, and the boat began to bear round as he steered for the landing-place a quarter of a mile away.

I looked up at him inquiringly, and he nodded at me.

"We can't help it, Herrick," he said; "if we stop afloat with the boat in this condition we shall have a serious accident. But we shall lose the junks."

"Oh!" I ejaculated, "and after all this trouble. We had been so successful too. Couldn't we repair the boat?"

"If we could run into a good boat-builder's we might patch it up, but we can do nothing here."

"Couldn't Ching show us a place?"

"I can't ask the scoundrel."

I winced, for I could not feel that Ching had deceived us, and for a few moments I was silent. Then a thought struck me.

"May I ask him, sir?"

Mr Brooke was silent for a while, but he spoke at last.

"I hate risking his help again, but I am ready to do anything to try and carry out my instructions. We ought to patrol the river here to wait for the junks coming down, and then follow them, even if it is right down to sea. Well, yes; ask him it he can take us to a boat-builder's, where we can get some tarpaulin or lead nailed on."

I wasted no time. "Ching!" I cried; and he looked up sadly, but his face brightened directly as he read mine.

"You wantee Ching?"

"Yes; where is there a boat-builder's where they will mend the boat directly?"

"No," he said; "takee velly long time. Boat-builder same slow fellow. No piecee work along. Take boatee out water, mend him to-mollow, next week."

"Then what are we to do?" I cried. "We want to watch the junks."

"Why no takee other fellow big boatee? Plenty big boatee evelywhere. Get in big sampan junk, pilate man no sabby jolly sailor boy come along. Think other piecee fellow go catch fish."

"Here, Mr Brooke," I cried excitedly; "Ching says we had better take one of these boats lying moored out here, and the pirates won't think of it being us. Isn't it capital?"

Mr Brooke gazed sharply at us both for a few moments, and then directed the boat's head as if going up the river again.

"Where is there a suitable boat?" he said hoarsely, and speaking evidently under great excitement, as he saw a means of saving the chance after all.

"Velly nice big boat over 'long there," said Ching, pointing to a native craft about double the size of our cutter, lying moored about a hundred yards from the shore, and evidently without any one in her.

"Yes, that will do," cried Mr Brooke. "Anything fits a man who has no clothes. Pull, my lads—give way!"

The men dragged at the oars, and I saw that since Ching had left off baling the water was gaining fast, and that if more power was not put on it would not be long before the boat was waterlogged or sunk.

In a minute we were alongside the boat, one of a superior class, possibly belonging to some man of consequence, and Mr Brooke had run the cutter along her on the side farthest from the shore, so that our proceedings were not noticed, as we made fast.

"Now then, tumble in, my lads," he cried; "take the oars and everything movable. Throw them in, our game and all. Here, Herrick, take both guns."

Everything was transferred in a very short time; and this done, Mr Brooke stepped aboard the little junk-like craft, gave his orders, and a line was attached to a grating, the other end to one of the ring-bolts. Then the craft's anchor-line was unfastened, and our painter hitched on to it instead. Next the grating was tossed overboard, with plenty of line to float it as a buoy and show where the boat had sunk, as it was pretty certain to do before long; and we, in our tiny junk, began to glide away with the tide, furnished with a serviceable boat, boasting of sails, even if they were not of a kind our men were accustomed to manage.

"Why, it is grand, Herrick!" cried Mr Brooke excitedly. "We shall get them after all."

"And all Ching's doing, sir," I said quietly.

"Ah, yes, perhaps; he is repentant now he has been found out. But we shall see—"

"That he is quite innocent, sir," I said.

"I hope so, my lad. Now, let's make sail, and beat about here, to and fro. We must keep a good watch for our two friends, and if they come down we can follow till we see the *Teaser* in the offing. We may, I say, capture them yet."

A sail was hoisted, and in a few minutes we found that the craft went along easily and well, answering to her helm admirably. Her high bulwarks gave plenty of shelter, and would, I saw, well conceal our men, so that we had only to put Ching prominently in sight to pass unnoticed, or as a Chinese fishing or pleasure boat.

'PULL, MY LADS.'

Just then I turned and found him close behind me, rubbing his hands.

"You ask Mr Blooke he likee Ching sit where pilate see him 'gain?" he said.

"I am sure he would," I replied.

He looked sad again directly, and just touched the sleeve of my Norfolk jacket with the long nail of his forefinger.

"Ching velly solly," he said.

"What about?"

"Mr Blooke think Ching fliends with pilates. Velly shocking; Ching hate pilates dleadfully; hollid men."

"Yes, I am sure you do," I said.

The Celestial's face lit up again directly, and he rubbed his hands.

"Ching velly—"

"Yes?" I said, for Mr Brooke called to me from the little cabin contrived for shelter in the after part of the vessel.

"Look here," he said, as I joined him, "we can keep below here, and command the river too, without being seen. Why, Herrick, my lad, this is capital; they will never suspect this Chinese boat to be manned by a crew of Her Majesty's Jacks."

"Then everything has turned out for the best," I cried eagerly.

"Humph! that remains to be proved, my lad. We've got to return and face Mr Reardon and the captain, and the first question asked of an officer who has been entrusted with one of Her Majesty's boats, and who returns without it, is— What have you done with the boat or ship? We—yes, you are in the mess, sir—have to go back and say that we have lost it."

"Why, the captain owned to Pat that a thing couldn't be lost when you knew where it was."

"I don't understand you, my lad," said Mr Brooke.

"Don't you remember about the captain's tea-kettle, sir, that Pat dropped overboard? It was not lost, because Pat knew where it was—at the bottom of the sea."

"Oh yes, I remember; but I'm afraid Captain Thwaites will not take that excuse."

"Why, she has gone down already, sir," I said, as I looked over the side for the boat we had left.

"Yes; but I can see the grating floating. The coxswain took his jacket out of the hole."

He pointed to the stout piece of woodwork which we had turned into a buoy, but I could not make it out, and I thought it did not much matter, for something else had begun to trouble me a great deal just then, and I waited very anxiously for my officer to make some proposal.

But it did not come at once, for Mr Brooke was planning about the watch setting, so as to guard against the junks coming down the river and passing us on their way out to sea.

But at last all was to his satisfaction, one man keeping a look-out up the river for the descending junks, the other downward to the mouth for the return of the *Teaser*, whose coming was longed for most intensely.

Then, with just a scrap of sail raised, the rest acting as a screen dividing the boat, we tacked about the river, keeping as near as was convenient to the spot where the *Teaser* had anchored, and at last Mr Brooke said to me, just in the grey of the evening—

"I'm afraid the lads must be getting hungry."

"I know one who is, sir," I said, laughing.

He smiled.

"Well, I have been too busy and anxious to think about eating and drinking," he said; "but I suppose I am very hungry too. Here, my lad, pass that basket along, and serve out the provisions."

"You likee Ching serve out plovisions?"

Mr Brooke frowned, and the Chinaman shrank away. I noticed too that when the food was served round, the men took each a good lump of salt pork and a couple of biscuits, Ching contented himself with one biscuit, which he took right forward, and there sat, munching slowly, till it was dark and the shore was lit up with thousands of lanterns swinging in shop, house, and on the river boats moored close along by the shore.

"Bad for us," said Mr Brooke, as we sat together astern steering, and keeping a sharp look ahead for the expected enemy.

"Why?" I asked.

"Getting so dark, my lad. We shall be having the junks pass us."

"Oh no, sir. Ching is keen-sighted, and all the men are looking out very eagerly."

"Ah, well, I hope they will not slip by. They must not, Herrick. There is one advantage in this darkness, though: they will not find us out."

The darkness favouring the movement, and so as to save time, ready for any sudden emergency, he ordered the men to buckle on their cutlass-belts and pouches, while the rifles were hid handy.

"In case we want to board, Herrick."

"Then you mean to board if there is a chance?" I said.

"I mean to stop one of those junks from putting to sea, if I can," he replied quietly. "The *Teaser* having left us, alters our position completely. She has gone off on a false scent, I'm afraid, and we must not lose the substance while they are hunting the shadow."

Very little more was said, and as I sat in the darkness I had plenty to think about and picture out, as in imagination I saw our queer-looking boat hooked on to the side of a great high-pooped junk, and Mr Brooke leading the men up the side to the attack upon the fierce desperadoes who would be several times our number.

"I don't know what we should do," I remember thinking to myself, "if these people hadn't a wholesome fear of our lads."

Then I watched the shore, with its lights looking soft and mellow against the black velvety darkness. Now and then the booming of gongs floated off to us, and the squeaking of a curious kind of pipe; while from the boats close in shore the twangling, twingling sound of the native guitars was very plain—from one in particular, where there was evidently some kind of entertainment, it being lit up with a number of lanterns of grotesque shapes. In addition to the noise—I can't call it music—of the stringed instruments, there came floating to us quite a chorus of singing. Well, I suppose it was meant for singing; but our lads evidently differed, for I heard one man say in a gruff whisper—

"See that there boat, messmate?"

"Ay," said another. "I hear it and see it too."

"Know what's going on?"

"Yes; it's a floating poulterer's shop."

"A what?"

"A floating poulterer's shop. Can't you hear 'em killing the cats?"

This interested me, and I listened intently.

"Killing the cats?" said another.

"Ay, poor beggars. Lor' a mussy! our cats at home don't know what horrible things is done in foreign lands. They're killing cats for market to-morrer, for roast and biled."

"Get out, and don't make higgerant observations, messmate. It's a funeral, and that's the way these here heathens show how sorry they are."

"Silence there, my lads," said the lieutenant. "Keep a sharp look-out."

"Ay, ay, sir."

Just at that moment, as the lit-up boat glided along about a couple of hundred yards from us, where we sailed gently up-stream, there was a faint rustling forward, and Tom Jecks' gruff voice whispered—

"What is it, messmate?"

"Ching see big junk."

There was a dead silence, and we all strained our eyes to gaze up-stream.

"Can't see nought, messmate," was whispered.

"Yes; big junk come along."

Plash! and a creaking, rattling sound came forth out of the darkness.

"It is a big junk," said Mr Brooke, with his lips to my ear; "and she has anchored."

Then from some distance up the river we saw a very dim lantern sway here and there, some hoarse commands were given, followed by the creaking and groaning of a bamboo yard being lowered, and then all was perfectly still.

What strange work it seemed to be out there in the darkness of that foreign river, surrounded by curious sights and sounds, and not knowing but what the next minute we might be engaged in deadly strife with a gang of desperadoes who were perfectly indifferent to human life, and who, could they get the better of us, would feel delight in slaughtering one and all. It was impossible to help feeling a peculiar creepy sensation, and a cold shiver ran through one from time to time.

So painful was this silence, that I felt glad when we had sailed up abreast of the great vessel which had dropped anchor in mid-stream, for the inaction was terrible.

We sailed right by, went up some little distance, turned and came back on the other side, so near this time that we could dimly make out the heavy masts, the huge, clumsy poop and awkward bows of the vessel lying head to stream.

Then we were by her, and as soon as we were some little distance below Mr Brooke spoke—

"Well, my lads, what do you say: is she one of the junks?"

"No pilate junk," said Ching decisively, and I saw Mr Brooke make an angry gesture—quite a start.

"What do you say, my lads?"

"Well, sir, we all seem to think as the Chinee does—as it arn't one of them."

"Why?"

"Looks biggerer and clumsier, and deeper in the water."

"Yes; tlade boat from Hopoa," said Ching softly, as if speaking to himself.

"I'm not satisfied," said Mr Brooke. "Go forward, Mr Herrick; your eyes are sharp. We'll sail round her again. All of you have a good look at her rigging."

"Ay, ay, sir," whispered the men; and I crept forward among them to where Ching had stationed himself, and once more we began gliding up before the wind, which was sufficiently brisk to enable us to easily master the swift tide.

As I leaned over the side, Ching heaved a deep sigh.

"What's the matter?" I whispered.

"Ching so velly mislable," he whispered back. "Mr Blooke think him velly bad man. Think Ching want to give evelybody to pilate man. Ching velly velly solly."

"Hist! look out!"

I suppose our whispering had been heard, for just as we were being steered pretty close to the anchored junk, a deep rough voice hailed us something after this fashion, which is as near as I can get to the original—

"Ho hang wong hork ang ang ha?"

"Ning toe ing nipy wong ony ing!" cried Ching.

"Oh ony ha, how how che oh gu," came from the junk again, and then we were right on ahead.

"Well," whispered Mr Brooke, "what does he say? Is it one of the pirate vessels?"

"No pilate. Big boat come down hong, sir. Capin fellow want to know if we pilate come chop off head, and say he velly glad we all good man."

"Are you quite sure?" said Mr Brooke.

I heard Ching give a little laugh.

"If pilate," he said, "all be full bad men. Lightee lantern; thlow stink-pot; make noise."

"Yes," said Mr Brooke; "this cannot be one of them. Here, hail the man again, and ask him where he is going."

"How pang pong won toe me?" cried Ching, and for answer there came two or three grunts.

"Yes; what does he say?"

"Say he go have big long sleep, 'cause he velly tired."

Mr Brooke said no more, but ran the boat down the river some little distance and then began to tack up again, running across from side to side, so as to make sure that the junks did not slip by us in the darkness. But hour after hour glided on, and the lights ashore and on the boats gradually died out, till, with the exception of a few lanterns on vessels at anchor, river and shore were all alike one great expanse of darkness, while we had to go as slowly as possible, literally creeping along, to avoid running into craft moored in the stream.

And all this time perfect silence had to be kept, and but for the intense desire to give good account of the junks, the men would soon have been fast asleep.

"Do you think they will come down and try to put to sea, Ching?" I said at last, very wearily.

"Yes, allee 'flaid Queen Victolia's jolly sailor boy come steam up liver and send boat up cleek, fight and burn junks. Come down velly quick."

"Doesn't seem like it," I said, beginning at last to feel so drowsy I could not keep my eyes open.

"So velly dark, can't see."

"Why, you don't think they will get by us in the darkness?" I said, waking up now with a start at his words, and the bad news they conveyed.

"Ching can't tell. So velly dark, plenty junk go by; nobody see if velly quiet. Ching hope not get away. Wantee Mr Brooke catchee both junk, and no think Ching like pilate man."

"Here, I must go and have a talk to Mr Brooke," I said; and I crept back to where he sat steering and sweeping the darkness he could not penetrate on either side.

"Well, Herrick," he said eagerly. "News?"

"Yes, sir; bad news. Ching is afraid that the junks have crept by us in the night."

"I have been afraid so for some time, my lad, for the tide must have brought them down long enough ago."

He relapsed into silence for a few minutes, and then said quietly—

"You can all take a sleep, my lads; Mr Herrick and I will keep watch."

"Thankye, sir, thankye," came in a low murmur, and I went forward to keep a look-out there; but not a man lay down, they all crouched together, chewing their tobacco, waiting; while Ching knelt by the bows, his elbows on the gunwale, his chin resting upon his hands, apparently gazing up the river, but so still that I felt he must be asleep, and at last startled him by asking the question whether he was.

"No; too much head busy go sleep. Want findee allee pilate, show Mr Blooke no like pilate. Velly 'flaid all gone."

How the rest of that night went by, I can hardly tell. We seemed to be for hours and hours without end tacking to and fro, now going up the river two or three miles, then dropping down with the tide, and always zig-zagging so as to cover as much ground as possible. The night lengthened as if it would never end; but, like all tedious times of the kind, it dragged its weary course by, till, to my utter astonishment, when it did come, a faint light dawned away over the sea beyond the mouth of the river, just when we were about a mile below the city.

That pale light gradually broadened, and shed its ghastly chilly beams over the sea, making all look unreal and depressing, and showed the faces of our crew, sitting crouched in the bottom of the boat, silent but quite wide-awake.

Then all started as if suddenly electrified, for Ching uttered a low cry, and stood up, pointing right away east.

"What is it?" I said.

"Two pilate junk."

We all saw them at the same time, and with a miserable feeling of despondency, for there was no hiding the fact. The river was wide, and while we were close under one bank they had glided silently down under the other, and were far beyond our reach.

Chapter Thirty Four
The Untrustworthy Agent

"Eaten, Herrick," said Mr Brooke in a low voice.

"Not yet, sir," I said.

I don't know how it was that I said those words. They came to my lips and I uttered them, making Mr Brooke turn round upon me sharply, in the grey light of dawn.

"What do you mean by that, boy?" he said.

"Mean? I don't—I—that is,"—I stammered; "I wouldn't give up yet, sir."

"What would you do? wait for them to come back?" he said bitterly.

"No," I cried, gaining courage; "go after them, sir."

"And attack and take them with this boat, Herrick?" he said, smiling at me rather contemptuously.

"Of course we couldn't do that, sir," I said, "but we might follow and keep them in sight. We should know where they went."

"Yes," he said, after a moment's thought; "but we may be away for days, and we must have provisions. What is to be done?"

"You likee me buy blead and fish, and plenty good to eat?" said Ching in rather a shrinking way.

"Yes," said Mr Brooke, turning upon the Celestial sharply. "Where shall we land you?"

"There," said Ching, pointing to the shore about a mile up from where we lay.

"But it's going back, and we shall lose sight of the junks, Ching," I said.

"Plenty blead there. Ching know the way."

"But one moment, Mr Brooke," I said; "are we sure that those are the right junks?"

"I feel sure," he said. "What do you say, my lads?"

"Ay, ay, sir, them's right," chorussed the men.

"Yes, Ching velly sure those pilate junk."

"I know one on 'em, sir," said Jecks, "by her great yard. I never see a junk with such a big un afore. Talk about the cut of a jib—I says, look at the cut of her mainsail."

"Well, we must have food and water, if we are going out of the mouth of the river," said Mr Brooke, and he turned the boat's head shoreward.

"No makee haste," said Ching deprecatingly. "Too soon, evelybody fas' asleep."

Mr Brooke gave an impatient stamp on the frail bamboo half-deck, but said no more for a few moments.

"We must wait if we are too soon, for it would be madness to go without food and water."

He was silent for a time, during which the men watched the distant junks, and as they stood out more and more boldly in the morning light, we compared notes, and made comments upon them, all growing more and more satisfied that these were the two of which we were in search.

"Yes, they must be," said Mr Brooke at last, after listening for some time to the men's conversation. "The very fact of their sailing in company is suggestive. Seems odd, though, doesn't it, Herrick?" he half whispered.

"What? their getting by us, sir, in the dark?"

"No; I mean, after making up my mind that this fellow Ching was a traitor, and that I would have no more to do with him, to find myself forced at every turn to rest upon him for help. Lesson for you, lad."

"In what way, sir?"

"Not to have too much faith in yourself. I am beginning to hope that I have been deceived about him, but we shall soon have proof."

"I feel sure you are misjudging him, sir," I said eagerly.

"Yes, with a boy's readiness to trust."

"But I feel sure he is honest, sir."

"Well, we shall soon see."

I looked at him for an explanation, and he smiled.

"I am going to give him some money, and send him ashore to buy provisions. If he is dishonest he will not come back."

"But he will come back," I said confidently.

"We shall see, my lad," he replied; and once more he was silent, after handing the tiller to me, and looking back longingly at the two junks, which were apparently making no way, for the wind was blowing dead now into the mouth of the river.

Early as it was, there were people stirring as we approached the landing-place Ching had pointed out, and he nodded with satisfaction.

"Allee light," he said, smiling. "Get plenty blead, meat. You fillee big tub with water;" and he pointed to a large rough vessel, and another which was a great earthenware jar.

"But where are we to get the water?" I said.

"Out o' liver. Plenty water in liver."

"We can't drink that peasoup," I said, as I looked over the side in disgust at the yellow solution of mud.

"Velly good water. Allee salt gone now. Plenty clear by and by."

"We must make the best of it, Herrick," said my companion; and then turning to Ching, he said rather sternly—

"Here are eight dollars: buy as much bread and cooked meat as you can, and get back as quickly as possible, when we set you ashore."

Ching nodded and smiled.

"Be velly quick," he said; "and you take boat lit' way out, and stop till come back."

"Of course; trust us for that, my man."

Ten minutes later we ran alongside some rough bamboo piles, to which about half-a-dozen Chinamen hurried, to stand staring at us. But Ching paid no attention to them. He only made a leap from the boat when we were a couple of yards from the platform, landed safely but with tail flying, and his blue cotton garment inflating balloon-like with the wind. Then he walked away among the houses, and one of our men pushed the boat off again, evidently to the intense wonder of the people, who stared hard to see a British sailor managing a native vessel; while two others, in a costume perfectly new to them, sat looking on.

Then our men were packed out of sight, some in the little cabin, others hidden at the bottom of the boat, beneath a matting-sail.

When we were about a hundred yards from the shore, a clumsy wooden grapnel, to which a heavy stone was bound with a twisted rope of bamboo, was dropped overboard, and then we lay in the swift tide, with the boat tugging at the line as if eager to be off on the chase the stern necessity concerning food kept us from carrying on at once.

"How these people do seem to detest us, Herrick!" said Mr Brooke, after we had been waiting patiently for about a quarter of an hour, impatiently another, but not quite in idleness, for, after tasting the river water to find that it was very slightly brackish now, the tub and the jar were both filled and left to settle.

"Yes, they're not very fond of us," I replied, as I noted how the numbers were increasing, and that now there was a good deal of talking going on, and this was accompanied by gesticulations, we evidently being the objects of their interest. "They can't have much to do."

Mr Brooke made no reply, but moment by moment he grew more uneasy, as he alternately scanned the people ashore and the junks in the offing.

"Oh," I said at last, "if we could only see the *Teaser* coming up the river!"

"I'd be content, Herrick," said Mr Brooke bitterly, "if we could only see the messenger coming back with our stores."

"Yes," I said uneasily, for I had been fidgeting a good deal; "he is a long time."

"Yes," said Mr Brooke, looking at me very fixedly, till I avoided his gaze, for I knew he was thinking of my defence of Ching.

"Perhaps the bakers' shops are not open," I said at last.

"Perhaps this is not London, my lad. It's of no use for you to defend him; I begin to feel sure that he has left us in the lurch."

"Oh, wait a little longer, please, Mr Brooke," I cried; and I vainly scanned the increasing crowd upon the platform and shore, and could see, instead of Ching, that the people were growing more and more excited, as they talked together and kept pointing at us.

"I shall not wait much longer," said Mr Brooke at last. "He has had plenty of time. Look here, my lads, we have plenty of water, and the business is urgent. You'll have to be content with a drink and a pull at your waistbelts."

"All right, sir," said the coxswain; "what's good enough for the orficers is good enough for us. We won't grumble, eh, mates?"

There was a low growl here, but not of discontent.

"Then in another five minutes, if our Celestial friend does not come back, we shall start. I'll give him that time."

"Beg pardon, sir; they're a siggling of us."

"Signalling! who are?"

"The Chinees, sir."

"Yes, look," I said; for, after a good deal of talking and shouting, one man was standing close at the edge of the landing-place, and beckoning to us to come closer in.

"Likely," I heard one of our men whisper. "Ducks."

"Eh?" said another.

"Dill, dill, dill; will yer come and be killed?"

"What do they want, Herrick? To inveigle us ashore?"

"I know, sir for the reason of their excitement now came to me like a flash, and I wondered that I had not thought of it before."

"Well, then. Speak out if you do know, my lad."

"That's it, sir. We've got a boat they know, and they think we're stealing it."

"Tut, tut, tut. Of course. That explains it. Very sorry, my friends, but we cannot spare it yet. You shall have her back and be paid for the use of it, when we've done with her."

The shouts, gesticulations, and general excitement increased, two men now beckoning imperiously, and it was evident that they were ordering us to come to the landing-place at once.

"No, my friends," said Mr Brooke, "we are not coming ashore. We know your gentle nature too well. But Ching is not coming, Herrick, so we'll heave up the grapnel and be off."

The crowd was now dense, and the excitement still increasing, but the moment they saw our coxswain, in obedience to an order given by Mr Brooke—in spite of an appealing look, and a request for another ten minutes—begin to haul up the rough grapnel, the noise ashore was hushed, and the gesticulations ceased.

"Five minutes more, Mr Brooke," I whispered; "I feel sure that Ching will come."

"Silence, sir," he said coldly. "It is only what I expected. The man knows he is found out."

By this time the boat was hauled up over the grapnel, and I shrank away in despair, feeling bitterly disappointed at Ching's non-appearance, but full of confidence in him—faith the stronger for an intense desire to make up to the man for misjudging him before.

Then the grapnel was out of the mud, and hauled over the side; the boat began to yield to the tide; and Mr Brooke stepped to the mast himself, being unwilling to call the men in the cabin into the people's sight.

"Come and take a hand at the rope here, coxswain," said Mr Brooke. "Mr Herrick, take the tiller."

But at the first grasp of our intention, as they saw the preparation for hoisting the sail, there was a fierce yell from the shore, and the people scattered to right and left.

"What does that mean?" I said to myself. But the next instant I knew, for they were making for different boats, into which they jumped, and rapidly began to unmoor.

"Humph! time we were off," said Mr Brooke. "Hoist away, man, I cannot do it alone."

"I am a-hysting, sir, but the tackle's got foul somehow. It's this here rough rope. The yard won't move."

"Tut tut—try, man, try."

"All right, sir, I'll swarm up the the mast, and set it free."

"But there is no time, my man. Haul—haul."

The man did haul, but it was like pulling at a fixed rope, and the sail obstinately refused to move, while to my horror there were no less than six boats pushing off, and I foresaw capture, a Chinese prison, and severe punishment—if we could not get help—for stealing a boat.

"All hands on deck," cried Mr Brooke, making use of the familiar aboard-ship order, and just as the first two boats were coming rapidly on, and were within a dozen yards, our Jacks sprang up armed and ready.

The effect was magical. Evidently taken by surprise, the Chinamen stopped short, and the boats all went on drifting slowly down the stream. But at the end of a minute, as we made no attack, but all stood awaiting orders, they recovered their confidence, uttered a shout to encourage one another, and came on.

"I don't want to injure them," Mr Brooke muttered, but he was forced to act. "Give them the butts of your pieces, my lads, if they try to lay hold of the boat. Mind, they must be kept off."

He had no time to say more, but seized the fowling-piece as the first boat was rowed alongside, and amidst a fierce burst of objurgations, in a tongue we could not understand, a couple of men seized the gunwale of the boat, while two more jumped aboard.

The men who caught hold let go again directly, for the butts of the men's rifles and the gunwale were both hard for fingers, and the Chinese yelled, and the two who leaped aboard shrieked as they were seized and shot out of the boat again.

But by this time another craft of about our own size had come alongside, and was hanging on to us, while four more were trying to get in, and others were pushing off from the shore.

We were being surrounded; and, enraged by our resistance, while gaining courage from their numbers and from the fact that we made no use of cutlass or rifle, they now made desperate efforts to get aboard.

Our men were getting desperate too, and in another minute there must have been deplorable bloodshed, the more to be regretted as it would have been between our sailors and a friendly power, when Jecks, after knocking a Chinaman back into his own boat with his fist, stooped and picked up the boat-hook we had brought on board from our now sunken cutter. With this he did wonders, using it like a cue, Barkins afterwards said, when I described the struggle, and playing billiards with Chinese heads. But, be that as it may, he drove back at least a dozen men, and then attacked one of the boats, driving the pole right through the thin planking and sending the water rushing in.

But we were still in imminent danger of being taken prisoners, and, as he afterwards told me, Mr Brooke was thinking seriously of sending a charge of small-shot scattering amongst the crowd, when two of our lads seized the sheet and began to try and hoist the matting-sail, and to my intense delight I saw it begin to go up as easily as could be.

I flew to the tiller, but found a big Chinaman before me, and in an instant he had me by the collar and was tugging me over the side. But I clung to it, felt a jerk as there was a loud rap, and, thanks to Tom Jecks, the man rolled over into the water, and began to swim.

"Now for it, my lads," shouted Mr Brooke. "All together; over with them!"

The men cheered and struck down with the butts of their rifles, the boat-hook was wielded fiercely, and half-a-dozen of our assailants were driven out of the boat, but not into the others, for they fell with splash after splash into the river. For our vessel careened over as the sail caught the full pressure of the wind, and then made quite a bound from the little craft by which she was surrounded.

Then a cheer arose, for we knew we could laugh at our enemies, who were being rapidly left behind; and, while some dragged their swimming companions into their boats, the others set up a savage yelling; gesticulating, and no doubt telling us how, if they caught us, they would tear us into little bits.

"Well done, my lads," cried Mr Brooke. "Splendid, splendid. Couldn't have been better. Excellent, Mr Herrick; ease her a little, ease her. We must have a reef in that sail. All left behind, then; no pursuit?" and he looked astern as our boat rushed through the water, and then he frowned, for one of the men said—

"Yes, sir; here's one on 'em from the shore coming arter us full sail, and she's going as fast as we."

And once more, as I looked behind me, holding on the while by the tiller, I seemed to see the inside of a Chinese prison after we had been pretty well stoned to death; for it was a good-sized boat that was gliding after us at a rapid rate, and threatening to overtake us before long.

Chapter Thirty Five
Mr Brooke's Error

"I did not see either of those craft with sails," I said to Tom Jecks, as we stood watching the following boat, which was evidently making every possible effort to come up with us.

"No, sir, 'twarn't neither o' them. I see 'em put off from a bit higher up," said Jecks. "My hye! they are in a hurry, sir. You'd better tell Mr Brooke he must shake out a reef instead o' taking one up."

"No; leave it to him, he doesn't like interference."

"No, sir, orficers don't, and it is their natur' to. But I say, sir, what a—murder!—what a wrench I give my shoulder."

"How?"

"Hitting one o' them pudding-headed Teapots, sir. Didn't hurt my knuckles, because his head was soft. Just like punching a bladder o' lard, but the weight on him wrenched the jynte."

"Wait till we get on board," I said, "and Mr Price will soon put you right."

"Bah! not him, sir," said the man scornfully. "I shouldn't think o' going to a doctor for nothing less than losing my head. It'll soon get right. Exercise is the thing, sir, for a hurt o' that sort. You and Mr Brooke give us a good job at them pirates out yonder, and I shall forget all about my shoulder."

"We'll try," I said laughingly. "But what were you going to say just now?"

"I, sir? nothin', sir."

"Oh yes; when you broke off."

"I broke off, sir?"

"Yes."

"To be sure. Yes, sir, I was going to say what a lesson it is for you, sir, as a young orficer, not to go pickling and stealing other folkses' boats. This here all comes o' taking boats as don't belong to you."

"Better than sitting in another till she sinks, Tom Jecks."

"Not so honest, sir."

"Rubbish! We haven't stolen the boat; only borrowed it."

"Ah, that's what them heathens don't understand, sir; and I don't know as I blames 'em, for it is rather hard for 'em to take hold on. S'pose, sir, as you was in London town, and a chap was to take your dymon' ring—"

"Haven't got one, Tom Jecks."

"Well, s'pose you had one, and he took it and sailed away as hard as he could go, sir. It wouldn't be very easy for you to tell whether he'd stole it or borrowed it, eh, sir?"

"Oh, bother I don't ask riddles now, we're so busy. Here: over we go."

"Lie to the windward, all of you," shouted Mr Brooke, who was now at the tiller. "More aft there; that's better."

For the boat had careened over to so great an extent that she had taken in a little water, and I felt that we were about to be capsized.

But she rose again and skimmed along rapidly for the mouth of the river, and I crept close to my officer again.

"Shall I take the tiller, sir?" I said.

"No, Herrick, I'll keep it for the present. I want to get all I can out of the boat, and keep up as much sail as possible without capsizing. It's wonderful what these clumsy things can do."

"Yes, sir, we're going pretty fast, but I'm afraid the one behind goes faster."

"She does, my lad, for her crew know exactly how to manage. I don't want any more fighting if I can help it, but if they do overtake us I think we can soon send them back again. Men seem much hurt? Do they complain?" he whispered.

"Only about bruises, sir. They seem to treat it as so much fun. I say, how that boat does sail!"

"Yes, and we can do no more here but keep steadily on. Yes, we can. Take a pull at that sheet, my lads, and flatten out the sail a bit."

"Ay, ay, sir;" and the sail was hauled a foot higher, and the sheet tightened, with the effect that we raced along with the water parting like a broad arrow before our prow, so that we seemed to be sailing along in quite a trough, and at times I wondered that we were not swamped.

But it was very exciting, and, like the others, I forgot all about a few contusions in the intense interest of the chase.

I went forward again to where Tom Jecks sat on the port gunwale, which was formed of one bamboo carefully lashed on with strips of the same material, and as there was nothing else to do, I shaded my eyes from the nearly level rays of sunlight, and had a good look at the distant junks.

"Yes, sir, that's them, sure enough," said the coxswain. "Wish we was twice as many, and had a good-sized gun in the bows."

"Why, it would kick the boat all to pieces, or sink her," I said.

"Oh, that wouldn't matter, sir."

"But it's some one else's boat that we've borrowed," I said, with a laugh.

"Ay, so it is; I forgot, sir. But we ain't got a gun, and I'm afraid we can't take them two junks alone."

"So am I, Tom Jecks," I said; "but we can follow them."

"Arter we've had another naval engagement, sir. I say, look astern; I do like the impidence of these here savages, chasing on us like this, and they're gaining on us fast."

"No; only just holding their own."

"Gaining, sir."

"No."

"Yes, sir."

I took a long look back at the boat, and counted the black caps and flattened limpet-shaped straw hats of the blue-jacketed men on board.

"Seven of 'em," I said half aloud.

"Eight, sir; I counted 'em twice. One on 'em is a-lying down now, but he was a-setting up a little while ago. Afraid we shall open fire, I expect."

"And that's what we shall have to do," I said. "A rifle bullet or two sent over their heads would make them give up."

"But they arn't pirates, sir, and you mustn't fire at 'em. Look at that now."

The pursuing boat was about two hundred yards behind us, and one of the Chinamen now stood up in the bows, holding on by a stay, waving his straw hat and gesticulating furiously.

"All right, Mr Shing po Num, or whatever your name is," said the coxswain in a low voice, "can't stop this time, we're in a hurry."

The man kept on gesticulating.

"Can't you hear what I say?" continued Jecks in a whisper. "We're in a hurry. Say, sir, that's the chap as belongs to our boat—I mean his boat, and he's getting wilder and wilder now to see us carry it off. Say, sir, arn't it a bit—what you may call it—to take it away?"

"A bit what?"

"Well, sir, what do you grand folks call it when some one does what we're a-doing on?"

"Unkind."

"No, sir; it arn't an un-anything."

"Cruel?"

"No, sir. Cause you see a boat arn't a beast."

"Oh, I don't know what you mean," I said impatiently.

"Yes, it is an un-something; I forgot, sir. I meant undignified—that's the word."

"He shall have his boat when we've done with it, and be paid for it too," I said. "English officers don't do undignified things."

"But it strikes me, sir, as there won't be no boat to pay for when the pirates have done with us. If we go alongside, do you know what they'll do?"

"Shoot."

"No, sir; pitch ballast into us, and sink us, as sure as we're here."

"Don't talk so much," I said impatiently. "Why, they've got another sail up, and are coming on faster."

"Yes, sir, that's right; and they'll be alongside on us in another ten minutes. Shall I pass the word along to the lads to spit in their fists?"

"What?"

"I mean, sir, I s'pose it won't be cutlasses but fisties, sir, eh?"

"Mr Herrick, you had better come and take the tiller," said Mr Brooke just then. "Don't attend to anything else. Your duty is to keep the boat running; we'll do what fighting there is."

"Very well, sir," I said, and I felt disappointed as I took the tiller, but felt better a minute later as I felt how I could sway the racing boat by a touch.

"Now, my lads, cutlasses and rifles under the thwarts. You take the oars to these men. Don't attack them, they are ignorant of our power. Only keep them off with a few blows."

The men eagerly responded to the words of command, and stood and sat about in the boat, each man armed with a stout, strong ashen blade, a blow from which would have sent any one overboard at once.

The chase, with our boat playing the part of hare, was exciting enough before, but it grew far more so now, for the men in the other boat were evidently determined, and two of them stood up with clumsy-looking hooks, and another with a coil of rope ready to lasso us, as it seemed to me. And as I sat there I felt how awkward it would be if the man threw a loop over my head or chest, and dragged me out of the boat.

Naturally enough, the thought of this alone was enough to produce in me an intense desire to stand up, instead of crouching down there holding the tiller, and forced into a state of inaction, wherein I was forbidden to move or raise a hand in my defence.

"I hope they'll give a thought to me," I said to myself, as I felt that in a very few minutes they would be alongside trying to leap on board, and from my position I knew that I must be in the thick of the fight, perhaps trampled upon, and pretty sure to receive some of the blows which came flying about.

I gazed firmly forward, knowing how much depended upon my keeping the boat's head straight, and determined, as I set my teeth, to do my duty as well as possible, but I could not help turning my head from time to time to look back at the pursuers, who began shouting to us, and jabbering in their own tongue, as they were evidently now at the highest pitch of excitement.

Not many yards behind now, and gradually lessening the distance. All was ready on board, and I saw Mr Brooke looking stern, and the men as they grasped their oars grinning at one another, and then looking aft at the enemy.

And as we raced, the water foaming behind, the bamboo mast creaking and bending, the mat-sail cracking and making curious noises as the wind hissed through the thick stuff, the trough we ploughed through the water seemed deeper, and my temples throbbed and my heart beat, while from time to time the water lipped over the bows, but not enough to warrant any change of course. And nearer and nearer the enemy came, their boat literally skimming over the water, six feet to our five, and I felt that the time had arrived.

One more quick glance over my shoulder at the eager faces of the Chinamen as they uttered a loud shout, another at the men ready for action; another over my left shoulder to see that the enemy was close upon us, and then I uttered a strange cry, and, bearing hard upon the tiller, threw the boat right up into the wind, the sail easing as we formed a curve in the water, our speed checked, and then we lay nose to wind, with the boat seeming to quiver and pant after her heavy run.

"Are you mad?" roared Mr Brooke, rushing at me, thrusting me aside so that I went down upon my back, and he was about to seize the tiller, when I shouted out, half-choking with laughter, panting too with triumphant delight—

"Don't, don't, don't! Can't you see—it is Ching!"

Chapter Thirty Six
Rest and Refreshment

Ching it was, and the men sent up a cheer as out pursuers grappled the side of our boat, held on, and our messenger came on board smiling.

"Velly muchee big job you catchee," he said. "Why, what fo' you lun along so fast?"

"Why, Ching," cried Mr Brooke, "what does this mean?"

"No get away. Muchee velly bad man. No get to boat. Allee fightee. Get 'nother boat, and come along."

"You couldn't get on board us again?"

"No; too many velly bad men. Plenty blead; plenty fish; plenty meat. Velly nice. All in boat. Velly long time catchee."

Our men laid down the oars with a great deal of care and precision, as if it was important that they should not be a quarter of an inch wrong, and our coxswain doubled himself up to indulge in a good long comfortable chuckle, while I could not help whispering to the young lieutenant—

"I say, Mr Brooke, I wasn't very far wrong?"

"No, my lad," he said, with a smile; "I give in. I was all prejudice against the poor fellow, but I was justified in a great deal that I said. Appearances were dead against him. There, I was too hasty."

Meanwhile the stores Ching had bought had been transferred to our boat, and he had told us a little about his adventures—how, when he had made his purchases, he had returned to the landing-place and found the crowd gathering, and heard the men declaiming against the foreign devils who had stolen the boat they were using. The people were growing so much excited that he soon found it would be impossible for him to go off with his load to join us, and as soon as he heard the most prominent of the men shouting to us to come ashore, he felt that his first duty was to warn us not to.

"Catchee allee. Takee off to plison. In plison velly hard get out again," he said, and then went on to tell us how he felt it would be best to hire a boat to come off to us from higher up the river, but in spite of all his efforts he could not get one and his stores on board till he saw the other boats push off to the attack; and then, when his men willingly tried to overtake us, urged on by promises of good pay, they had been mistaken by us for enemies.

"But velly good boat, sail velly fast. You tink it Ching coming?"

"No, of course not," I said.

"No, not tink it Ching. Send boat 'way now? Ching go?"

"No, no," said Mr Brooke eagerly. "You will stop with us."

"You no velly closs with Ching now?"

"Cross? No; very grateful."

"You no tink Ching like velly bad man pilate?"

"I think you a very good, faithful fellow," said Mr Brooke, and the Chinaman's face lit up.

"Send boat 'way now?"

"Stop; I must pay the men."

Ching shook his head.

"No, Ching pay. Velly clebby pay money. Two dollar pay men."

He went back into the other boat, and, producing some money from up his sleeve, he settled with the men, who nodded, smiled, and, as soon as Ching had returned on board, were about to push off, when Mr Brooke stopped them.

"Tell them we shall return the boat as soon as we have done with it."

"Yes; no go steal boat. Plenty boat in steamy-ship. Tell them capen give dollar, eh?"

"Yes, tell them that."

"You likee other boat and men?"

"Well, I don't know," said Mr Brooke, hesitating, as if he thought some use might be made of such a fast-sailing craft.

"Ching askee."

He entered into a short conversation with the boatmen, who smiled at first, then scowled, stamped, and gesticulated.

Ching nodded and turned to us.

"Say, go to big steamy-ship and Queen Victolia jolly sailor, but no to see pilate. 'Flaid cut off head."

"Then they must go; send them off."

The men laughed, nodded at us in the most friendly manner, then hoisted their sail and went back up the river. Then, provisions being served out, our lads sat eating and chatting, while our boat sped seaward towards where the two junks lay windbound not many miles away, or else waiting for some reason, one which Mr Brooke decided at last to be for reinforcements.

"Yes," he said, as I sat munching away at some pleasantly sweet-tasted bread which Ching had brought on board, "depend upon it, we shall see boats or a small junk go out and join them by and by."

It is curious how old tunes bring up old scenes. Most people say the same, but at the risk of being considered one who thinks too much of eating, I am going to say that nothing brings up old scenes to my memory more than particular kinds of food.

For instance, there is a flat, square kind of gingerbread which we boys used to know as "parliament." I cannot ever see that without thinking of going to school on sunny mornings, and stopping by one particular ditch to bang the wasps with my school-bag, swung round by its string. It was only the seniors who sported a strap for their books; and in those days my legs, from the bottom of my drawers to the top of my white socks, were bare, and my unprotected knees in a state of chip, scale, and scar, from many tumbles on the gravelly path.

Then, again, pancakes will bring up going round the stables and cowhouse in search of stray new-laid white eggs, which I bore off, greatly to the disgust of the great black cock, with the yellow saddle-hackles and the tall red serrated comb.

Fish naturally bring up the carp in the muddy pond which we used to catch, and gloat over their golden glories; or the brazen small-scaled tench, with all the surroundings at Norwood, where the builder has run riot, and terraces and semi-detached villas—I hope well drained—cover the pool whence we used to drag forth miniature alligators with a worm.

I could go on for pages about those recollections, but one more will suffice:— Sweet cakey bread always brings up Mother Crissell, who must have made a nice little independence by selling us boys that sweet cake dotted with currants, some of which were swollen out to an enormous size, and lay in little pits on the top. These currants we used to dig out as *bonnes bouches* from the dark soft brown, but only to find them transformed into little bubbles of cindery lava, which crunched between the teeth.

And so it was that, as I sat sailing along at the mouth of that swift, yellow, muddy Chinese river, munching the sweet cakey bread Ching had brought on board, and gazing from time to time at the geese we had shot and had no means of cooking, memory carried me back to Mother Crissell's shop, and that rather bun-faced old lady, who always wore a blue cotton gown covered with blue spots and of no particular shape, for the amiable old woman never seemed to have any waist. There was the inside of her place, and the old teapot on the chimney-piece, in which she deposited her money and whence she drew forth change.

And then, in a moment, I seemed to be back in the great playground; then away on to the common, where we hunted for lizards amongst the furze, and got more pricks than reptiles. I saw, too, the big old horse-chestnuts round by the great square pond where you could never catch any fish, but always tried for them on account of the character it had of holding monsters, especially eels as big and round as your arm. I never knew any one catch a fish in that pond, but we did a deal of anticipation there, and watched the dragon-flies flit to and fro, and heard the rustle of they transparent wings. Splendid ones they were. First of all, there came early in the summer the thin-bodied ones, some of a steely-blue, some dark with clear wings, and with them those with the wings clouded with dark patches. Then came the large, short, flat-bodied, pointed-tailed fellows, some blue, some olive-green. Late in the season, affecting the damp spots of the common among the furze bushes more than the pond, came the largest long-bodied flies, which hawked to and fro over the same ground, and played havoc among their prey.

You could hear the school-bell from there—the big one in the turret on the top of the great square brick mansion; and in imagination I saw that pond, and the dragon-flies, lizards, and furze, the shady finger-leaved chestnuts, and even heard that bell, while the sweet cakey bread lasted; and then I was back in the Chinese boat on the Chinese river, for Ching leaned over me with something in rice-paper.

"You likee bit piecee flesh meat?"

"What is it?" I said, looking hard at the rather tempting brown meat with its white fat.

"Velly nice," he said. "Got pep' salt. Velly good."

"Yes," I said; "but is it good? I mean something I should like to eat?"

"Yes; loast lit' piggee; velly nice."

He was quite right—it was; and after I had finished I went forward to see if I could get something to drink. Jecks was inspecting the big earthen vessel with a tin baler, and I appealed to him.

"How is the water?" I said.

"Well, sir, yer can't say quite well thankye, 'cause it arn't right colour yet, and it's got a sort o' fishing-boat flavour in it, as puts yer in mind o' Yarmouth market at herring time, but it ain't so pea-soupy as it were, and it might be worse. Try a tot, sir?"

"Yes," I said; "I'm so thirsty, I must have a drop."

He dipped the baler in carefully, and brought it out dripping.

"Has anybody else drunk any?" I said.

"Oh yes, sir, all on us; and I says to you as I says to them, you shut your eyes, sir, and think you've been eating bloaters, or codfish, or fried sole. Then tip it down quick, and you'll says it's lovely."

"Ugh!" I ejaculated, as I looked down into the baler, "why, it looks like a dose of rhubarb."

"Well, it do, sir, a little; but you're a spyling of it a deal by looking at it first. You shut your eyes, sir, as I said; me and my mates thought as it's good strong water with a deal o' what some people calls nootriment in it."

"None for me, thank you," I said, handing back the tin.

"Bring me some water, Mr Herrick, when you've done," said Mr Brooke from where he sat holding the tiller.

"Yes, sir," I said; and, holding the baler to my lips, I took a hearty, hasty draught, for it was cool and refreshing to my dry mouth and throat, and, that done, I refilled the baler and took it aft.

"Humph! rather muddy, Herrick," said Mr Brooke, smiling; "but one can't carry a filter about at a time like this."

He tossed off the water without hesitation, gave one of the men the tin to take back, and then altered the course of the boat a little, so as to hug the shore.

"We must not let the pirates suspect that we are following," he said.

"What are we going to do, Mr Brooke?" I said.

"You should never question your commanding-officer about his strategy," he replied, with a smile; and I was about to apologise, but he went on, "There's only one thing to do, my lad, keep them in sight, and I hope that at any time the *Teaser* may appear. When she does, she will in all probability run by those junks without suspecting their nature, then we come in and let them know the truth."

"But suppose the *Teaser* does not come into sight?"

"Then our task is clear enough. We must hang on to the track of the junks till we see where they go. Depend upon it, they have two or three rendezvous."

"Think they have telescopes on board?" I said.

"It is extremely doubtful; and if we keep Ching always well in sight, I don't suppose they will notice us. They will take us for a fishing-boat, that's all."

By this time the sun was pouring down his beams with scorching violence, and we were glad to give up the tiller to one of the men, and get into the shelter of the cabin, just beyond which we found that Ching was busy at work plucking one of the geese.

"Why are you doing that?" I asked.

"Velly good to loast."

"But we've got no fire."

"Go 'shore, make fi', loast all, and come back on board."

"Yes, it will be a good addition to our stock of provisions, Herrick," said Mr Brooke, smiling. "Your friend Ching is going to turn out a benefactor after all."

Chapter Thirty Seven
Jack Ashore

All was quiet on the junks, not a man being visible as we sailed out of the river and along the south shore of the estuary; and now, after a long examination, Mr Brooke declared that there couldn't be a doubt as to their being the ones we had seen up the branch river when we were in the trap.

"The rig is too heavy for ordinary traders, Herrick," he said; and he pointed out several peculiarities which I should not have noticed.

Ching had been watching us attentively, and Mr Brooke, who evidently wanted to make up now for his harsh treatment of the interpreter, turned to him quietly—

"Well, what do you say about it, Ching?"

The interpreter smiled.

"Ching quite su'e," he replied. "Seen velly many pilate come into liver by fancee shop. Ching know d'leckly. Velly big mast, velly big sail, go so velly fast catchee allee ship. You go waitee all dalk, burn all up."

"What! set fire to them?"

"Yes; velly easy. All asleep, no keepee watch like Queen ship. No light. Cleep velly close up top side, big wind blow; make lit' fire both junk and come away. Allee 'light velly soon, and make big burn."

"What! and roast the wretches on board to death?"

"Some," said Ching, with a pleasant smile. "Makee squeak, and cly 'Oh! oh!' and burn all 'way like fi'wo'k. Look velly nice when it dalk."

"How horrid!" I cried.

"Not all bu'n up," said Ching; "lot jump ove'board and be dlown."

"Ching, you're a cruel wretch," I cried, as Mr Brooke looked at the man in utter disgust.

"No; Ching velly glad see pilate bu'n up and dlown. Dleadful bad man, bu'n ship junk, chop off head. Kill hundleds poo' good nicee people. Pilate velly hollid man. Don't want pilate at all."

"No, we don't want them at all," said Mr Brooke, who seemed to be studying the Chinaman's utter indifference to the destruction of human life; "there's no room for them in the world, but that's not our way of doing business. Do you understand what I mean?"

"Yes, Ching understand, know. Ching can't talk velly quick Inglis, but hear evelyting."

"That's right. Well, my good fellow, that wouldn't be English. We kill men in fair fight, or take them prisoners. We couldn't go and burn the wretches up like that."

Ching shook his head.

"All velly funnee," he said. "Shoot big gun and make big hole in junk; knockee all man into bit; makee big junk sink and allee men dlown."

"Yes," said Mr Brooke, wrinkling up his forehead.

"Why not make lit' fire and bu'n junk, killee allee same?"

"He has me there, Herrick," said Mr Brooke.

"Takee plisoner to mandalin. Mandalin man put on heavy chain, kick flow in boat, put in plison, no give to eat, and then choppee off allee head. Makee hurt gleat deal mo'. Velly solly for plisoner. Bette' make big fi' and bu'n allee now."

Mr Brooke smiled and looked at me, and I laughed.

"We'd better change the subject, Herrick," he said. "I'm afraid there is not much difference in the cruelty of the act."

"No, sir," I said, giving one of my ears a rub. "But it is puzzling."

"Yes, my lad; and I suppose we should have no hesitation in shelling and burning a pirates' nest."

"But we couldn't steal up and set fire to their junks in the dark, sir?"

"No, my lad, that wouldn't be ordinary warfare. Well, we had better run into one of these little creeks, and land," he continued, as he turned to inspect the low, swampy shore. "Plenty of hiding-places there, where we can lie and watch the junks, and wait for the *Teaser* to show."

"Velly good place," said Ching, pointing to where there was a patch of low, scrubby woodland, on either side of which stretched out what seemed to be rice fields, extending to the hills which backed the plain. "Plenty wood makee fire—loast goose."

I saw a knowing look run round from man to man.

"But the pirates would see our fire," I said.

"Yes, see fi'; tink allee fish man catch cookee fish."

"Yes, you're right, Ching. It will help to disarm any doubts. They will never think the *Teaser's* men are ashore lighting a fire;" and, altering our course a little, he ran the boat in shore and up a creek, where we landed, made fast the boat under some low scrubby trees, and in a very short time after a couple of men were placed where they could watch the junks and give notice of any movement. The others quickly collected a quantity of drift-wood, and made a good fire, Ching tucking up his sleeves and superintending, while Mr Brooke and I went out on the other side of the little wood, and satisfied ourselves that there was no sign of human habitation on this side of the river, the city lying far away on the other.

When we came back, Ching was up to the elbows in shore mud, and we found by him a couple of our geese and a couple of ducks turned into dirt-puddings. In other words, he had cut off their heads, necks, and feet, and then cased them thickly with the soft, unctuous clay from the foot of the bank; and directly we came he raked away some of the burning embers, placed the clay lumps on the earth, and raked back all the glowing ashes before piling more wood over the hissing masses.

"Velly soon cook nicee," he said, smiling; and then he went to the waterside to get rid of the clay with which he was besmirched.

Mr Brooke walked to the sentinels, and for want of something else to do I stood pitching pieces of drift-wood on to the fire, for the most part shattered fragments of bamboo, many of extraordinary thickness, and all of which blazed readily and sent out a great heat.

'MAKES A BIT OF A CHANGE, SIR.'

"Makes a bit of a change, Mr Herrick, sir," said Jecks, as the men off duty lay about smoking their pipes, and watching the fire with eyes full of expectation.

"Yes; rather different to being on shipboard, Jecks," I said.

"Ay, 'tis, sir. More room to stretch your legs, and no fear o' hitting your head agin a beam or your elber agin a bulkhead. Puts me in mind o' going a-gipsying a long time ago."

"'In the days when we went gipsying, a long time ago,'" chorussed the others musically.

"Steady there," I said. "Silence."

"Beg pardon, sir," said one of the men; and Tom Jecks chuckled. "But it do, sir," he said. "I once had a night on one o' the Suffolk heaths with the gipsies; I was a boy then, and we had hare for supper—two hares, and they was cooked just like that, made into clay balls without skinning on 'em first."

"But I thought they always skinned hares," I said, "because the fur was useful."

"So it is, sir; but there was gamekeepers in that neighbourhood, and if they'd found the gipsies with those skins, they'd have asked 'em where the hares come from, and that might have been unpleasant."

"Poached, eh?"

"I didn't ask no questions, sir. And when the hares was done, they rolled the red-hot clay out, gave it a tap, and it cracked from end to end, an' come off like a shell with the skin on it, and leaving the hares all smoking hot. I never ate anything so good before in my life."

"Yah! These here geese 'll be a sight better, Tommy," said one of the men. "I want to see 'em done."

"And all I'm skeart about," said another, "is that the *Teaser* 'll come back 'fore we've picked the bones."

I walked slowly away to join Mr Brooke, for the men's words set me thinking about the gunboat, and the way in which she had sailed and left us among these people. But I felt that there must have been good cause for it, or Captain Thwaites would never have gone off so suddenly.

"Gone in chase of some of the scoundrels," I thought; and then I began to think about Mr Reardon and Barkins and Smith. "Poor old Tanner," I said to myself, "he wouldn't have been so disagreeable if it had not been for old Smith. Tanner felt ashamed of it all the time. But what a game for them to be plotting to get me into difficulties, and then find that I was picked out for this expedition! I wish they were both here."

For I felt no animosity about Smith, and as for Tanner I should have felt delighted to have him there to join our picnic dinner.

I suppose I had a bad temper, but it never lasted long, and after a quarrel at school it was all over in five minutes, and almost forgotten.

I was so deep in thought that I came suddenly upon Mr Brooke, seated near where the men were keeping their look-out. He was carefully scanning the horizon, but looked up at me as I stopped short after nearly kicking against him.

"Any sign of the *Teaser* sir?" I said.

"No, Herrick. I've been trying very hard to make her out, but there is no smoke anywhere."

"Oh, she'll come, sir, if we wait. What about the junks?"

"I haven't seen a man stirring oh board either of them, and they are so quiet that I can't quite make them out."

"Couldn't we steal off after dark, sir, and board one of them? If we took them quite by surprise we might do it."

"I am going to try, Herrick," he said quietly, "some time after dark. But that only means taking one, the other would escape in the alarm."

"Or attack us, sir."

"Very possibly; but we should have to chance that." He did not say any more, but sat there scanning the far-spreading sea, dotted with the sails of fishing-boats and small junks. But he had given me plenty to think about, for I was growing learned now in the risks of the warfare we were carrying on, and I could not help wondering what effect it would have upon the men's appetites if they were told of the perilous enterprise in which they would probably be called upon to engage that night.

My musings were interrupted by a rustling sound behind me, and, turning sharply, it was to encounter the smooth, smiling countenance of Ching, who came up looking from one to the other as if asking permission to join us.

"Well," said Mr Brooke quietly, "is dinner ready?"

Ching shook his head, and then said sharply —

"Been thinking 'bout junks, they stop there long time."

"Yes; what for? Are they waiting for men?"

"P'laps; but Ching think they know 'bout other big junk. Some fliends tell them in the big city. Say to them, big junk load with silk, tea, dollar. Go sail soon. You go wait for junk till she come out. Then you go 'longside, killee evelybody, and take silk, tea, dollar; give me lit' big bit for tellee."

"Yes, that's very likely to be the reason they are waiting."

"Soon know; see big junk come down liver, and pilates go after long way, then go killee evelybody. Muchee better go set fire both junk to-night."

"We shall see," said Mr Brooke quietly.

He rose and walked down to the two sentinels.

"Keep a sharp look-out, my lads, for any junks which come down the river, as well as for any movements on board those two at anchor. I shall send and relieve you when two men have had their dinner."

"Thankye, sir," was the reply; and we walked back, followed by Ching.

"That last seems a very likely plan, Herrick," said Mr Brooke. "The scoundrels play into each other's hands; and I daresay, if the truth was known, some of these merchants sell cargoes to traders, and then give notice to the pirates, who plunder the vessels and then sell the stuff again to the merchants at a cheap rate. But there, we must eat, my lad, and our breakfast was very late and very light. We will make a good meal, and then see what the darkness brings forth."

We found the men carefully attending to the fire, which was now one bright glow of embers; and very soon Ching announced that dinner was cooked, proceeding directly after to hook out the hard masses of clay, which he rolled over to get rid of the powdery ash, and, after letting them cool a little, he duly cracked them, and a gush of deliciously-scented steam saluted our nostrils.

But I have so much to tell that I will not dwell upon our banquet. Let it suffice that I say every one was more than satisfied; and when the meal was over, Ching set to work again coating the rest of our game with clay, and placed them in the embers to cook.

"Velly good, velly nicee to-day," he said; "but sun velly hot, night velly hot, big fly come to-mollow, goose not loast, begin to 'mell velly nasty."

As darkness fell, the fire was smothered out with sand, there being plenty of heat to finish the cookery; and then, just when I least expected it, Mr Brooke gave the order for the men to go to the boat.

He counter-ordered the men directly, and turned to me.

"These are pretty contemptible things to worry about, Herrick," he said, "but unless we are well provisioned the men cannot fight. We must wait and take that food with us."

Ching was communicated with, and declared the birds done. This announcement was followed by rolling them out, and, after they had cooled a bit, goose and duck were borne down to the boat in their clay shells, and stowed aft, ready for use when wanted.

Ten minutes later we were gliding once more through the darkness outward in the direction of the two junks, while my heart beat high in anticipation of my having to play a part in a very rash and dangerous proceeding—at least it seemed to be so to me.

Chapter Thirty Eight
Information

It was too dark to make out the junks, but their direction had been well marked, and Mr Brooke took his measures very carefully.

"Perfect silence, my lads," he said. "Perhaps the lives of all here depend upon it. Now, the sail half up; Jecks, hold the sheet; the others sit in the bottom of the boat. Every man to have his arms ready for instant use."

There was a quick movement, a faint rattle, and then all still.

"Good; very prompt, my lads. Mr Herrick, come and take the tiller, and be ready to obey the slightest whispered command."

I hurriedly seated myself by him in the darkness, and waited while our leader now turned to the last man to receive his orders.

"You, Ching," he said, "will go right forward to keep a good look-out, ready to give a whispered warning of our approach to the junks. Do you know what a whispered warning means?"

"Yes; Ching say see junk so lit' voice you can't hear him."

The men tittered.

"Silence! Yes, you understand. Now go, and be careful. But mind this, if our boat is seen and the pirates hail, you answer them in their own tongue; do you understand?"

"Yes; 'peakee Chinee all along."

"That will do."

Ching crept forward, and we were gliding along over the dark sea before a gentle breeze, which, however, hardly rippled the water.

"Keep a bright look-out for the *Teaser*, Jecks. We may see her lights."

"Ay, ay, sir."

Then on and on in a silence so deep that the gentle rattle and splash of the sea against our bows sounded singularly loud, and I almost felt drowsy at last, but started back into wakefulness on Mr Brooke touching my arm and whispering—

"I reckon that we shall be very near them in another ten minutes. I want to sail round at a little distance."

I nodded, but doubted whether he could see me in the intense darkness, for there was not a star to be seen, the sky being covered with low down black clouds, which seemed to be hanging only a short distance above the sea. Right away behind us was a faint glow telling of the whereabouts of the Chinese city, but seaward there was no sign of the *Teaser's* or any other lights, for it was like sailing away into a dense black wall, and I began to look forward more and more anxiously as I thought of the possibility of our running with a crash right on to the anchored junks.

But I was under orders, and waited for my instructions, keeping the light craft as straight on her course as I could contrive, and grasping the tiller with all my strength.

All at once there was a faint rustling, and suddenly I felt Ching's soft hand touch my knee, and I could just make out his big round face.

"Listen," he said.

Mr Brooke's hand was laid on mine, and the tiller pressed sidewise slowly and gently, so that the boat glided round head to wind, and we lay motionless, listening to the dull creak and regular beat of oars a short distance to the north. Then came a faint groan or two of the oars in their locks, but that was all. We could see nothing, hear no other sound, but all the same we could tell that a large boat of some kind was being pulled in the same direction as that which we had taken.

"Men going out to the junks," I said to myself, and my heart beat heavily, so that I could feel it go *throb throb* against my ribs. I knew that was what must be the case, and that the men would be savage, reckless desperadoes, who would have tried to run us down if they had known of our being there.

But they were as much in the dark as we, and I could hear them pass on, and I knew that we must have been going in the right direction for the junk. Then I had clear proof, for all at once there was a low, wailing, querulous cry, which sent a chill through me, it sounded so wild and strange.

"Only a sea-bird—some kind of gull," I said to myself; and then I knew that it was a hail, for a short way to the southwards a little dull star of light suddenly shone out behind us, for the boat had of course been turned.

There was the answer to the signal, and there of course lay the junk, which in another five minutes we should have reached.

Mr Brooke pressed my arm, and we all sat listening to the beating of the oars, slow and regular as if the rowers had been a crew of our well-trained Jacks. Then the beat ceased, there was a faint rattling noise, which I know must have been caused by a rope, then a dull grinding sound as of a boat rubbing against the side of a vessel, and lastly a few indescribable sounds which might have been caused by men climbing up into the junk, but of that I could not be sure.

Once more silence, and I wondered what next.

Mr Brooke's hand upon mine answered my wonderings. He pressed it and the tiller together, the boat's sail filled gently once more, and we resumed our course, but the direction of the boat was changed more to the north-eastward. We were easing off to port so as to get well to the left of the junks, and for some distance we ran like this; then the hand touched mine again, and the rudder was pressed till we were gliding southward again, but we had not gone far when Ching uttered a low warning, and I just had time to shift the helm and send the boat gliding round astern of a large junk, which loomed up above us like ebony, as we were going dead for it, and if we had struck, our fragile bamboo boat would have gone to pieces like so much touchwood, leaving us struggling in the water.

"I don't see what good this reconnoitring is doing," I said to myself, as I sat there in the darkness wondering what was to happen next; but sailors on duty are only parts of a machine, and I waited like the rest to be touched or spoken to, and then acted as I was instructed. For from time to time Mr Brooke's hand rested upon mine, and its touch, with its pressure or draw, told me at once the direction in which he wished me to steer; and so it was that, in that intense darkness, we sailed silently round those junks, going nearer and nearer till I knew exactly how they lay and how close together. But all the while I was in a violent perspiration, expecting moment by moment to hear a challenge, or to see the flash of a match, the blaze up of one of the stink-pots the junks would be sure to have on their decks, and then watch it form a curve of hissing light as it was thrown into our boat.

But not a sound came from the junks we so closely approached, and at last, with a sensation of intense relief, I felt Mr Brooke's hand rest on mine for some time, keeping the rudder in position for running some distance away with the wind, before the boat was thrown up again full in its eye, and we came to a stand, with the mat-sail swinging idly from side to side.

Hardly had we taken this position, when once more from the direction of the river came the low beat of oars. As we listened, they came on and on, passed us, and the sounds ceased as before just where the junks were lying.

This time there was no signal and no answering light, the occupants of the boat finding their way almost by instinct, but there was a hail from the junk to our left, and we could distinguish the murmuring of voices for a time, and the creaking of the boat against the side as the fresh comers climbed on board.

"Ah, good information, Mr Herrick!" whispered Mr Brooke. "We have seen nothing, but we know that they have received reinforcements, and now in a very short time we shall know whether they are going to sail or wait till morning."

"How?" I said.

He laughed gently.

"Easily enough. They will not sail without getting up their anchors, and we must hear the noise they make."

"But I don't quite see what good we are doing," I whispered.

"Not see? Suppose we had stopped ashore, we should not have known of these men coming to strengthen the crews, and we should not have known till daylight whether they had sailed or were still at anchor. This last we shall know very soon, and can follow them slowly. Why, if we had waited till morning and found them gone, which way should we have sailed?"

"I'm very dense and stupid, sir," I said. "I had not thought of that."

"Allee go to s'eep," whispered Ching; "no go 'way to-night."

"What's that mean?" said Mr Brooke in a low voice; and I felt his arm across my chest as he pointed away to the left.

I looked in that direction, and saw a bright gleam of light from the shore.

"Our fire blazing up, sir," said Tom Jecks softly.

"Yes, I suppose so," said Mr Brooke thoughtfully; and as we watched the bright light disappeared, but only to appear again, and this was repeated three times.

"That can't be our fire," said Mr Brooke.

"Fliends on shore tellee pilate what to do," said Ching, with his face close to us.

"What do you mean?" said Mr Brooke.

"Ching know. Show big lamp. Mean big junk going sail mollow morning, and pilate go long way wait for them."

"Why? Couldn't they stay here and wait?"

"No; silk-tea-ship see pilate junk waiting for them, and come out lit' way and go back again. 'Flaid to sail away."

"Yes, that sounds reasonable," said Mr Brooke thoughtfully.

Then all at once there came over the black water a peculiar squeaking, grinding sound, followed by a similar noise of a different pitch.

"Pilate not going to s'eep; allee look out for light and go sail away d'leckly."

"Yes, we have not wasted our time, Herrick," whispered Mr Brooke. "They're getting up their anchors."

"And are we going to follow them, sir?" I said softly.

"Yes, my lad; our work has only just begun."

Chapter Thirty Nine
Tricked

They were singularly quiet, these people on board the junks, I suppose from old experience teaching them that noise made might mean at one time discovery and death, at another the alarming of some valuable intended prize.

This quietness was remarkable, for as we listened there was the creaking and straining of the rough capstan used, but no shouted orders, no singing in chorus by the men tugging at the bars; all was grim silence and darkness, while we lay-to there, waiting and listening to the various faint sounds, till we heard the rattling of the reed-sails as they were hauled up. Then we knew that the junks were off, for there came to us that peculiar flapping, rattling sound made by the waves against a vessel's planks, and this was particularly loud in the case of a roughly-built Chinese junk.

"Are you going to follow them at once?" I said in a whisper.

"Yes, till within an hour of daylight," was the reply. "Now, be silent."

I knew why Mr Brooke required all his attention to be directed to the task he had on hand—very little reflection was necessary. For it was a difficult task in that black darkness to follow the course of those two junks by sound, and keep doggedly at their heels, so as to make sure they did not escape. And then once more the slow, careful steering was kept up, Mr Brooke's hand guiding mine from time to time, while now for the most part we steered to follow the distant whishing sound made by the wind in the junk's great matting-sails.

All at once, when a strange, drowsy feeling was creeping over me, I was startled back into wakefulness by Mr Brooke, who said in an angry whisper—

"Who's that?"

I knew why he spoke, for, though half-asleep the moment before, I was conscious of a low, guttural snore.

"Can't see, sir," came from one of the men. "Think it's Mr Ching."

"No; Ching never makee nose talk when he s'eep," said the Chinaman, and as he spoke the sound rose once more.

"Here, hi, messmate, rouse up!" said the man who had before spoken.

"Eh? tumble-up? our watch?" growled Tom Jecks. "How many bells is—"

"Sit up, Jecks," whispered Mr Brooke angrily. "Next man take the sheet."

There was the rustling sound of men changing their places, and I heard the coxswain whispering to the others forward.

"No talking," said Mr Brooke; and we glided on again in silence, but not many yards before a light gleamed out in front.

"Quick, down at the bottom, all of you! Ching, take the tiller!"

We all crouched down; Ching sat up, holding the tiller, and the light ahead gleamed out brightly, showing the sails and hulls of the two great junks only fifty yards away, and each towing a big heavy boat. There were the black silhouettes, too, of figures leaning over the stern, and a voice hailed us in Chinese, uttering hoarse, strange sounds, to which Ching replied in his high squeak.

Then the man gave some gruff order, and Ching replied again. The light died out, and there was silence once more.

"What did he say?" whispered Mr Brooke.

"Say what fo' sail about all in dark?"

"Yes, and you?"

"Tell him hollid big gleat lie! Say, go catchee fish when it glow light."

"Yes."

"And pilate say be off, or he come in boat and cuttee off my head."

Mr Brooke hesitated for a few moments, and then reached up, took the tiller, and we lay-to again for quite an hour.

"Only make them suspicious if we are seen following, Herrick. Let them get well away; I daresay we can pick them up again at daybreak."

But all the same he manipulated the boat so as not to be too far away, and arranged matters so well that when at last the dawn began to show in the east, there lay the two junks about six miles away, and nothing but the heavy sails visible from where we stood.

We all had an anxious look round for the *Teaser*, but there were no tell-tale wreaths of smoke showing that our vessel was on her way back, and there seemed to be nothing for us to do but slowly follow on along shore, at such a distance from the junks as would not draw attention to the fact of their being followed, till we could catch sight of our own ship and warn our people of the vessels; or, failing that, lie in on the way to warn the junk which Ching believed would sail from the river before long.

Mr Brooke reckoned upon our being provisioned for two days, and as soon as it was light he divided the little crew into two watches, one of which, self included, was ordered to lie down at once and have a long sleep.

I did not want to lie down then, for the drowsy sensations had all passed away; but of course I obeyed, and, to my surprise, I seemed to find that after closing my eyes for two minutes it was evening; and, upon looking round, there lay the land upon our right, while the two junks were about five miles away, and the boat turned from them.

"Have you given up the chase, Mr Brooke?" I said.

"Yes, for the present; look yonder."

He pointed towards the north-west, and there, some three miles distant, and sailing towards us, was another junk coming down with the wind.

"Another pirate?" I cried.

"No, my lad; evidently the junk of which Ching told us."

"And you are going to warn her of the danger, sir?"

"Exactly; we can't attack, so we must scheme another way of saving the sheep from the wolves."

As we sailed on we could see that the fresh junk was a fine-looking vessel, apparently heavily laden; and, after partaking of my share of the provisions, which Ching eagerly brought for me out of the little cabin, I sat watching her coming along, with the ruddy orange rays of the setting sun lighting up her sides and rigging, and brightening the showy paint and gilding with which she was decorated, so that they had quite a metallic sheen.

"Take a look back now," said Mr Brooke. "What do you make of the pirate junks?"

"They seem to be lying-to, sir," I said.

"Then they have seen their plunder, and the sooner we give warning the better. She must turn and run back at once, or they will be after and capture her before she can reach port again."

Just then I saw him stand up and give a sharp look round, his face wearing rather an anxious expression.

"You can't see the *Teaser*, sir?" I said.

"No, my lad; I was looking at the weather. I fear it is going to blow a hurricane. The sky looks rather wild."

I had been thinking that it looked very beautiful, but I did not say so. Certainly, though, the wind had risen a little, and I noticed that Tom Jecks kept on glowering about him in a very keen way.

Just then Mr Brooke shook out the little Union Jack which we had brought from our sinking boat, and held it ready to signal the coming junk, which was now only about a mile away, and came swiftly along, till our leader stood right forward, holding on by a stay, and waved the little flag.

"Three cheers for the red, white, and blue!" muttered Tom Jecks. "Look at that now. We in this here little cock-boat just shows our colours, and that theer great bamboo mountain of a thing goes down on her marrow-bones to us, metty-phizickly. See that, Mr Herrick, sir?"

"Yes, Tom," I said excitedly; "and it's something to be proud of too."

For, in obedience to our signals, I saw one of the many Chinamen on board wave his hands as he seemed to be shouting, and the great vessel slowly and cumbrously rounded to, so that in a few minutes we were able to run close alongside.

"Tell them to heave us a rope, Ching," said Mr Brooke, and the interpreter shouted through his hands, with the result that a heavy coil came crashing down, and was caught by Tom Jecks, who was nearly knocked overboard.

"We said a rope, not a hawser," growled the man, hauling in the rope. "Better shy a few anchors down too, you bladder-headed lubbers!"

"Now, say I want to speak to the captain," said Mr Brooke.

A showily-dressed Chinaman leaned over the side of the huge tower of a poop, and smiled down on us.

"Are you the captain?" cried Mr Brooke, and Ching interpreted.

"Say he the captain," said Ching; "and you please walkee up top sidee big junk."

"Yes, it will be better," cried Mr Brooke. "Come with me, Herrick. You too, Ching, of course. There, keep her off a bit, Jecks, or you'll have the boat swamped."

He seized the right moment, and began to climb up the junk's side. I followed, and Ching was close at my heels, the clumsy vessel giving plenty of foothold; and we soon stood upon the deck, where some dozen or so Chinese sailors pointed aft to where the captain stood, bowing and smiling.

We had a rough set of bamboo steps to mount to the clumsy poop-deck, and there found the captain and half-a-dozen more of his men waiting.

"Now, Ching, forward," I said. But he hung back and looked strange.

"Don't be so jolly modest," I whispered; "we can't get on without you to interpret."

At that moment there came a loud hail from our boat, invisible to us from where we stood, and there was a tremendous splash.

"What's the matter?" cried Mr Brooke, making for the side; but in an instant the attitude of the Chinaman changed. One moment the captain was smiling at us smoothly; the next there was an ugly, look in his eyes, as he shouted something to his men, and, thrusting one hand into his long blue coat, he made a quick movement to stop Mr Brooke from going to the side.

'"JUMP, JUMP," YELLED CHING.'

The various incidents took place so quickly that they almost seemed to be simultaneous. One moment all was peace; the next it was all war, and the warnings I heard came together.

"Pilate! pilate!" shouted Ching.

"Look out for yourself, my lad! Over with you!" roared Mr Brooke, as I saw him dash at the Chinese captain, and, with his left fist extended, leap at the scoundrel, sending him rolling over on the deck.

"Now!" cried Mr Brooke again, "jump!"

"Jlump! jlump!" yelled Ching; and with a bound I was on the great carven gangway, just avoiding three men who made a rush for me, and the next moment I had leaped right away from the tower-like stern of the huge junk, and appeared to be going down and down for long enough through the glowing air before striking the water with a heavy splash, and continuing my descent right into the darkness, from which it seemed to me that I should never be able to rise again.

At last my head popped out of the dark thundering water, and, blinking my eyes as I struck out, I was saluted with a savage yelling; the water splashed about me, and I heard shots; but for a few moments, as I looked excitedly round, I did not realise that I was being pelted with pieces of chain, and fired at as a mark for bullets.

But in those brief moments I saw what I wanted: Mr Brook and Ching safe and swimming towards me, and the boat not many yards behind them, with two of our men at the oars, and the others opening fire upon the people who crowded the side of the junk, and yelled at us and uttered the most savage throats.

"This way, Herrick, my lad," panted Mr Brooke, as he reached me. "Ah! did that hit you?"

"No, sir, only splashed up the water; I'm all right!" I cried; "the bullet didn't touch."

"Swim boat! swim boat!" cried Ching excitedly.

But our danger was not from the water but the sharp fire which the Chinese kept up now, fortunately without killing any of us. Then the boat glided between us and the junk, ready hands were outstretched from the side, and I was hauled in by Tom Jecks, who then reached over and grasped Ching by the pigtail.

"No, no touchee tow-chang!" roared the poor fellow.

"All right; then both hands and in with you."

"Lay hold of the sheet, Jecks!" cried Mr Brooke, who sprang over the thwart to the tiller, rammed it down, and the sail began to fill, but only slowly, for the towering junk acted as a lee, and all the time the men yelled, pelted, and fired at us.

"Look out, my lads; give it to them now. Make fast the sheet, Jecks, and get your rifle. Ten pounds to the man who brings down the captain!" roared Mr Brooke. "Here, Herrick, my gun!" he cried; and, handing it to him, I seized mine, thrust in two wet cartridges with my wet fingers, and, doubting whether they would go off, I took aim at a man on the poop, who was holding a pot to which another was applying a light.

The next minute the pot was in a blaze, and the man raised it above his head to hurl it right upon us, but it dropped straight down into the sea close to the junk, and the man staggered away with his hands to his face, into which he must have received a good deal of the charge of duck-shot with which my piece was charged.

Excited by my success, I fired the second barrel at a man who was leaning over the bulwarks, taking aim at us with his great clumsy matchlock, and his shot did not hit any one, for the man dropped his piece overboard and shrank away.

As I charged again, I could hear and see that our lads were firing away as rapidly as they could up at the crowded bulwarks, while Tom Jecks was making his piece bear upon the deck of the high poop whenever he could get a shot at the captain; and now, too, Mr Brooke was firing off his small-shot cartridges as rapidly as possible, the salt water not having penetrated the well-wadded powder enclosed in the brass cases.

By this time we were fifty yards away from the junk, and gliding more rapidly through the water, which was splashed up about us and the boat hit again and again with a sharp rap by the slugs from the Chinamen's matchlocks.

The men were returning the fire with good effect as we more than once saw, and twice over one of the wretches who sought to hurl a blazing pot of fire was brought down.

"They can't hurt us now," I thought, as I ceased firing, knowing that my small-shot would be useless at the distance we now were, when I saw a spark of light moving on the poop, and then sat paralysed by horror as I grasped what was going to take place. It was only a moment or two before there was a great flash and a roar, with a puff of sunset-reddened smoke, hiding the poop of the junk; for they had depressed a big swivel gun to make it bear upon us, and then fired, sending quite a storm of shot, stones, and broken pieces of iron crashing through the roof of our little cabin, and tearing a great hole in our sail.

"That's done it!" shouted Tom Jecks, giving the stock of his rifle a heavy slap.

"You've hit him?" cried Mr Brooke.

"Yes, sir; I caught him as he stood by watching the cannon fired."

"Yes, that's right," cried Mr Brooke, shading his eyes and gazing hard at the scene on the high poop, where, in the last rays of the setting sun, we could see men holding up their captain, who was distinctive from his gay attire and lacquered hat, which now hung forward as the scoundrel's head drooped upon his breast.

"Cease firing!" said Mr Brooke, for we were a hundred yards away now, and rapidly increasing the distance. "We can do no more good. Thank you, Jecks. Now then, who is hurt?"

There was no reply.

"What, no one?" cried Mr Brooke.

"Yes, sir: why don't you speak out, Tom Jecks? You got it, didn't you?"

"Well, so did you; but I arn't going to growl."

"More arn't I, messmate. It's nothing much, sir."

"Let me see," said Mr Brooke, as we sailed steadily away, while the junk still remained stationary; and, after a rapid examination, he plugged and bound a wound in the man's shoulder, and performed a similar operation upon Tom Jeck's hind-leg, as he called it, a bullet or slug having gone right through the calf.

I could not help admiring the calm stolidity with which the two men bore what must have been a painful operation, for neither flinched, but sat in turn gazing at his messmate, as much as to say, "That's the way to take it, my lad; look at me."

This done, Mr Brooke turned his attention to the wound received by the boat, where the charge from the swivel gun had gone crashing through the top of the cabin and out at the side. It was a gaping wound in the slight planking of the boat, but the shot had torn their way out some distance above the water-line, so that unless very rough weather came on there was no danger, and we had other and more serious business now to take up our attention.

For Ching pointed out to us a certain amount of bustle on board the junk, which was explained by a puff of smoke and a roar, as simultaneously the water was ploughed up close to our stern.

"Not clever at their gun drill," said Mr Brooke coolly, as he took the helm himself now, and sent the boat dancing along over the waves, so as to keep her endwise to the junk, and present a smaller object for the pirate's aim.

"That's bad management under some circumstances, Herrick," he said, smiling. "It's giving an enemy the chance of raking us from stern to stem, but I don't believe they can hit us.—I thought not."

He said this smiling, as the water was churned up again by another shot, but several yards away upon our right.

Another shot and another followed without result, and by this time we were getting well out of range of the swivel gun, a poor, roughly-made piece, and our distance was being rapidly increased.

"Going away!" said Ching, as we saw the great mat-sails of the junk fill.

"Or to come in chase—which?" said Mr Brooke quietly. "It does not matter," he added; "we shall soon have darkness again, and I think we shall be too nimble for them then."

"Beg pardon, sir," said Tom Jecks.

"Yes, what is it? Your wound painful?"

"Tidy, sir; but that warn't it. I was only going to say, look yonder."

He pointed right away east, and, as we followed his finger with our eyes, they lit upon a sight which would have even made me, inexperienced as I was, think it was time to seek the shelter of some port. And that something unusual was going to happen, I knew directly from Mr Brooke's way of standing up to shelter his eyes, and then, after gazing for some time in one direction, he turned in that of the great Chinese port we had so lately left.

Chapter Forty
Another Enemy

For as I looked towards the horizon away to the east, a curious lurid glow spread upward half-way to the zenith, and for the moment I thought that in a short time we should see the full-moon come slowly up out of the sea. But a few moments' reflection told me that we were long past the full-moon time, and that it would be the last quarter late on in the night. The sea, too, began to wear a singular aspect, and great frothy clouds were gathering rapidly in the south. And even as I looked there was a peculiar moaning sigh, as if a great wind were passing over us at a great height, though the sea was only just pleasantly rippled, and a gentle breeze was sweeping us rapidly along and away from the great junk, which now seemed hazy and distant, while those we had watched so long were quite out of sight.

"Feel cold?" said Mr Brooke quietly. "I ought to have told you to take off and wring out your clothes."

"Cold, sir!" I said wonderingly. "I hadn't thought about it; I was so excited."

"Yes; we had a narrow escape, my lad. It is a lesson in being careful with these cunning, treacherous wretches. You made sure it was a trader, Ching?"

"Ching neve' quite su'e—only think so," was the reply, accompanied by a peculiar questioning look, and followed by a glance over his right shoulder at the sky.

"No, I suppose not. I ought to have been more careful. They threw something down at the boat as soon as we had mounted: did they not, Jecks?"

"Yes, sir; I see it coming. Great pieces of ballast iron, as it took two on 'em to heave up over the bulwarks. I just had time to give the boat a shove with the hitcher when down it come. Gone through the bottom like paper, if I hadn't. But beg pardon, sir, arn't we going to have a storm?"

"Yes," said Mr Brooke quietly; "I am running for the river, if I can make it. If not, for that creek we were in last night. Take the tiller, Mr Herrick," he said, and he went forward.

"Going blow wind velly high. Gleat wave and knock houses down," said Ching uneasily.

"Yes, my lad; we're going to have what the Jay-pans calls a tycoon."

"No, no, Tom Jecks," I said, smiling.

"You may laugh, sir, but that's so. I've sailed in these here waters afore and been in one. Had to race afore it with bare poles and holding on to the belaying-pins. Tycoons they call 'em, don't they, Mr Ching?"

"Gleat blow storm," said Ching, nodding. "Hullicane."

"There you are, sir," said Jecks. "Hurricanes or tycoons."

"Typhoons," I said.

"Yes, sir, that's it, on'y you pernounces it different to me. Don't make no difference in the strength on 'em," he continued testily, for his wound was evidently painful, "whether you spells it with a kay or a phoo. Why, I seed big vessels arterwards, as had been blowed a quarter of a mile inland, where they could never be got off again."

"Yes, I've heard of that sort of thing," I said. "They ride in on a great wave and are left behind."

"Lookye here, sir," whispered the coxswain, who seemed to ignore his wound; "I don't want to show no white feathers, nor to holler afore I'm hurt, but if I was you, I should ask Mr Brooke to run straight for the nearest shore—say one o' them islands there, afore the storm comes; you arn't got no idea what one o' them tycoons is like. As for this boat, why, she'll be like a bit o' straw in a gale, and I don't want to go to the bottom until I've seed you made a skipper; and besides, we've got lots more waspses' nests to take, beside polishing off those three junks—that is, if they're left to polish when the storm's done."

"Stand up, Mr Herrick," cried the lieutenant. "Look yonder, due north. What do you see?"

I held the tiller between my knees as I stood up and gazed in the required direction, but could see nothing for a few minutes in the dusk.

"Can't you see?"

"Yes, sir, now. Small round black cloud."

"Yes, of smoke."

"Ay, ay, sir, I see it," said one of the sailors. "Hooray! it's the *Teaser* with the wind blowing hard astern and carrying the smoke of her funnel right over her and ahead."

"The *Teaser* or some other steamer; and she's running fast for harbour. Let's see: those are the Black Gull Islands to port there. Were you with us when the cutter's crew landed, Jecks?"

"Yes, sir; I rowed stroke-oar, sir."

"To be sure. The second one from the north had the highest ground."

"Yes, sir; but you couldn't land for the surf and the shark-fin rocks, if you remember."

"Exactly; and we rowed along the south channel till we found a sheltered sand-cove, where we beached the cutter, and then explored the island. We must make for that channel, and try to reach it before the storm comes down. We could not get half-way to the river, and, thank heaven, the *Teaset* will soon be in safety."

"No, sir, you couldn't make no river to-night."

"It will be dark too soon."

"Not to-night, sir," said Jecks sturdily.

"Yes, man; there will be no moon."

"No, sir; but in less nor an hour's time the sea 'll be white as milk, and all of a greeny glow, same as it is some still nights in port. There won't be no difficulty, sir, about seeing."

"But you think it will be hard to make the channel?"

"I hope not, sir, but I'm afraid so; we can only try."

"Yes, we can only try," said Mr Brooke slowly, as he came and sat beside me. "And we must try, Herrick—our best. For this is no night to be out in almost an open boat."

"Then you think there is danger, sir?" I said anxiously.

"No, Herrick," he replied, smiling; "sailors have no time to think of danger. They have enough to think about without that. We must get in the lee of that island to-night, and it the storm holds back, and the little boat spins along like this, we ought to do it."

"And if it doesn't, sir?"

"If it doesn't? Ah, well, we shall see. Stand by, two of you, ready to lower that sail at a moment's notice."

"Ay, ay, sir," was the ready reply as two of the men changed their places; and just then I looked at Ching, to see that his face was lit up by the reflection of the strange light on our right and behind, which grew more striking, while away before us the land disappeared, and we were gazing at a bank of clouds of an inky black.

The effect was very curious: behind us the dull coppery glow becoming fainter minute by minute, as the darkness increased the blackness before us; and one's instinct seemed to warn one to turn from the black darkness to sail away towards the light. Tom Jecks took the same idea, and said, in an irritable whisper, exactly what I thought—

"Seems rum, sir, don't it, sir?—makes believe as that's the best way, when all the time the wussest looking is the safest."

Just then, after a glance round, Mr Brooke uttered another warning to the men to be ready, and settled himself down to the tiller.

"Sit fast, all of you; the hurricane may be down upon us at any moment now."

I looked at him wonderingly, for it was painfully still, though the darkness was growing intense, and the great junk seemed to have been swallowed up by the clouds that hung low like a fog over the sea.

"There will be such a turmoil of the elements directly," continued Mr Brooke in a low voice, but only to me, "that I don't suppose a word will be heard." Then aloud, "Look here, my lads; I shall try and run the boat high upon the sands at the top of some breaker. Then it will be every man for himself. Never mind the boat—that is sure to be destroyed—but each man try to save his arms and ammunition; and if the two wounded men are in difficulties, of course you will lend a hand. Now then, one more order: The moment I say, 'Down with the sail,' drag it from the mast, and two oars are to be out on either side. The wind will catch them and send us along, and I want them to give a few dips to get on the top of a roller to carry us in."

"Ay, ay, sir."

"That's all."

His words in that terrible stillness sounded to me as almost absurd, for the sea was still calm, and save that sighing in the air of which I have before spoken, there was no further sound; and at last I said to him—

"Do you really think we shall have a hurricane?"

"Look at the sky, my lad," he replied; "and take this as a lesson to one who will have men's lives depending upon his knowledge and skill some day. If ever there were signs of an awful night in the Chinese seas, it is now. Hark at that!"

"Guns! The *Teaser!*" I exclaimed excitedly.

"Heaven's artillery that, my lad," he said solemnly. Then in a whisper, "Shake hands! I'll help you all I can, Herrick, but heaven knows how we shall be situated soon."

I felt a strange sensation of awe creep over me, as he gripped my hand warmly, and then snatched his away, and sat up firm and rigid, turning his head to the east as all now became suddenly black—so dark that I could hardly see the men before me and the sail. But still we glided rapidly on over the long smooth rollers, on and on toward the islands, which lay a short distance from the mainland.

"It will be all guess work," whispered Mr Brooke. "I am keeping her head as near as I can guess for the channel, but the breakers will soon be our only guide."

Then came the heavy roar again, which I had taken for guns, but it did not cease as before, when it sounded like a sudden explosion. It was now continuous, and rapidly increasing.

"Thunder?" I asked in a low voice.

"Wind. Tremendous. It will be on us in five minutes."

But even then it seemed impossible, for we were still sailing swiftly and gently along towards the channel between the islands, and the roar like distant thunder or heavy guns had once more ceased.

"We shall get to the shore first after all," I whispered.

"No."

At that moment there was a sensation as of a hot puff of air behind us. It literally struck my head just as if a great furnace door had been opened, and the glow had shot out on to our necks.

"Here she comes," growled Tom Jecks; "and good luck to us."

And then, as if to carry out the idea of the opened furnace, it suddenly grew lighter—a strange, weird, wan kind of light—and on either side, and running away from us on to the land, the sea was in a wild froth as if suddenly turned to an ocean of milk.

"Down with the sail!" shouted Mr Brooke, who had held on to the last moment, so as to keep the boat as long as possible under his governance; and quickly as disciplined men could obey the sail was lowered, and as far as I could see they were in the act of stowing it along the side, when it filled out with a loud report, and was snatched from their hands and gone.

"Any one hurt?"

"No, sir," in chorus.

"Oars."

I heard the rattle of the two pairs being thrust out. Next Mr Brooke's words, yelled out by my ear—"sit fast!" and then there was a heavy blow, heavy but soft and pressing, followed by the stinging on my neck as of hundreds of tiny whips, and then we were rushing along over the white sea, in the midst of a mass—I can call it nothing else—of spray, deafened, stunned, feeling as if each moment I should be torn out of my seat, and as if the boat itself were being swept along like lightning over the sea, riding, not on heavy water, but on the spray.

Then all was one wild, confusing shriek and roar. I was deafened; something seemed to clutch me by the throat and try to strangle me; huge soft hands grasped me by the body, and tugged and dragged at me, to tear me from my hold; and then, two arms that were not imaginary, but solid and real, went round me, and grasped the thwart on which I sat, holding me down, while I felt a head resting on my lap.

I could see nothing but a strange, dull, whitish light when I managed to hold my eyelids up for a moment, but nothing else was visible; and above all—the deafening roar, the fearful buffeting and tearing at me—there was one thing which mastered, and that was the sensation of being stunned and utterly confused. I was, as it were, a helpless nothing, beaten and driven by the wind and spray, onward, onward, like a scrap of chaff. Somebody was clinging to me, partly to save himself, partly to keep me from being dragged out of the boat; but whether Mr Brooke was still near me, whether the men were before me, or whether there was any more boat at all than that upon which I was seated, I did not know. All I knew was that I was there, and that I was safe, in spite of all the attempts made by the typhoon to drag me out and sweep me away like a leaf over the milky sea.

It cannot be described. Every sense was numbed. And if any lad who reads this were to take the most terrible storm he ever witnessed, square it, and then cube it, I do not believe that he would approach the elemental disturbance through which we were being hurled.

There was a rocky shore in front of us, and another rocky island shore to our left; and between these two shores lay the channel for which we had tried to make. But Mr Brooke's rule over the boat was at an end the moment the storm was upon us, and, as far as I could ever learn afterwards, no one thought of rocks, channel, saving his life, or being drowned. The storm struck us, and with its furious rush went all power of planning or thinking. Every nerve of the body was devoted to the tasks of holding on and getting breath.

How long it lasted—that wild rush, riding on the spray, held as it were by the wind—I don't know. I tell you I could not think. It went on and on as things do in a horrible dream, till all at once something happened. I did not hear it, nor see it, hardly even felt it. I only know that something happened, and I was being strangled—choked, but in another way. The hands which grasped my throat to keep me from breathing had, I believe, ceased to hold, and something hot and terrible was rushing up my nostrils and down my throat, and I think I then made some effort with my hands. Then I was being dragged along through water and over something soft, and all at once, though the deafening, confusing noise went on, I was not being swept away, but lying still on something hard.

I think that my senses left me entirely then for a few moments—not more, for I was staring soon after at the dull light of white water sweeping along a little way off, and breathing more freely as I struggled hard to grasp what it all meant, for I did not know. I saw something dim pass me, and then come close and touch me, as if it sank down by my side; and that happened again and again.

But it was all very dream-like and strange: the awful, overwhelming, crushing sound of the wind seemed to press upon my brain so that I could not for a long time think, only lie and try to breathe without catching each inspiration in a jerky, spasmodic way.

I suppose hours must have passed, during which I stared through the darkness at the dull whitish phosphorescent glow which appeared through the gloom, and died out, and appeared and died out again and again, passing like clouds faintly illumined in a ghastly way, and all mingled with the confusion caused by that awful roar. Then at last I began to feel that the rush of wind and water was passing over me, and that I was in some kind of shelter; and when I had once hit upon this, I had as it were grasped a clue. I knew that I was lying on stones, and saw that rising above me was a mass of rock, which I knew by the touch, and this stone was sheltering me from the wind and spray.

"We must have reached the shore safely, then," I said to myself, for my head was getting clearer; "and—yes—no—I was not hurt. We were all saved, then."

At that point a terrible feeling of dread came over me. I was safe, but my companions?

The shock of this thought threw me back for a bit, but I was soon struggling with the confusion again, and I recalled the fact that I had felt some one touch me as he sank down by my side.

Arrived at this point, I turned a little to look, but all was perfectly black. I stretched out my hand and felt about.

I snatched it back with a cry of horror. Yes, a cry of horror; for, though I could not hear it, I felt it escape from my lips. I had touched something all wet and cold lying close beside me, and I felt that it was one of my companions who had been cast up or dragged ashore—dead.

Shivering violently, I shrank away, and stretched out my hand in the other direction—my left hand now, with my arm numbed, and my shoulder aching when I moved it, as if the joint had become stiffened and would not work.

I touched somebody there—something cold and smooth and wet, and drew my hand away again, when, as it glided over the sand, it touched something else round and soft and long, and—yes—plaited. It was a long tail.

"Ching!" I ejaculated; and, gaining courage, I felt again in the darkness, to find that it grew thinner. I tried again in the other direction, and once more touched the round wet object, which did not seem so cold, and then the next moment a hand caught mine and held it.

I was right; it was Ching. I knew him by his long nails.

Not alone! I had a companion in the darkness, one who was nearly as much stunned as I, for he moved no more, but lay holding on by my left hand, and for a time I was content to listen to the savage roar of the wind. But at last, as my brain worked and I mastered the sensation of horror, I began to feel about again with my right hand, till I touched the same cold, wet object I had encountered before.

It was an arm, quite bare and cold; while now I could not withdraw my hand, but lay trembling and shuddering, till I felt that perhaps I was not right—that any one lying dead would not feel like that; and my hand glided down to the wrist.

I knew nothing about feeling pulses only from having seen a doctor do so, but by chance my fingers fell naturally in the right place in the hollow just above the wrist joint, and a thrill of exultation ran through me, for I could distinctly feel a tremulous beating, and I knew that my imagination had played me false—that the man was not dead.

Chapter Forty One
After the Typhoon

The repugnance and horror gave way to a sensation of joy. Here was another companion in misfortune, alive and ready to share the terrible trouble with us, but who was it?

I tried to withdraw my left hand from Ching's grasp; but as soon as he felt it going, he clung to it spasmodically, and it was only by a sharp effort that I dragged it away, and turned to the side of my other companion, and began to touch him. There was the bare arm, but that was no guide; the face helped me no more; but the torn remnants of his clothes told me it was not Mr Brooke, and my heart sank. I felt again, and my hand encountered a drawn-up leg, and then I touched a bandage. It was Tom Jecks, who had been wounded by the fire from the junk.

I could learn no more. I tried to speak; I shouted; but he made no sign, and I could not even hear my own cries. The darkness remained profound, and the deafening roar of the wind kept on without cessation.

But, feeling more myself at last, I determined to crawl about a little, and find out whether any more of our crew were near us. Then I hesitated; but, summoning courage, I crept on my hands and knees, passed Ching, and then crouched down nearly flat, for I had crept to where the shelter ceased, and to have gone on would have been to be swept away.

To test this I raised one hand, and in an instant I suffered quite a jerk, and each time I repeated the experiment I felt more and more that to leave the shelter meant to die, for the power of the blast was appalling.

Crawling back, I proceeded in the other direction, and found that I could go what I guessed to be quite a dozen yards, feeling more and more in shelter. Then all at once I reached a point where the wind came through what afterwards proved to be a narrow pass between two masses of rock, and I shrank back disheartened at the barrenness of my search.

In that black darkness it was very difficult to find my former position, even in so confined a space, and I found myself completely going wrong, and into the rushing wind, the effect being horribly confusing again. But, after lying flat down on the sand, which kept flying up and nearly blinding me, I grew more composed, and, resuming my search once more, found where my two companions lay; and, after touching our wounded sailor, and finding him lying as I had left him, I began to think of what I could do to help him, but thought in vain. To give help was impossible in the midst of that awful storm, and, utterly exhausted now, I sank back and reached out my left hand once more to try and touch Ching.

He was on the alert, and caught my hand in both his, grasping it firmly, as if, boy as I was, he would gladly cling to me for protection; while I, in my horror and loneliness, was only too thankful to feel the touch of a human hand.

Then, amid the strange confusion produced by the roar of the wind and thunder of the waves whose spray hissed over our heads, I lay wondering what had become of Mr Brooke and the others—whether they had reached the land, and were screened behind the rocks as we were; then about the *Teaser*—whether she had been able to make the shelter of the river before the typhoon came down upon them in all its fury.

I seemed to see the men at their quarters, with the spars lowered upon deck, the boats doubly secured, and everything loose made fast. I fancied I felt the throb of the engines, and the whirr of the shaft, as it raced when the stern rose at some dive down of the prow; and the sharp "ting-ting" of the engine-room gong-bell struck on my ears above the yelling of the storm, for wild shrieks at times came mingled with the one tremendous overpowering roar.

Then I began thinking again about Mr Brooke, and whether, instead of lying there in shelter on the sand, I ought not to be striving with all my might to find him; and all at once the roar over my head, the thunder of the breakers somewhere near, and the hiss and splash of the cutting spray, seemed to cease, and I was crawling about the shore, over sand and rocks, and through pools of water, to find Mr Brooke, while Ching followed me, crying out in piping tones, "Velly long of you. Windee blow allee way." But still I toiled on, lying flat sometimes, and holding tightly to the rocks beneath me, for fear of being snatched up and sent whirling over the sea.

Then on again, to come to a mass of rock, up which I climbed, but only to slip back again, climbed once more and slipped, and so on and on till all was nothingness, save that the deafening roar went on, and the billows dashed among the rocks, but in a subdued far-off way that did not trouble me in the least. For my sleep—the sleep of utter exhaustion—had grown less troubled, the dreamy crawl in search of Mr Brooke died away, and I slept soundly there, till the sun glowing warmly upon my face made me open my eyes, to find Ching's round smooth yellow face smiling down at me, and Tom Jecks nursing his leg.

I started up in wonder, but sank back with a groan, feeling stiff and sore, as if I had been belaboured with capstan bars.

"You feel velly bad?" said Ching.

"Horribly stiff."

"Hollibly 'tiff; Ching lub you well."

Before I knew what he was about to do, he seized one of my arms, and made me shout with agony, but he moved it here and there, pinching and rubbing and kneading it till it went easily, following it up with a similar performance upon the other. Back and chest followed; and in ten minutes I was a different being.

But no amount of rubbing and kneading did any good to my spirits, nor to those of our companion in misfortune, whose wound troubled him a good deal; but he sat up, trying to look cheerful, while, with my head still confused, and thought coming slowly, I exclaimed—

"But the storm—the typhoon?"

"Allee blow way, allee gone," cried Ching, smiling; "velly good job. You feel dly?"

I did not answer then, for I felt as if I could not be awake. I had been lying in the lee of a huge mass of rock, amid stones and piled-up sand, upon which the sun beat warmly; the sky overhead was of a glorious blue; and there was nothing to suggest the horrors of the past night, but the heavy boom and splash of the billows which broke at intervals somewhere behind the rock.

At last I jumped up, full of remorse at my want of thought.

"Mr Brooke—the others?" I cried.

"We were talking about 'em, sir, 'fore you woke up," said Jecks sadly; and I now saw that he had received a blow on the head, while he spoke slowly, and looked strange.

"And what—"

"I'm afraid they're—"

'THEN YOU SAVED ME, CHING?'

"Allee dlowned; velly much 'flaid."

I groaned.

"I don't know how we managed to get ashore, sir," said Jecks faintly. "I think it was because there was so little undertow to the waves. When the boat struck, it felt to me as if I was being blown through the shallow water, and I shouldn't have been here if I hadn't come up against Mr Ching, who was pulling you along."

"Then you saved me, Ching?" I cried.

"Ching takee hold, and pullee here. Velly pull wolk. Him get hold of tow-chang, and pullee him both together."

"That's right, sir. I snatched at anything, and got hold of his tail, and held on. But you don't mind, Mr Ching?"

"No; mustn't cut tow-chang off."

"Let's try if we can find the others," I said; and, taking the lead, I walked round the mass of rock which had sheltered us, to gaze out at the heaving sea, which was rising and falling restlessly; but there was no white water, all was of a delicious blue, darker than the sky, and not a sail in sight.

To right and left extended a low cliff, at whose feet lay huge masses which had fallen from time to time; then an irregular stretch of sand extended to where the waves came curling over, the swell being very heavy, and the only trace of the storm to be seen was the way in which the sand had been driven up against the cliff, so as to form quite a glacis.

We could see about half a mile in either direction, but there was no sign of our companions, and my heart sank again. There were, however, here and there, ridges of rock, running down like breakwaters into the sea, and about which it fretted and tossed tremendously; and, in the hope that one of these ridges might hide our friends from our view, I climbed to the top of the highest piece of rock I could reach, and took a long and careful survey.

"See anything, sir?" said Tom Jecks.

"No," I replied, "nothing. Yes; about a quarter of a mile on there's a spar sticking up; it may be the boat's mast."

I came hurriedly down, and my announcement was enough to set my companions off, Jecks limping painfully through the loose sand, climbing rocks, and finding it no easy task to get over that so-called quarter of a mile, which, like all such spaces on the sea-shore, proved to be about double the length it looked, while the nearer we got the higher and more formidable the ridge seemed to grow, completely shutting out all beyond, where it ran down from the cliff at right angles into the sea.

All at once, as I was helping the coxswain over an awkward stone, the poor fellow being weak and rather disposed to stagger, but always passing it off with a laugh and an "All right, sir, I shall be better after breakfast," Ching uttered an ejaculation, and pointed to something that the sea had washed up, and was pouncing upon again like a cat to draw it back.

My heart seemed to stand still, but a horrible fascination drew me to the spot along with the Chinaman, for my first thought was that it was the body of Mr Brooke.

"Not jolly sailor boy," said Ching; and I felt a peculiar exaltation. "Not Mis' Blooke. Pilate man dlowned. Ching velly glad."

We turned away, and continued our route, for I shrank from going into dangerous breakers to try and drag the man out, and my companion was too weak. As to its being one of the pirates, it seemed possible, for I knew that one, if not two, had gone overboard in the fight, and it was probably one of these.

We trudged on and reached the ridge at last, to find it bigger and more precipitous than I had expected. It ran out evidently for hundreds of yards, its course being marked by foam and fretting waves, and I was just thinking what a fatal spot it would be for a vessel to touch the shore, when I reached the top and uttered a startled cry, which brought the others to my side; for there was the explanation of the presence of the drowned Chinaman! Spreading away for a couple of hundred yards, the shore was covered with timbers, great bamboo spars, ragged sails, and the torn and shattered fragments of some large Chinese vessel; while, before I could shape it in my mind as to the possibilities of what vessel this could be, though certain it was not the *Teaser*, Ching said coolly—

"That velly good job. That big junk blow all to pieces, and allee bad pilate man dlowned. No go choppee off poor sailor head now. No 'teal silk, tea, allee good thing, and burnee ship. Velly good job indeed; velly bad lot."

"You think it was the junk which cheated us?"

"Yes, velly muchee same. Look, allee paint, lacquee, gold. Allee same junk; no use go find um now. No get head chop off for killee sailo'. Allee bad pilate allee dlowned."

"Hold hard there, sir," whispered Tom Jecks. "I can hear people talking. Quick! squat, hide; there's a lot on 'em coming down off the cliff."

We had just time to hide behind some rocks, when a party of about twenty Chinamen came cautiously and slowly down on to the sands, and Ching whispered as he peeped between the fragments of rock—

"Not allee pilate dlowned. Come along look at junk; take care; choppee off allee head; must hide."

Ching was quite right, and I was awake to the fact that we three were prisoners on a little desert island, and in company with a gang of as savage and desperate enemies as man could have.

Chapter Forty Two
For Dear Life

It was all clear enough: the great junk which had so deceived Mr Brooke and Ching had been cast ashore and shattered, these men having escaped and been exploring the island, or perhaps they were only coming down now from the spot where they had taken refuge after being cast ashore.

"Why, Ching," I whispered, "perhaps there are more of them about!"

"P'laps," he replied.

We dared not move, but remained there watching; and it now became pretty evident that the men had come down to examine the wreck, for they began to hurry about, chattering away as they searched in all directions amongst the fragments, one or another setting up a shout from time to time, which brought others to him. Then we saw them drag out now a chest from the sand in which it was bedded, now a cask; and soon after there was a burst of excitement over something we could not make out; but it was evidently a satisfactory find, for they bore it up from the sea to the soft, warm, dry sand, and all sat down round about it.

"Find something velly good to eat," whispered Ching. "Now allee velly busy; come along, hide."

It was very good advice; and we followed him down from the ridge, and in and out at the foot of the cliff, seeking for some place of concealment; for I had not a doubt about our fate if we were seen. In fact, I did not breathe freely until the great ridge and several masses of rock were between us; and only then, a good half-mile away in the direction from which we had come, did we venture to speak above our breath.

"Velly big pity," said Ching, whose face was all in wrinkles. "Velly muchee wish back at fancee shop."

"Let's find a place before we talk about that," I said.

"Yes; soon findee place."

"Here, what is it, Jecks?" I cried, catching our companion's arm; for he suddenly gave a lurch as we struggled through the loose sand, and nearly fell.

"Bit done up, sir," he said, with a piteous smile. "Wound in my leg makes me feel sick, and the sun's hot. Is there a drop o' water to be got at anywhere?"

I looked round at the glowing sand and rocks with a feeling of horrible despair coming over me. Yes, there was water—hundreds and thousands of miles of water, blue, glistening, and beautiful in the calm morning, but none that we could give a parched and fainting man to drink.

"Try and creep along a little farther," I said. "Let's get you in hiding, and then Ching and I will search for some and bring it—"

As I spoke I remembered that I had nothing that would hold water, and I felt constrained to add—

"Or fetch you to it."

"All right, sir," said the man, with a weary smile; "allus obey your officers."

Ching went to his other side, and supported him some fifty yards farther, our way now being through quite a chaos of rocks, which had been loosened in bygone times from the cliff above. Then, so suddenly that we were not prepared, the poor fellow dropped with his full weight upon our arms, and we had to lower him down upon a heap of drifted sand.

"No go, sir," he said softly; "I'm a done-er."

"No, no; rest a bit, and we'll find a cool place somewhere. I daresay we shall see a cave along here."

"Can't do it, sir," he said feebly; "I've kep' on as long as I could. It's all up. Never mind me. If those beggars see you, they'll have no mercy on you, so go on and try and get away."

"Yes; velly muchee makee haste. Pilate come soon."

"Yes, sir; he's quite right, sir. You two cut and run."

"And let them come and murder you, while we go?" I said.

"Well, yes, sir," said the poor fellow faintly; "there's no good in having three killed when one would do."

"Look about, Ching," I said sharply. "Is there any place where we can hide?"

"No," he replied disconsolately. "Only place for lit' dog; no fo' man."

"You can't do it, sir," said our poor companion. "Good-bye, sir, and God bless you; you've done all a orficer can."

"Oh, have I? I should look well when Mr Reardon or the captain says, 'What have you done with your men?'"

"Don't! stop a-talking, sir," he cried, clinging to my hand. "You know what these beggars are, and you'll have 'em on to you, sir."

"Yes; and we shall have them on to you if we don't find a place soon. Here, Ching, don't run away and leave us;" for I could see the interpreter climbing up a gap in the cliff.

"He's quite right, sir; you go after him. I tell you it's all over and done with me. If you got me along a bit farther, I should only go off all the same. It's all up. Now, pray go, sir. It's no use to stay."

"Hold your tongue!" I cried angrily; for with the feeling on me strong that the pirates might be down on us directly, and the only thing to do was to set off and run for my life, the poor fellow's imploring words were like a horrible temptation that I was too weak to resist.

"I must speak, sir," he whispered, with his eyes starting, and his lips black and cracked by the heat and feverish thirst caused by his wound. "There, you see, Mr Ching's gone, and your only chance is to follow him."

I looked up, and just caught sight of one of the Chinaman's legs as he disappeared over the edge of the cliff to which, high up, he had crawled. And once more the desire to escape came upon me, but with increased strength, that made me so angry at my weakness that I turned upon the poor fellow almost threateningly.

"Will you hold your tongue?" I whispered hoarsely.

"Will you go, sir?" he pleaded. "I tell yer it's all up with me, and the Teapots can't hurt me worse than what I've got now. Arn't got your dirk, have you?"

"No; why?"

"'Cause it would ha' been an act o' kindness to put me out of my misery, and save me from being cut to pieces by them there wretches. Now, sir, good-bye, and God bless you, once more! Tell the skipper I did my duty to the last."

I broke down as I sank on my knees by the poor fellow; and I didn't know my voice—perhaps it was being husky from the heat-as I said to him, very chokily—

"And if you get away, tell the captain I did my duty to the last."

"Yes, sir; but do go now."

I jumped up again, ashamed of the blinding tears that came for a few moments into my eyes.

"Look here," I said; "if you weren't so weak, I'd kick you, old a man as you are. Likely thing for a British officer to sneak off and leave one of his men like this!"

"But the beggars are coming, I'm sure, sir."

"Very well," I said gloomily, "let them come. It's all very well for a full-moon-faced Chinaman to go off and take care of himself, but it isn't English, Tom Jecks, and that you know."

The poor fellow hoisted himself a little round, so that he could hide his face on his uninjured arm, and as I saw his shoulders heave I felt weaker than ever; but I mastered it this time, and knelt there with a whole flood of recollections of home, school, and my ambitions running through my brain. I thought of my training, of my delight at the news of my being appointed to the *Teaser*, of my excitement over my uniform; and that now it was all over, and that in all probability only the sea-birds would know of what became of me after the Chinamen had done.

Then I thought of Ching's cowardice in leaving me alone with the poor wounded fellow like this.

"I knew he wasn't a fighting man," I said sadly; "but I couldn't have believed that he was such a cur."

At that moment there was a quick scrambling sound, which made me start to my feet, and Tom Jecks started up on his elbow.

"Here they come, sir," he gasped. "Now, sir," he whispered wildly, "do, pray, cut and run."

"With you," I said resolutely.

He made an effort to rise, but fell back with a groan.

"Can't do it, sir. Without me. Run!"

I put my hands in my pockets without a word, and then started, for a voice said—

"You think Ching lun away allee time?"

"Ching!" I cried, grasping his arm.

"Yes; no good. Can't findee big hole to hide. Ching tumblee down off rock, and hurt him."

"Much?" I said.

"Yes, plentee plentee. Time to go now. Pilate all come along this way."

He passed his hand involuntarily straight round his neck edgewise, as if thinking about how a knife or sword would soon be applied.

"You saw them?" I cried.

"Yes," he said sadly. "Allee come along. You lun away now with Ching?"

"I can't leave Tom Jecks," I said. "Off with you, and try and save yourself. Never mind us."

Ching looked at the injured sailor.

"You no get up, lun?" he said.

"Can't do it, mate," groaned the poor fellow. "I want Mr Herrick to make a dash for his life."

"Yes, velly good. You makee dashee you life, Mr Hellick."

"No, I stay here. Run for it, Ching; and if you escape and see the captain or Mr Reardon again, tell him we all did our duty, and how Mr Brooke was drowned."

"Yes, Ching tellee Mr Leardon evelyting."

"Then lose no time; go."

"No; Ching velly tire, velly hot; wantee bleakfast, flesh tea, nicee new blead. Too hot to lun."

"But I want you to save yourself," I said excitedly.

"Yes; allee save evelybody, alleegether. Ching won't go leave Mr Hellick."

"Ching!" I cried.

"Hush! No makee low. Lie down likee lit' pigee in sand. Pilate come along."

His ears were sharper than mine; for, as I dropped down at full length in the sand upon my chest, I saw him drag a good-sized stone in front of his face to screen it, while I, in imitation, rapidly scooped up some of the sand and spread it before me, so as to make a little mound of a few inches high, just as a couple of the junk's crew came into sight about a hundred and fifty yards on our left, and as close down to the sea as the billows would allow. Then a few more appeared; and at last the whole party, walking almost in single file, and looking sharply from left to right as they came.

There was a space of about sixty yards from the face of the cliff to the edge of the water, and the shore, after about twenty yards of perfect hard level, rapidly rose, the interval being a rugged wilderness of rock half buried in the driven sand.

It was up nearly at the highest part of this chaos of rocks, where we had been seeking along the cliff face for a cavern, that we three lay, many feet above the level strip by the sea; and there were plenty of rocks protruding from the sand big enough to hide us; but it could only be from a few of the men at a time. To the others I felt that we must be so exposed that some one or other must of necessity see us if he looked our way.

There was no need to whisper, "Be silent," for we lay there perfectly motionless, hardly daring to breathe, but forced, fascinated, as it were, into watching the long procession of our enemies, walking along, chattering loudly, and every now and then stooping to pick up something which had been driven up by the sea.

At times I saw them gazing right in our direction, and then up, over us, at the cliff with its patches of grey-green vegetation; but fully half of them passed by without making a sign of being aware of our presence, and hope began to spring up of the possibility of their all going by without noticing us.

The next moment it seemed impossible, and my heart sank as one active fellow stepped toward us, apparently coming straight to where we lay, and appearing to be watching me all the time.

And now more strongly than ever came the feeling that I must leap up and run for my life, though I knew that if I did the mob of Chinamen would give chase, like the pack of savage hounds that they were, and never give up till they had run me down; and then—

I felt sick with the heat of the sun, and the horror of my position. There, say it was all from the latter cause; and the rocks, sea, pirates, all swam before me in a giddy circle, with only one clear object standing out distinct upon the sands—imagination, of course, but so real and plain before my dilated eyes, that I shuddered at its reality—it was myself, lying in the baking sunshine, after the pirates had overtaken me and passed on!

It was very curious in its reality, and so clear before me that I could hardly believe it true, when the man who was coming toward us suddenly stooped, picked up something, and then turned and went back to his position in the line.

For I had not calculated in my excitement upon the deceptive nature of the ground upon which we lay, with its large masses of rock and scattered fragments of endless shapes, some partly screening, some blending with our clothes as we lay motionless; and above all, upon the fact that our presence there was not expected. Otherwise there might have been quite another tale to tell.

Even when I knew that they were passing on, I hardly dared to draw my breath, and lay still now, with my head pressed down sidewise in the sand; till at last I could keep from breathing no longer, and the dry sand flew at one great puff.

I lay trembling the next moment, fearing that the sound would bring the bloodthirsty wretches back, hot and eager to hack to pieces the foreign devil who had escaped from their clutches the day before; but the sound of their voices grew more and more faint, till the last murmur died away, and I raised my head slowly, an inch at a time, till I could gaze along the strand.

There was nothing visible but the scattered rocks, sun-bleached sand, and the dark, smooth surface over which the foaming water raced back each time a glistening billow curved over and broke. And in proof that the enemy were some distance away, I could see the pale-feathered, white-breasted gulls passing here and there in search of food, while able at any moment to spread their wings and escape.

Chapter Forty Three
Our Refuge

"Oh deah me!" said Ching in his most squeaky tones, "I velly hungly. You like nicee bleakfast, Mis' Hellick?"

"Don't speak to me as if I were a baby, Ching," I cried angrily.

"No; speak like to offlicer, Mr Hellick. You likee bleakfast—something good eat?"

"I hadn't thought of it before, Ching," I said, feeling rather ashamed of my angry tone; "but I am faint, and I suppose that is through being hungry."

"Yes; Ching go down among locks and sand, see if he find something eat."

"No, no," I cried excitedly; "it would be madness."

"Eh? you tinkee Ching mad?" he said, with a smile.

"Oh no; but you would meet some of the pirates."

"No; allee gone 'long shore. Not come back long time."

"But it is too risky. Perhaps some of the wretches are waiting."

"No; allee velly wicked—velly bad men. Feel 'flaid stop all alone. 'Flaid see men again headee chop off. Pilate allee keep together. No come long time; Ching go find something good eat."

"But if they come on the cliffs and look back, they might see you."

"Yes; might see Ching flom velly long way topside lock chop. Then think—"

"Think, yes, of course."

"Not allee same you think. See Ching? Yes; see John Chinaman in blue flock allee torn, long tow-chang; that's all."

I did not grasp his meaning for a moment.

"Oh, I see," I cried at last; "you mean that if they did see you, they would think it was one of their own crew?"

"Yes; think one of own clew. But Ching not pilate."

"Of course. Then there would be no risk. You shall go, but we must find some place where we can hide."

"Mis' Hellick help soon makee velly nicee place."

"Wait a minute," I said. "Couldn't we climb up on the cliff like you did?"

"Yes, Mr Hellick climb, but no cally jolly sailor boy, Tom Jeck, allee way."

"No; we must make a place here if we cannot find one."

He walked up to the face of the cliff, but there was no spot at all likely to answer the purpose till he had gone about fifty yards, when he turned and signalled to me.

I crept close up to the cliff, and then stooped down, after a timid look in the direction taken by the pirates, and found Ching standing by a piece of the rock which had split away from above, fallen clear, and then its top had leaned back against the rock face, leaving a narrow rift between its base and the cliff, through which we could see the light dimly, some twelve or fourteen yards away, but it was only a faint gleam showing that the far end was nearly closed.

"Velly nice beautiful place; ought to come here last night."

"Yes, capital. We can hide here; and once inside, if we had arms, we could keep the wretches at a distance."

"Don'tee want fight now," said Ching, quietly. "No swold, no shoot gun, no jolly sailor boy. Wantee eat and dlink."

"Yes; let's get poor Jecks here at once."

"You go fetch him; tly to walkee now: Ching go fetch eat, dlink."

He hurried off toward the ridge, while I went back to my wounded man, who seemed to be lying asleep, but he opened his eyes as I approached.

"We've found a place," I said. "Do you think you can limp a little way?"

He tried to rise, and fell back with a moan, but upon my placing my arm under his, he made a fresh effort, and stood upright, taking step for step with mine, till I had him right up to the narrow opening of our shelter, into which he slowly crawled, and then spoke for the first time, but in a hoarse voice I did not know—

"Water."

"I'll try," I said; "don't stir from there till I come back."

Creeping along close under the cliff, I soon reached the ridge, and was about to mount, but dropped down and hid, for I saw something move in the direction taken by the pirates.

A minute's investigation, however, showed it to be some bird on the strand, and I began to climb, reached the top, took a careful observation in both directions, and then up at the cliff, and,—lastly, looked out for Ching.

I soon espied him running out after a retiring billow, then running in again, and continuing this several times as if he were a boy at play. Finally, however, I saw him go splashing in after a wave, and then come hurrying back dragging something, which he drew right ashore.

There he stopped, panting, and looking back, caught sight of me, and signalled to me to come.

I hurried down, reached him amongst the piles of broken timber and rubbish, and found that he had secured a wooden box, one end of which had been battered upon the rocks, laying bare the bright glistening tin with which it was lined; and I realised directly that he had found what for us was a treasure, if we could tear open the tin, for the case bore the brand of a well-known firm of English biscuit-makers, and doubtless it was part of the loot taken from some unfortunate British merchantman.

"You helpee me cally?" he said.

For answer I took hold of one end of the case, and we bore it right up, through the thick sand, close under the cliff, where we placed it behind a big stone.

"You gottee big stlong knife?" cried Ching.

I took out a big-bladed knife, opened it, and found no difficulty in thrusting it through the soft tin and cutting a long gash. Then I cut another, parallel, and joined two of the ends, making a lid, which, upon being raised, showed that the biscuits were perfectly unharmed by the salt water.

"Fillee allee pockets," cried Ching; and I proceeded to do so, while twice as many as I could stow away disappeared under his garments.

"Now," I said, "we must find water and get back."

"Waitee minute; p'laps pilate come back; no·have bliskit."

He dropped down upon his knees, and began tearing away the sand from behind the stone, after which he dragged the case into the hole, and tossed the sand over it at a tremendous rate, ending by completely covering it and looking up at me with a smile of satisfaction.

"Now for water," I said eagerly.

"Yes, Ching find water;" and we tramped back, the loose dry sand falling in and obliterating our footprints.

Ching led the way to a pile of tangled wreck-wood, and took out a jar covered with bamboo basket-work, and having a cross handle—a vessel that would probably hold about half a pailful.

"Ching find—float flom junk," he said; and then, with a knowing smile, he led the way to where the ridge joined the cliff; and, unable to contain myself when, he stopped and pointed down triumphantly, I fell upon my knees, and placed my lips to a tiny pool of clear cool water, which came down from a rift about forty feet above my head in the limestone rock, and, as I drank the most delicious draught I ever had in my life, the water from above splashed down coolly and pleasantly upon the back of my head.

"Ching hear can go *tlickle, tlickle*," he said, stooping in turn to get a deep draught before filling the vessel, and then leading the way back over the ridge, and out of the hot sunshine into the place where our poor companion lay upon his back, muttering hurriedly words of which we could not catch the import.

This was a fresh difficulty, for he could not be roused into sitting up to drink; and at last, in despair, I scooped up some water in my hand, and let it trickle upon his half-parted lips.

The effect was instantaneous; they moved eagerly, and, ceasing his muttering, he swallowed more and more of the water, till he must have drunk nearly a pint, and now sank into a more easy position fast asleep, and breathing easily.

"Ha!" I exclaimed. But I said no more, Ching's hand was placed over my lips, and he held me back, staring hard all the time towards the tall narrow outlet of our shelter.

For the moment I thought that this was some cowardly attack—one is so prone to think evil of people rather than good; but he stooped down, placed his lips to my ear, and whispered the one word—

"Pilate."

Then a loud burst of talking came upon us, sounding as it doubled by striking and echoing from the rocks. My blood ran cold once more, for I thought that my exclamation had been heard, and that the enemy was talking about and watching the opening of our shelter.

Then the noise grew louder, and some dispute seemed to be on the way, while, what was worse, the sounds did not pass on, showing that the crew of the junk, for I felt that it must be they, had returned and stopped just in front of where we crouched.

Where we were was dark enough to keep any one from seeing us if he looked in from the bright sunshine; but I knew that, sooner or later, if the men stayed where they were, some one was sure to come prying about, and would see the place. How long, then, would it be ere we were discovered, and had to meet our terrible fate after all?

"You thinkee get out other way?" said Ching at last, with his lips to my ear.

"I think not," I whispered back.

"Mustn't look out this way," he whispered again. "You go light to end and look see if pilate going stop."

I was so eager to get an observation of the enemy, that I hurriedly crept along the narrow passage. I say hurriedly, but my progress was very slow, for I had to worm my way over fallen stones, some of which were loose, and I was in constant dread of making a sound which might betray us.

But I got to the end in safety, and had to mount up over a large narrow wedge-like piece which filled up the end; the opening, dim and partly stopped with some kind of growth outside, being quite ten feet from the sandy bottom.

And all this while the murmur of voices from outside came indistinctly, till I was at the top of the wedge, when the talking grew suddenly louder.

I hesitated for a few moments, and then, feeling sure that I was safe, I placed my face to the opening, parted the tough plant a little, and then a little more, so as not to attract attention; and at last, with a bright yellow daisy-like growth all about my face, I peered out, to see that the enemy had quietly settled down there to smoke, not thirty yards from our hiding-place, while some were settling themselves to sleep, and again others to eat biscuits similar to those we had found.

They evidently meant to stay, and if our wounded companion began his delirious mutterings again, I knew that, although a fellow-countryman might be spared, my career was at an end.

I crept down cautiously, and told Ching all I had seen; whereupon he nodded his head sagely, and placed his lips to my ear.

"Plenty big stone," he whispered. "Plenty sand; velly quiet; 'top up hole."

I shrank from making any movement, but, softly and silently, Ching crept nearly to the opening by which we had entered, and began moving the fragments embedded in sand, which formed the flooring of our narrow refuge, turning over peat shaley pieces, and laying them naturally between us and the light, and, after planting each heavy piece, scooping up the dry sand with both hands, and pouring it over the stone. Then another piece and another followed, awkward bits so heavy that he could hardly lift them; and, gaining courage, I let to as well, pulling blocks from out of the sand where I knelt, and passing them to him.

He nodded his satisfaction, and we both worked on slowly and silently, building up till the erection became a breast-work, rapidly growing narrower as it rose higher; the sand poured in, filling up the interstices and trickling down on the other side, thus giving our rugged wall the appearance of being a natural heap, over which the dried sand had been swept in by the storm.

I was in agony as we worked on, expecting moment by moment to hear a stone fall, or a loud clap of one against another; but Ching worked in perfect silence, while the busy chattering of the men without kept on, and then by slow degrees grew more smothered as our wall arose; while as it progressed our shelter grew more gloomy.

There was plenty of material to have made a wall ten times the size, whereas, roughly speaking, ours was only about four feet in length from the fallen rock to the base of the cliff, and sloped inward till, at breast height, it was not more than two feet, and from there rapidly diminished till Ching ceased, and breathing hard, and wet with perspiration, he whispered to me —

"No leach no higher; can'tee find now."

It was so dark that we could only just see each other's faces, but in a short time we became so accustomed to the gloom, that we could watch the changes in Tom Jecks' countenance as he lay sleeping, by the faint rays which stole in over the top of our cavern, and through the tuft of herbage which grew high up at the other end. But the heat was terrible in so confined a space, and, exhausted as I was with lifting stones and scooping up sand, there were moments when everything appeared dreamy and strange, and I suppose I must have been a little delirious.

I was sitting panting with the heat, resting my head against the rock, listening to the breathing of Tom Jecks, and wondering why it was that something hot and black and intangible should be always coming down and pressing on my brain, when I started into wakefulness, or rather out of my stupor, for Ching touched me, and I found that he had crept past Tom Jecks to where I had made my seat, and had his lips close to my ear.

"Hoolay!" he whispered. "Flee cheahs! Pilate all go away! Go up see."

Chapter Forty Four
Within an Ace

Ching's words sent a thrill of delight through me, rousing me, and bringing me out of my half-delirious state.

Without a word, I crept cautiously up to my look-out place, listening to the loud shouting and gabbling of the Chinamen as I got nearer to the tuft of greeny growth, which I parted without so much hesitation now, and, looking out, I could see that by the warm glow of the late afternoon sun which made me shrink back with my heart sinking, and creep down again to Ching.

"Yes?" he whispered. "Allee going 'way?"

"No," I replied, with my lips to his ear; "they are carrying up boards and pieces of the wreck and sails, and making themselves a shelter. They are going to stay."

Ching drew his breath with a low hiss, and was silent for a few minutes. Then, quite cheerfully, he whispered—

"Velly bad job. Don'tee want bad wicked pilate here. Nevy mind: come, eat blisket, dlink watee. Muchee best place. Muchee better than pilate. Then go have good long s'eep."

We stole back to where the biscuit and water vessel had been placed for safety; but when Ching handed me some biscuits I felt as if I could not eat, though a little water refreshed me.

"No dlinkee much; no get more till pilate gone."

I shuddered as I thought of the consequences of being without water in that stifling place, but the simple refreshments did me a wonderful amount of good, and, after dipping my handkerchief in the vessel and squeezing a few drops from time to time between Tom Jecks' lips as he began to mutter, he dropped off to sleep again.

I sat listening then to the smothered sounds from without, where the enemy were evidently very busy, and I was just dropping off again into an uneasy slumber, when I started into wakefulness, for there was a loud shout from the opening we had blocked up, and I felt that all was over. They had found the way in, and in a few moments we should be dragged out.

Directly after there was the babble of several other voices, and a discussion went on in Chinese, not a word of which could I understand. Then, to my utter wonder, the voices which had come over the top as if speaking close by me, suddenly ceased, and I could hear the *pad pad* of bare feet on the sands.

"Velly neally catchee catchee, and choppee off head," said Ching softly. "Begin to be velly solly for poor Mis' Hellick. Pilate say, 'Heah good place, make hole s'eep in.' 'Nothee pilate say, 'Big fool; allee wet damp; wildee beast live in hole, and allee 'tink. Come back, makee better place.'"

It was a narrow escape, and it was long enough before my heart calmed down, left off throbbing, and I fell asleep.

Utter exhaustion had done its work, and my sleep was deep and dreamless. Once my eyes had closed, they did not open again till long after sunrise the next morning, when I lay there puzzled, and wondering where I was and what was the meaning of the murmur of voices apparently from somewhere overhead.

Ching's voice chased away the remaining mists.

"You had velly good s'eep?" he whispered. "Feel muchee better?"

I did not answer, only squeezed his hand, and turned to see how Tom Jecks was, but he did not seem to have stirred, and we then ate sparingly of our biscuits, and drank more sparingly of the water.

"Must be velly careful," Ching said again; "no get more till pilate gone 'way."

That day went by like a portion of some feverish dream. My head burned and throbbed; my thirst grew terrible in the hot, close place, and Ching owned to suffering terribly in the same way; but the faithful fellow never touched a drop of the water, save when the evening came, and we partook together of our rapidly-diminishing store of biscuits, the very touch of which on my lips increased the agony of my thirst.

And all the while we were awake to the fact that the Chinamen had an ample supply of food and water, for they kept dragging up to the camp they had formed casks and chests which had been washed up from the wreck of their junk; and when I climbed up and looked out, I could see them apparently settled down and resigned to their fate, until some friendly junk came along or they could surprise another, feasting away, or playing some kind of game with stones.

"Waitee lit' bit," Ching whispered. "Allee s'eep, and Ching get eat dlink."

But I felt certain that he would be caught, and begged him not to go till we were absolutely driven by hunger and thirst; and so that day passed, with the rock growing hotter, and the air too stifling almost to breathe, while, to my horror, I found that Tom Jecks was growing more and more feverish. At times he began to mutter so loudly that we were obliged to throw my jacket over his face to prevent the sounds from drawing the attention of the enemy.

I believe I was half-delirious all that day, and when the night came our little supply of water was running so low that Ching asked if he had not better climb over the wall and go and fetch some more.

"No," I said; "it means discovery. We must wait."

I dropped soon after into a heavy stupor-like sleep, and this time I was the first to wake and see the sun's rays stealing in through the growth in the rift. Ching was sleeping calmly enough, but Tom Jecks had been tossing about, and lay in a very peculiar position, which startled me—it looked so strange. But Ching woke just then, and, nodding and smiling, he helped me to turn our poor companion back, when we found him flushed and excited, muttering angrily, quite off his head.

"Nevy mind; pilate get tired; go to-day," whispered Ching. "Get bettee soon. Now have bleakfast. Waitee bit: Ching makee butiful bleakfast, chicken, toast, egg, nice flesh tea. There. On'y 'nuff blisket for to-day. Ching go out to-night get plenty blisket, plenty watee, plenty—plentee—oh, deah—oh, deah!"

"What is it?" I whispered.

"Oh deah! Not drop watee left. You get up dlink allee watee?"

"No; did you?"

"No. Ching see. Pooh Tom Jeck knock over with arm."

It was only too evident, for the water vessel had been laid upon its side, and the sand beneath was soaked.

"Ching velly solly," said the Chinaman softly. "No gettee more watee till quite dalk."

My head sank against the rock, and I hardly stirred the whole of that day. Ching pressed me to eat some of the remaining biscuits, but I could not touch them, only rest my burning head there, and try to think of what was to come. Ching would certainly be caught if he ventured out, for the enemy never all lay down to sleep together; and, what was worse, I felt convinced, though in a confused way, that sooner or later the delirious mutterings and talkings of Tom Jecks must be heard.

I can only remember patches of that day. The rest is all burning heat and wandering away amongst grass and flowers and purling streams, whose trickling I seemed to hear.

It was getting well on in the afternoon, I suppose, that Tom Jecks' fever came to a height. He muttered, and then began to talk angrily, but in an incoherent way, and his voice grew so loud that at last I roused myself and went up to the look-out, to watch whether it was heard without.

But the Chinamen heard nothing, only sat or lay about, talking or sleeping. It was getting close upon evening, for the sunshine was warm and golden, and cast long shadows from the rocks and the cliff above us over the level sand.

How beautiful it all looked! that golden sea, with a distant sail here and there. And now suddenly I found that there was a great deal of excitement amongst the Chinamen, who were talking loudly.

My head was hot and confused, but I soon saw the reason why, and hope began to revive, for about a couple of miles out I could see two junks standing in, and my heart throbbed again with excitement as I noted their rig, and could feel certain they were the pair we had watched through that strange night.

"I must go and tell Ching," I said to myself. "Those junks will take the wretches off. Only a few more hours, and we shall be safe."

"Stand by, my lads! Look out! Storm's coming down upon us. Now then; every man for himself."

I turned cold with horror. Just then, too, when we were so near to safety. For the words were Tom Jecks', roared in a hoarse voice in the height of his delirium, and I saw that they were heard outside.

For the Chinamen who were sitting sprang up, sword or knife in hand; those who were looking out to sea or making signals faced round, stood staring at the cliff for a few moments as if startled, and then, as Tom Jecks' voice rose again, but in muffled tones, for Ching had thrown himself upon the poor fellow to stifle his utterances, the pirates uttered a yell, rushed to the opening, tore down the sand and stones, and Ching and Tom Jecks were dragged out on to the sand.

They had not seen me for the moment, but there was a shout directly, a man jumped up, caught me by the leg, and I was dragged along and out into the soft evening sunshine, to be forced down upon my knees close to where Tom Jecks lay, and Ching was being held, for he was struggling wildly with his captors, and talked excitedly to the fierce wretches who crowded round us.

Ching was evidently pleading for mercy, not for himself but for me. I knew it, for he kept pointing to me; and finally he made a bound, got free, and leaped to me, throwing his arms about my waist.

"No killee; shan't killee," he cried wildly; and then, turning round, he yelled at our captors in his own tongue, abusing them in his rage, and threatening them with his clenched fist.

But it was all in vain: a dozen hands were at him; others seized and held me. Ching was dragged away vociferating wildly, thrown down, and three men sat upon him, while another knelt down, twisted his hand in the poor fellow's tail, and held his head fast.

I don't think they meant to kill him, their rage being evidently directed at us; and I saw, with a peculiar kind of fascination, one man with a big sword come close to me; another, armed with a similar blade, go to where Tom Jecks lay, held down by three others.

IT WAS NOT THE FALLING OF THE SWORD ON MY POOR OUTSTRETCHED NECK.'

I can hardly describe my sensations. Five minutes before, I was horribly frightened; the cold perspiration stood upon my forehead; my hands were wet, and my legs sank under me. But now, all the fear had gone. I knew I was to die, and I remembered the execution I had seen in that great enclosure, when with one *whisk* of the sword the executioner had lopped off head after head. It would not take long, I thought, and a curious exaltation came over me as I began to think of home, and at the same time my lips uttered the word "Good-bye," which was followed by a prayer.

I did not cease muttering those words as I felt myself forced into a kneeling position, and saw that Tom Jecks was being treated in the same way. And somehow, as I prayed, the thought would come to me that the poor fellow would not feel or know anything about what was going to happen.

Just then, as the man with the big sword approached Tom Jecks, and I was watching, I did not see but I knew that the other was close behind me and a little on my left. But it did not trouble me any more than it did to know that the fierce wretches were all gazing excitedly at us, and in a high state of delight at being able to slay two of their foes.

It takes long to describe all this, but it happened very quickly.

The man had raised his sword to strike at Tom Jecks, and I shuddered and looked aside, to see the great shadow of a man on the sand at my feet, and there was a sword raised close by me.

At the same time Ching uttered a wild shriek, and the man who held his tail forced the poor fellow's head down in the sand, but in vain; he wrenched his head sidewise, raised it, and looked towards the cliff, while I flinched slightly, for the shadow moved, as he who made it drew back to strike.

Crash!

No: it was not the falling of the sword on my poor outstretched neck, but a volley from the top of the cliff, fired by twenty of our brave blue-jackets, and half-a-dozen of the pirates fell shrieking on the sands.

I turned faint, but I recovered my senses as I saw Ching spring up, rush at a man on the sand, snatch up his sword and run to me.

"Quick!" he cried; "jump up; fight!"

Almost mechanically I obeyed him, and snatched a knife from the hands of one of the fallen men to defend my life, just as a second volley rolled forth from the cliff, directed at the pirates as they ran toward the ridge.

For there was no need for us to fight—our enemies were in full retreat; and, as I looked up at the cliff, I could see our men drawn-up, and they were signalling evidently to some one out of sight.

The next minute we were hailed.

"Which is the way down?"

"This way," cried Ching excitedly; and he ran south, pointing to the rift by which he had climbed the cliff, while I stood there—giddy, helpless, and at last sank down on my knees beside poor Tom Jecks, who was still muttering something about the storm.

I recovered, however, enough to watch our men descending the rift—a perilous, break-neck place; but they did not hesitate, and in a few minutes all were down, formed up, and came toward us at the double.

And now for the first time, at the head of those familiar faces, I saw Mr Reardon, who thrust his sword into his sheath as he drew near and literally rushed at me.

"My dear boy!" he cried, giving me quite a fatherly hug; "thank God, we were just in time."

I could not speak—I was too giddy; but I tried to look my thanks.

"Not hurt, are you?"

"No, sir; only faint."

By this time the last of the pirates had passed over the ridge, and I felt irritated with Mr Reardon for not going in pursuit. But he did not read my countenance; he called one of the men out of the line, made him give me some water from his bottle, and bent down on his knees by poor Tom Jecks.

"Ha!" he said; "fever from a wound. Give him some water too, my lad."

He sprang to his feet then, and I understood why he had not gone in pursuit of our enemies, for just then there was a sharp volley from over the ridge somewhere.

"Ha! that's got them," said Mr Reardon, turning to me. "We divided, my lad! half of us came along the top of the cliff, the other half along the shore."

There was another volley, and I saw Mr Reardon smile as he gave the orders, and out flashed the men's cutlasses, and were fixed with a quick tingling rattle on the muzzles of their rifles.

"Here they come, sir," cried the warrant officer at the far end of the line.

"Yes, my lad, and we're ready for them. Now, one volley as soon as they are together, boys, and then the blades. Bayonet every wretch who does not throw down his arms."

A low murmur ran along the little line, and I saw our men's eyes flash in the evening sun.

But the excitement was not complete, for, gathering strength now, and recovering from the shock I had received, I was watching the pirates scrambling over the ridge in haste, as if pursued, when there was a concussion of the air, a heavy boom, and I saw the *Teaser* come into sight, passing through the channel south of where we stood. Then there was a quick puff of smoke, another heavy boom, and I saw that she was going full speed, leaving a black stream of smoke behind her, in chase of the two junks, one of which was about a quarter of a mile away, the other about a mile farther.

They were evidently taken by surprise, for the men were hurriedly hoisting sail, and, as I learned afterwards, the *Teaser* had been quite hidden till she rounded a little promontory at the mouth of the channel between the first and second islands — the channel for which we had so vainly steered on the night of the storm.

The firing went on steadily, the crash of the great shell following the report of the piece, but I had nearer and more exciting work to see close at hand; and once more my heart beat high, as the pirates gathered together, and, seeing the danger before them, paused for a moment or two at the foot of the ridge slope, looked to right to see only the perpendicular cliff, to left to see the sea, and then, uttering a savage yell, came tearing on.

"Fire!" roared Mr Reardon, when they were about fifty yards distant, and I saw several fall and others stagger and halt.

But the others continued their wild dash like men, and were met by our lads, who advanced with their cutlass-bayonets at the charge.

There was a loud cheer, a savage yelling, and I saw the blades flashing in the golden sunshine as they met. Then a minute's fierce encounter, with men falling, and then half-a-dozen turned and fled back for the ridge, but only to stop and turn to their right, making for the sea.

For the ridge was lined with blue-jackets and marines, and shot after shot was fired at the flying men, who without hesitation plunged into the sea and swam out a few yards, while our lads pursued them, but only to halt on the hard wet sand, where the waves now gently rippled.

There was a strange fascination in the scene, and I watched the six shaven heads of the swimming pirates till the first threw up his hands, battled the air for a few moments, and went down. The others turned and slowly swam shoreward till they could wade, when they approached our men and flung their weapons on the sand in token of surrender.

There was a triumphant shout at this, and then another—a loud and frantic cheer. For the firing of the *Teaser* had been going on rapidly, and all at once the first junk was seen to heel over, and gradually settle down, leaving the sea strewn with fragments of timber, to which the crew were left clinging; while the gunboat raced on, sending shell after shell rapidly at the other, till she was nearly alongside, when there was a tremendous roar, following the crashing into her of a shell, and the second junk flew up in fragments.

The shell had reached her little magazine of powder; and then the work of mercy began.

I was watching the boats being lowered when I heard a shout from behind, and, looking round, saw the second line of our blue-jackets advancing from the ridge. To my great joy, I saw with them those whom we had mourned as drowned, while the next minute Mr Brooke had me by the hands, and I heard a strange gulping noise, ending in quite a howl.

I looked sharply round, and saw Ching seated on the sand, wiping his eyes with his sleeves.

"What's the matter, Ching—hurt?" I asked.

"No, not hurt, Mis' Hellick; Ching so velly glad."

Chapter Forty Five
"Huzza!"

By the time the *Teaser's* boats had picked up those of the wretches who wished to be saved, I had learned from Mr Brooke how, when the boat struck, he and the others had clung to her and been swept along through the channel, the fierce current carrying them round the point, and at last into comparative shelter, where finally they reached the shore right on the far side of the island.

Thence, after a great deal of climbing, they made their way toward the channel to come in search of us; but they had to fly for their lives, finding that the island was in possession of the wrecked crew of the junk.

They lay in hiding all that day and the next. That evening, in answer to signals, a fishing-boat picked them up, half-dead with thirst, and by the use of a few Chinese words and signs, and the showing of money, the men were prevailed upon to take them up to the river, where, to Mr Brooke's great delight, he found the *Teaser* at her old anchorage uninjured, she having escaped the fury of the typhoon, just passing into the river before it came down in its full violence.

Captain Thwaites had been anxiously awaiting the return of the boat from up the river, for, in spite of all inquiries, he had been unable to get any tidings of her till just as Mr Brooke arrived, to find the owners of the boat he had taken, on board making application for payment.

They were dismissed with a promise of full restitution, and, while steam was being got up, a boat was lowered, the floating grating which acted as a buoy found, the cutter recovered, and then the *Teaser* sailed for the river's mouth and came in search of us, Mr Brooke still clinging to the hope that we had escaped. In the offing the two junks were seen and recognised, evidently on their way to pick up their shipwrecked friends.

First of all, the strong party of blue jackets and marines was landed, while the *Teaser* went round the back of the island, to reach the channel and take the pirate junks by surprise.

Thorough success, as I have shown, attended the manoeuvre, and soon after we were on board, where, after a few congratulatory words from our busy captain, I found Barkins and Smith eager to welcome me back, and quite ready to forgive me for having what they called "such a glorious lot of adventures," on account of the share they had had in the sinking and blowing up of the two pirate junks.

"Yes," said Barkins, after I had told my experiences on the island, "that was all very well; but oh, my lad, you should have been here when we attacked those junks! It was glorious—wasn't it, Blacksmith?"

"Lovely! But don't say any more to the poor fellow; it will only make him mad."

We returned to the river, where our prisoners were landed, and we three lads had more than one spell on shore before we left that port, notably being in the city on the night of the Feast of Lanterns; but though we had several more brushes with pirates, they were all trivial affairs with small junks, the destruction of the last three being the crowning point of our achievements. Indeed, this and the sinking of another in search of which, upon excellent information, Captain Thwaites had suddenly gone after we had set out on our shooting expedition, and in which engagement Smith assured me he had greatly distinguished himself, were such blows to the piratical profession that its pursuers were stunned for the time.

We remained upon the coast for another six months, and then: were ordered home, to the great delight of everybody but Ching, who parted from us all very sadly.

"You think Mr Leardon like to take Ching see Queen Victolia?" he said to me one day in confidence.

"I'm afraid not," I replied seriously.

"Ching velly solly," he said. "Plenty lich man now! plenty plize-money! Ching wear silk evely day in Queen Victolia county. You no tink captain take Ching?"

"I'm sure he would not," I said.

"Ching velly good interpleter; velly useful man."

"Very; you've been a splendid fellow, Ching!"

He smiled, and a fresh idea struck him.

"You tink Queen Victolia like Ching teach lit' plince and plincess talk Chinese?"

Again I was obliged to damp his aspirations, and he sighed.

"What shall you do when we are gone, Ching?" I said.

"Open fancee shop again. Sell muchee tea, basket, shell, culios, fo' Inglis people. Glow tow-chang velly long. Wait till Mr Hellick come back with jolly sailo' boy, fight pilate."

And with that understanding, which was doomed never to be fulfilled, we parted.

For the next morning the men were singing—

"Huzza! we're homeward bou-ou-ound. Huzza! we're homeward bound."

And homeward we all—including Tom Jecks, who soon recovered from his injury—returned in safety, HMS *Teaser* steaming gently one summer day into Plymouth Sound; and this is her log—my log—written by a boy. But that was years ago, and I'm an old boy now.